THE
STARS
BELOW

VEGA JANE BOOK FOUR
A NOVEL BY

DAVID BALDACCI

 SCHOLASTIC PRESS | NEW YORK

To Spencer and Collin, this series was always for you and so it is
fitting that the final chapter is dedicated to the both of you.
I love you and love that you both are READERS!

Copyright © 2019 by Columbus Rose, Ltd.

Library of Congress Cataloging-in-Publication Data available

ISBN 978-1-338-26393-0

10 9 8 7 6 5 4 3 2 1   19 20 21 22 23

Printed in the U.S.A   23
First edition, March 2019

Book design by Elizabeth B. Parisi

"The most effective way to destroy
people is to deny and obliterate their
own understanding of their history."

— George Orwell

"Things may look different to you than
they did before. I've had that experience
myself. But don't let appearances fool
you. There's only one reality."

— Haruki Murakami

"Drinking a wind of danger new and deep,
Staring on Vega with a piercing eye,
And gather up his slender hooves and leap
From crag to crag down Chaos, and so go by."

— Edna St. Vincent Millay

At Last

I CRIED OUT, *"RIGAMORTE!"*

My cast spell impaled the Maladon directly in the chest, cleaving it as though fine steel had been my weapon of choice. However, the incantation was far deadlier than even the purest of forged metals. He toppled forward to the dirt. He would never move again. He would never hurt anyone else again.

I felt a smile creep to my lips at his demise.

I did not like killing others. But I had no problem with vanquishing evil.

Then I turned my attention to my remaining opponent. He was backed against a wall and was looking at me murderously but with an underlying expression of fear.

He raised his wand and shot a spell at me.

I flicked it away with a wave of my wand, the Elemental.

He shot another spell at me and then another.

I blocked them easily, almost casually.

His wand now quivered in his shaking hand.

"Who the bloody hell are you?" he screamed at me. *"What* the bloody hell are you!"

I advanced on him. I was no longer smiling. My face was iron, my will the same.

I said, "My name is Vega Jane. And I'm the last thing you will ever see before you go to your personal Hel, Maladon."

My wand moved so fast that he had no ability to block what I was about to do.

"Rigamorte!"

This battle was over.

I looked around at the five bodies.

They were all Maladons and they were all dead.

They thought I was walking into a trap, but the trap was all mine, carefully conceived and flawlessly executed.

As was my habit after battling these creatures, I confiscated all their wands and crushed them to bits with an *Impacto* spell.

Killing had once been very difficult for me.

Yet in war, you either killed or you died. And we were very clearly in a war.

I was nearly eighteen now. I had been gone from my hometown of Wormwood for almost three years. It felt like three hundred.

I looked around at the darkness of night. I was about five miles from the town of True, near a tiny village that I had used to set my trap for my enemies.

I had brought no one with me for the simple fact that I needed no one else to do this. I preferred to rely on myself with tasks such as this one. That way I only had myself to worry about.

Besides which, our numbers had fallen considerably, and I did not want to risk more losses if I could avoid it.

War was not pretty or safe. People died all the time. That was why they called it war.

I cast the *Pass-pusay* spell and tapped my leg with my wand.

I was instantly transported back to my ancestral home, Empyrean.

It looked just as it had when I had first seen it.

Built of stone and wood, it was enormous and rambling, like a huge boat on land. To me it was also a pillar of strength and stability.

And refuge.

I passed through the front door and entered the massive front hall.

All of Empyrean was immense and stylishly outfitted. The ceilings were twenty feet high, the rooms large enough to hold a hundred people easily. The stone walls were bedecked with the portraits of long-dead men and women, all of them powerful sorcerers and sorceresses. The furnishings were of the highest quality, and though many centuries old, they were in first-rate shape. The rugs were colorful and luxurious, so thick your feet couldn't help but sink into them. And yet there were nooks and crannies throughout where one could find privacy. And peace.

The entire property was kept sparkling clean by the staff, headed up by the suit of armor named Pillsbury.

Empyrean was exactly the same, except for one thing: the occupants.

It had started out with just me and my friends Delph, Delphia, and Petra Sonnet.

And of course my faithful dog, Harry Two.

Then we had found and recruited an army of fifty former slaves to help us fight the Maladons.

And they had fought, well and good.

But now nearly half of them were dead.

Thus, the air of loss hung deeply over Empyrean, as did the smoky smell from the fires we conjured in the massive fireplaces. We had all trained together, lived together, eaten together and fought together.

And, unfortunately, died together.

As I moved through the front hall, Tobias Holmes walked in on one flesh-and-bone leg and a wood-and-metal one that I had conjured for him, to replace the leg he had lost to a Maladon curse. He was tall and good-looking, with curly brown hair and an angular face fronted by two large and luminous blue eyes. He met me with a smile.

"Good hunting, Vega?"

I nodded. "It all went well, Tobias. Five fewer Maladons. How are things here?"

"Petra just got back with Artemis and Regina. Miranda and some others are still out, but it was just a scouting expedition, as you know, so no worries there."

"And how did it go with Petra?" I asked, heartened by the fact that he would not be smiling if there had been another loss.

"The mission was a considerable success," replied Tobias. "The Elite Guard posted on the northern end of Greater True will have to make do without their guns."

I nodded and moved on.

Pillsbury was the next one to greet me. His armor appeared to be, if anything, far shinier than when we had first met. He and Mrs. Jolly, the cook in the form of a broom, kept Empyrean running like a finely tooled instrument.

"Delighted to see that you have returned safe and sound, Mistress Vega."

"Thank you, Pillsbury. Everything all right here, I trust?"

"No problems, unless you count an oven reluctant to warm itself to the degree of perfection demanded by Mrs. Jolly. She's making the loaves of bread for breakfast."

"I am amply confident that Mrs. Jolly will soon sort it out."

I proceeded up the stairs and down the hall to my room.

Awaiting me there, as he often did, was Harry Two.

He sat up on my bed and watched me with his mismatched eyes, one blue and one green. Part of his ear was missing from when he had saved my life, which he very often did.

I rubbed his damaged ear and pushed my nose into his thick, soft fur, filling my nostrils with his scent. As bad a day as I ever had could be partially cured by this simple measure. My dog just seemed to calm me whenever I needed it.

I undressed because killing blokes was a dirty business and I needed to wash up.

Across my shoulders and down the backs of each of my arms was Destin, my magical chain, which greatly increased my physical strength and, more important, allowed me to take flight.

I had magically embedded it into my body some time ago. I was the one who used it almost exclusively. And instead of wearing it around my waist, it seemed more prudent to make it a part of me. If others ever needed it, it was but a simple spell to free it from my skin.

The links moved silently and fluidly as I rolled my shoulders to ease the tension there.

I moved over to the looking glass and studied myself.

I had grown to my full height now, my shoulders broad and my arms ropy. I ran my gaze up and down my frame. I had scars on my arms, legs and belly from Maladon strikes. And there was one at the nape of my neck that had very nearly done me in. I perhaps could have magically removed them, but I had chosen not to try. They were all marks of battle, and I wanted my skin to chronicle every one of them.

There was another, more practical reason for retaining them. They all represented near misses at death. I never wanted to forget how close it was to me. To all of us here. We all carried the detritus of battle. This made us realize that we had to be perfection itself to survive.

I examined my face closely. Though I hadn't yet celebrated my eighteenth year alive, it seemed to me that I looked older. Far older. Tiny lines had whittled themselves around my eyes, forehead and mouth.

I sighed. War certainly did not make one prettier.

Next, I moved over to one wall and studied the marks I had placed there.

I knew exactly how many of them were cut into the plaster.

I raised my wand, and with a quintet of rapid movements, I added five more slashes to the wall, representing the Maladons I had discharged this night.

I stepped back and surveyed the wall.

It was simply rows of marks, yet each represented a life taken.

I suddenly had to turn away before the sight sickened me. They were Maladon deaths, it was true, but they were still dead. And while I could smile when they fell at the tip of my wand, I would not celebrate their destruction.

I washed, changed into my nightclothes and then fell asleep in my bed.

In what seemed like minutes, but I knew was actually hours because the sun was well up, I heard the sound of a knock on my door.

It was Delph, my best mate from Wormwood.

He was very tall, and very fetching-looking.

Delph was not magical like Petra and I. But he was a fighter still and had qualities, talents and skills that neither Petra nor I possessed. He was calm when I tended to be excitable, and thought things through in ways that I never could.

"Pillsbury told me you were back, but I wanted to let you sleep." He glanced at the wall. "How many?" he asked.

I sat up, resting my back against the enormous wooden headboard. "Five," I replied tersely. "Why?"

He sat on the bed and scratched Harry Two's ear.

"You never really told me about Wormwood," he said abruptly.

This was not the first time he had said this. It might as well have been the hundredth.

"I told you all you needed to know, Delph. It's gone. They're all gone. They killed everyone, including your father. I saw their graves. And as I told you, I buried Thansius."

"That's not exactly so," he countered. "They killed every-one *except* your brother."

"At least there was no grave for my brother. But, in truth, I have no idea if he's alive or dead."

These words suddenly caught at my heart, and I had to look away from him. I had lost many friends in the war and that had hardened me. Yet John was my brother. John was my family.

Delph stood. "But why would they take John, if that indeed is what happened?"

I rose from my bed and faced him from a foot away. Though I was tall, Delph was six and a half feet high, so he towered over me. "You've asked me that before. And I've asked myself that a thousand times, Delph. I keep coming up with a thousand different answers."

Delph said, "It *would* make sense in one way."

"What way?" I said bluntly.

"Well, at first I thought they might be using John to hold over your head, you know. If you don't surrender, they'd hurt John. But they haven't done that, Vega Jane, though they've had ample time. So there must be another reason."

"Such as?"

"Morrigone was teaching John back in Wormwood. She'd taken him under her wing, so to speak, because he was so smart and all with books and such."

"I told you that. But it was terrible stuff that she . . ."

My voice trailed off, and I looked in horror at Delph.

"Are you saying that they took my brother to . . . to . . ."

I couldn't say it. Not for the life of me.

"To maybe make him into a Maladon?" said Delph. "A right powerful one. Judging by what a sorceress you are, I 'spect that John might make an equally powerful sorcerer."

"But why just John? Why not take all in Wormwood for that purpose?"

"John was so smart, Vega Jane. And . . . he seemed to like . . . you know . . ."

"You mean he liked all those horrible things that Morrigone was teaching him?" I said stiffly.

"Well, you told me that yourself."

"But, Delph, he was just a little boy. He didn't know any better. He liked to fill his head up with . . . stuff," I finished quite lamely. In my mind's eye, all I could see was a little boy with feet too large for him shuffling along while holding my hand. I would pick him up every day after Learning, and I would bring a snack for him because he was always hungry. My brother had been painfully shy and kind and bighearted. I knew that he had changed while with Morrigone, but my most lasting memories of him had always been as a shy little boy holding my hand.

Delph interrupted my thoughts. "Well, he's not a little boy now. He's very nearly fifteen. The same age you were when you ran away from Wormwood with me."

This was absolutely correct. Indeed, John was far closer to being a man now than he was to being a boy.

If they'd captured him from Wormwood, my brother would have been with the Maladons for quite some time.

"You're right, Delph," I said contritely. "He is a man by now. I just don't know what sort of man he is." I felt my lips begin to tremble and I turned away from him.

An instant later I felt Delph's large arm around me, squeezing me to him.

In my ear I heard him whisper, "It's okay, Vega Jane. We're going to find him. And . . . and regardless of what sort of shape he's in, we're going to bring him back to what he was."

"You . . . can't know that," I said haltingly.

"But I can promise to do all I can to make it happen."

I turned and looked at him, touched his cheek with my hand. "You're my best friend, Delph. You always have been."

He smiled. "You were the *only* friend I had, Vega Jane. And a ruddy great one you are."

He got that certain look in his eye that I well knew. In fact, I'm sure I had a similar look in mine.

Our lips instinctively found each other, and we kissed. I felt his arm circle my waist and squeeze gently. I ran my hands over his broad shoulders. I had to stand on tiptoe to do this.

When we separated, my eyes were heavy and I could see his were as well.

His arm lingered around my waist, and I placed my hand on his chest.

"You had better go," I said, conscious that I still had my nightclothes on. "I . . . I can smell food downstairs. You must be hungry."

"I am, Vega Jane," he said, staring directly at me. "But I'll go have my meal."

As soon as he said the words, his face turned crimson and he started to stutter, as he once had back in Wormwood.

"I-I m-m-mean . . ."

I put a calming hand on his arm. "I know *exactly* what you meant, Delph." I spun him around and gave him a hard push to the door. "Now go eat."

After he left me, I sat back on my bed and tried to catch my breath, which had suddenly abandoned me. The only thing I seemed to be able to think of was Delph with his arm around me, looking at me as he had.

Later, I walked down to the kitchen and had my breakfast. It had been a long night, and the few hours of rest had done nothing to ease my lethargy. But I had no time to be weary.

I had just finished my meal and Mrs. Jolly had just left with my dirty dishes when Petra walked in. Our eyes met, and in that look, there was much that was communicated. It just seemed to be that way with Petra and me.

She was about a year older than me. And like me, she too appeared older still. The shirt she wore had no sleeves and I could see the marks and scars up and down both arms. My gaze ventured to her burned hand from a wand mishap, and then to the gap between her fingers, where one of them had been torn away by the Elite Guard back in Greater True.

I said, "Tobias told me that you had returned. And that the Elite Guard had lost their muskets."

She nodded. "They'll make others. But it will take time. However, those gits are far from our biggest problem."

"I know that," I said a bit abrasively. For whatever reason, I was constantly on my guard with Petra. I always felt instantly combative with her. The fact was, she brought out the absolute worst in me at times, though I knew she would die in order to save me. It was quite an odd relationship.

"I heard your journey was also a successful one," she said, sitting down across from me.

10

"If five dead Maladons are any measure, then yes, it was."

There was a subtle barrier between us that I assumed would always be there. Maybe it was because we were so similar. Maybe it was because we both cared deeply for Delph. I knew that Petra had actually loved him, and it must hurt her very much to know that her feelings were not reciprocated. She had moved on to another man, Nicholas Bonham. However, he had died a year ago in battle. Unfortunately, with Petra right next to him. I imagined that she felt guilt for surviving. Just as she had when we had lost her friend Lackland Cyphers back in the Quag.

"That makes four hundred of them dead, then," said Petra, eyeing me so intently, I assumed that this conversation was building up to something of importance, at least in her eyes.

"Just that," I said.

"We'll be burying Alabetus tomorrow," Petra informed me.

Alabetus Trumbull had lost his life two days ago, at the hands of a gang of Maladons who had tricked him into an ambush.

That had been the impetus for my journey last night, to avenge Alabetus's murder. We had to let the Maladons know very clearly that we would never yield. That we would kill far more of them than they did of us.

"I know that," I said. "I will speak of course. He will be terribly missed."

"As will the twenty others who preceded him," said Petra, her gaze still on me.

I sat back, and now my gaze held on her. So *this* was where Petra was going.

"I fully realize that we have lost nearly half our number," I said sharply.

Petra sat forward and plunged in. "Four hundred to twenty-one. That's nineteen Maladons to every one of ours."

11

"I can do the mathematics," I replied coolly.

"But you know we've discovered that there are thirty times more Maladons than there are of us. That only leads to one outcome, Vega. We can't win this way."

"We're still trying to find magicals among the countryside," I said.

"We've found none in all this time. None since we rescued that lot from Greater True."

When I said we were at war with the Maladons, that was true. But there had been no great battles on broad fields. No titanic clashes of sorcery. We simply hadn't the numbers for such a style of combat. So, our war was a series of small skirmishes. Ambushes, tactical missions, two-on-two, four-on-four. Small encounters, almost all of which we had won, but as Petra had pointed out, the eventual outcome with such a strategy was inevitable. A war of attrition was always won by those with superior numbers.

"We can't attack them outright," I said. "We can't try and invade Maladon Castle. We would be slaughtered."

"I know that."

"Then what do you suggest?"

"I'm not sure I have anything to suggest. But I would say that until we figure out our eventual goals, we need to do everything we can to keep what army we do have left safe and intact. If we lose even a few more, it won't matter what we do in the future. We'll still have lost."

What she said was undoubtedly true. And yet if we stopped fighting?

"I'll think about it, Petra," I said.

She started to say something, a sharp retort I could tell from the look on her face. But she apparently bit back these words, simply nodded, rose and left.

A minute passed while I closed my eyes and tried to push the fatigue from my bones.

A slim figure came rushing toward me. "Vega! Vega!"

I opened my eyes. It was Miranda Weeks. She and her group must have returned from their scouting expedition.

Miranda was the youngest of our number, but she had grown taller and stronger with the passage of time. Initially, she had been timid and unsure of herself, and her magical ability had been pretty much nonexistent. But she and her wand had reached common ground, and now she was one of the best warriors we had. At Delph's suggestion, I had not allowed her to engage in combat with the Maladons at first. But our shrinking numbers and her heightened skills had led me to reverse that judgment about six months ago.

"Yes, Miranda?"

"You must come."

"Come? Come where?"

"To the village where we just were."

I half rose from my chair. "Why? What happened?"

"The villagers saw her."

"Who did they see?"

"Your mother."

An Unexpected Ally

PETRA WAS ON my left, Miranda on my right, as we appeared out of clear air on the outskirts of the small village.

My wand was in my hand, and I motioned for the others to hold theirs at the ready.

"Show me," I said tersely to Miranda.

I followed her along a winding path until I saw smoke curling upward from a chimney.

Petra was ten feet behind me, guarding our rear flank. We went into every situation like this with the thought that we would have to fight our way back out.

"There," Miranda said, pointing to a small thatch-roofed cottage about fifty feet in front of us. "The woman in there was the one who told me."

I marched up to the door, half expecting a trap. My thoughts went briefly back to the wall in my bedroom, and to how many more slashes I might add to it before the day was done.

I rapped on the door and listened, my wand twitching expectantly as the sounds of footsteps approached.

Petra and Miranda were on either side of me, about eight feet away. From there, they could see any attack coming and take action to defend our position.

The door opened, and an old woman peered out. Her gaze dropped to my hand, and when she saw my wand, her eyes widened.

"Y-you're not them blokes?"

I looked at her, momentarily unsure what she meant. Then it struck me.

"No, I'm not like them. I hate them. I'm here to ask you about someone." I pointed at Miranda. "You talked to her about a woman you saw?"

The old woman swiveled her gaze to Miranda. She nodded. "That's right."

"And did the woman call herself Helen?"

She nodded.

I needed to make sure, so I pulled something from my pocket.

It was an engraving of my mother. I held it up for the woman to see.

"Is this her?"

"Oh, yes, that's her all right." She looked from the engraving to me, and her jaw slackened.

"What is it?" I asked.

"Well, it's just that she looks like *you*, dearie."

I was taken aback by this until I realized it was perfectly natural that a mother and daughter should resemble each other.

"We're family," I said vaguely, putting the engraving away. "When was she here?"

"Yesterday, it was."

"Can you tell me anything else about her? Why was she here? What did she want?"

Out of the corner of my eye, I saw Petra keeping a sharp lookout. On the other side of me, Miranda was doing the same.

Their wands were pointed in front of them, and they made arcs with them in the air, ready to fire at anything threatening.

Their consummate training and attention to detail allowed me to concentrate fully on the woman.

She said, "Well, this *Helen* was looking for an herb. Healing herb I call it, though she used a different name. I didn't quite catch it."

My heart skipped a beat. "Healing herb? Why? Was she injured?"

"Not so's I could tell. I mean she looked all right enough. Though she was terribly thin, and her face was quite, well, careworn. Poor thing."

"Maybe the herbs were for someone else. Are you sure she was alone?"

"Well, there was no one else with her that I could see."

"Did she mention someone else's name? A man? Hector?"

"No, nothing like that."

I held up my wand. "Did she have one of these?"

The woman shuddered, and a hand flew to her bosom.

"No, she did not."

I studied her. "Did other people show up with these? Around the time Helen was here?"

The woman nodded. "Bloody men in them suits and hats. Awful people."

"What did they want?"

"Well, I don't know exactly what they wanted. But they were asking questions left and right, about any strangers hereabouts."

"And what did you tell them?"

Her features became confused. "I . . . I don't really remember. That's all right fuzzy."

I nodded. I could easily see what had happened. They had no doubt cast the *Subservio* spell over her and magically compelled her to tell them all that she knew. And then they had performed a spell to wipe out her memory. I took heart that their spell had not been entirely successful.

"This healing herb, did you have any of it?"

The woman shook her head. "But I told her there was plenty growing down by the river."

"Where is the river?"

She pointed to her left. "Down that way about a half mile. Can't miss it, dearie."

I rushed off before she even had the chance to close her door.

Petra and Miranda were right behind me.

"Take my hands," I said when we were out of sight of the village.

They gripped me, and we all three rose into the air.

After a short flight, I spotted the winding water and set us down next to it.

I looked around, uncertain whether my mother was nearby or not.

Miranda said, "I bet these are the herbs she was talking about."

They were green-and-red leafy plants growing all around the riverbank.

I barely looked at this vegetation before my gaze returned to the trees across the river. The waters were calm. The woods silent. This put me on my guard.

Just about every fight I had been in had commenced with near silence.

"So the Maladons showed up when your mum came to the village," said Petra.

I nodded, still studying the trees. "She must have the mark on her. They tracked her that way."

"Well, if she has the mark and has done nothing to cover it, it's a wonder the Maladons haven't captured her after all this time."

"I agree. But they haven't, so she must be doing something to circumvent that."

"And your father?" asked Miranda.

"If my mother was uninjured, the healing herb might have been for him," I noted, worry creeping into my voice. If my father was injured, was it serious? Could he even now lie dying?

I bent down and gathered some of the healing herbs and put them in my pocket. When Miranda looked at me quizzically, I said, "Just in case she didn't have time to collect it herself."

"Oh, right."

"What do we do now?" asked Petra. "Look for them, I suppose."

I didn't answer her. I was still staring at the trees. Was something in there?

Someone?

"Vega?" said Petra in a firmer tone.

I came out of my musings and turned to her.

"Do we look for them?" she asked again, though I had heard her the first time.

I nodded and took their hands and we soared over the water, landing gently on the opposite bank.

The three of us stared at the dense forest facing us. I'm sure we were all thinking the same thing: Are there Maladons lurking in there, just waiting to strike? That's what constant battle does to you. It makes you untrusting. It makes you bloody *paranoid*.

Before the others could move, I charged forward into the dense thicket, my wand at the ready. They immediately followed but spread out into a triangle pattern, as I had trained them to do. If we had been clumped together, one spell could have finished us all off. We had gone about a hundred feet or so into the forest when I spotted it.

The piece of cloth fluttering in the breeze. As I cautiously approached, I could see that it had snagged on a prickly bush.

I freed the cloth and held it up. As Petra and Miranda drew closer, I sniffed it. "This belongs to my mother."

"You're sure?" asked Miranda in a small voice.

I nodded and pressed the cloth fragment against my nostrils again, once more breathing in her scent. Though it had been years since I'd seen my mother, with that one inhale of breath, memories of her came flooding back.

But when I turned the cloth over, the breath froze in my lungs.

There was blood.

Petra observed this and said, "She might have used that cloth to dress his wound, or maybe some got on her when she was helping him. And then it got snagged on that bush when she went to seek the herbs."

While they were speaking, all I could see was my father lying gravely injured in the woods.

"*Crystilado magnifica,*" I said, pointing my wand in front of me.

All I saw were more trees close-up.

Until something flickered in front of my sight line.

The spell came at me so fast I barely had time to deflect it.

It hit a tree and exploded, burning a deep hole in the wood.

I didn't have to tell Petra or Miranda what to do. It had become second nature to both of them.

They each assumed a defensive posture about ten feet on either side of me and slightly behind me. Next, I tossed the ring of invisibility that I wore at all times to Petra. She slipped it on her finger and spun it around, activating the invisibility shield. She used her wand to cast a golden lasso connecting herself to Miranda, ensuring that the youngest member of our army would be invisible too.

I soared into the air to make myself a target.

This would give the pair of them the opportunity to rain spells upon our opponents once they gave away their positions by firing at me. This had been a tried and true tactic of ours.

I shot spell after spell into the trees, hoping that one of them would find the enemy. Regardless, they would have to return fire at some point, I thought.

But nothing happened.

I looked down at where I knew Petra and Miranda were. Their gazes would be fixed on the tree line, awaiting the spells to come upward at me so they could draw down on their targets.

I stared back at the trees. This was bewildering. Had the Maladons figured out our strategy and were now using it against us? Lying in wait for us to reveal ourselves?

I used another magnification spell to see well into the trees below. But I could make out nothing useful.

This was getting bloody frustrating. I wanted to attack and decimate the Maladons, not hover in the air, waiting for something that might never come.

But then I thought two could play at this game.

I flitted to the ground and used a spell-cast lasso to attach myself to Petra and Miranda, thereby rendering myself invisible as well.

Petra whispered, "Who do you think is out there?"

I was about to answer, when my chest seized up. Bloody Hel, had I just fired spells at my parents? Were they the ones in the forest, perhaps hurt or ill? Had I just added to their misery? And were they simply casting spells to defend themselves, perhaps thinking that *we* were Maladons?

I thought quickly. How could I communicate with them? I had to be careful. If Maladons were out there, I didn't want to somehow give them the upper hand.

Finally, an idea hit me.

I used my wand to draw something on the cloth I had found. It was a picture of my mother's favorite flower. She'd kept one in a vase at our home back in Wormwood. It had a very distinctive look, and I was sure she would recognize it. Underneath the drawing I wrote, *I love you, Mum. Vega.*

I willed my wand to its full golden size so it resembled a lance. I attached the cloth to the Elemental and said, "Take this to my mother, if she's in there."

I tossed the Elemental into the air, and it soared away.

As it disappeared into the distance, my breaths started coming more rapidly. I had felt this way when I had finally found my grandfather Virgil. I prayed that I would have far more time with my parents than I'd had with him.

A minute passed and both Petra and Miranda exchanged anxious looks with me.

Had I just made a colossal blunder?

Then I saw the Elemental heading back. Though I was invisible, that didn't deter the spear from finding me and landing right back in my hand.

The cloth was still attached. It had not found my mother. And it would have if she were in there. So, it had to be someone else. Someone magical.

Maladons? Or . . . ?

I willed the Elemental to wand size.

And not a moment too soon.

I lashed out with it just in time to stop the spell. It ricocheted off my wand's shield incantation and went spinning off into the trees. I stared out ahead of me.

How in the world? They couldn't see us. Or could they?

"Move," I called out to Petra and Miranda. We took to our heels and fled a hundred yards to the left.

I waited, my breath coming in bursts.

Who the bloody Hel was out there? Might they have seen the Elemental leave or return to the invisibility ring and targeted us that way? But why had they waited so long?

The next moment, a voice shouted, "No," just as another spell headed our way but fortunately passed well to our right.

As I lowered my wand, it occurred to me that the voice sounded familiar, though I'd heard it utter only one word.

The next words dispelled any doubts as to who was speaking.

"No, Archie. Can't you see? That's not a Maladon you're casting spells at. It's Vega."

The voice left me dumbstruck.

And my numbness only increased as two people appeared out of thin air at the edge of the wood. It was the woman who had taught me to be a sorceress.

Astrea Prine, and her only living child, Archie, who had once tried to murder me.

Blimey.

Once More, the Bloody Prines

I HAD PETRA SPIN the ring back around so that we all became visible.

Astrea Prine looked exactly as she had when I left her, now over two years ago. Her son, Archie, looked exactly the same as well.

She was petite with dark hair cut in bangs and looked to be in her twenties. She was actually over eight hundred years old and one of the most powerful magical beings I'd ever encountered.

Archie was taller and thin but with looks that showed quite clearly that Astrea was his mother.

Seeing them both now was absolutely stunning.

"What are you doing here?" I exclaimed as Petra and Miranda looked warily at the newcomers, their wands held at the ready.

And I kept one eye on Archie since he'd just tried to curse me into an early grave again.

Astrea said, "There was nothing left for me to do in the Quag."

I stiffened. "You know about Wormwood, then?"

"Of course I do, Vega. It was my job to keep it safe." She paused. "I obviously failed."

"It wasn't your fault," I said tersely. "The Maladons discovered and exploited a seam in the barrier you concocted."

"Regardless, Wormwood is no more. Thus, Archie and I came here to see what we could do to defeat the Maladons."

"How did you break through the barrier?" I asked. "I sealed it afterward."

She hiked her eyebrows. "I am rather something more than simply a *competent* sorceress, Vega. You should know that by now."

I felt myself blush, but then my features hardened. This woman *had* taught me to be a sorceress. But she hadn't seen how much I had changed in the last two years, how much I had experienced and overcome. She didn't know that my wand, after saying its respectful good-byes to its previous owner, had become one with me, immeasurably increasing my confidence and, with it, my magical power.

"My apologies," I said in an overly formal tone.

"I found the gash despite your *sealing* it," she said. "Of course *you* created the opening when you breached the wall on your way through into this world. That was what you were referring to before, wasn't it?"

She didn't have to say the second part of this thought, for there was assuredly a second part.

And also how the Maladons found their way in, *allowing them to slaughter all* your *fellow Wugmorts.*

Petra said nervously, "Vega, I don't think we should just be standing here talking about these things. We're completely vulnerable."

I nodded, because she was exactly right. But I had one last query that I needed an answer to now.

"Have you seen a woman around here who looks like me?"

"No, I have not seen your mother, Vega. Nor have I seen your father."

I frowned. I had forgotten that Astrea knew about my parents.

Astrea answered my look. "Yes, Vega, I assumed they must have ended up here somehow. They did not pass through the Quag. They found another way."

"The Maladons call them the Campions," I said proudly. "Like we've been doing, they've been fighting the Maladons."

"Which is what Archie and I have been doing as well."

My jaw dropped. "You've been fighting the Maladons?"

Archie spoke up. "That's who we thought you were."

"Have you killed any?" I asked pointedly.

"An even dozen," she said. "But we keep looking for more. Bloody Bowler Hats."

I looked down at the cloth in my hand, then at the surrounding woods. If my parents had been here, they apparently no longer were.

"Vega?" hissed Petra anxiously. "We should go."

"Come with us," I said to Astrea. "We can provide shelter and I'll introduce you to the others."

"You have others?" said Astrea, looking interested.

"I have an army," I said. "I can explain in more detail later."

"Where are you staying?" she asked.

I lowered my voice. "Just come with us. You'll see." But then a thought struck me as I looked down at my gloved hand. "The Maladons can track the mark of the three hooks," I said. "You must have that mark on your hands."

Astrea said dismissively, "It is taken care of, Vega." She held up her hand, and Archie did the same.

I was stunned I had not noticed it before. Their hands looked metallic.

"A simple spell," she noted. "But effective."

25

"When did you learn of their ability to track you that way?" I asked.

"From the first Maladon we encountered. I forced him to tell me." She added casually, "Before I dispatched him."

I roped all of us together and then used the *Pass-pusay* incantation to carry us to Empyrean.

As soon as we alighted on the front steps, covered by my ring of invisibility, Astrea gasped.

I looked over at her to see tears spilling down her cheeks as her gaze ran along the stretch of the stone facade. Never had I seen Astrea this overwhelmed. She was not a woman who showed emotion. Yet now, it was plain to see what this place had meant to her.

"It's really still here?" she said, her voice quavering.

"I'tis," I said. "Come inside. I doubt things have changed a whit since you were here last."

She slowly approached the wooden front door. With every glance, it seemed a fresh memory from the past was forming in her mind.

Inside, we were met by quite a few people, including Delph.

When he saw Archie, he charged forward, ready to fight.

"No, you don't, you bloody git!" shouted Delph, his fists balled.

Archie brandished his wand and seemed about to cast a spell.

I sent a blaze of light thundering into the ceiling to get their attention and shouted, "No, Archie! Delph, it's okay. He's no longer, well, *confused*."

Delph halted his charge but looked suspiciously at Archie, who gazed defiantly back at him, his wand twitching in his hand.

My spell and the raised voices had brought everyone else flooding into the hall, including Pillsbury and Mrs. Jolly.

I introduced Astrea and Archie to everyone. I left out the part that she was not nearly so young as she looked, though many did seem puzzled that she seemed to be the same age as her *son*.

As the others dispersed and went back to what they had been doing, Pillsbury marched forward and extended a crisp salute to Astrea.

"Madame Prine, it has indeed been a long time."

I glanced at Pillsbury in surprise. "You know each other?"

She said, "Pillsbury ran Empyrean with a firm hand back then, though not as a suit of armor. That came later, did it not, Pillsbury?"

"It did indeed, Madame Prine."

Astonished by this, I said, "What were you before then?"

"I was a man," said Pillsbury simply.

"Do you mean they turned you into a suit of armor?" I said, the revulsion clear in my tone and on my features.

"A man dies, Mistress Vega," said Pillsbury. "An enchanted suit of armor lives forever. And that was what was called for. Oh, I did so willingly."

I said, "But who enchanted you?"

"Your ancestor, Jasper Jane."

"Jasper Jane!" exclaimed Delph, who, along with Petra, had lingered behind.

Pillsbury stared up at Delph. "Yes. It was necessary. Empyrean had to be kept safe. Master Jasper well knew that centuries might pass before things were made right, if they ever were. Thus, there had to be those who would remain here to take care of Empyrean."

I looked at Astrea. "But why didn't you come here directly after leaving the Quag?" I asked. "You obviously knew of its existence. Your portrait hangs on the wall here."

"I was not the one who enchanted it, thus I did not know its location."

"Who did, then? Alice and Gunther were dead before it became enchanted."

"Jasper also provided the protective incantations," said Astrea. "He knew the darker side of magic better than the rest of us. And as Pillsbury has already said, he wanted to ensure that Empyrean survived. It was his ancestral home after all. It meant everything to him, and his sister. He would have done anything to protect it. And he did."

"I guess I can understand that," I said. "But why didn't he inform you of this?"

"It was a tumultuous time, Vega. It's not like Jasper and I had the time or opportunity to sit down over tea. We were literally fleeing for our lives with a great deal to accomplish in a very short period of time."

I nodded. This seemed to make sense.

"How did *you* find your way here, Vega?" she asked.

I held up my wand. "The Elemental led me here."

She nodded. "Of course. You see, it is the Elemental's home as well, having belonged to Alice."

Petra said, "Look, I know it's a nice home and all, but would the Maladons finding this place back then have mattered all that much?"

Now Astrea's piercing gaze bored into Petra. "Matter all that much?" she said forcefully. "As you have no doubt discovered, there is much magic in this place. In addition to it being his beloved home, Jasper also believed that it would provide a safe haven one day for his descendants who had taken up the fight. That of course turned out to be spot on. Also, the golden wand of the slain Bastion Cadmus hangs on the wall. We would never want that instrument to fall into the hands of the Maladons."

I interrupted her.

"His wand no longer exists. I magically broke it apart and sent its pieces to provide wands to my army," I said. "Fifty wands from one."

I had only once before absolutely stunned Astrea. Back at her cottage I had unleashed a magical blast without a wand, resulting in Astrea being blown off her feet and flung into a wall.

Well, I had just stunned her for a second time with only the *magic* of my words.

"You . . . you created fifty wands from Bastion's one?"

"Yes."

"How? There is no incantation known that would accomplish that."

"I know. I created my own spell to do so."

She continued to stare at me in a way that was making me feel quite uncomfortable. "I see, Vega," she finally said.

"Yes, I think you do," I said firmly as she continued to gaze at me. "I have seen and talked to Uma Cadmus's spirit. And also to Alice," I added.

Astrea's jaw slackened. "You have seen Alice?"

"I have."

Astrea put out a hand to the wall to steady herself.

Archie said worriedly, "Mum? You okay?"

With an effort, Astrea composed herself. "Yes, of course. It's just that I never thought I would see dear Alice again. I never . . ."

"Well, now you can," I said, staring at her curiously.

29

"And how is she?" asked Astrea anxiously.

"Unsatisfied" was the only word I could come up with.

Pillsbury, who had hovered in a corner of the room, stepped forward.

"Madame Prine, would you care for some food, a bath, some clean garments and a soft bed upon which you could regain your energy?" He swiveled his visor around to Archie. "And for your son too of course."

Astrea shot Archie a look and nodded. "Yes, Pillsbury, that would be very welcome. Our beds have been the dirt and our food only what we could scrounge."

She and Archie followed Pillsbury upstairs.

Astrea turned back around and looked down at me.

Again, it seemed as though she could peel away my skin and look right into my head and heart. She had both irritated and intimidated me when we had first met. Her confidence seemed to be limitless. Yet I had ended up more than holding my own. So why did I feel like a schoolgirl once more?

It was so disconcerting that I turned and walked off, though I could still sense her watching me.

Petra and Delph followed, peppering me with questions.

"Not now," I said. "We can talk later about it."

"But, Vega Jane," began Delph.

"Not now!" I barked.

I raced down the stairs to a room I knew well. The last time I had gone there, I received the most shocking and terrible news of my life. That Wormwood and all those in it were gone.

Still, I needed to talk to someone.

A dead someone.

Sometimes, they know far more than those of us still alive.

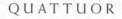

The Rival

A LICE?"

I looked around the drab, shadowy interiors of the room. It was here that I had first encountered the ghost or spirit or whatever it was of Alice Adronis, my people's fiercest warrior. I had seen Alice do battle, watched her die. Been given the Elemental by her. And she had known me by name. That was one thing I wanted to ask her about. I hadn't all this time because, well, I guess I was afraid of what her answer might be.

"Yes, Vega?"

She had appeared behind me, still wearing the chain-mail armor in which she had perished on the battlefield. Her mortal wound still gaped in her chest. Each time I saw it, my own chest hurt.

"I have news."

"I already know."

"You know? How?"

She glanced down at my wand, which I had slid through my belt.

The Elemental had once belonged to her, but it no longer acknowledged that. It was my wand, pure and simple.

Or maybe not.

"What the wand can see, I can see also," she said.

I looked down at the Elemental, feeling a bit betrayed.

"So, you know that Astrea is here?"

She nodded. "I expect her to come and see me, soon."

"She told me you two were friends."

"I'm sure she told you many things."

"She taught me how to be a sorceress."

"She was always an able mentor."

"I owe her for that," I said slowly.

"You owe no one anything" was her surprising reply.

"How do you mean?"

"You came to Astrea's cottage by your own courage and ingenuity. You took her lessons and made the most of them. But your magical ability was always inside you, Vega. Astrea merely allowed it to find purchase. And then you left her and made your way across the Quag. You came here, and you have been fighting the Maladons with bravery and honor all this time. I repeat, you owe no one anything. Including me."

"Do you trust her?"

"I have long trusted Astrea."

"So why are you telling me these things, then?"

"Astrea has her own way of doing things. She does not take the advice of others often, or with . . . grace."

"She let me change her mind and cross the Quag."

"Yes, she did. And how did that turn out . . . for her?"

"I . . . I don't know what you mean."

"When you've thought deeply enough about this, Vega, come back and see me."

She vanished.

"No, wait," I cried out. "I wanted to ask you something else."

But she did not return.

"Vega, you git. Why didn't you just ask her the most important question first?"

Depressed, I headed back upstairs.

IT WAS A ritual I dreaded.

We were all lined up, dressed in our finest clothes.

I was at the head of the line.

I looked at the wooden coffin containing the mortal remains of Alabetus Trumbull.

We were in the rear grounds of Empyrean, which had been returned to its past glory by the loyal enchanted outdoor staff. It was a beautiful day with nary a cloud in the sky. But there were no beautiful thoughts in my head or my heart.

Only a deep sense of loss.

In my mind's eye, I could see Alabetus smiling or making a quip over a meal. I could see him fighting alongside me against the Maladons. I could also see him grip the hand of Regina Samms, with whom he had grown very close.

We would be burying Alabetus next to Regina, for she had succumbed in battle one month earlier.

Alabetus had never been the same after her death. And I suspected that the loss of Regina had driven him to take more and more risk in fighting the Maladons, as a way of avenging her death. And finally, that had ended in his own demise.

I pulled my cloak tighter around me, stepped in front of the coffin and briefly eyed the grave that had been dug by the outdoor staff. Their marbleized forms stood off to the side at respectful attention.

I eyed the long line of graves previously dug. Today we would be adding Alabetus to this depressing number.

I shook off these thoughts and turned to the crowd facing me.

Petra and Delph stood side by side.

Harry Two sat beside them.

On the far right were Astrea and Archie.

She wore robes of emerald green, while Archie was more plainly dressed in a somber brown.

Astrea gave me a little nod, as though letting me know it was okay to start.

I frowned at this. It wasn't like I needed her permission.

I cleared my throat and began.

"Alabetus will be much missed, just like all the others," I said, my gaze drifting to the row of graves. "He fought bravely and ably by our sides. He gave his life in the fight against the Maladons. He will always be remembered as the fine warrior and good person that he was."

At this Mrs. Jolly used one of her wooden appendages to place a large hankie next to her eyes, while Pillsbury patted her gently with his metal hand.

"I know that our losses have been heavy," I continued. "But with each of our fallen, we have forcefully let it be known to the Maladons that we will fight to the very end. And that we will triumph over them. There will be no stopping us."

I paused and fought back an urge to become strident in tone, to rally my troops. I could see in the grief-stricken faces riveted on me that this was not the time nor place to do so.

"I want each of us to reflect on our loss and to think, each and every day, of Alabetus and the others we have lost. I want us to keep them in our heads and hearts. And devote ourselves to making sure that none of them will have died in vain.

"But Alabetus was far more than a soldier fighting in a war, no matter how honorable that battle is. He was a son. He was a person. He had hopes and dreams of a better future." I

34

cast my gaze sideways to peer at Regina Samms's grave. "He wanted to fall in love, marry and raise a family of his own. He wanted to have a life free from fighting, free from war. He wanted to live in peace, as we all do."

I turned to the coffin and placed both my hands on it. I closed my eyes and bowed my head.

"Alabetus, I believe that you can hear me. I want you to know that we all miss you and will never forget you. And that we will fight on. In your name and in that of the others we have lost. We send your remains into the grounds of Empyrean, a haven of comfort, safety and fellowship. As to your spirit, it will remain always with us. It will help us in the days and months to come. It will make us better warriors. And better *people* when peace arrives for us all. Good-bye, Alabetus, honored brother."

I raised my wand. All those behind me did the same.

We sent waves of light into the air.

I lifted Alabetus's coffin with an incantation and placed it gently into the grave.

With a sweep of my wand, the mound of dirt next to the grave moved and covered it.

I bowed my head, said a silent prayer, then lifted my head and turned to the others.

As was our usual custom, I said, "Do any here wish to say a few words?"

At other such burials, we usually had one or two who came forward.

For the last two interments, though, no one had stepped forward. As I looked over the downcast faces, I thought such would be the case here until she stepped up.

"*I* would like to speak."

I looked in surprise at Astrea Prine.

Her gaze was not on me; rather it was directed at all the others.

She walked forward until she stood directly in *front* of me.

Flustered by this, I stepped awkwardly to the side as Astrea turned to face the others.

"My son, Archie, and I did not know Alabetus, but it is quite clear that he was a fine man and a worthy warrior. He fought with great bravery and died a hero to the cause. We wish his spirit peace." She paused, and I could see her features take on a hardened expression.

She pointed her wand at the row of graves. "There lies nearly half your number."

I stiffened because I had some inkling of where she was going with this. I shot Delph a glance. He had the exact same look on his face as I'm sure I did on mine. When I looked at Petra, she was simply staring curiously at Astrea, waiting for her to proceed.

Astrea said, "I have been through a war with the Maladons before, many centuries ago. I fought against them as you are doing now."

I looked around the group and saw, to my considerable dismay, that the others were listening raptly.

Astrea continued. "Because of that, I know them better than anyone here." She glanced at me. "Even better than Vega Jane."

I felt my face begin to burn, but I remained silent. I had no wish to create an altercation at such a sacred ceremony.

"I have come here to help in the fight," she continued. "My son has accompanied me. We have not been here long, but we have succeeded in killing a dozen Maladons already."

I looked around and saw that most here seemed impressed with that number, though I had killed far more Maladons than that myself.

She pointed at me. "Vega is a fine sorceress and warrior." She smiled at me, and I found myself having to return the gesture.

Her next words struck the smile from my face.

"She should be because I trained her."

I once more looked around the crowd and saw many surprised countenances. Some glanced at me before turning their attention back to Astrea.

"Yes, I trained her, and while I believe that all of you have received instruction, I may be able to augment that education and convey onto you the benefit of my magical ability and fighting experience." She glanced at me. "You may find it as useful as Vega did. Without it, I'm sure she will concede that it would have been impossible for her to reach this point in the war."

I felt quite frustrated by her words. First, because she was undoubtedly right. And second, because I did not want to concede this point, at least not to the others.

She continued. "You have fought hard and well through what I am sure are many skirmishes and battles."

She waited for those listening to slowly nod at her words. I had to admit, the woman could indeed mesmerize a crowd.

She said, "But winning one or two battles is not of paramount concern. Nor is counting up how many Maladons you may have killed." She paused as she surveyed the crowd. "What is of critical importance is to have a strategy to win the *war!*"

She said this last word so fiercely that several in the crowd jumped.

"The Maladons outnumber you on a vast scale. This is undeniable. At your current mortality rate, the conclusion of the war is inevitable." Here again, she paused. "You will lose."

I shot a glance at Petra. Had she been talking to Astrea?

Had she expressed the same concerns to her as she had to me? The sudden sense of betrayal I felt was palpable.

Astrea once more surveyed the crowd as a few grumbles in opposition to her words were heard.

"No, no, this is not a reflection on you," Astrea said. "Or your fighting ability. Or your heart. It is simply a reflection of you being outnumbered. We had the same problem before, when we fought the Maladons."

I could hold my silence no longer.

"And you *lost* your war, did you not?"

Astrea turned to face me. The look on her features was, well, it was not pleasant.

"We did indeed lose that war. Which is why I'm here. To make sure that history does not repeat itself. I have valuable knowledge of the Maladons. I can make sure that the mistakes we made against them are not made by you. Or any *more* mistakes," she added.

I again felt my face burn.

Then Astrea said something that almost made me raise my wand and strike.

"I can lead you to victory."

I again shot a glance at Delph. He looked outraged by her words.

Yet when I looked at Petra, she, once more, merely looked curious, even intrigued.

Well, enough was enough, I thought. Alice Adronis's words came ringing back to me. I owed no one anything, least of all bloody Astrea Prine.

I took a step forward. "That is all well and good. We would be foolish not to accept *help* from such an experienced sorceress. You can supplement the training they have received and suggest to us different tactics and strategies. And any information you can provide us on the Maladons, the techniques, weaknesses, ploys they tried in the past, would also be invaluable in aiding our effort. You can work directly *under* Delph and me in implementing these things."

I even managed a benign smile while saying these things.

I was so proud of myself, because what I really wanted to do was blast Astrea Prine into a million pieces.

Astrea looked around at the others. Their features were easy enough to read.

They were all in agreement with what I had just said.

"Very well, Vega," she said, returning my smile. "We will work well *together* now."

"I'm sure of it," I said pleasantly, even as the Elemental shook aggressively in my hand. Perhaps it was channeling Alice!

"Can we commence with a discussion after dinner?" she offered.

"That sounds absolutely smashing," I replied, perhaps laying it on too thick.

She grimaced rather than smiled, turned and stalked off, with Archie quickly following her, though he kept shooting glances back at me.

The git. Like mother, like bloody son!

While the rest of the group quickly dispersed and headed back to the house, I stayed behind with Delph and Petra.

"What the Hel was that about?" exclaimed Delph.

I whirled on Petra. "Did you speak to Astrea before this?"

"Just to say hello," she said. "Why?"

"Because she was making the same argument about us being outnumbered that you did."

"Well, you don't have to be a bleeding genius to come up with that one, do you?" she said in a sarcastic tone.

I gazed at her suspiciously, but finally that look faded. She

39

seemed perfectly sincere, and it was usual for Petra to wear her true feelings right on her sleeve. Deception, fortunately for me, was not her strong suit.

Delph said, "She was trying to . . . to take over like, Vega Jane."

"I *know* that, Delph," I snapped.

"But she made some good points," added Petra.

Of course you *would think that, Petra Sonnet,* I thought.

"I mean, she must have experience if she's fought them before."

"Yes, well, considering that her *experience* is over eight hundred years old, I'm not at all sure how useful it will be today. I would think the Maladons have altered their tactics over such a long stretch of time."

"You put her in her place, Vega Jane," observed Delph.

"Oh, Delph, you know what she's like. She won't stop."

I thought back to what Alice had told me. She trusted Astrea, but she also had intimated that I hadn't thought through everything about the woman. Well, the last few minutes had showed me she was right about that.

I had been battling the Maladons for two long years.

And now it seemed that I would have to add the woman who'd taught me to be a sorceress to my already-long list of adversaries.

Wonderful.

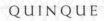

The Curse of Elythia

OUR MEAL THAT night was delicious.

Right up until the moment Astrea turned to me and said, "Now, it's time we talked, Vega."

It was not a request. It was a command.

And it made my skin creep and my blood turn molten.

Yet I smiled and escorted her to the library, giving a shake of my head to Delph when he glanced at me with a face that said *Do you want me to come too?*

I closed the stout doors behind Astrea, or I attempted to, but Archie burst in, almost causing the wooden door to hit me in the face.

Scowling, I shut the door behind him, strode across the room and took my seat behind my desk. I considered it *my* desk because it was where I conducted my work and the business of both running Empyrean and also my army. There was a lot to do and orders needed to be thought through and then given.

As I settled in my seat, Astrea sat across from me while Archie hovered at his mother's shoulder.

"Yes, Astrea? You wished to talk about something?" I said expectantly, keeping my tone polite and my features pleasant. Yet I was gritting my teeth, for I well knew what she was going to say.

"I didn't want to say this in front of the others of course, Vega," she began.

This only confirmed my expectations.

"I'm sorry?" I said, playing stupid.

"You have not yet turned eighteen, correct?"

"I have not. But when I do, I'm sure you and Archie will wish me a happy birthlight," I added cheekily.

She didn't take the bait on that one. She said, "I was thirty when the war with the Maladons commenced. And Alice was a bit older."

I frowned. I hadn't expected her to throw Alice's age in my face.

"Thank you for telling me. Is that all?" I started to rise from my seat, just to see her reaction.

It was Archie who took *my* bait when his mother showed more proper restraint.

"No, it bloody well isn't!" he exclaimed.

I looked at him, all knotted fists and furrowed brow. I smiled benignly at him.

"Do you wish to tell me something, Archie?" I almost tacked on *dear* to his name, but then thought better of it.

He pointed a finger at me.

"The Quag."

"Yes?"

"Gone, destroyed."

The Quag had been created to protect those in my village of Wormwood from the Maladons. And also to keep us from leaving Wormwood. Astrea and my ancestor Jasper Jane had carried the laboring oar in so doing. The Quag was full of dangerous beasts. And there were Five Circles in the Quag that served as obstacles to anyone trying to cross it. Each circle had unique elements designed to defeat anyone coming within that sphere. It had very nearly defeated me.

"I am well aware of that, though I wouldn't say the Quag is gone. It was still there when I flew over it."

"Wormwood, then. Totally destroyed. All dead."

I let the smile slowly erode from my face.

I stood so that I was taller than Archie. Astrea was comically short, though a far more powerful magical being than was her son.

I rolled my shoulders and stretched my arms. Though it made no sound, Destin's links moved just under my skin. Astrea had no idea that I embedded the chain within me. And I didn't want her to. But just feeling it there was quite comforting.

"Thansius wasn't dead when I got there. The Maladons made him dig all the graves and then simply left him to die without a proper burial. Did *you* know that?" I asked. I let my gaze drift to Astrea because I wanted there to be no misunderstanding that she was also included in this discussion.

"We were *not* aware of that, Vega," said Astrea solemnly. "All we saw were the graves."

"So you visited there?"

"Of course. I was the Keeper of the Quag. It was my duty."

"Yes, well, you carried out your duties admirably, Astrea — right up until the end."

She looked as though I had slapped her, and with my words, I had.

Jumping to his mother's defense, Archie exclaimed, "Do you deny that what happened to Wormwood and all those in it was *your* fault?"

Despite his accusation, I kept my gaze on Astrea. It was clear to me that despite Archie being the speaker, it was Astrea actually making these inquiries. I didn't want her to think of letting Archie do the talking. I was fooled by her ploy.

"Do you deny allowing me to cross the Quag with the full knowledge that my plan was to escape it and come here?"

I now shot Archie a glance and saw the git deflate like a split bag of flour. He glared at me for a moment and then looked helplessly at his mother.

She said, "I do not deny that, Vega." She clasped her hands together. "But Wugs died. All of them. Horribly. I will never be able to banish those graves from my memory. Never."

Now my lips started to tremble. Her sincere words had done something that Archie's inane bluster could not. Make me feel guilt. And I was guilty. My breaking out of the Quag had allowed the Maladons a way in. They had, in turn, murdered my fellow Wugs. I was at least complicit in this, if unknowingly.

But how unknowingly, Vega? Did you never think of this possibility? You knew your freedom from the Quag could mean death for those left behind.

I put a hand on the desk to steady myself. I actually felt like I would vomit. But I had to appear strong in front of Astrea. Fortunately, she chose to break the silence.

"But that is water under the bridge, Vega. It cannot be changed. It is something we will both have to live with."

"So where does that leave us?" I asked.

"With having to win this war," she said simply.

"I am doing my best," I said quite sincerely. "We have inflicted great damage on them."

"It is not enough," she replied. "There are far too many of them."

"I am aware of that," I said wearily. I had no desire to revisit this old argument.

"It is not simply about their superior numbers, Vega."

44

This caught my attention. I focused on her. "What else?"

"Tell me what you have learned since you have been here. What you have seen. Where you have gone."

I sat back in my chair, pointed my wand at the fireplace and ignited a fire there. I sensed this might take some time.

I drew a long breath and began. After I'd finished answering her queries, I found something in Astrea's face I had not expected to see, at least this early in the conversation: respect, though it was coupled with an overlay of wariness.

I hunched forward. "Now, it's true that we have lost nearly half our army, and the prospects of adding to our magical number are not promising. Our options are to hunker down here, not engage the Maladons and preserve our numbers; continue what we are doing; or become even more aggressive in our battle strategies."

Astrea nodded appreciatively. "You have evidently given this a great deal of thought, Vega, and I commend you for the informed way you have gone about your duty."

"Thank you," I said, but I was wondering what would come next out of her mouth after such praise. What did come next was something I would never have anticipated.

"Let me ask you something, Vega, and think carefully before you answer."

"All right," I said, quite curious now as to what her query would be.

"Have you seen any children among the Maladons?"

My eyes widened.

"I thought as much," she said, in answer to my look.

"There are young boys in Greater True who march under the banner of the Maladons, but they carry mortas, or guns rather, and aren't magical. Other than that, I have seen no children. None at all."

"And have you seen any *female* Maladons at the castle?"

"No, only men," I replied in a hollow tone.

"Yes. I thought that too."

"But I don't understand," I said. "Were there not young Maladons *and* female Maladons back in your time?"

"Though they had not adopted the Maladon name yet, the answer is yes, Vega. Of course there had to be both young and female Maladons, else their number would have died off long since. A male cannot bear children, even by magic."

"So what would explain their absence?" I asked.

"I don't have a definitive answer for you, Vega, but I *do* have a theory."

"I'd like to hear it."

"Necro had a wife."

"And a son, Jason."

"Yes, Jason. Necro's wife I knew well. Her name was Elythia. She loved Jason more than life itself."

"And did she love Necro?"

Astrea didn't answer right away. "I think that Elythia understood what Necro was, or at least what he had become."

"You mean he wasn't always . . . evil?"

"I won't go that far. But there are degrees of evil. And Necro exceeded all of them by the time war came. But there is something else."

"What?"

"I can't be sure of this, you understand. When it was evident that the war was to commence, I had very little contact with Elythia. But I did see her one final time; this was after Jason had been found dead. As I told you before, they blamed his death on us."

"But you think it was Necro who killed him. You told me that. To ensure that the war started."

46

"That's right. And I wasn't the only one who thought that."

"You mean on our side?"

"No, I mean that's also what *Elythia* believed as well."

I was dumbstruck by this. "How do you know that?"

"Because she came to my home on the night that Jason's body was found. That was the last time I ever saw her. She was inconsolable. And she told me that she believed Necro had murdered his own son, though she had no proof."

"Okay, so she knew her husband better than he probably thought she did. But how does that connect to the Maladons having no women and children?"

"Elythia was chosen by Necro to be his wife primarily because of a belief about Elythia and her past. It was long rumored that Elythia was actually not only a sorceress of exceptional power and skill, but also . . . a *goddess*."

I looked at her blankly. "What is a goddess?"

"I guess I can explain the difference by this: We were born with magical ability, and we worked hard to harness that ability and increase our skills at it. A god or goddess is also born with supernatural ability, but they need not expend any energy in gaining skill or power. It is simply there, and at exponentially more powerful levels than any sorcerer or sorceress possesses."

I thought about this. "My grandfather was an Excalibur. He was endowed at birth with certain powers and knowledge of his past. It's sort of like that?"

"Yes, though we are and your grandfather was *human*, Vega."

"And goddesses are not?"

"Let's just say that they are something more than human."

"So their power is infinite? They can do whatever they want?"

"Why do you ask that?"

"Isn't it obvious? If Elythia is all-powerful and she believed that Necro killed her son, why didn't she simply destroy Necro?"

"I don't know, Vega. I just don't know."

"Did Necro know this about Elythia? That she was possibly a goddess?"

"I'm sure that Necro was aware. And to his thinking, having a mate with such strength must have been intoxicating. I have no doubt that he desired very much to see if he could siphon her power and place it onto himself."

I thought this sounded very much like what the Maladons had done to my grandfather and the other magicals they had captured. Sucking out their magic and placing it in those blasted bottles. Perhaps to use later.

Astrea continued. "To my knowledge, he never succeeded in that. Though Elythia let Necro lead his people, I believe that she knew exactly what he was. She was not about to let him gain access to her powers. And I believe that she found a way to get back at him for what he had done."

"How?"

She paused for a moment. "*This* is my theory." She paused once more, her features growing strained. "I believe that she used her powers to make all female Maladons barren from that point on. No more children for them after her husband had taken from her the only child she would ever have. And shortly after Jason's death, Elythia simply vanished and was seen no more."

I took a few moments to absorb this stunning information. "Okay, that would explain why there are no young Maladons. But not why there are no female Maladons. I mean Necro is still alive, so he must be taking something like the Elixir of Life. All of his followers must have too since they couldn't have children."

"Think about it, Vega. Necro, for all his evil, was and is a very smart person. He eventually had to discover what Elythia had done. And so what does he do in retaliation?"

As the truth hit me, my jaw fell.

"Are you saying . . . ?"

She nodded. "I'm saying that Necro *killed* all the Maladon women, who, after Elythia's curse, he saw as being useless to him."

"Useless?!" I exploded. "The git. Does he not know that women make exceptional warriors? Look at you. And Alice! You two could best any Maladon out there."

She shook her head. "For him, women were only good for bearing children, male children preferably."

"Then he's not only evil, but stupid beyond belief!"

Astrea and I shared a knowing smile.

Two women perfectly attuned to dwelling in a world dominated, for no good reason, by men.

"And that," said Astrea, "will be his downfall."

SEX

The Past of My Future

I T WAS VERY late as I stared into the depths of the lingering fire in the library.

All others had long since retired to their beds, except for Harry Two, who sat alertly next to my chair.

Yet I could not sleep. I could barely think. But *think* was the very thing I had to do. Perhaps more deeply than I ever had before.

The revelation about Elythia and her curse had supplanted my anger at Astrea for her trying to usurp my authority and leadership. Though I well knew I would have to revisit that issue with her later.

As the flames flickered in front of my eyes, an idea occurred to me.

In my mind, I said her name. I called out to her that I needed desperately to speak to her.

The next moment Uma Cadmus was hovering next to me, the daughter of Bastion and Victoria Cadmus. Her beauty was something beyond belief. Her face was flawless, every element in perfect proportion to its neighbor. Her blond hair was thick and luxuriant and pooled down over her shoulders as though laid precisely in marble. Her eyes, though, were like chips of ice that the sun had struck at just the right angle, producing a fiery blue that one could literally not draw their gaze from.

And she was also dead.

She had once told me that she was neither ghost nor spirit, but merely represented the emotion of regret.

"Yes, Vega?" she said to me now.

I looked at her curiously. She was always a bit misty, and in spots one could see right through her. But she seemed more transparent than ever.

"Uma, are you all right?"

"I am neither all right nor not all right," she replied dully.

I didn't bother to argue about such a starkly contradictory statement. "I just meant that, well, you look a little less visible tonight."

She looked down at herself and then back up at me. "I am fading," she said simply.

"But why?"

She appraised me sadly. " 'Tis no matter. What is it that you want, Vega?"

I decided to plunge ahead. I told her about what Astrea had said about Elythia, the women she presumably struck barren and there being no young Maladons.

She hovered there without speaking for a few moments, the beats of her heart represented by a pulsing of light from her somewhat transparent chest. She was right — she was fading. Even her exquisite eyes, her most remarkable feature in my estimation, were not quite as striking as they had been. It was as though the light that forged them was dying out.

"What do you want to know from me?"

"First of all, is Astrea correct in what she says?"

"I have no way of knowing. I was dead by the time it would have happened. I killed myself with stones in my pockets when I found out my love, Jason, was dead. The ends of our lives were only separated by a few minutes."

I looked askance at her. "But you're not really dead, Uma. You're here. You can talk to me. You see things. At least tell me about Elythia."

The pulse in her chest beat ever brighter. It was as though the light was returning to her for a bit.

"Jason was far more like his mother than his father."

"She was a good person, Elythia?"

"I admired her, and also pitied her."

"Being married to Necro, you mean?"

She nodded.

"Why would she choose such a mate?" I asked.

"Necro wasn't always like he turned out to be. Or if he was, he hid it well. I was told that he was kind as a boy, gentle as a young man. But then something happened to him. By that time, he and Elythia had married. It was too late."

"What do you think happened to him, to make him so terrible?"

"I think that magic brought out all the most awful impulses that he had. He thirsted for power. Before he came to lead what are now the Maladons, there were no divisions between our people. We were as one. But Necro slowly changed all that. He created the Maladons in his own fiendish image."

"And Elythia? What did she think of all that?"

"She loathed the man her husband had become. But she was wedded to him for life."

"But that makes no sense to me," I replied heatedly. "Astrea described her as a goddess with powers far beyond the magic that we and the Maladons possess. Such a person could do as she pleased. And if she loathed Necro, she could easily be rid of him."

"What you say makes perfect sense, Vega. Yet I have no answer for you. I do know that Elythia chose not to leave him. Or harm him."

"Okay, go on."

"And then there was Jason of course. That was what she focused her entire life on: making sure that Jason did not become like his father."

"And she succeeded."

When Uma said nothing, I repeated, "And she succeeded, right?"

"Jason was the love of my life, Vega."

"I know. You've told me that."

I fell silent waiting for her to speak. When she didn't, I said, "Do you believe that Necro killed Jason?"

"It is an accepted fact."

"But you said you were dead only a few minutes after he breathed his last. How could you know who had killed him? Did someone tell you that it was Necro?"

She glanced up at me, anger flitting across her features. "We have spoken before about this."

"Not really, no. I have been told by others what *might* have happened. That Necro murdered Jason and then blamed it on our kind so that war would be sparked. But no one has provided me any evidence to support that. Pillsbury told me that Necro slit Gunther Adronis's throat, and the facts seem to back that up. But you and I have not spoken about exactly *how* Jason died."

"He was stabbed."

"I know that! But if not by Necro, then by whom?"

"I don't know, because I wasn't there!"

"You suspect no one?"

"His father, Necro. But you know that."

"I know that Elythia thought he had done it. Which is why she cursed the Maladons, barring their women from having children."

53

"What does it matter exactly how Jason died?"

I studied her, never having seen Uma this agitated before.

"Have you ever seen him after his death?" I asked.

She froze. "What?"

"You came here after your death, and I can see you. Alice Adronis is here. Morrigone is here, at least in spirit, or something like that. That means that the dead can come back. So, has Jason appeared to you?"

The next moment, Uma was gone.

Still, I had my answer.

She really didn't know if Necro had killed his son. And she didn't know why Elythia never retaliated against Necro though she believed him the murderer of her only child.

But I needed to know more. And I needed to ask the question that I had failed to ask before.

I returned to the room in the bowels of Empyrean, where I had first met Alice Adronis. I wanted to ask her several things, including the query I had not gotten around to asking her before she vanished from me last time.

It was dark in here, but it was a curious darkness, one unlike any I had ever experienced before. It seemed to have great depth, with seams of lurking light within the blackness, magically inspired, no doubt.

However, I had not come here to learn how light could be part of darkness.

"Alice? Alice, I need to speak with you."

When she didn't appear, my anger got the better of me.

"I bloody well need to speak to you, Alice Adronis. And I'll wait here for the rest of my life if that's what it takes!"

I felt the air around me turn to what felt like fire. The only thing I had ever experienced comparable to the sensation was when Necro hardened the air around me at Maladon Castle.

I leapt back.

And there she was, advancing on me like I had seen her — astride a great, flying steed — charge her opponents on that battlefield all those eons ago.

Her face was full of fury. If she had possessed the Elemental, I felt certain it would be pointed directly at me now, a hideously complicated curse on her lips.

"I am not accustomed —" she began.

Before she could finish, I held up the Elemental, not threateningly of course, but as symbol of the connection between us.

"I want to win, Alice. I want to win this war, *my* war against the Maladons. But I need your help to do so."

My frank words seemed to drain all the fury from her.

She nodded at me to continue, though her cold features made it clear that she was not necessarily agreeing to help me.

I composed myself and said, "You gave me this, the Elemental, on that battlefield that I traveled to when I ventured back in time. That battlefield was where you died."

"This of course I already know," she said tersely.

"But what *I* don't know is how you knew my name. You called me Vega. You gave me this, as though it were predestined that I should possess it. But I went back in time, Alice. I hadn't even been born yet, not for over eight hundred years, when you called me by name. When you gave me this, apparently certain that I was the rightful possessor of it. So how did you know all that?"

She gave me an appraising look, as though weighing what I had just said against how much she should reveal in answer.

" 'Tis a complicated question, Vega," she said in a low voice. The tone astonished me because it seemed to carry with it an element of uncertainty, something I had never associated with the woman.

55

"Then I'll try my best to understand it," I said quickly.

"Time is a tricky thing indeed. It separates generations, but it also *connects* those from different eras."

I looked at her curiously. "How can time separate but also connect?"

"We are family, Vega. My blood runs in your veins. You must have noted the resemblance between us."

I looked down at myself and then back up at her.

"We do look alike."

"But that is not all of it. It is far more than how we *look*. Though we are separated by the eons, there is a strand of even more powerful connectivity between us that we refer to as *Empchon*."

I shook my head. "I don't know what that means. And it doesn't explain why you knew my name."

In answer, she put her hand to her chest, where her gaping, mortal wound was plain to see.

"Do you think it was mere coincidence that you appeared on that battlefield on the very day that I perished?"

I had never thought about this before. I thought it *had* just been happenstance.

"Due to the laws of Empchon, what you needed to see in the past is what you saw. And you needed to see . . . me. On the very day of my death. So I could give you that."

She pointed at the Elemental. "It is not merely a wand, as I'm sure you have learned."

"It's saved my life more times than I can remember," I said. "Both as a wand and as a spear."

"You would not have survived your time in Wormwood, then, without it?"

"No," I said. "If not for the —"

I stopped and blanched as what she was trying to tell me finally dug its way into my apparently slow-moving thoughts.

"You gave me the Elemental . . ."

"To allow you to survive, Vega. So you could one day be *here*."

"To fight the Maladons," I said.

She nodded. "It is Empchon. Sometimes known as the Fates. It is preordained. No one can control it. One must obey it. That is all."

"So, you knew when you saw me on the battlefield that I was the one to lead us now?"

She nodded. "It was why I fought to keep you alive that day. I took risks that I otherwise might not have taken."

The message underlying her words took a bit of time for me to grasp.

The color slowly drained from my face. *Took risks you otherwise might not have taken?* "Alice, are . . . are you saying that if I hadn't appeared on the battlefield that day that you would not have . . . ?"

I pointed at her mortal wound.

She stared at me, seeming unwilling to answer my query.

"Alice!"

" 'Tis a small price to pay, Vega. Our war was lost at that point. We all knew it. Though some of us stubbornly refused to admit it," she added. "Myself included."

"But how could you possibly have known my name?"

In answer, she snapped her fingers, and in the palm of her hand appeared a delicate tiny bird, nearly as transparent as she was.

"What is this, Vega?"

I looked at the creature. "It's a bird."

"How do you know that?"

"Because, well, because what else could it be?"

She snapped her fingers, and the bird vanished.

"You were the bird that came to me that day. Appearing on a battlefield and in an era where you had no other reason to be. And I thought, who else could it be, other than you, Vega Jane, my descendant?"

"I still don't understand." And I truly did not. I didn't consider myself dim-witted, but I was feeling such.

"Then let me make it crystal clear." She paused. "Your ancestor Jasper Jane?"

"What of him?"

"You have met his spirit?"

"Yes. He helped save my life in the Quag."

"He was a brilliant man, expert in many magical fields, including the darker ones inhabited by the Maladons. Shortly after the war with the Maladons commenced, he too took a trip through time. But not to the past."

"Then he went into the future?" I said.

"It is the only alternative," she said tersely.

"And what did he see in the future?" I said, slowly, though the answer was dawning on me as I asked the question.

"He saw . . . *you*."

The Dog in the Nighttime

THE REVELATION THAT Jasper had seen me in the future had been a stunning one. But what Alice had refused to tell me was what Jasper had seen of me. I had implored her to do so, but she had vanished without answering.

I walked mutely back to my room that night and spent the next several days in a sort of mental limbo. Nothing that I had learned from either Astrea or Alice could aid me in my principal endeavor: winning the war against the Maladons.

I had canceled all missions and had my dwindling forces alternating polishing their fighting skills and resting. But that was no strategy. While we sat here twiddling our thumbs in essence, the Maladons were out there, plotting to finish us off. Even now they could be devising ways to find and penetrate Empyrean. They had done so with the dome around the Quag. And if they could do that, then nowhere, not even Empyrean, was safe.

Thus, I had sentries posted day and night whose sole job was to watch for any suspicious activity. But it was not enough. At some point we would have to leave the relative safety of Empyrean and take up the fight once more. Only, I still had not conceived of a way to do so that would not result in our absolute destruction.

It did not help my mood that I also saw Astrea talking to quite a few of the others, in the halls, in the library, and over meals. I frowned whenever I saw this. Once, she saw me watching, and she merely smiled and continued on with her conversation with Anna Dibble.

When I questioned several of my warriors as to what they had discussed, they all said that Astrea was only interested in their confrontations with the Maladons, how they fought, what sort of tactics they used, what their magic was like in battle. What spells did they seem particularly vulnerable to and that sort of thing. They were universal in telling me that Astrea was highly complimentary of what I had accomplished, and was in no way trying to undermine my authority.

I could not maintain that her queries were unreasonable. She could just be updating her knowledge of the Maladons from the days when she had taken up her wand against them.

I discussed with Delph what Alice had told me, one night after everyone else had gone to bed.

"They have control of garms and jabbits," I said. "They can make the Elixir probably forever. Whereas, we can't."

"Well, we'll just have to beat them before we die," said Delph.

"Easier said than done. And now Astrea is here to, I don't know, second-guess me on everything."

"We follow you, Vega Jane, not bloody Astrea."

"Thanks, Delph."

As I rose to leave, Delph took my hand.

He said, "Have you thought about life after the Maladons are no more?"

I felt myself taken aback, because I hadn't thought about it at all.

My look had evidently been answer enough because Delph said, "I have. I mean, you have to make plans, right?"

I stroked his hand with mine. "What sort of plans are you thinking about, Delph?"

I expected him to grow reticent, or hem and haw or be confused, because while Delph is brilliant and can articulate things I never could, he sometimes places his very large foot in his mouth when discussing things of a highly personal nature, which is where I believed he was going with this.

Yet he surprised me.

"My plans include you, Vega Jane. Being with you, until I breathe my last."

My eyes widened and then moistened as I grasped all of what he was saying. But I was terrified too because of the phrase he had used: *breathe my last.*

"We, um, we have, I mean, don't you think we have time to, um, sort those things out, Delph?" I said. Now it was me with my big foot in my mouth.

"Do we?" he said, his gaze fixed on mine. "I think we have a great many things, but time may not be one of them."

"I . . . I know."

"I just want you to think about it, okay?" he said, gripping my hand tightly.

"I will, Delph. I promise."

I sighed and took my leave of Delph, heading to my room. I was all wonky in the head. So wonky that I almost didn't see him coming.

He stepped from the shadows so suddenly that I had half drawn my wand from my pocket.

"Don't do that again," I snapped. "Unless you want a curse dangling around your neck."

Archie Prine didn't look the least bit put off by my warning.

61

"We need to talk, Vega."

"What about?" I snapped. My thoughts were still back with Delph and all that his words had done to affect me. I didn't want to have to focus on this git now.

"You needn't take that tone with me. We are on the same side after all. You act like I'm your enemy or something. It's not fair."

"Oh, I'm sorry, Archie," I said with mock contriteness. "I guess it must have to do with the time you tried to bloody well *murder* me."

"I had my reasons," he said offhandedly. "And I didn't actually end up murdering you, did I?"

This bloke was really something.

"Not for want of trying. If it weren't for Delph, I would be dead at your hands."

Delph again.

I think we have a great many things, but time may not be one of them.

"Vega, are you listening to me?" Archie snapped.

Delph's image vanished from my thoughts, and I focused on Archie. "What do you want? I'm busy."

"You've been very cavalier with my mother's offer to lead our forces."

"Really? I thought I was pretty clear that I had *rejected* her *offer.*"

"She is far more experienced than you are in a war with the Maladons. You have to admit that."

"Eight hundred years ago, yes. But I've been battling them for the last two years. And my blokes have killed far more of them than they have of us, so there."

"But as she pointed out, that is a losing proposition."

"Your mother didn't have to *point* it out. I was well aware of it. So, unless you can ruddy conjure me some more magical folks who will fight with us, or else make the Maladons lay down their wands or better yet bloody well disappear, then I'm not sure how Astrea can lead any more effectively than I can."

"She is a great sorceress."

"So am I," I said heatedly. "I've faced Endemen and Necro and been outnumbered a dozen to one and survived. And, unless you forgot, your mother *lost* her war. So, Archie, tell me why should I assume the outcome will be any different *this* time?"

I struck home with this point. Archie's face scrunched up in uncertainty and confusion.

I decided to take the opportunity to put an end to this nonsense. "Now, if you'll excuse me." I pushed past him and went to my bedroom and slammed the door behind me.

"What a git!" I said to Harry Two, who lay on my bed. I really was seething. Astrea and Archie seemed to have completely discounted the fact that I had been fighting the Maladons all this time and had more than held my own. Indeed, if I had fifty more warriors, I was convinced we would wipe the field with them. But I didn't have fifty more warriors. I didn't have five more.

I sat on my bed and stroked Harry Two's head. My dog had an amazing power to calm me, and calm was what I needed right now.

"It's a real conundrum, Harry Two. It seems impossible, it really does. I can make neither heads nor tails of it, but I have to, in the end. We have to find a way to beat these blokes."

In answer, Harry Two did something unexpected. He rose, hopped off the bed, went to my wardrobe set against one wall and scratched at the door. He had never done this before.

I rose and crossed the room. "What is it, Harry Two? What's the matter?"

His answer was to scratch more furiously at the door.

I opened it and he pawed at a drawer inside. I opened the drawer, and a smile creased my features.

I pulled out the old parchment and closed the drawer. Embedded inside the parchment was a sometimes cranky but more often helpful spirit, or some such oddity. Actually, I had no idea what the thing calling himself Silenus actually was, but I was glad Harry Two had drawn my attention to him.

"Thanks, Harry Two."

Only, Harry Two remained staring at the wardrobe. But I didn't really focus on this because I was excited about the prospects with Silenus.

I carried the roll back over to the bed, sat down and touched the parchment.

"Silenus? I'd like to talk to you."

A moment later, a face appeared on the paper. The features were old, but the eyes were very sharp indeed. I had found that there was much wisdom in Silenus.

"Yes, Vega?"

I explained to him my dilemma.

"I can see no way to defeat the Maladons by staying the course that we're on. Even with the addition of Astrea and Archie, that only gives us two more wands in battle. It's not enough. By my calculations, by the time the last of us fall, there will be hundreds of Maladons left. I would appreciate any advice you have to give me."

Silenus mulled over this for a long minute. I went from looking at him hopefully to gazing at him helplessly.

When I glanced at Harry Two, he was paying us no mind, but still sat staring at the wardrobe door.

Finally, Silenus spoke. "You are assuming that you can summon no others to your aid."

64

"If I can find my parents, that would be helpful, but apparently one of them is injured, and I have no way to locate them."

Silenus looked at me in a disappointed fashion. "Have you *tried* to find them?"

I felt my face flush. "Of course I have."

"How have you done so?"

I sputtered, "I almost found them when a scouting expedition I sent out was told that my mother had been looking for some healing herbs. I immediately went to the spot and searched for her. I found a bit of cloth with some blood on it that I know belonged to her."

"But you did not find her."

"No, that was when I ran into Astrea and Archie."

"So, you stopped searching at that point?"

I felt my face flush once more. "There was no sign of them. I tried to send my mother a message, but she didn't reply. And I . . . I had to get Astrea and Archie back here to safety."

"Really? Why was that? Could you not have employed them to help you search further for your parents? After all, the blood on the cloth indicated that they were in some peril, did it not?"

I simply stared at him. I had come to him for help, and all I was getting were accusations about my poor performance with regard to finding my parents.

"I believe that I did all I could." The defensiveness in my voice made me feel all the more guilty, because I suddenly realized that he was right.

Silenus did not even deign to answer this statement.

After a few moments of silence, I said tersely, "Can you not help me, then?"

"I think, Vega, that the best thing you can do is think about what you want to accomplish and study the tools you have at your disposal to meet your goals."

"What do you think I've be—"

I stopped because Silenus had vanished.

"Git!"

I stuffed the parchment back into the drawer and slammed shut the wardrobe door.

I was breathing so heavily I felt as though I might be sick to my stomach.

"Well," I said to the walls of my bedroom. "I guess I better simply carry on and see what can be done, since certain people do not wish to help me."

I undressed and climbed into bed.

Harry Two usually curled up next to me, but this time he didn't. He was sitting on the floor still staring at my wardrobe.

I sat wearily up in bed and looked at him. Whenever Harry Two did this, it meant he wanted me to do something. But I was simply too knackered.

"Harry Two," I said. "Come to bed. I've already tried to talk to Silenus. It was no help, and I'm not going to bother with him again."

My dog didn't move.

I angrily punched my pillow into a more comfortable shape and slumped back.

Time ticked by. Every once in a while, I would glance over at the wardrobe.

Harry Two was sitting there like a rock, staring at it.

But there was nothing in there that he could need. I just thought he was being stubborn about something.

I slumped back again.

An hour passed, and it must have been about three in the morning when I heard a scratching sound.

I looked up, and Harry Two was sliding his paw up and down against the door of the wardrobe.

I sighed, slowly climbed out of bed and stood next to him with my hands on my hips.

"Harry Two, what is wrong with you? What are you trying to tell me?"

He scratched at the wood again.

"There's nothing else in there that you would want."

He ignored me and scratched again.

I opened the door. "See? It's just clothes."

The next moment I watched in amazement as he leapt up and snagged something off a wall peg in the wardrobe.

Stunned, I could see that it was the bit of bloody cloth of my mother's that I'd found in the woods the day I'd run into Astrea and Archie. It still had the flower and message that I had etched into the fabric with my wand.

With the cloth in his mouth, my dog rushed over to the door and stared at it.

Realization as to what Harry Two wanted to do spread over me.

Excited, I quickly dressed, grabbed my wand and opened the door.

Harry Two raced down the stairs to the front door. No one was about at this late hour. We stepped outside, I harnessed him to my chest, twisted the ring of invisibility around and we took to the air.

A Visible Event

I HAD BEEN SUCH an idiot not to think of this myself.

I well knew the power of smell that dogs had.

I used the *Pass-pusay* spell to take us directly to where I had found the cloth.

We landed, and I unharnessed Harry Two but created a magical tether so that he would remain invisible along with me.

I had no idea who might be around. I already knew that Maladons had visited this area, and they might come back at any time. Hence, my wand was held at the ready, even as I rushed after Harry Two, who was nimbly sprinting over the uneven terrain.

He must already have the scent of my mother in his nostrils, I thought excitedly. He bounded around a tree and then up an incline slicked with rain on top of low ground cover. I struggled up after him. When he reached the top, Harry Two stopped and gazed around, sniffing the air with his big nostrils, sucking in what I hoped was a replenished portion of my mother's scent.

But Harry Two seemed confused. He turned and looked up at me. In his mismatched eyes, I saw uncertainty, and this made my spirits wilt. Had we come here for nothing?

I peered around the area. It looked just the same as the last time I had been here. I took a few tentative steps forward and risked calling out to my parents.

"Mum, Dad, are you out there? It's me, Vega. Can you send me a signal? I want to help you."

There was no response.

I pondered what to do and finally decided to do a bit of reconnaissance. I led Harry Two back to the cottage where I had gone earlier. There was a light on inside, which seemed strange for the time of night.

I approached cautiously and knocked on the door, my wand at the ready while Harry Two was showing his fangs.

Right before the door opened, I turned the ring around so that Harry Two and I became visible once more.

The door creaked open, and the same old woman appeared there.

"You've come back," she said.

I nodded. "I came looking for Helen, my mother."

The old woman nodded.

"Have the others been back since I was last here?" I asked.

She shook her head. "But I'm afraid they will return."

I happened to look over her shoulder and saw something small and huddled in front of the meager blaze burning in the stone fireplace.

"Who's that?" I asked.

"My grandson."

"Where are his parents?"

"They were taken."

"Did they have the mark on their hands?"

"Marks? No."

"Does he?" I asked, glancing at the huddled figure.

She looked puzzled. "There is something there, yes. It's faint."

I said, "Can I speak with him?"

She nodded and stepped aside to let me pass.

I approached the boy, who I could hear had a racking cough.

"He's sick?" I asked the woman.

"Since yesterday."

"What's his name?"

"John."

I nodded and drew closer.

He had my brother's name, though he was far younger. By the size of him, he looked to be perhaps six or seven at most.

"John, my name is Vega. I can make you feel better." I took the Adder Stone from my pocket. The Stone held the magic of a powerful sorceress. You waved it over the injured or sick person, thought good thoughts and it could heal pretty much anything. But if you ever thought bad thoughts while using it, I had been told the results would be catastrophic. Fortunately, I had no desire to use it for harm.

I said, "This can make you feel better."

He coughed some more but wouldn't look at me.

I drew even closer.

"Can you look at me?"

John didn't move.

I walked past and turned to look at him.

He was bent over, rocking back and forth.

I held up the Adder Stone and waved it over him, thinking good thoughts.

To my shock, he continued to cough and rock.

I looked down at the Stone. What was going on?

I knelt down in front of the boy.

"John. Can you hear me?"

He nodded.

"Can I see your hand?"

He slowly held out his right hand. On it I could see the faint traces of the mark of the three hooks.

I slowly let go of it.

His fingers reached out and touched my ring.

As I felt his skin slide against mine, it sent shivers down my spine.

"John, can you look at me?"

He slowly lifted his head.

And I received the greatest shock of my life.

My brother, John, was staring back at me.

I leapt back and gasped, "John!" I felt the tears roll down my face. "John, it's me, Vega."

I went to hug him. "It's me."

My arms wrapped around him.

And the next moment I was clinging to air.

And I was no longer in the cottage. I was standing by the forest with Harry Two next to me.

I looked around in amazement. And then I stared down at my hands. Hands that had just been about to wrap around my brother.

He was gone. I was breathing so hard that I could barely stand.

What had just happened? How was any of this possible? Had I been hallucinating?

I felt something behind me and turned to stare.

It was the old woman.

"Where is John? Where is my brother?" I called out.

She didn't answer me.

The hairs on my arms started to rise, something I never took as a good sign.

I looked back at Harry Two. My dog was no longer staring out across the woods. His full attention was on the woman. He gave off a low growl, and I saw his hackles rise. He bared his fangs.

I also never took that as a good sign.

"Stay, Harry Two," I whispered. "Stay."

I turned back and drew closer to the woman.

I remembered to turn my ring around so that I would become invisible.

"Why are you here?" I asked.

She just stared at me. I mean she was looking directly at me though she couldn't possibly see me!

The next moment I had catapulted into the air, pulling Harry Two with me by virtue of the magical tether.

There were so many spells shooting at where we had just been standing that they seemed to blur together into one massive blast of light.

I leveled out and zipped forward, pulling Harry Two toward me and buckling him into his harness. We soared over the forest as spells hurled skyward. I rolled and banked and dove and rose to avoid them.

What the Hel was going on? How could they see me? And where was my brother?

I tapped my leg and said, *"Pass-pusay."*

The vision of Empyrean was firmly in my mind.

I expected my feet and Harry Two's paws to land on the solid stone porch of my ancestral home and to be safe from this nightmare.

That did not happen.

The fear seized up in my throat. I felt frozen even though I was hurtling along at an incredible velocity.

I tapped my leg again and again and said the words over and over.

"Pass-pusay. Pass-pusay."

A spell shot right over my head.

I looked behind me, and my spirits dropped right through the dirt.

Endemen, Necro's most trusted fighter, was right behind me along with at least twenty Maladons in pinstripe suits and bowler hats.

I shot a glance at my hand where the mark of the three hooks was. Maladons, we had found, could trace us through that mark. That's why I wore the glove that Alice Adronis had given me, because it prevented the Maladons from tracking me that way.

Then I looked at the ring of invisibility that had once belonged to my grandfather, who had, in turn, been given it by Colin Sonnet, Petra's ancestor.

It had given me protection for so long that I really took it for granted.

But now, as I looked down at it, I was horrified.

My ring was glowing a dull red. It had never done that. I looked back over my shoulder at the oncoming Maladons.

It was clear.

They could see me!

Then I thought back to the creature before the fire. It had touched my finger.

No, it had touched my *ring*. And somehow disabled its power.

I smacked my leg with my wand again and muttered the incantation, *"Pass-pusay."*

Again, nothing happened.

How could they stop my incantation?

Another spell struck, and Harry Two howled.

I looked down at him as he hung limply from the harness. "Harry Two. No!"

At the same instant, I felt the very air around me commence to harden, just like it had done back at Maladon Castle.

I was panicking now because I knew that this must mean Necro was somewhere nearby. I was unafraid of Endemen because I had bested him before. But Necro was a different matter altogether.

And now he was going to kill me.

That must be how the *Pass-pusay* incantation had been stopped.

I found it harder and harder to breathe.

I felt my body growing limp.

So this was how it was going to end.

I stroked the limp Harry Two's ear.

I'm sorry, Harry Two. I'm so sorry for being so bloody stupid.

I was at a point now where I could no longer stay in the air. I felt myself flip over, and then I was in a long, steep dive.

The only result would be impact with the ground. And that would be that.

I closed my eyes and said my good-byes.

Good-bye, Delph. Please forgive me for leaving you. And do your best. Good-bye, Petra. Take care of Delph. And beat the Maladons to dust. Good-bye . . .

Out of the corner of my eye, I saw the streak of light heading my way.

I knew that this had to be a killing spell. They were taking no chances apparently that the collision with the ground would do me in.

I braced myself for impact.

And then it struck me.

And I was gone.

Her, Finally

THE SENSE OF falling this time was beyond anything I had ever felt. Even when I was first learning to fly with Destin and had my share of hard encounters with the dirt after tumbling from lofty heights.

But when I finally stopped dropping, there was no hard collision with the ground.

I opened my eyes and looked around.

I felt Harry Two's body lying on top of me.

"Harry Two!"

He just hung limply in his harness.

A hand passed in front of me, reached out to my dog and rubbed something against his fur.

I looked wildly around to see who it could be. But it was dark; all I could glimpse was a silhouette.

"Who are —" I flinched when I saw a wand tip appear and tap the spot where the hand had touched my dog.

I was about to pull my wand, when I felt something. I felt something absolutely wonderful.

Harry Two was moving. I could hear his heartbeats against my chest.

"Harry Two! You're alive!"

He licked my face, and I hugged him.

And then every single part of me froze as if I had been struck by the *Paralycto* spell.

"M . . . Mum?"

My mother, Helen Jane, was staring back at me as she slowly lowered her wand.

I had not seen her for over three years. And she looked like she had aged twenty. I barely recognized her. Yet it *was* my mother.

Her fingers graced my cheek.

"Vega, thank the Steeples that you are unharmed."

I sat up and unbuckled Harry Two.

Then I stood on shaky legs, held out my arms and hugged my mother so tightly I thought we might both burst.

I felt her thin, strong arms hug me back. I buried my nose in her hair and breathed in her scent. I started to sob. And she did too. We both stood there shaking together for I don't know how long.

When we drew apart, I took her in fully, as she did me.

"You saved my life," I said. I looked at her wand. "The *Rejoinda* spell?"

She gave a teary smile and nodded. "Slightly modified. It was born of necessity," she added.

"Someone told me all magic is born from that."

Then I realized what was missing.

"Where's Dad?"

Her smile faded. "Come. I will take you to him. It's not far."

She held out her hand, which I immediately took. I was now taller and physically stronger than my mother. But it was as though I was once more a little girl reaching out for her mother to guide her.

I glanced at the back of her hand and saw the mark of the three hooks.

"The Maladons can track you that way," I warned.

"They can no more," she said. "We turned the link upon itself such that the trace creates a confusion incantation only in a Maladon. That allows us to take distinct advantage. It was your father who thought of it."

"That *is* quite clever," I said admiringly, thinking that my grandfather Virgil had done something very similar to overcome the challenges of his mark.

Harry Two trailed behind us.

"How did you save Harry Two?" I asked. "I have a magical healing stone, but I had no chance to use it."

"Healing herbs paired with a bit of magic did the trick," she said. "Where separately they would have failed."

"Was that also born out of necessity?"

"Everything here is, Vega. Everything."

"So, is Dad okay?"

I felt my entire body tremble as I asked this.

"Let's just wait until we get there, Vega."

I did not take this as good news. The euphoria I had felt at finding my mother was fading to despair.

"How did you know I was even near you?" I asked.

"*Crystilado magnifica*," she replied. "The Maladons keep coming back to this area, so I maintain a constant watch. I saw them appear earlier. They went to that cottage and did something to the old woman who lives there. Then I saw the Bowler Hats show up. They only come around when something significant is about to happen. So I kept watching." Her hand twitched inside mine. "That's when I saw you in peril." She paused and said, "*He* is nearby."

"You mean Necro?" I said.

She nodded.

I thought about this. "I did not think he ever left Maladon Castle."

"I didn't think that he did either," she said.

"You've been there?"

"To see it. But not to go inside."

As we were walking, I said, "Shouldn't we be prepared for the Maladons to follow us?"

"I have taken precautions," she said. "We are safe, for now."

"Even against Necro?"

"Powerful as he is, he is not infallible," she replied in a firm tone. This boosted my spirits considerably.

I squeezed her hand, not believing my good fortune at having been reunited with her at last.

"I have been looking for you and Dad," I said. "Ever since you left Wormwood."

I hesitated as anger swelled up inside me. I quickly pushed it back down. Now was not the time to bring up my parents abandoning me and my brother back in Wormwood. I'm sure there was a good explanation.

"We have been looking for Virgil," she said. "We had no idea that you were here, Vega. I was never more stunned in my life than when I saw you tonight."

I nodded and said in a shaky voice, "Virgil is dead. Killed by Necro."

My mother stopped walking and simply stood there staring out into the darkness. I felt the pulse in her hand start to race.

"Virgil is dead?"

"Yes. He told me he was never able to find you."

She started walking again and pulled me along.

Before I could say anything else, we had passed over a rise in the ground and she stopped.

Down below, there was a little glen, but that was all.

"Is Dad somewhere around here?"

She nodded.

She waved her wand, and the air in front of us seemed to shimmy. We passed through what felt like a barrier.

"Boundary incantations," explained my mother as I nodded in understanding.

Revealed in front of us was a small shack with a curl of smoke escaping from its stone chimney.

She moved her wand again, and the door opened.

She walked through and beckoned me to follow.

I did so.

And screamed.

I was looking down at this . . . thing lying on a cot. It was not much bigger than a newborn with a head half again larger than it should have been for the size of the body. It was very pale, and its appendages were bent and twisted. It was quietly sobbing.

Though it was hideous to look at, I could not help but feel sorry for the piteous creature.

"What is that wretched thing?" I asked my mother.

"That wretched thing," she said, "is your father."

DECEM

A Friend in Need

I DON'T REALLY REMEMBER transporting my mother and father to Empyrean. I know that my feet hit the front steps. I know that my wand opened the door. I know that we were greeted by Delph, Petra, Astrea and many others.

And all the while I carried in my arms, and wrapped in a blanket, my father.

Dropping my cloak on the floor and telling the others I would explain fully later, I took him and my mother to an upstairs bedroom. I laid my father on the bed and looked down at him.

"What happened?" I gasped. I had been too shocked to ask when I first found out this pitiable creature was Hector Jane.

My mother sat on the side of the bed and gently rubbed her husband's forehead with her hand.

"We were surprised by a group of Maladons. We fought our way clear, but as we were escaping, two Maladons sent spells at us. Before they hit your father, they collided and their mingled magic struck him." She cast her gaze down at the little bundle on the bed. "And this was the result."

"When did it happen?"

"Two months ago." She shook her head in misery. "I have tried everything I could think of to bring your father back, but nothing has worked. At least he is still alive. Which gives us a chance of restoring him to what he was."

I had a sudden thought. I took the Adder Stone from my pocket.

"As I said, this is a healing stone. It has the magical power of a sorceress embedded inside it. It might help."

I waved it over my father and thought absolutely good thoughts. And though we both stared at him anxiously, absolutely nothing happened.

"It was a worthy try, Vega."

I nodded and put the Stone back in my pocket.

My mother looked around in wonder. "What a beautiful place this is."

I quickly explained to her about Empyrean.

"You are safe here," I said. "Both of you. And we will do whatever we can to try and bring Dad back to what he was."

She nodded but said nothing.

I studied my mother more closely. After having lost her so long ago, and after searching for her ever since, it was unfathomable to me that she was sitting on a bed in Empyrean while I stood next to her. It was almost as if we had never been apart. But when I looked down at my wretched father, it was quickly apparent that we had been separated for far too long.

My mind wandered back to the days in Wormwood. John was still a child, and I was not yet ten. We had a good life. We all lived in our home and I had not yet started work.

I still went to Learning back then, and my parents would walk us there every morning and return in the evening to take us home. My fingers would interlace with either my mother's or my father's. They would ask what we had learned that day, and I would do the answering. My brother was still painfully shy and would simply stare at his too-large feet and nibble on whatever snack our parents had brought us. I would rail against what we were being taught, or rather what we were not being taught, for even back then I was suspicious that much about our history was being kept from us.

My mother would listen carefully while my father would snatch anxious glances at the both of us. She could have told me to stop asking such questions, but she never did. Instead, she had said, "Keep raising your hand and keep asking, Vega. That is the only way you will ever get answers."

And I had. Right up until the time they kicked me out.

We would spend the evening cooking our last meal of the day together in the tiny kitchen, which, back then, seemed as big as Empyrean's to me. My mother was quite a fine cook, and though we hadn't much in the way of coin to buy the food they sold on the High Street, we ate very well indeed.

And then our happiness had been blasted away when my parents were struck down by a curse from Morrigone and placed in the Care.

I leaned into her. "Mother, it's so good to have you back. I can't believe you're really here."

My mother smiled at me. "I can hardly believe it either, Vega, my dear, sweet child. Though you are clearly no longer a child. You are a woman." She looked me over. "And if I had to hazard a guess, you have grown into a fine sorceress and warrior."

"I've had my share of battles."

"Who leads you?" she asked.

I was a bit taken aback by her query, but then I supposed it was certainly a fair one. My mother had no idea about what had taken place with me.

"I am the leader," I said.

She looked at me, clearly surprised. "Indeed?"

I suddenly felt my face redden. Had she supposed a man was in charge?

"Yes. I fought my way across the Quag with Delph and my dog, Harry Two, after escaping from Wormwood. Then I fought my way through this place. I have personally killed over a hundred Maladons," I added for good measure.

She looked at me, shocked. "Over a hundred Maladons?!"

At first, I didn't think she believed me, but then she smiled. "Your grandfather always said that you were special, Vega. That you would do great things."

I didn't smile at her remark because Virgil had never told me that.

"My holy Steeples," she cried out. "I must be losing my mind. Where is John? Did he come with you into the Quag? Or is he still back in Wormwood? If he's here, you must fetch him so I can see my *son*."

I stood there frozen as she looked up at me.

"Is . . . is John not here, then?"

I shook my head. "No, he's not."

I saw the light go out in my mother's eyes. "Is . . . he . . . ? Please, don't tell me . . ."

"He's not dead. At least not that I know." I sat down on the bed and took her hand in mine. Of course my mother would want to know of John's fate. And I should have thought of this and prepared a proper response. But, being a git, I hadn't.

"I have been back to Wormwood," I said.

"And?"

Now I had to force myself from tearing up. "It no longer exists. The Maladons were able to pierce the Quag, reach Wormwood. And destroy it. They killed all. Thansius died in my arms. They had left him behind half-dead and blind to dig the graves."

As I recalled this horrible scene, my eyes welled with tears.

"But you said John was not dead."

"There was no grave for John," I replied. "I have no proof of this, but I believe . . . I believe the Maladons took him."

She shuddered and looked like she might be sick. "But why?" she exclaimed.

"John is exceptionally bright," I began. And then I plunged in and told her how Morrigone had taken John under her wing. How he had helped design the wall to keep us in. And I spoke a bit about the dark subjects he had found so fascinating.

"He had changed, Mum, by the time I left. John was still in there somewhere, but so were many other things in him too. Things I did not recognize."

I watched, shocked, as she withdrew her hand from mine and looked away from me.

"And so you just left your brother in the clutches of that . . . woman?" she said coldly.

My jaw slackened. "There was nothing I could do. It would have been impossible for me to have taken John."

"I saw Delph downstairs. You managed to bring him. But not your brother? Your own flesh and blood."

I felt my face flame. This was the last thing I would have expected from my mother. Blaming me for not rescuing John. And my parents hadn't taken their own "flesh and blood" when they had left Wormwood, had they?

But then doubt began to creep into my mind. Was my mother right? Had I callously abandoned my brother? Did I try hard enough to find a way to bring him along? I *had* managed to take along Delph and Harry Two.

"We were very nearly all killed as it was when we fled Wormwood," I said. "And since that time, we have been nearly killed dozens of times. John would never have survived."

She looked at me, and I had never seen such an expression

on my mother's face. It was bitter and angry and something I never thought my mother could possibly be — ugly.

She snapped, "You can't possibly know that. And better death for him than to be in the hands of the accursed Maladons."

This statement shocked me to my core. But, again, as I thought about it, I believed my mother had a point. Wouldn't I choose death over being a prisoner of the Maladons?

But what my mother really didn't understand, despite my words, was that John *had* changed. He was no longer an innocent little boy. He had grown into someone I didn't recognize. Someone, dare I even think it, who could choose the side of the Maladons over us.

"So how long have they had him?" she said, still looking at me with a face full of fury and betrayal.

"Two years, possibly."

I saw her demonstrably tremble at my answer. "My . . . poor . . . son," she said, her words coming out in long gasps.

I tried to get my emotions under control but only half succeeded. "You must be hungry. I will have food brought up. And you can clean up and rest." I looked at my father. "I . . . what nourishment does he require?" I asked lamely.

"He will have a bit of mine," she said tersely. "That will be fine. Thank you, Vega," she added coldly.

I nodded. "All right. I have some things to attend to. If you need anything at all."

"I'm sure whatever arrangements you have devised will be fine, Vega," she said, her words holding not a trace of warmth.

It was as though I was speaking with a complete stranger.

The fate of John had driven a block of granite directly between us.

I had dreamed many times of finding my parents. Not a single time had I ever imagined it to be like the reality facing me now.

I left without another word and fled to my room down the hall. I slammed the door shut, threw myself on the floor and lay there sobbing and quaking for how long I wasn't sure.

When I finally sat up, I was drained. My limbs were weak, my thoughts muddled and my spirits crushed.

There came a knock on the door.

I closed my eyes and said nothing in response. I just wanted whoever it was to go away.

"Vega Jane?"

It was Delph, and I did not want to talk to him or even see him.

"Not now, Delph. Please. I just need to be by myself for a bit, okay?"

Several minutes of silence were followed by another tapping on the door.

"Delph, please, just go away."

"It's not Delph. It's Petra."

I shook my head in frustration. "What is it, Petra?"

"I heard, Vega. I heard what was said."

Stunned by this, I slowly got to my feet, crossed the room and yanked open the door.

"You heard *what* precisely?" I snapped.

"I think this might be done better in private," she replied quietly.

I glanced down the hall to see several people staring at us.

I stood back and let her pass. Then I shut the door and faced her.

"You heard what?!"

"You and your mother."

"So, you were spying on us?" I said accusingly.

"No, I came to your room to bring you this."

She held up the Elemental. "It was in your cloak. You left it on the floor of the hall."

I blinked and took it from her.

"Thank you. But that doesn't explain how you heard my mother and me speaking."

Surprisingly, she pointed to my wand. "I don't know how it worked, Vega, but I heard everything through your *wand*."

I looked down at the Elemental, a sense of fear and also betrayal going through my mind.

"What, do you mean like I sent a wand wire? But that makes no sense. I didn't even have my wand with me."

Petra shook her head. "I think whether you have your wand or not, it's a part of you. It's almost as if it was sensing what you were going through, Vega. When I was holding it, I . . . well, I felt sadness coursing through me."

I continued to stare dully at my wand. That had also been the case with Alice. Whatever the Elemental saw, or presumably heard, was also communicated to her.

"Did anyone else hear?" I said slowly.

"No, just me. And I would never mention it to anyone else," she added hastily. "Never."

"Thank you for that."

I turned away from her. But I felt so lost, so full of despair, that I was unsure of what to do or say.

"I'm sorry, Vega."

I waved this off. "I don't need pity, Petra."

"Nor am I offering any. I feel sorry for you *and* your mother. It's not the same thing as pity."

I shot her a quick glance.

She sat down on the edge of my bed and looked at me.

"What your mother said any mother would have said, in the heat of the moment. But I'm sure she is regretting her words."

"You can't possibly know that," I retorted.

"Perhaps. But it's more likely than anything you might be thinking right now. And I also know that what you're feeling is tremendous guilt. Because I've felt it too. I know what you're going through, Vega."

I studied my feet. "But when it happens, you feel that it's only happening to *you*."

"There is something we can do," she said.

"What?"

"We can try to find your brother."

"I *have* been trying to find him! Everywhere I go I look for him, ask questions of people. I've cursed Maladons I've come across to try and get information. Nothing has worked."

"It may be that he's being kept at Maladon Castle."

"He might be," I agreed. I looked down at my ring. "And they used some spell to make my ring not work. They could *see* me, Petra. If not for my mother's quick thinking, I wouldn't be here. I'd be dead."

She looked stunned by this revelation.

I went on gloomily. "Which means I can't use invisibility to get inside the castle anymore. And if I can't do that, how can I go there and look for John?"

"We can attack the place," she suggested, though I could tell it was done halfheartedly.

"And be slaughtered for our troubles?" I replied, shaking my head. "I can't ask anyone here to do that, not even for my brother. It's not right or fair to them."

"There must be a way," she said.

I mulled this over. "If my brother is alive, what are they doing to him? It's been two years, Petra. They could have . . ."

Petra gripped my hand. "From what you've told me of your brother, I think they will find it harder to break him than they might believe."

"But no one can escape Necro forever," I said. "I have felt his power."

"You have to believe in your brother, Vega. And we have to come up with a way to help him."

I nodded, knowing that she was right.

"And we need to help your father too."

"My mother said she's tried everything."

"She may have, but *we* haven't."

I looked up at her even as I squeezed her hand. "Thank you, Petra. You're a good friend."

"As you are to me, Vega."

"We do share a bond of blood," I said, smiling weakly.

"I think we share a lot more than that," she said.

Light Not So Bright

I COULDN'T SLEEP AFTER all that happened. It was still dark outside when I found myself in Jasper Jane's laboratory high atop Empyrean. It was as though he had just that moment upped and left his digs, though I knew that had occurred about eight centuries ago. And though I had met his spirit back in the Quag, I had no idea how my ancestor had died.

I had come here tonight with one purpose: to find a cure for my father.

I looked around the stacks of old musty books, and the shelves of bottles and fragile scientific instruments. And then there were the pots full of only Steeples knew what. Scattered on every surface were ancient pieces of parchment on which lurked Jasper's spidery handwriting, which spread across page after page like the creeping cover of some poisonous vine. For some reason, from all of this, I drew a sense of calm. As though whatever I was searching for *must* be found within the room's confines.

This heartened me, and by the light of numerous candles, I began my hunt for something that would restore my father to me. I also had another incentive. If I could bring him back, I thought it possible that my mother would forgive me for the neglect of my brother. And if John was at the castle, and I was able to rescue him, he might be able to provide information that we could use to defeat the Maladons.

As time passed and the sun slowly rose outside the window, I yawned and stretched and slumped wearily over the thick tome I had straddled across my lap.

The creak of stairs right outside the door made me look around.

A few moments later Astrea Prine appeared in the doorway.

"I thought I might find you here," she began.

"And why was that?" I inquired from my spot on the dusty pine plank floor.

She looked around the untidy study. "Because you have a problem and you have sought the antidote, as it were, from here." She glanced back at me. "Am I correct?"

I grudgingly nodded and closed the book I was holding.

I stood, towering over her.

"I've yet to find it, unfortunately."

"And what if it does not lie here?"

"Then I shall look elsewhere."

"Your poor father. A commingled spell, I understand? Nasty business."

I scowled. "And who do you understand that from?" I demanded.

"You needn't look so bothered, Vega. I spoke with your mother before I searched you out. She was up early seeing to your father. I explained to her who I was and offered my help."

My scowl slowly faded. "Do you know a lot about commingled spells?"

"Not all that much for the simple fact that they are rare, and that's a good thing, for one cannot accurately predict what the result will be when two separate spells clash together with the ricochet impacting someone a moment later. Magic is complicated enough as it is."

"Have you ever reversed the effects of a commingled spell?"

She pursed her lips as she seemed to mull over this query.

"Well, either you have or you haven't."

"Actually, Vega, it isn't that simple, because you don't always know that a spell *has* been *commingled*. On the battle-fields during our war with the Maladons, I saw many strange results. Were they the results of a commingled spell? I couldn't tell you for certain because I was too busy fighting for my life and the lives of my compatriots. War is not always convenient. In fact, it never is."

I looked away, embarrassed. She was all too right about that.

"But," she said, "we can certainly make attempts to diagnose the problem."

"How do we do that?" I said with interest.

"The most critical thing is not to go in willy-nilly and try antidote incantations without understanding the underlying problem. That could do even more harm than the original clustered spells."

"I could see that," I said. "But how do we diagnose it?"

"By examining your father. And by finding out every detail we can from your mother about how the curses were initially cast."

"I'm not sure how much she might remember."

"Well, we must help her to do so. It is imperative to finding an anti-incantation."

Astrea looked around Jasper's study. "I remember this place and Jasper so very well. He was always up here mixing brews and reading his books and coming up with spells. I would sometimes simply watch him. I have never seen a more passionate practitioner of magic in my life."

"His creation of the Fifth Circle nearly did us all in," I said.

"Jasper was always very clever," she said with a smile.

"He was bloody dangerous is what he was," I retorted. Then it struck me. Astrea must know the answer to my question. "What happened to Jasper? How did he die? If he helped you create the Quag, he must have survived the war and gone into hiding with you."

"He *did* survive the war, and he did take his place in the Quag. You may have seen his home there?"

"Yes, of course. Jasper's spirit appeared before me. At first, he did not want to help me, but I told him something that changed his mind."

"What was that?"

"That *you* had supported my decision to escape the Quag and take up the war against the Maladons once more."

She fixed an unwavering gaze upon me. "I'm glad I could be of assistance with Jasper. But I'm surprised that such a thing would have persuaded him to help you."

"Well, it did. And I would like to know how he died."

"I don't know how he died, Vega."

I frowned. "How could you not know?"

"My place of settlement was located before one entered the circles. Jasper's was deeply embedded within the circles. I never once saw him after we came to create the Quag."

"Never?" I said skeptically.

"Never."

"Do you at least have a guess, then, as to how he perished?"

"He may not have elected to take the Elixir of Life. He could simply have died from old age."

I thought this doubtful, but the expression on Astrea's face clearly showed that she did not wish this conversation to continue. And I needed her help with my father. But I had to ask one more question.

"Alice told me that Jasper had gone into the future once. And that he had seen . . . well . . . me."

"Indeed?" she said placidly.

"You don't seem surprised."

"Truly, nothing surprises me anymore."

"Did Jasper ever talk to you about seeing me in the future?"

"No, Vega, he never did," she said dismissively.

"Well, thank you for enlightening me to the extent you did."

"Now, let me think about your father's situation for a bit, and then we can meet with your mother."

I looked away again.

"Vega, is something the matter?"

"Um, it might be better if *you* met with my mother alone, at least the first time."

"I see," said Astrea. "Are you sure?"

"Quite sure."

I wasn't looking at her, but still, I could feel her penetrating gaze upon me.

"Well, I'll leave you to it," she said.

I could hear the creaks of the stairs as she made her way back down.

I strode over to the window and looked out onto the beginnings of a spectacularly beautiful day. The flowers were in full bloom, the tree canopies were bursting with leaves rippling in a pleasant breeze. The emerald-green lawn of Empyrean seemed to stretch into infinity. But I well knew that it did not. Not far away the Maladons lurked. If they could find this place, they would slaughter us.

But I knew why they had not been able to thus far.

I raised my wand and muttered, *"Exposadus."*

I could see every color of the rainbow swirling and whipping around Empyrean. I knew that I could see them only because I was not a Maladon. The protection spells had been set up with this precaution in mind, Pillsbury had told me. If a Maladon were to see the spells, it would have defeated their purpose in the first place: It would have clearly shown that there was something here to protect.

I put my wand away and the colors instantly vanished.

"Keep us safe until we finish the Maladons," I murmured.

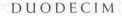

A Dash of Hope and Trouble

THAT EVENING, I ate alone at the far end of the dining room. By the time I entered the space, most others had finished their meals and gone back to their rooms.

I looked up from my plate of sausages when he walked in.

I inwardly groaned, something I had never done before upon seeing him.

Delph headed directly over to me.

I took up a sausage on my fork and bit into it, my gaze on my plate.

He sat down heavily next to me.

"Vega Jane?"

I still did not look at him. "Yes, Delph?" I said calmly.

"We need to discuss things."

"Such as?"

"I've spoken with Helen."

"Have you, now? And what did my mother say to you?" I asked coldly.

"Will you at least grant me the favor of looking at me while we talk?" said Delph, throwing my icy tone right back at me.

I glanced up sharply and at the same time I put my fork down. "There, is that satisfactory?" I said, gazing sternly at him.

He sat back and studied me, his thick arms crossed over his broad chest.

"As I said, I've spoken with Helen and I've also seen your father."

"You mean you've seen what he has become."

"Yes." He paused. "Your mother has not given up hope, nor should you."

"And who says I've given up hope?!" I snapped. "I've only just bloody found them, Delph. I've given up *nothing*."

Delph knew me so well, he could easily perceive the hollowness behind my biting words.

"I'm glad to hear that," he said, giving me credit where I — and no doubt he — knew none was due.

"I also spoke to her about John."

My hostile look faded. "About John?"

"Yes. She wanted to know things about John, before we left Wormwood."

"And what did you tell her?"

"I told her the truth, Vega Jane. She deserves nothing less."

"And what *was* the truth, Delph? According to you?"

He looked at me as though I was speaking gibberish. "That you did all you could to protect and then save John. That you risked your life for him. That you suffered terribly because of Morrigone taking him away. That you were torn apart by what had become of him. That you did not want to leave him. That if you hadn't escaped Wormwood, you would either be dead or in prison. And that you had no ability to take your brother with you. It would have been impossible."

My mouth kept falling farther and farther open as Delph continued to speak.

"You . . . you said all that to her?"

"Yes, I did. Because she needed to not only hear it, but *understand* it."

"And what was her response?"

He glanced away for a moment before looking back at me. "It was a lot to take in, Vega Jane. I'm not sure she had a response. But I'm sure that she will, given time."

I looked back down at the remains of my meal. My appetite had suddenly vanished.

"I'm not sure that time will help, but I do appreciate what you did, Delph. Truly I do. Reuniting with my parents has not been what I had hoped for."

Well, that was a bloody understatement!

He gripped my hand. "Just like your father, your brother is not lost to us, Vega Jane. What a grand thing it will be to fully reunite the Jane family, eh?"

I glanced at him. In all my family issues, I had lost sight of the fact that Delph would *never* reunite with his remaining family. His father, Duf, lay murdered and buried back in what remained of Wormwood. Why did I have to be so close-minded about things? It was like I looked simply at injustices against me and didn't consider the effects of such on other people. And I was also quite cognizant of the fact that my ripping through the dome around the Quag had allowed the Maladons to slaughter all Wugmorts, Duf included.

"Delph, I know I've said it before, but I am so sorry about Duf."

He shrugged. "I think if my father had had a choice in the matter, he would have wanted us to do what we did, Vega Jane."

"But did we have the right to make the decision, Delph? To break out of the Quag? To allow the Maladons a way in?"

"First, we had very little choice in the matter. If we had stayed in the Quag, we would be dead. Second, we had no idea that breaking through that wall would enable the Maladons to do what they did."

"I didn't even think about that possibility."

"Leisurely thinking through all possibilities is a pastime best left for when you're not fighting for your life."

I had to smile at the wisdom of his words, but still it all gnawed at me. Wugs *had* died because of what I did.

"There is no guarantee that my father will be restored, or that my brother will come back to us," I pointed out.

"None a'tall," he agreed. "But I do have some thoughts as to your *brother*."

"I already know your thoughts. You believe that he was taken by the Maladons for some hideous purpose."

"But I could have been wrong."

I sat up straighter. "How?"

"We assumed that the Maladons have him. Based on what precisely?"

I looked at him incredulously. "Based on his being the only one in all of Wormwood who did not have a grave."

"Well, the Maladons taking him would be one explanation."

"One?" I exclaimed. "It's the *only* explanation."

"Look at it another way. *We* escaped Wormwood. Could not your brother have done the same thing?"

I gazed at him as though my loyal friend had gone completely nutters.

"Why would John have escaped from Wormwood?"

"Same reason we did. We figured it out, right? That we were meant to stay there, like prisoners. Well, your brother was smart, maybe smarter than both of us put together. So why couldn't he figure it out too, eh?"

I gaped, but then my mouth snapped shut. Could what he was saying be remotely possible?

"I guess that might be so," I said slowly. "But if he did escape, where is he?"

"There might be one person here who knows."

The answer flashed through my mind.

"Morrigone!"

WHEN DELPH AND I burst into her lair, Morrigone was not alone.

Astrea Prine looked up at me from where she was perched on a chair. Morrigone's spirit was standing in front of her.

I glared at the shimmering image of Morrigone, and she glared right back at me.

"I understand that you have found your mother and father," said Morrigone tensely.

"They found *me*. My mother saved my life."

"I am glad for that," said Morrigone casually.

I looked at Astrea. "I would like to have a private word with Morrigone."

"All right. I have things to occupy me. I will go now and speak to your mother *alone* as you desired."

I bristled at this, as it seemed to be uttered simply to make me uncomfortable.

I waited until I heard the door close behind her before turning to Morrigone.

"Yes, Vega?" she said in an unfriendly tone.

"My brother, John?"

"What of him?"

"There was no grave for him back in Wormwood."

"The Maladons killed all who remained in Wormwood."

"I know that," I said impatiently. "So, was John there or not when it happened?"

"It was a very difficult time, Vega."

"Was he, or wasn't he?" I demanded more hotly.

"The night before the Maladons attacked us, John came to tell me that he wanted to leave Wormwood."

"Why?"

"He wanted to find *you*."

"Me? Why?"

"You're his sister."

"He did not seem to feel that way while I remained in Wormwood," I said heatedly. "He seemed quite happy to stay with *you*."

"If you think that, you did not understand your brother," she replied evenly.

I sat down in the chair that Astrea had occupied. "Did you let him go?"

She laughed lightly. "I could hardly have stopped him."

I gazed at her, puzzled. "Why not? You were magical."

"I couldn't stop you from leaving, though your magical gifts were nascent at the time. Well, your brother was a bit farther along than you, I must say."

She seemed to be gleeful about putting me in my place.

"So, he left Wormwood before the Maladons got there?"

"I don't know, Vega. He was living at your old home. He insisted on moving there shortly after you left."

"I saw my house when I went back. The Maladons had desecrated it. But they hadn't destroyed it."

"Interesting," said Morrigone cryptically.

Delph said, "Did you see John when the Maladons came?"

"All I saw were four hideous Maladons showing up at my house, pointing their wands at me and —" She broke off and looked away for a moment. "So, no, I didn't see anyone else die, only . . . myself."

I said quite sincerely, "That must have been horrible."

"I would not wish it on anyone," she replied.

"I saw your house after the Maladons were there. Much of it was destroyed. But I looked at John's room. All the hideous things on his walls were gone."

"Because he had taken them with him."

"But otherwise the room was undamaged."

"Interesting," she said again.

"Why do you keep saying that?" I blurted out.

"Because it *is* interesting."

"How so?"

"Your house, where John went to live? And his old room at my home? Both undamaged by the Maladons? It makes one wonder why, that's all."

"And why do you think the Maladons didn't touch those spaces?" asked Delph.

"I can only speculate."

"Do so," I said bluntly.

"Maladons can sense things that perhaps we can't. Evil things, I mean. Or the *potential* of evil."

I felt my cheeks growing warm because I knew exactly where she was going with this.

Morrigone continued. "When they got to John's room, and also his old home, they might have sensed some of the things that had been there. His pictures and his books."

"The evil things," I said.

"Yes. And they might even be able to sense the thoughts of the person who had inhabited those spaces."

"So you're saying —"

But she cut me off with a wave of her hand. "No, I am not. What the Maladons lack is an appreciation of nuance, of subtlety."

"I don't understand."

102

"For them, there is only light and dark. There is nothing in between."

"So you're saying that they might have interpreted John's *curiosity* about dark matters as him being evil?"

"It's certainly possible."

I mulled things over for a bit. "Okay, did John say where he was going to go if he left Wormwood? Did he have a plan? Or any idea what he would be facing?"

"He had some idea, because I told him." She eyed me closely. "I know I did not grant you the same privilege, Vega."

"I'm glad that you could at least aid him," I said sincerely.

"I wished nothing but the best for your brother. I'm sorry that I didn't act the same with you."

"But you *did* let me escape from Wormwood. Why?"

Morrigone studied the floor for a long moment before suddenly glancing up to stare fully at me.

"I could sense that things were changing. And . . . and I thought you had a better chance of finding out why. That is why I let you go." She paused. "As I told you back in Wormwood, I did admire you, Vega. In their ignorance, our fellow Wugs worshipped me and ridiculed you."

"*I* worshipped you, Morrigone," I said.

"Until you came to your senses and saw me for what I was. A fraud, a shell, a failure." Her pale, ethereal cheeks seemed to light with heat at this frank admission.

"I never considered you to be a failure," I said. "Far from it. You had a job, and you tried to do it to the best of your abilities."

"Thank you for saying that." She paused. "Thus, to sum all this up, it could very well be that your brother is out there somewhere."

I tapped my foot against the stone floor. "Morrigone, why

103

did you take him under your wing, into your house, and show him the . . . the awful things that you did?"

"I had nothing to do with that," replied Morrigone, surprising me. "He found them himself."

"Where?"

"Inside the Council building."

"The Council building!" I cried out.

"He was there working on the plans for the wall. He was searching for some books to help him with his task. He told me that he found a secret cache of parchment and a large box of dusty tomes and drawings. I do not know who put them there. It must have been from long ago. All I know is that John was fascinated by what he saw and read about."

"But why didn't you take them away from him? Tell him these things were wrong and horrible and evil?"

"I *did* tell him, Vega."

"But you didn't take those horrid things away from him. They were in his room. In your house."

"Because I knew that merely taking them away would do no good. You can't make someone be good, Vega. Just as you can't make someone evil."

I drew several calming breaths, looked at Delph and then said to Morrigone, "Do you have any idea where John is now?"

"I do not, Vega. I swear to you that I do not."

I looked wearily at the wall in front of me.

"What will you do now?" asked Morrigone.

I had no answer to give her.

The Problem of the Ring

I RETREATED ALONE TO my room and lay back on my bed to contemplate many things. Chiefly, if my brother was out there somewhere, either in this world or back in the Quag, I needed to find him. Only I had a problem.

It rested on my hand.

My broken ring of invisibility.

I thought back to the creature posing as my brother when he was a child. The creature had befouled my ring. This had led to a sudden, awful thought that had occurred to me when I had left Morrigone. Since the Maladons had used an image of my brother in their trap, did that mean they indeed had John?

To answer that question, I needed to repair my ring.

And right now, I could only see one way to do that.

I took out my wand, tapped it against my leg and said, *"Pass-pusay."*

A moment later I was in the Quag, at the spot where Jasper Jane had made his home inside a large stone building.

I walked toward the enormous doors of the place and pointed my wand at them.

"Ingressio."

The doors swung open. I passed through and used my wand to close them behind me.

I looked alertly around the interior of the vast place.

"Hello?" I called out.

When I received no answer, I called out once more.

"Yes?"

I looked up to the top of the staircase. My ancestor was wearing the exact same clothes he'd had on when I had been here last. A long robe, open in front, revealing a breastplate underneath bearing the stamp of the three hooks, our symbol, which he had told me represented peace, hope and freedom. Precisely in that order.

"Jasper, it's me, Vega Jane. I was here before."

He swept down the stairs and came to stand in front of me.

"You have escaped the Quag, then?"

"I have."

"I had wondered why everything had changed," he said. "The Quag. Its power and, with it, its relevance has gone."

"Yes, well," I began, and then could think of nothing else to say.

"And what have you discovered outside the Quag?" he asked.

"Well, I was this very morning in your old laboratory at Empyrean."

"Empyrean?" he exclaimed. "You were at Empyrean? Our ancestral home?"

"There is only one Empyrean," I replied.

He paused and studied me. "Why were you in my old laboratory?"

In answer, I held up my ring.

"A man named Colin Sonnet gave this to my grandfather when my grandfather ventured into the past. Sonnet owned a shop of curiosities, and this apparently was one of them. It renders the wearer invisible. But the Maladons have done something to it, such that it no longer works. I was wondering, well, I was wondering if you could think of a way to fix it?

Because in order to defeat the Maladons, I need for it to work properly."

"Colin was quite the collector of antiquities."

I stiffened. *Colin?* "Wait, do you, or rather, *did* you know Colin Sonnet?"

"He was one of my best mates."

I considered my next question carefully. "You went into the future once, didn't you?"

"Did I?"

"Alice Adronis told me that you did. And she told me something extraordinary."

"What was that?"

"That you saw *me* upon your venture into the future."

"Did she indeed?"

"She did indeed. What exactly did you see of me?"

"I cannot tell you, Vega."

"Why not?"

"Revealing things that have not taken place is not allowed. If I were to attempt it, the consequences would be unimaginable."

"But you're already dead. What do you care about consequences?"

"Not consequences for me, Vega. Consequences for *you*."

"Me?"

He nodded. "But you are here about your ring?"

I studied him for a long moment and shook my head clear. "Yes. I need to set it right. Do you have any suggestions as to how I can do that?"

He mulled over this for a bit.

"I know one person who can help you."

"Who?" I said eagerly.

"Colin Sonnet, of course."

Eon Redux

BACK IN **W**ORMWOOD.
It was the very last place I wanted to be.

Here, there was only death. I could smell it, taste it, even hear it in the imagined moans from the dead and buried.

As I flew over the Hallowed Ground, where we laid our deceased in the dirt, I had to look away.

Yet I now believed that my brother had not perished here. Whether he was out there alone, or a prisoner of the Maladons, I didn't know. And though my mother and I had agreed that it would be better to be dead than be a prisoner of the Maladons, I had come to reconsider that conclusion.

If John *was* a prisoner, that meant he was alive. And that, in turn, meant I had a chance to get him back.

I landed in front of the destroyed doors of Stacks and walked toward it.

Stacks was my old workplace, where I had labored as a Finisher. It had also once been Bastion Cadmus's home. It had been magically transported here when Wormwood had been created.

I had already seen what the Maladons had done to Stacks. Knocked down the doors, toppled the turrets, demolished Julius Domitar's office and desecrated my workstation.

I had been trapped in Stacks once with a pair of jabbits in pursuit of me. I knew that jabbits no longer inhabited the place, but as I walked through the dark empty halls, my heart began to race nonetheless.

I marched up the damaged staircase to the second floor and made my way down to the end.

Here, there had been a small wooden door with a screaming Wugmort made from metal as the doorknob. It was through this portal that I would make my way to the past.

Only there was no door now and no screaming Wugmort doorknob, only a solid wall.

Undeterred by this, I pointed my wand at the wall and said, *"Exposadus."*

Absolutely nothing happened.

I incanted the magnification spell to see if I could look on the other side of the wall.

It didn't work.

I tapped my wand against my leg and muttered the *Passpusay* spell, my destination being on the other side of the wall.

Again, nothing.

I took a step back and pondered what to do.

Then something took ahold of me.

Back at Empyrean, I had followed Uma down to the very bowels of the place. She had passed through a solid wood door, but when I had attempted to turn the doorknob and open the portal, I had been unable to. I had stood there like a fool for the longest time until I realized this might be a test.

I had managed to open the door using something I had always held in abundance: imagination.

And the imagined thoughts I used had been based on the jabbits chasing me through Stacks. I had conjured all those awful memories and forced myself to really believe that I was in peril, that I needed the door to open or else I was lost.

I closed my eyes, set my mouth in a firm line and attempted to do this again.

Since I was in the very place where the jabbits had actually hunted me, it was not all that hard to bring these terrifying memories back to vivid life.

My heart started to race, my breaths grew ragged. Sweat appeared on my forehead. My legs ached from my imagined flight from these deadly predators.

In my mind, when they almost had me, I opened my eyes.

My face plunged in disappointment.

There was still no door. And thus, no screaming-Wug doorknob.

"Bloody Hel!" I yelled in disappointment. I kicked the wall, which sent a jolt of pain flying up my leg.

The next moment I froze.

Screech. Screech.

I slowly turned around.

There was only one creature I knew of that made that vile sound.

As I stood there frozen, it came into view.

This was one of the largest jabbits I had ever seen, nearly twice as long and three times as broad as a normal one. The hundreds of heads on its trunk were all looking right at me as it slithered down the hall.

How had a jabbit gotten in here?

Then I realized how.

The separation between Wormwood and the Quag was no more. Creatures could come and go as they pleased.

As I thought this, I could not take my eyes off the jabbit coming for me.

My breath came in gasps; fear-induced sweat poured off my body. My heart was pounding so fast I could near nothing else.

Except the creature's screeches. The last thing you hear before you die.

Out in the Quag I had faced many jabbits. And I had defeated them all.

But there was something different in this place.

Stacks was where I had worked as a young Wug. Here, I had always lived in stark fear of the creatures from the Quag.

I had my wand now, but my hand felt paralyzed.

I fell back. I could not think of a single spell to cast, though I knew many that would have vanquished the beast. I could summon the Elemental to its full size and hurl it at the jabbit. But my tortured mind would not allow the precision of thought this required.

My only thought was to flee.

Just as the jabbit reared up to strike, I whirled around.

There was the door.

And there was the screaming Wug.

I reached out, turned the knob, opened the door and threw myself inside.

I slammed the door behind me.

The door had held before against the jabbits. I prayed that it did so now.

I shrank back and waited.

Moments went by and I listened intently for the screech. Or the jabbit slamming its massive body against the tiny door.

Yet neither happened.

I let out a long, painful breath. I had gone from mighty sorceress to scared little girl faster than I ever thought possible. If that was not a lesson in humility, I didn't know what was. But at least I was alive.

I slowly stood, turned and walked into the darkness until I reached a vast cave.

I thought back to what I had said on my first trip here, in order to summon what I required.

"I need answers and I need them now," I shouted.

"Hello?" the voice said instantly.

I turned to see a small, hooded figure walking toward me. As before, he carried a wooden staff in one hand and a lantern in the other.

It was Eon, the guardian of time.

"Eon, it's me, Vega Jane."

"Why have you returned?" he asked.

I looked around. "Eon, do you not realize that Wormwood has been destroyed? There's no one left."

The little creature looked at me blankly. "I do not understand."

I decided not to pursue it. I supposed none of that mattered to the bloody guardian of time.

"I'm here because my grandfather Virgil went back in time."

"Yes, he did. He was the only traveler other than you to do so."

"Right. Well, he received this ring when he traveled into the past." I held it up for him to see. "I want to go back to where he did, because I need to see Colin Sonnet, the bloke who gave him this ring, so that he can, well, fix it up. Okay?"

Once more, Eon simply stared blankly at me.

"So, can you arrange that?" I asked hopefully.

"I have no control over *where* one goes, either in the future or the past, Vega."

My hopes fell. "What? But then how *is* it determined?"

"I would say that where one ends up either in the past or

the future depends on the traveler himself. Or *herself*," he added quickly.

He took something from his pocket and held it out.

I saw instantly that it was a key.

"By your own words now, you obviously have a need once more," said Eon. "Take this key and fulfill it."

An Old Friend When New

I TENTATIVELY APPROACHED THE fiery gates that would allow me to go back in time. I inserted the key in the lock, the gates opened and I braced myself. In my mind I held the name Colin Sonnet. I hoped that was enough.

Turns out, it wasn't. Not even close.

When I passed through the gates, I was instantly embraced by what appeared to be clouds hovering a foot above the ground. This had happened to me before, so I was unafraid.

When the mists cleared, I was in the middle of a forest, but I heard voices nearby. I headed toward these sounds as I looked around, trying to determine where I was.

I cleared a thicket of tall poplars and stopped.

I had happened upon what looked to be a small village. It was really just a set of rudimentary huts made of clay with thatched roofs. I saw some women tending to large cauldrons hung over small fires. There were men sharpening blades on long spears and some feathering arrows they placed in leather quivers. Folks were chatting amiably together, but in the way they would continually look around, I saw they were nervous about something.

And then I received the shock of my life when she walked around the corner of one of the thatched homes and came into my view.

It was Petra. Younger, smaller, but it was clearly Petra Sonnet.

She was overly thin, and her hair wasn't as long as it was now. But she carried herself with pride, and her eyes were focused and intent. Though small and skinny she looked hardened and tough. Her clothes were dirty, as was her skin. Over her shoulder she carried some creature that was clearly dead.

She deposited it with one of the women tending a cauldron.

Then I was able to see the bow over Petra's shoulder, and the small quiver of arrows on her back. When I had first met her in the Quag, she had carried a far more formidable crossbow.

She had evidently killed the creature for food.

I looked around to observe whether anyone could actually see me. When it was clear that they could not — several people had seemed to look full at me without reaction — I stepped forward into the clearing and studied Petra, who had sunk down upon her haunches and was dipping a metal cup into a bucket of water. She took a long drink and gazed moodily around.

It suddenly struck me. So that was why everyone was on their guard.

This was the Quag. And these people had all been trapped here when the Quag was created to conceal Wormwood. Or at least their ancestors had been. Although it was quite possible, in fact even certain, that some of the ones ensnared in the Quag had been Maladons. As I had learned, the transition had been a bit chaotic. I felt pity for all those left to fend for themselves in this awful place, whether they had Maladon blood or not.

As I continued to watch Petra, something curious happened.

A man passed by her, glared at Petra and called her a filthy name.

Surprisingly, she did nothing.

A few moments later, a group of children not that much older than she came to stand in front of her. A tall boy, his hands clenched into fists, stepped forward.

"What you be doing?" he snapped.

She glanced up at him. "What does it look like I *be* doing? I'm drinking water."

"Who says you can do that?" barked the boy.

She stood and left her bow and quiver on the dirt.

"Who says I can't?"

"I bloody well do."

"And why is that?"

"My mum says you're spawned from the Quag. She says your mother is a garm and your father a foul wendigo."

"You're a filthy beast," spat a girl.

"You know my mother and my father, and they're not either of those things," replied Petra firmly.

"You lie!" shouted the boy. "All lies!" He pushed her.

I saw Petra cock her fist. And the next thing I saw, the boy was on the ground and Petra was on top of him pounding away.

But then men rushed over and pulled her off, roughly cuffed her and threw her to the dirt.

"Be gone with you, beast," said one of the men.

And Petra got to her feet and ran off.

The mists covered me again and I did not know where I would be going next.

When the clouds cleared, I was standing next to a river. I could hear the water rushing by.

There were several children there. They were yelling and pointing at someone.

I looked around and saw that a very small boy had fallen into the river and was hanging on to a limb from a tree that had partially collapsed into the water. It was clear he could not hold on much longer, and the current was deadly swift.

I started to run toward the river, though I wasn't sure what I could do. I wasn't sure I could even grip the child and pull him free.

But before I got there, I heard a splash.

I looked and saw Petra swimming frantically toward the boy.

She was older now, perhaps fourteen. But she had grown to nearly her full height. Petra reached the boy and grabbed him by the arm. She swam back to the shore and helped him out of the water.

I expected the others to applaud her for the courageous thing she had done.

But that did not happen.

Instead, they jeered at her, calling her ugly names. Even the little boy she had saved ran away from her.

I looked at Petra and my heart went out to her. But she never shed a tear, even though I felt my own eyes grow watery at the scorn she was receiving.

Petra turned and walked off, while the others skipped along behind her, keeping up their torrent of vitriol.

The mists crowded up over me again before I could go after her. Yet they cleared rather quickly.

I heard the sounds of weeping. I was once more in the middle of trees, and it took a few moments for me to get my bearings.

Petra sat on a rock, her face in her hands, sobbing.

I looked at my wand and wondered if there was any spell I could summon that would make her feel better.

Before I could act, though, a man appeared from the tree line and approached her.

He was tall and exceedingly thin and his features were haggard. I suppose all who lived in the Quag were under-nourished and also suffered from the anxiety that comes from living in a place where so many horrible creatures could kill you at any moment. At first, I tensed because I thought he might attack her. But his features were kindly, and he said softly, "Petra?"

She lifted her head enough to see him.

"Petra, I heard what happened. Are you all right?"

"I'm fine, Uncle."

Uncle, I thought. This bloke must be the relative Petra told me about. The one who was magical and possessed a wand. And he, I knew, would later die at the hands of a garm that Petra would kill, only too late to save him.

He sat down beside her and stared into the distance.

"The young ones can be cruel," he said.

She sat up straight, her face puffy and her eyes reddened. "It's not only the young."

Her uncle nodded. "You're different from the others, Petra. We have had this discussion before. I believe that they can sense that."

"I don't want to be different."

"There is absolutely nothing wrong with being different. It would be a dull place indeed if all were the same."

When she didn't respond, her uncle gave a searching look around and then pulled something from his pocket.

It was his wand.

"You really have no choice in the matter, as I had no choice," he said.

She looked at the wand.

"What bloody use is it?"

"It has a great many uses, as you well know."

"I wish . . . I wish I didn't know how to use it."

"Many people would love to have the ability you and I have, Petra."

"It helps no one."

"You're wrong there. We have spoken of this before. I have shown you."

"They hate me. Because . . ."

"Because you can make things happen that are inexplicable? I experienced the exact same thing when I was your age. But I had someone who showed me that I was actually not odd, but special."

"*That* makes you special?" she said coldly, indicating his wand.

"A mere possession cannot really make one special, Petra. It's how you live your life that does it."

Blimey, I thought. Silenus from the parchment had told me that the bloke was definitely a Maladon, because the wand he had given to Petra was that of a Maladon. But Petra's uncle didn't sound evil. He actually appeared to be quite sensitive. And this completely turned upside down my opinion of Maladons. Could some of them be good? I supposed I had known the answer to that question all along. Petra was at least part Maladon and she was good. In fact, I could have some Maladon in me. And I considered myself *quite* good.

"I have something for you, Petra," said her uncle.

I watched as he slowly reached in his pocket and pulled it out.

119

I had seen the object before, many times.

It was Petra's wand. She had told me that her uncle had given it to her. It had part of his fingernail embedded in the wood.

To my surprise she shook her head. "I don't want that, Uncle."

But her uncle seemed not at all shocked by her refusal.

"I can understand why you feel that way, but let me explain something."

She watched him, patiently waiting. As did I.

He held the wand up. "You saved a child today from death. You did so at great personal risk. You did so despite knowing that your actions would be jeered instead of cheered. It takes a very special person to do that. And that is why, today, I give you your wand. Because you have earned it, my very dear Petra."

She stared at her uncle with a look that shook my heart, it really did. It was as though all the hurt and taunts and ugliness that Petra had faced all this time were seeping out of her for one divine moment.

She reached out and gripped the wand.

"Thank you, Uncle," she said.

And then the mists covered me once more.

Colin Sonnet

I FLINCHED BECAUSE SOMEONE passed so close to me that we almost collided. I stepped back and nearly slipped. I looked beneath me to see cobbles, and ahead of me to see a stone building.

It was one among many in a long line strung out down a broad boulevard. It was like the High Street back in Wormwood, only far nicer. As I watched people come and go, there was a widespread sense of peace and prosperity.

I blinked when I saw the sign of the storefront.

ARCANE ARTIFACTS, ET ALIA, COLIN SONNET, PROPRIETOR

Someone opened the door to head into the shop, and I slipped in behind this person, a tall, strongly built man in a luxurious burgundy cloak.

As the door opened, a bell had tinkled.

I looked around the shop and tried to take it all in, but it was really not possible to do so because there was so much to see.

Long, low counters were on every wall. Under the glass I saw objects all lined up in perfect rows. I drew closer to inspect the contents.

There were aged coins, fat leather books, pieces of what looked to be bones together with the entire skeletons of small beasts. There were myriad rolls of parchment next to sparkling ink sticks, and necklaces made of chain mail alongside jewels of every conceivable color. An eyeball of some creature's sat next to another creature's lethal-looking fang. A metal hand leaned against a shimmering bottle of liquid that smoked and sparked inside its container.

On the walls above the counters were fastened all manner of things: heads of beasts, shields of metal, spears, swords, lances, a metal ball with pointy spikes. A full suit of armor hung from the ceiling. Stuffed winged creatures, both large and small, were suspended on long chains from the rafters. They seemed about to soar across the room and attack me. One of them looked like the dreads that had chased me back in the Quag. A full black carriage sat against one wall. Next to that was a mirror that reflected nothing in the shop, but held the image of a dark sky with shiny stars scattered across its face like flower petals along a path.

The floors were piled high with crates overflowing with interesting objects: an assortment of weapons and instruments and devices that seemed to hold scientific potential; hats and cloaks and gloves; long glass tubes filled with colorful liquids. And in a cage was an assortment of live small animals and birds, all surprisingly getting along swimmingly.

"Colin, how are you?"

I snapped my head around to stare at the man in the burgundy cloak as he greeted a small, thin younger man who had emerged from behind a curtain. The younger man had a full head of red hair and a pair of finely wrought golden spectacles that sat halfway down his long, slender nose.

"Gunther, I am never better, thank you."

I blinked again. *Gunther? Was this Gunther Adronis, Alice's husband?*

He was tall and broad shouldered, and as he turned to look around the shop, my suspicions were confirmed. This was indeed Gunther Adronis. I had seen his portrait back at

Empyrean. I had also seen his body in a silver coffin. Pillsbury had told me how Necro had murdered Gunther in his home, slitting his throat. I shivered with the thought that the man I was staring at would die a violent death.

Then I studied Colin Sonnet. For some reason, I had imagined he would be muscular and fierce-looking. However, his appearance was far more like a scholar's than a warrior's. He was certainly nothing like Petra.

Colin adjusted his spectacles and looked up at the tall Gunther. "And how is Alice?"

Gunther's hearty smile receded. "It has been difficult. Losing a child during its birth."

"It is the worst possible occurrence for a parent, Gunther. You have my deepest sympathies. My wife will be coming by later with some food and other things, and to sit with Alice."

"Thank you, Colin. But I think Alice needs to be alone, at least for now. She is . . . complex."

"But she is also very strong. The strongest person I know."

"And I as well," replied Gunther firmly.

My jaw had sagged as this conversation had gone on.

Alice had lost a child?

"The Janes are a hearty family," said Colin. "With many offspring."

"Yes. And we will continue to try. Alice wants to be a mother. She hopes for a daughter."

Colin smiled. "She is one of the few. Yet I agree with her sentiments. Men, I fear, are revered far above their qualifications."

"Which is why she seeks a daughter," replied Gunther. He next looked at something in one of the counters while Colin attended him.

I crept over to the cage and stared at the creatures inside. One had a puffy, furry face, and was about the size of my hand. One of the birds had wings of gold and a beak about six inches long. There was a beast sleeping on the floor of the cage. It was long and muscular with curly golden hair. When it yawned, I could see row after row of teeth the shape of needles. It opened its eyes, and when a fluttering bird came within reach of its fangs, I feared the worst. But the thing just rolled over and went back to sleep after leisurely scratching itself.

That would never have happened in the Quag, I knew.

A few minutes later, Gunther finished his business and left.

I drew closer to the counter with the intent of seeking Sonnet's counsel on the ring.

And then something occurred to me.

Vega, you git, you're invisible. Not because of my ring, but because I had gone back in time. How could I have him help me, if he couldn't even see me?

In despair, I looked at the counter where Sonnet was returning some items that Gunther had been examining.

My gaze fastened on one item there.

It was my ring! Or at the very least it was its twin. However, it should have not been a surprise. My grandfather had gotten his ring from Colin, probably from this very shop. So there could well be a spare.

As I stood there, an incredible thing happened. A white light shot out from the ring under the glass and impacted the ring on my finger.

"I'm sorry, I didn't see you come in. May I help you?"

I looked at Colin, who was now staring directly at me.

I looked around to make sure he was actually speaking to me, but there was no one else in the shop.

"That was Gunther Adronis, was it not?" I managed to say.

He nodded and looked at me closely. "You know Gunther?"

"I know Alice Adronis."

124

He looked me over. "There is actually a resemblance between you. Are you related to the Janes?"

"Distantly."

"They are a fine family. Gunther and Alice live at her ancestral home, Empyrean, a wonderful estate not too far from here."

"I have heard of it," I said.

"And how can I help you?"

"Um, yes, I was wondering if you could assist me with my ring."

I took it off and set it on the counter.

He glanced at it and then gave me a sharp look.

"How did you come by it?" he asked.

"My grandfather gave it to me." This was perfectly true, even if the actual event had occurred far into the future.

"And his name?"

"Virgil."

"And your name? You did not give it before."

"Vega. I do not hail from here," I added quickly. "But I was passing through and noticed your shop." I glanced around. "It is quite wonderful."

He smiled. "Many have found it so."

"The creatures in the cage over there?"

"They are pets to be brought into homes."

"The one on the floor with all the needle-sharp teeth?"

"That would be Amadeus. He is a canine. They are quite loyal, and harmless to others. But not if their loved ones are threatened in any way. Then they can become quite fierce."

I glanced back over at Amadeus. So that was what a canine looked like over eight centuries ago. They had changed quite a bit.

"Rightly so," I said. "I have a canine who is quite like that."

He nodded and gingerly touched the ring. "Fascinating."

I said, "I see you have one nearly identical to it."

Colin nodded. "Yes. I have had it for a very long time. I must say that it is quite surprising to see a spare such as this. I thought there to be only one in existence."

His comment startled me. Could that ring under the counter and my ring be the same? Virgil would not come for his ring for quite some time. But then again, he might already have come, since I was wearing the ring he had given me. Time travel! My poor head swirled with the complications of it.

"It *is* quite a nice ring," I said.

"And what help do you need with it?"

I had prepared for this question, but right now my ready explanation seemed quite nonsensical. As I stared back at him, the eyes behind the specs seemed to grow to enormous proportion, giving me the uncomfortable impression that he could see into my mind.

I opted for the truth, or at least some of it. "This is no ordinary ring," I said.

"How do you mean?"

"Magic is borne from necessity."

"I would not argue with you on that point. But what of it?"

I recalled exactly what my grandfather had told me that Sonnet had told him when he had given Virgil the ring. "It can be the result of the confluence of mystical powers coming together at just the right moment. Quite a phenomenon of serendipity, but magic is often that way."

Colin stared at me over the rims of his specs. "I have written books on the field of sorcery."

"I know. I have read at least one."

"And how did you come by it?"

"A friend. I found it to be very helpful, particularly for those who hate dark sorcery, but are concerned that one day they may need to fight against it."

His gaze sharpened at my words.

"You are quite young to have such thoughts."

"I may be young in body, but I can assure you that I am mature beyond my years when it comes to the potential wickedness of others."

His gaze flicked to my ring on the counter. "I see. Yes, I think I see quite clearly what you mean."

I picked up the ring, placed it on my finger and then spun it slowly around, so the tip was facing down.

"I take it you can still see me," I said.

He nodded slowly. "And I take it you do not wish to be seen?"

"That's right. The ring, unfortunately, was subject to an . . . interference by another. This apparently has stripped it of its true abilities. I was wondering if you could repair it."

"And you wish it to have its power returned so that you can . . . ?"

"Deal with the wickedness of others," I replied.

I took the ring off and handed it to him.

"Can you help me?"

He looked down at the ring before fixing his gaze upon me. "I can certainly try. But it will take some time. When it is about to grow dark, you will return. I trust you have other things to do in the interim?"

"I will *find* other things to do."

He bowed and disappeared behind the curtain with my ring.

And I headed back out into the past to see what I could see.

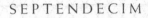

Full Circle

I WAS GLAD OF my long cloak because others here were wearing similar clothing. I passed down the road fronting the shops, keeping to the footpaths, for horses and carriages steadily rumbled past. The time for motorcars was apparently far into the future, although people did pop in and out on the street as wands tapped legs and the incantation *Pass-pusay* was uttered.

I looked for but could not detect an air of anxiety among the populace. I wondered how long it would be before the war with the Maladons was to commence. Was it far enough away that I would not see any signs for it? Although, Colin Sonnet had seemed to understand my words when I mentioned fighting wickedness.

I stopped and pressed myself against one wall as a man and woman approached with a little boy skipping along behind them.

It was Astrea Prine and probably her husband. And the little boy looked an awful lot like the man I now knew as her son, Archie.

Astrea, because of the Elixir of Life, had not changed a jot, which is how I had so easily recognized her. However, she was much taller. She had told me that the weight of centuries had physically compressed her body. She wore a long green cloak.

I felt my features grow somber. With all her magical ability Astrea did not know, could not know, what I did: that her life and that of her family's were to be torn apart fairly soon. She seemed happy and carefree now, which only added to my misery at the dismal upheaval that would constitute her future.

"You worry too much, my dear," her husband was saying to Astrea.

"That is an absurd statement," she retorted.

"War is unthinkable. Things will be worked out. Necro is a good man or I am much wrong."

"You are much wrong, then. Nothing can be worked out with *him*."

So, I thought. My question had been answered. It seemed the war was drawing near.

Her husband sighed and pointed to some articles in a window. "Look, Archie, the hat you wanted."

He and Archie went inside the shop while Astrea waited outside.

I tentatively approached her.

"Yes?" she said brusquely, eyeing me up and down in a severe way.

"You're Astrea Prine."

"I know I am. And who are you?"

"No one important."

I stared at her. I had to fight the impulse to warn her of what was to come. I remember Jasper telling me of the dire consequences for Astrea if I were to do that. But would they be more terrible than what was actually in store for her?

I said, "Do you know Alice Adronis?"

"I do," said Astrea, her gaze still scrutinizing me in an unsettling way.

"I understand that she has lost her child?"

129

Now Astrea eyed me suspiciously. "And how did you come to know that?"

"I was in Colin Sonnet's shop when Gunther Adronis came in. I overheard him tell Colin."

"You should not eavesdrop," Astrea said sternly.

"I wasn't eavesdropping. Gunther has a booming voice."

"That he does," agreed Astrea, her features relaxing a bit. "And men often do not know when to keep silent on certain subjects."

"I heard your husband say that war was unthinkable. But apparently you don't believe him?"

She studied me closely. "Who exactly are you? Tell me. Now," she added imperiously.

"You don't know me. I'm a stranger, only having just arrived here."

Before I could say more, a man approached down the street. He was elegantly dressed all in black. He was rather tall with wide shoulders, and long slender legs. His chin jutted out and was bracketed by a solid jaw. A thin line of hair lay above his top lip. His eyebrows were narrow and followed the slope of his wide eyes.

Then my focus was drawn to his clothes, and I flinched.

Unlike the other men I had seen, who were outfitted in cloaks, this gent was dressed neatly in a three-piece pinstripe suit, tie and bowler hat.

He tipped his hat at Astrea, revealing immaculately combed hair parted down the middle.

"Madame Prine, how wonderful to see you."

She looked back at him with a face of granite. "Necro," she said stiffly.

This attractive and well-dressed man was Necro? That foul creature I had seen on his horrible throne at Maladon

Castle? Yet it had to be, because now it was clear to me where Endemen and his henchmen had acquired their choice of clothing.

He glanced at me, and in those eyes, I could see past the good looks and suave manners. They were twin dots of pure silky black, so dark that they appeared fathomless. I could see myself falling through them into the pits of Hel, which was the only place such eyes could possibly lead.

"And who might your young friend be?" asked Necro, glancing at me. "I don't believe that I know her."

"I only just met her myself," said Astrea. When I looked at her, she had a worried expression. For some reason, I took it to mean that she was worried for me!

Necro took me in with those black eyes. "A lovely addition to our humble town?" he said smoothly. However, his words made me want to retch, because his gaze ran up and down my figure in a way I did not care for.

"Just passing through," I said.

"Well, I hope that we meet again." He tipped his hat once more and was off.

We will meet again, I said to myself.

I looked at Astrea, who was still staring after Necro with disgust in her features.

"If I were you, Madame Prine, I would prepare for war," I said, with a long glance at the back of Necro.

She flinched and said, "What do you know of anything?"

"A lot more than you probably think. Heed my words, for they are both well intended and well founded."

With that I hurried after Necro.

He turned down one street and then another. I kept close enough to see his actions, but not so close as to arouse the man's suspicions.

We reached a part of the town that, though as fashionable as the one I had just left, had taken on a coldness that had not been present before. As I looked up at the sky, it had darkened. Was it just a storm coming in? Or was something else happening?

The people hereabouts were uniformly dressed in dark garments. And while they looked normal, there was something in their countenances that told me that I had ventured into the world of the Maladons, even if they were not yet called that.

People greeted Necro as he walked along. It was clear that he was both well-known and popular with this crowd.

As I watched, Necro crossed the street and approached a couple walking from the opposite direction.

I slowed and took in this pair, realizing who they were a moment later.

"Jason," cried out Necro to the tall, handsome youth.

This was Necro's son. And the woman he was holding hands with was Uma, Bastion Cadmus's ethereally lovely daughter.

"Father," said Jason perfunctorily.

Necro tipped his hat to Uma, who glanced nervously away.

"You are looking as lovely as ever, Uma," said Necro, in a way that struck me as rather creepy.

"Thank you," said Uma, her gaze still averted.

"So, have you set your wedding date yet?" asked Necro.

This puzzled me because I had always understood that Necro had not approved of this union.

"Not yet," said Jason with a glance at Uma. "But it will be soon."

"Splendid," said Necro. "We will anxiously await that happy time. Until then." He tipped his hat again and was off once more.

I crossed the street and slowly approached the pair as they remained standing there.

"Hello," I said.

They both looked at me. "Hello," said Jason, and Uma nodded and smiled at me.

It was deeply unsettling to me that I knew that both of these beautiful young people were doomed. Jason would be stabbed to death and Uma, in her personal agony, would drown herself. And again, as with Astrea, I was tempted to warn them of what was coming for them. But Jasper's words came back to me once more, and I held my tongue.

Instead I said, "I heard that man say that you are getting married?"

"Yes," said Jason, with a shy glance at Uma.

"That's wonderful. I'm sure you'll be very happy together." I had to fight back tears because I knew their marriage would never come to pass.

"Thank you," said Uma, who was now looking at me strangely. "Do I know you?" she asked.

Not yet, I thought to myself. "No, I've just arrived here."

"Well, it's not often that one receives well wishes from a stranger. You must have a very kind heart. Perhaps we will see more of you?" she added with an enigmatic smile.

"Perhaps," I said noncommittally.

"I'm Uma and this is Jason. What is your name?"

"Vega."

"A curious name, but enchanting," said Uma. "Do you have family here?"

"I might," I said evasively. "That man who was just here?"

"Jason's father," said Uma, her disgust thinly veiled.

"He seems delighted at your upcoming marriage."

"Yes, he does seem to be," replied Jason.

I looked at Uma, who said, "Yet not everything is as it seems."

I shot Jason a look, but he seemed not to have heard her words.

"Well, good-bye, Vega," said Uma, who was looking chastened at her remark. "I hope that we meet again."

As I left them, I looked back and watched as they walked away, hand in hand.

I took my wand from my pocket, tapped it against my leg and said, "*Pass-pusay.*"

My destination was clearly in mind.

Empyrean.

But not the Empyrean with which I was familiar.

I landed in front of the place. It looked much like it did in my time, though it was obviously much newer. The grounds were sumptuous and inviting. I glimpsed large marble statues set in strategic places, and wondered if they had served as the inspiration for the enchantment of the outside staff at the Empyrean I currently inhabited. The stone-and-wood house sat there looking as unmovable as a star in the sky.

The sky!

I looked up and the sun was shining and the coldness I had felt in the part of town I had just left was gone, replaced with an inviting warmth.

As I peered out from under the cover of the tree line, I started.

A tall woman was striding purposefully along a path on the right side of Empyrean. She turned and headed in my direction.

As she drew closer, I could see who it was.

I stepped clear of the trees and called out to her.

"Hello?"

Alice Adronis stopped walking and looked up.

She was dressed not in chain mail, a warrior ready for battle, but in a long lavender cloak. Her face was strained, and I knew why. The horror of losing a child was printed upon every square inch of it.

My gaze fell to her breast, where I knew her mortal wound would eventually strike her down. It was such a disturbing thought that I had to glance away, shaken.

"Who are you?" she asked, her brows knitted together, her countenance stern and searching. "What are you doing here?"

I looked up as I drew closer to her.

"My name is Vega."

"But what are you doing here?"

"I seem to have lost my way." I paused. "Are you Alice Adronis?"

She stiffened but answered, "I am."

"I'm sorry for your loss."

She drew her cloak closer around her. "How do you know of it?" It was more a snarl than a statement.

"I saw your husband in town."

"He told a stranger . . . about my loss?" she said in disbelief.

"No, please don't be angry with him. He told Colin Sonnet at his shop. I just happened to be there when he did."

Alice looked over my shoulder. "I did not know that Gunther had gone to town."

I stood there feeling immensely awkward.

I took another step forward. "I have traveled far to obtain assistance from Colin to repair a ring of mine."

"Then you have chosen well. Colin is excellent in the field of curiosities."

I nodded and looked around. "Your home is truly beautiful."

Alice drew a bit closer, and I saw her eyes widen when she took me in fully.

"Do I know you?" she asked.

"No," I said quickly. "Have you lived here long?"

"Empyrean will always be my home."

Yes, it will, Alice, I thought.

Her features softened and she said, "Are you hungry? Would you like some sustenance?"

"That would be very kind," I replied.

We headed to the house. The door opened as we approached it.

We passed through and it closed behind us.

I looked around and marveled at the fact that Empyrean had not changed a jot. A tall, portly man dressed in a servant's livery slipped into the room and said, "Madame Alice, lunch is ready in the dining hall."

"Thank you, Pillsbury."

I nearly fell over as I beheld the true form of Pillsbury, before he was conjured permanently into a suit of armor.

I found myself growing sad at the sight of the flesh-and-blood Pillsbury, now a metal carcass still alive eight hundred years later. While I believed that Empyrean was a beautiful home, I didn't think anyone should have to care for *any* place for that long.

Alice led me down the passage and into the large dining hall.

A tall, thin white-haired woman with long limbs and enormous blue eyes came in, pushing a serving cart.

"Mrs. Jolly, we have a guest for lunch."

I was prepared for this and barely flinched as I took in the current Mrs. Jolly and concluded that she indeed had the willowy shape of a broom.

"Right you are, Madame Alice. There is plenty, for I had assumed Master Gunther would be here."

"He has gone into town," said Alice. "Though he failed to tell me."

I said, "He thought you perhaps needed to be alone."

Alice shot me a hard look that slowly softened. "Well, perhaps he was right."

The meal was placed before us, and Mrs. Jolly left the room.

We began to eat. I was ravenous, though I noticed that Alice ate only a few bites with absolutely no enthusiasm.

I said, "I have never had a child, but I can only imagine how hard it must be to lose one."

I saw her hand shake a bit before she answered. " 'Tis hard. Perhaps the hardest thing I've ever faced, and I have confronted many hard things in my life." She glanced at me. "Where do you come from?"

"A place far from here, but very much like it."

"You look quite familiar to me," said Alice. "I noted it outside, and the sense is even stronger inside my home."

"I suppose we might have met somewhere, sometime," I replied cautiously. Before she could pursue this line of inquiry, I added, "I saw Necro in town."

I saw her lips purse and her eyes blaze.

"And what did you think of him?"

"I think I have never seen a more evil bloke in my life."

She lifted her gaze to mine. "You are wise beyond your years."

"I saw Astrea Prine in town as well. She seems to understand this. But there are others, her husband for example, who do not."

Alice sat back and studied me. "For coming from a faraway place, you seem to have a deep understanding of our politics."

"I have the advantage of being in a similar situation of my own."

I wanted to tell her this *situation* was taking place eight hundred years into the future, but I thought that might have been a bit awkward over lunch!

She wiped her mouth with a napkin. "Indeed."

"I also saw Uma and Jason. They seem very much in love."

"I daresay they *are* very much in love." She hesitated and then continued. "But love cannot conquer all."

"Truer words were probably never spoken," I said. I looked around the room. "I can understand your desire to fill such a wonderful place as this with the sounds of happy children. And you will no doubt accomplish that."

I had never heard of Alice having children, but I had no desire to say that to a woman who had been so cruelly bereaved.

"Thank you. You never told me your surname."

"No, I didn't."

What I did next was perhaps a huge gamble, but for some reason it felt like the right thing to do. Alice had told me about the concept of Empchon or the Fates. She said there was a connectivity between us. Well, I was going to put that theory to the test right now!

I took out my wand and set it on the table.

Alice's gaze was immediately transfixed by it. That the wand was the Elemental was unmistakable. Then she looked up at me.

Her features were so hard that they appeared to be like the statuary that sat outside the grounds of Empyrean. I had never seen her eyes like that, knuckles of iron that seemed too large to be contained by mere sockets.

"Who are you?" she said in a hushed tone.

I laid my gloved hand over hers. She flinched because she had to know that I wore what had once been her glove. "Someone who will always be your friend, Alice. Always. You will fight your fight. And I will fight mine."

The next moment I was cursing myself because the mists covered us, and I was back standing in front of Colin's shop.

It was dark now, and as I opened the door, the bell tinkled.

Colin was behind the counter working on something. As I approached, he held up the ring. "I believe that it will comport with your requirements now."

"Wonderful," I said, smiling.

"And what might those requirements be?"

We both turned to see Necro standing there. I had not heard the bell tinkle, yet there he was.

I said, "A ring has many uses, does it not?"

He stepped forward, his disingenuous smile far deadlier than the fanged face of a jabbit.

"Does it? I should think it only has the one, as adornment for the finger."

I slipped the ring on my hand. "Well, that may show you have much to learn." I looked at Colin. "I can assume that serendipity has struck once more?"

"Most assuredly, it has."

"What do I owe you for your services?"

He held up his hands. "It was my pleasure to do so, Vega."

"I insist that I provide you something in return."

"I think that you have already done so."

I glanced at Necro, who was hanging on every word of this exchange.

I nodded at Colin. "I thank you for both your expertise and your comprehension."

139

I left the shop and Necro immediately followed.

"You interest me greatly, *Vega*," he said.

I winced. I wished that Colin had not used my name in front of the man. I turned to him. "Do I? I wonder why?"

"Perhaps we can have dinner together? I know an excellent place. We can have a discussion."

"I can't imagine what we would talk about."

"Can't you?"

I smiled. "Actually, I can."

And then the mists came once more, and the greatest enemy of my life disappeared.

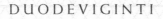

DUODEVIGINTI

Stones in Water

W AS YOUR TRIP successful?" Eon asked as I appeared in front of him.

I twisted my ring around. "Can you see me now?"

"No."

I returned the ring to its original position.

"Then my trip was successful."

"What will you do now?" he asked.

"What needs to be done," I replied.

I tapped my leg, muttered my incantation and a moment later I was standing on the steps of Empyrean.

As I looked it over, I had a new appreciation for the place, having seen it centuries before.

When I opened the door and stepped inside, Pillsbury greeted me. I looked at him too in a different way, having seen him without his armor. With a sudden impulse, I kissed his metal visor. If steel could blush, then Pillsbury just had.

"Mistress Vega? Are . . . are you all right?"

"I'm smashing, Pillsbury. And I just want you to know how very much I appreciate all that you do here for us."

He gave a short bow. "It is my true pleasure to serve you," he said.

When he straightened, he added, "I was unaware that you had gone out."

"It was sort of a last-minute decision."

"Do you require anything? Food? Drink?"

I shook my head. "I had something to eat, thank you."

It was eight centuries ago, but who was counting, I thought as I headed to find Delph.

I finally found him up in Jasper Jane's old laboratory poring over books.

"What are you doing, Delph?" I asked.

He looked up from a dusty tome. "Trying to find something that will help your dad. Where have you been?"

I sat down next to him on one of the tall stools around Jasper's worktable.

"I've been traveling."

He shot me a look. "Traveling? Where?"

"Back in time."

He slammed shut the book. "Vega Jane. Blimey!"

I slowly went through all that I had done while I had been gone, including getting my ring repaired. And all those whom I had met along the way.

As I spoke, poor Delph's jaw dropped lower and lower until I feared it might smack into the table.

When I finally finished, he gave me such a look of both reproach and wonder that I snapped, "What, Delph?"

"You shouldn't have gone by yourself," he readily replied. "We talked about you doing such."

"But I was going into the past, there was no danger."

"Like when you were nearly killed on that battlefield where you saw Alice? And you said they could all see you this time. Well, except for Petra."

"Um, right. Well, I wasn't hurt this time."

"Necro, eh?"

"Yes."

"And you said he looked all, well, normal?"

"Except for his eyes. You could tell in them, Delph, of the evil to come."

He sat back, looking exhausted just by hearing of my adventure.

"And Astrea when she was young. And Alice and her mate, Gunther. And Uma and Jason."

He leaned forward and looked curious. "Right. But you said that Necro seemed to want them to get married."

"I frowned. I was puzzled by that too."

"And you saw Petra being shunned by others because she was different. Reminds me of somebody."

"Who?" I asked curiously.

"*You*, Vega Jane."

"I'm sure she had great difficulty" was my diplomatic reply, ignoring his comment about me.

"And she overcame it," he said. "Like you did."

Okay, enough was bloody well enough. I blurted out, "We took an oath, Delph. Apparently, some of my blood rests in her now, and some of hers was wicked into me. But I'm never going to be best mates with Petra, no matter how much you may want that."

My words were fierce, and I expected some sharp retort, but Delph simply nodded in agreement.

"I understand that, Vega Jane. And you don't have to be best mates. You just have to trust each other."

"I *do* trust Petra. I've trusted her with my life. And she's done the same with me."

"Then there's no problem, is there?" he said matter-of-factly.

I once more started to say something and then realized that Delph had outsmarted me, boxed me in with no way to get out.

"I suppose not," I said unenthusiastically.

"So with the ring tidied up, what's your plan?"

"To find John," I replied.

He nodded. "That is all well and good, Vega Jane. And I know with your mum and dad here that's uppermost in your thoughts, and finding John would please all of us, especially your mother."

"But?" I said.

"I'm trying to find a way to cure your dad, and I know that Astrea is looking into it too. But we're fighting a war."

I stood and put my hands on my hips. "What are you saying, Delph? Don't be mealymouthed about it. Just say it."

"You're our leader. So you need to lead us."

I had a reply all ready, but suddenly the words seemed jargoled in my mouth. Still, I had some ammunition I could use in this argument. And I decided to do just that.

"Delph, if the Maladons do have John and are preparing to use him on their side, then we would be far better off with him on our side."

Delph seemed taken aback by my argument.

"And how will you do that?" he asked, seemingly genuinely curious.

"With the ring I can poke around here and there. I may see or hear something that could help us locate him."

"Will I be allowed to come along on these little excursions?"

"Why, of course, Delph, perish the thought that I might manage it on my own."

I grinned to show him that I was not being serious in the least. Well, maybe a bit, but he needn't know that.

However, Delph did not return my smile. His gaze was downcast.

"What's wrong, Delph?" I said.

"Nothing."

"Obviously something is. Look, things haven't changed. We're still best mates."

"You're right, Vega Jane, things *haven't* changed."

And he left me there, wondering what the Hel had just happened.

Still puzzled, I walked down the stairs and out into the rear gardens.

I had not seen Petra since I'd been back, and truth be known, I didn't really want to see her right now. I had been witness to some very personal memories of hers, and I was afraid that something in my features would betray this intimate knowledge. Then I would find myself either guilt-ridden or hounded by her to reveal what I knew.

Thus, I sought solace in the sun and the gardens.

As I strolled along, I heard a noise that immediately drew my attention for two reasons: First, I could not see the source of it. And second, it was the sound of someone weeping.

I hurried along a path that intersected twin rows of hedges and plunged into a thicket of trees. Once clear of those, I reached a large pond. And sitting on the grass by the water was Uma, or rather her nearly transparent image. I had never seen her outside of Empyrean. In the sun she was far paler, mostly an outline really, of what she had once been.

I hurried up to her.

"Uma, are you all right?"

She would not turn her face to me, but I was certain she was the source of the weeping.

"I'm fine, Vega. Fine," she added firmly, apparently to convince herself as well as me.

And before I could ask her anything else, she was gone.

145

I looked out over the surface of the pond. It was quite lovely, with nary a ripple to mar it.

"Where she done it."

I quickly turned around to see one of the statuary that worked in the grounds — this one was a large horse — staring at me from the copse through which I had come.

"I'm sorry?" I said, mightily confused.

"Where she done it," said the horse.

It was quite unsettling to find myself conversing with a horse made of marble, but there you are.

"Who?" I replied, rather stupidly.

"Mistress Uma. Where she done it. Killed herself." The horse raised a knobby foreleg and indicated the waters of the pond.

I whipped around to stare at the smooth surface once more.

"*This* is where she walked into the water with stones in her pockets? Were you here when it happened?"

The horse nodded its enormous head. "Was working out here, I was. Well, I wasn't a horse then, was I? I was a bloke, name of Tom Pittman. Just started working at Empyrean, I had. See them bushes right there? I was cutting 'em back, when I heard a splash. I turned around and there she was, walking into the water. Then, before I could take a step, she'd gone under. I jumped in, swam around some looking for her. But weren't no use. Dark in there, and mucky, it is. And deep. And it's got vines and such. Nearly drowned myself, them clutching at me. By the time I got out and found help, it was too late. They pulled her out. Dead she was. Pale as ice."

I looked around at the lovely setting, which had now been transformed into something ugly and depressing in my mind.

"But why here? At Empyrean?"

The horse shook its head. "Dunno."

146

And then the beast turned and cantered off.

I walked to the edge of the water and peered into its depths. In my mind's eye, I conjured the image of Uma placing large stones in her pockets, staring at the water and then making the decision to simply walk into the depths and end her life.

How sad and dispirited she must have been. I had felt very low at many times in my life. But never once had I considered ending my life. There had been too many times when some- one *else* was trying to do that for me, I suppose, to ever contemplate doing it myself.

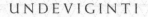

A Time for Words

AT DINNER THAT night my depression deepened.

A little over half my army was still alive, and as I looked around the dining room at them, it was clear that a certain melancholy had set in. Though they had fought valiantly, my order that no further missions would be undertaken for the foreseeable future had apparently dampened morale. And who could blame them? I hated inactivity too. Yet our numbers were so small that to attempt additional skirmishes with the Maladons would be insanity itself. Even one more loss would be too many.

The other cause of my depression was sitting across from me.

My mother had not once looked my way since she had come down for the meal. She spoke to Delph, had even said hello to Petra, and thanked Mrs. Jolly for the fine food. She exchanged a few words with Astrea and with the silent and morose-looking Archie next to her.

But for her own daughter, there had been nothing. Not a word, not a glance.

I would normally have felt anger at such a slight, but this was my mother. She had suffered terribly. Her husband was a shell of his former self with no clear path to recovery. Her only son had vanished, perhaps into the hands of the Maladons.

And she blamed me for this, rightly or wrongly.

Normally decisive on any dilemma presented to me, I felt paralyzed.

"Delph said you went into the past."

I looked up to see Petra's gaze upon me. I gave Delph a quick glare and then realized that I had not told him to keep news of my adventure secret.

I laid down my fork and knife as all eyes around the table settled upon me, save my mother's. She continued to eat her meal, her gaze downcast.

"I did. I was able to get my ring repaired." I paused. "Your ancestor Colin Sonnet did a fine job."

I could see from her lack of surprise at this statement that Delph had also told her this.

"Clearly not a Maladon, then," she said. I could almost taste the triumph in her words.

I could have said something like *Well, at least not a full-blooded one,* but common sense stopped me. Also, I didn't want to have to duel Petra over my supper.

"I also met Necro."

At this, I felt everyone in the room stiffen, including Astrea and my mother.

I looked at Astrea. "I also spoke with you, Astrea. I saw your husband. And I saw Archie as a young lad skipping along the cobbles."

"Indeed?" she said quietly. "You would have thought I would remember that."

"Well, it was over eight hundred years ago," I replied, forcing a smile. I could not get over the sense that this woman would undermine me given the opportunity. But there was something in her look that told me she *did* remember this meeting. I decided to test this theory.

"You had on a bright red cloak."

"No, it was the —"

She fell silent, her face pale and her look one of chagrin at how I had tricked her.

"Then you must also recall that I informed you that you were correct that war was coming?" My query was met by stony silence and a blank stare.

"Time works in funny ways," I continued. "It's hardly a linear thing. And sometimes it seems to make no sense a'tall. Alice called it Empchon, or the Fates." I looked at Astrea. "You undoubtedly are aware of these things, are you not, Astrea?"

Once more she met my question with silence.

"When I met her, I told Alice something that probably left an impression on her." I took out my wand and held it up. "I showed this to her. Alice knew it was her wand. Perhaps that's why she gave it to me on that battlefield right before she died. And also why she told me I needed to survive."

I glanced once more at Astrea. "When I met you in the Quag, did you remember me?"

Delph said, "But, Vega Jane, you just went back in time today. We met Astrea in the Quag long before that."

"I told you time works in unusual ways," I replied. "But in one way it works very simply. What came before, came before, regardless of when it occurred. Am I not correct, *Madame Prine?*"

"Tell her off, Mum," barked Archie. "What does she know, eh?"

I ignored this and said, "I believe you did remember my warning, which is perhaps why you allowed me to leave your imprisonment and cross the Quag. You knew Alice had given me the Elemental. You actually showed me that it was also my wand. And because of the power that I showed during one of our *confrontations*, you knew that I was perhaps the best chance for eventual victory?"

All eyes in the room passed from me to Astrea.

"Mum," snapped Archie. "Tell her —"

She held up a hand and he was instantly silenced.

She fixed me with what should have been an unnerving look, but I was so focused on what I wanted to hear her say that it had no impact upon me.

She seemed to sense this and looked away.

"I have spoken with Alice since I have come here, Vega. She remembers you well from that battlefield. She gave you the Elemental, her most cherished possession, for which she sacrificed much to gain, because she saw in you something that she no doubt saw in herself."

"What was that?"

This question came from none other than my mother.

I glanced at her, but my mother's gaze was upon Astrea.

"Indomitability," said Astrea simply, now staring directly at me.

"Surely, there are many with that trait," said my mother.

"Not to the degree required," responded Astrea.

"And pray tell, what is the difference?" asked my mother.

"Suffering," said Astrea immediately.

I said, "We have all suffered, Astrea. Everyone around this room, yourself included. Many here were slaves, their minds and freedoms gone. Petra lived in the Quag under the most severe conditions imaginable. Delph was cursed as a child and lost his father to the Maladons. You and your family existed in the Quag for centuries doing your duty." I paused and looked at my mother. "And my mother was cursed along with my father. And now he lies upstairs unrecognizable to her. I might say that rather than having suffered the most, I have suffered the least among us."

To my surprise, Astrea simply nodded. "All that you say is true, Vega."

"Well, then?" I asked.

"Why did you leave Wormwood? Why did you fight your way across the Quag? Why do you fight still?"

"Because I wanted the truth. I wanted to make things right. I wanted to take back what had been so cruelly taken from our kind. I want everyone here, and all those out there whose lives have been stolen by the Maladons, to have those lives back!"

"So your suffering included perhaps the most difficult element of all."

"What?" I asked.

"You suffer not simply for yourself, as most do. You have placed the suffering of all those here, and all those others of which you speak, upon your shoulders. For every one of us who falls on the battlefield, for all the souls lost in Wormwood, for every life that is snuffed out by the Maladons, you blame yourself. You wonder how you could have prevented it. You wonder how you can keep us all safe." She shot Delph a glance. "You take risk after risk, alone, not wanting to enlist your friends for fear that they will not survive. You fight not for yourself, Vega. You fight not for personal glory, as others of our kind undoubtedly did." She paused and when she next spoke, her voice rose higher. "You fight for us all. And that is why you lead us, Vega. Because you have taken our pain, our suffering, our loss . . . as your own. Peace. Hope. Freedom."

I felt dizzy at her words. Dizzy and stunned. Of all the people I would have expected to say something like this, Astrea would not have even made the list.

All I could think to say was, "Precisely in that order."

Astrea smiled benignly. "Precisely in that order. Although I have always considered hope to be the strongest among them. Because without that, we cannot have the other two. And that's what you do, Vega. You give us hope."

Now my mother did look at me. Her lips trembled, and I saw tears clutching at her eyes.

I felt the same physical reaction happening to me.

She abruptly rose and hurried from the room.

"Go after her, Vega."

I turned to see Petra staring at me with a sense of urgency. "She's your mum, and she needs you. As much as you need her right now, I reckon."

I gave her a grateful look, excused myself, and rushed from the room.

I ran into Pillsbury in the hall.

"My mother?" I began.

He pointed down the hall toward the rear door.

"I hope it goes well," he said kindly.

I hurried to the door, and a few moments later I was rushing down the path.

My mother was sitting on a bench among the roses. It was the same bench where I had comforted the young Miranda Weeks, seemingly centuries ago.

Lurking in the background was the same horse statue that had spoken to me earlier after my encounter with Uma.

I gave him a look that made him instantly clear off.

I stopped in front of my mother. She was staring at the ground and weeping.

"Mum?" I said tentatively.

She did not look up. But she said, "Oh, Vega, how very sorry I am."

I sat down next to her and put an arm around her quivering shoulders.

"It's all right."

"No, it's really not. I have acted appallingly to you. My own flesh and blood."

"It's not easy. And you've been through so much."

She wiped her eyes, sat up and took my hand. She managed a brief smile before her eyes welled up once more with tears, matching my own. "I have thought about you every day since we parted ways in Wormwood, Vega."

"It was the same for me. Every day."

My mother suddenly looked wistful. "We were wrong, Vega. To leave you and John. No matter what we thought we could accomplish here, to abandon our children . . . it was inexcusable."

"You wanted to change things. You wanted to fight the Maladons. I'm sure you would have come back to get us."

She gripped my hand more tightly. "We would have, Vega. But I am your mother and I had a choice. And . . . the choice I made was the wrong one. There is nothing more important to me than you and your brother. Nothing. Your father and I gave you both life. We had a duty, bound from love. And we abandoned that duty."

"For something perhaps greater," I said, trying to make her feel better.

"There is nothing greater, Vega, or at least there shouldn't be."

We sat there in silence for a few long moments. All I could hear was our breathing. It seemed that nothing else existed but the two of us.

Finally, I held my ring up. "I will find John."

"No, *we will find your brother.*"

"But Dad?"

"Your father is alive and surrounded by those who love him and will care for him. Our son is guaranteed neither of those things. We have to find him, Vega. We must."

"We will."

My mother smiled sadly at me.

"What?" I asked, confused by her look.

"My little girl is all grown up."

"I had no choice," I replied.

Her smile faded. "I know, Vega."

She slowly reached out and held me in her arms.

I felt the tears slide down my face.

And I held on to my mother with all my strength.

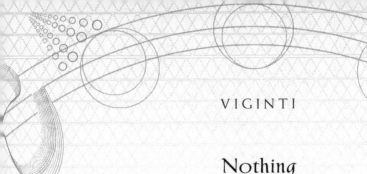

Nothing

THE NEXT MORNING, Astrea summomed me to her room before breakfast. Needless to say, and despite her words from the previous evening, this did not make for the beginning to a good day. Were we going to go back and forth for eternity?

I knocked on her door and Archie answered. He scowled at me and then stepped back, allowing me to pass by.

Astrea was sitting at a large table with books and parchment scattered across it.

She barely looked up when I walked in.

"Yes?" I said expectantly.

Astrea glanced up from a piece of parchment on which she was scribbling with an ink stick.

"How did things go with your mother last night?"

"They went fine," I said tersely.

"Now, Vega, there's no reason to take that tone or attitude."

"*You* summoned *me*," I retorted. "Was it just to hear how it went with my mother?" When Astrea didn't answer immediately, I turned toward the door.

"I'm very glad things went well with your mother."

I turned back and my features softened. I don't know if it was her genuine-sounding words, or the fact that I was just tired of being angry. "What you said last night at dinner was . . . helpful," I conceded.

"It was also the truth. Isn't it nice when the truth also can be helpful *and* make one feel good?"

Her frank statement brought an involuntary smile to my lips. "I suppose it is," I agreed.

Astrea pointed to her books and parchment. "I have interviewed your mother most carefully."

"About what?" I asked, drawing closer to her.

"About the *exact* circumstances leading up to your father becoming as he currently is."

I sat on the edge of her bed while Archie hovered in the background.

"And what were the exact circumstances?" I asked.

"I will *show* you. It's so much more instructive that way."

She took out her wand and pointed it against one wall.

Appearing there were three figures.

"Your father and the two Maladons with whom he was fighting. According to your mother, the Maladon on the left fired off a *Jagada* spell, whilst his mate hurled a *Paralycto* curse."

She moved her wand around, and the figures moved as well. Light shot out from the two Maladon silhouettes.

"What caused them to collide?" I asked. "My mum never said."

"Ah, well spotted," said Astrea. "Now, your mother, in an attempt to assist your father, set forth a shield spell, but the two spells hit it at a heightened angle. So, instead of absorbing the twin blow, the shield spell caused the two Maladon curses to meld together, and thus entwined, they deflected off and, unfortunately, hit your father."

She flicked her wand, and I watched as this very thing happened with the figures on the wall.

I shuddered at the impact of the commingled spell on my poor father.

"But how did they get away with my father so badly injured?"

"Ah, well, that goes to your father."

"My father!" I let my thoughts hark back to the image of my father as he now was. "But he was out of the fight."

"Not quite. Before the spell hit him, he managed to get off a spell of his own. He had a bare second whilst the two Maladon curses were encountering your mother's shield incantation. And he made good use of it, sending off a spreading *Impacto* spell that caught both of the Maladons full on. With them both incapacitated, your mother was able to get to your father and extricate them before Maladon reinforcements arrived."

I let out a long gasp, having just realized that I had been holding my breath the whole time.

"So, how does that help you?"

Astrea sat back in her chair and surveyed the mass of materials in front of her. "I began my researches in earnest last night in the library here, and also in Jasper's laboratory, and I have continued consulting the appropriate materials this morning."

"And?"

"And it is devilishly tricky, Vega. Devilishly tricky."

I leaned back, for I had unconsciously edged forward in anticipation of her answer.

"So, there is no hope?" I exclaimed.

She smiled encouragingly. "There is always hope, my child. And I am quite clever about these things. We had many unusual injuries during our war with the Maladons. Now, each situation is tricky, but, upon further rumination on the matter, I believe I have before unraveled one or two results of commingled spells."

"It can be done, then?" I cried out, feeling hopeful once more.

However, Astrea's features turned grim. "I would be remiss in not making something perfectly clear to you, Vega."

I felt my smile fade along with my hope. "What?"

"In attempting to reverse the effects of such a thing as this, I only have a single chance to get it right."

"What happens if you don't get it right?" I said, though I thought I knew the answer.

"If we don't get it right, Vega, your father will probably die. That is just how these things are. You see, the commingled spells are in his body, and while they have injured him greatly, the rest of their magic is actually still intact but has not yet fully deployed upon him."

My spirits sank to my knees. "You're saying that the two spells are like some sort of potential explosion waiting inside him?"

"Yes. And if we get it wrong, those spells will almost surely be fully unleashed. The effects cannot fail to be deadly."

I glanced over at Archie. I'd never seen him so serious. I looked back at Astrea. "But we can't leave him as he is," I said.

"I thought you would say that," she said, cheering up a bit. "Which is why I have been working so diligently on trying to get the antidote incantation exactly correct."

"How long will it take?"

"I can place no timetable on it, Vega. But when I am ready to proceed, I will inform you and your mother of everything I have learned and what I intend to do. And, with a bit of luck, we hopefully will restore your father to what he was."

I slowly nodded.

"I do not know your father of course," continued Astrea. "But I do know you, I daresay. And if father is anything like daughter, I would think that your father would be willing to

159

take the risk of death over remaining as he is now. But I will leave that decision up to you and your mother."

I slowly nodded once more. "I appreciate you doing all this."

"Of course. And I will do it to the best of my ability. But you have pressing matters before you."

I glanced up at her, unaware of to what she was referring.

"You have an army to command, Vega. You have the Maladons to defeat."

"Then you —"

She held up her hand. "You bested me at dinner last night, you know. Drawing me out as you did. That's not easy to do, is it, Archie?"

I looked at Archie, who smiled and said, "Rather impossible, Mum." Then inclining his head at me, he added, " 'Cept for Vega."

I felt astonished by his positive comments about me, and a smile tugged my lips upward.

"Thank you, Archie. When I came in, I thought you were angry with me."

"I'm just angry in general, Vega. I've missed a lot in my life, no matter how long it's been. I don't blame Mum anymore," he added quickly, as Astrea seemed about to speak. "And I can't say I wasn't happy about you being allowed to escape the Quag when I hadn't been. But I understand the choices that were made."

I looked at Archie in a new light.

Just when you thought you had someone figured out . . .

Astrea had been staring at her son, but turned her attention to me.

"I did not answer your query last night, Vega, for I was feeling vain and taken advantage of by your quicker wit. But I will answer it now." She paused and seemed to choose her

160

words with great care. "Like reversing the effects of commingled spells, the matter of time is devilishly tricky. I do not pretend to understand it. I doubt that Eon, though he is one who administers the very nature of time, is fully cognizant of all that is encapsulated over the ages, particularly when one manages to travel from one time to another."

"But did you know me in the Quag at your cottage, because I met you *yesterday back in time?*" It sounded funny how I said it. And truth be told, my mind could not come to grips with what I was even asking.

"At the time, consciously, I can't say that I did. Subconsciously? That is a whole other matter, Vega. And then one gets into the concept of parallel universes, holes through the eons and other matters of such complexity that I daresay no one has ever fully comprehended the possibilities."

"I see."

"Regardless, when I met you in the Quag, I did not need a long-ago memory of our meeting to understand one thing."

"What was that?"

"The same thing that Alice recognized when she saw you on that battlefield. That you were a force to be reckoned with. A force of good. A hope for all of us."

"Thank you."

"So I will focus on your father, and you can spend your time and energy on how we defeat the Maladons."

"I would still like to seek your counsel."

"And you are very welcome to it. As you probably know, I have queried the others on Maladon fighting techniques and strategies. I have to say that they have evolved over time. This contingent of bowler-hatted blokes, in particular. I see that they have adopted Necro's preferred method of dress as their battle uniforms."

"They have. And they are led by a Maladon named Endemen. He seems to be Necro's second-in-command."

"Now, that is a new thing. I wonder from whence Endemen came?"

"I'd much prefer to focus on where he's going."

She looked at me quizzically.

"To extinction," I finished.

The End of Endemen

WHEN THE DARKNESS came that night, I had one compelling thought: It was time to use my ring to look for my brother.

I used a wand wire to talk to Victus, the slave who resided at Maladon Castle. He had not seen anyone matching my brother's description, but he also told me that there was a great deal of activity going on at the castle.

"Something is happening, Vega," he said, his tone low and anxious. *"I know not what, but something is in the works."*

This troubled me greatly, for when there had been such activity in the past, Wormwood had been destroyed by the Maladons.

The next question was who I should take with me. I couldn't go alone. I had promised Delph that I would not.

Then I remembered our discussion. *My mother.*

I immediately went to her room and explained what I wanted to do.

"I will have Mrs. Jolly look after your father," she said immediately. "And I will be ready in five minutes, Vega."

I descended the stairs, so absorbed in my thoughts that I bumped into him on the way down.

It was Archie.

"How are things going with the antidote?" I asked.

"Mum doesn't really talk to me about it. But she's totally absorbed in it."

"I have every confidence in her ability to reach a solution." In my mind, I conjured an image of my father. "He can't remain as he is."

"If anyone can help him, Mum can."

He glanced at me nervously.

"What?" I said in response.

"I guess I'm eager to show that I can help in the fight against the Maladons. I certainly never thought I would have the chance."

"But you and Astrea have been fighting them, ever since you left the Quag."

"It's been more her than me. I mean, I *can* fight. She trained me up as she did you. But there's a difference between training for something and actually doing it."

"I know that well enough."

I studied Archie for a long moment, and a thought entered my head that surprised even me.

"Archie, how would you like to accompany me and my mother on a trip to Maladon Castle?"

He looked as surprised at hearing my request as I probably felt making it.

"When?"

"Now."

To his credit he didn't shrink from this rather ominous offer.

"I'm ready, Vega."

"We'll be under my ring of invisibility of course. I want to see if John is there."

"Your brother?"

"Yes, he might be their prisoner."

"I'll be back in a jiff," he said. "I just need to get my cloak and my wand."

He set off while I considered what I had just done. Well, either it would be successful or we'd all be dead.

"BLIMEY, IS THAT it?"

We had just landed in front of Maladon Castle when Archie spoke.

I nodded as I surveyed what was going on in front of us. There was activity with Maladons running hither and thither, as there had been on a previous visit of mine here.

My mother was on my other side. She stared at the castle with interest. She had told me that she and my father had seen the castle, but never been inside. Well, that would change tonight.

"The gates are open," I whispered. "Let's slip through, but keep close to me. And if you must speak, keep your voices low. We're invisible, but they can still hear us."

"Right," said my mother while Archie simply nodded.

We made our way forward and managed to ease through the gates after a column of cloaked Maladons. Once inside, I led them down a side passage.

"You know your way around here?" Archie whispered as we stopped at the intersection with another corridor.

"Somewhat," I said. "I haven't been all over the place, but enough to figure things out."

"Where shall we start?" my mother asked.

When I looked at Archie, he was as rigid as a tree, with his wand gripped so tightly in his hand that I was afraid he might snap it in two.

I smiled and said, "First, Archie, relax, before you keel over."

He let out his breath, and I could see his body loosen. "Sorry, Vega."

"No need to apologize. I was the same way on my first visit here. It takes a bit of getting used to, if one ever does."

I looked at my mother. "Are you okay?"

She nodded. "I'm not afraid, Vega, though I guess I should be. I just want to find John and get us all back safely."

"That's the goal. Keep your wands at the ready at all times."

I led them through a series of corridors. We occasionally passed a Maladon or two, but luckily no garms and jabbits, who could smell us.

"Where are we going?" Archie asked.

"There's a room here where they stripped our kind of their magic. John might be there."

We reached the room where I had found people trapped behind mirrors while their magic was sucked from them and collected as dust in bottles.

I used a magnification spell to see behind the door. There was no Maladon keeping guard inside.

I opened the door, and we stepped through, closing the door behind us.

I heard the moans instantly. I shot a glance at one of the mirrors and was struck dumb by what I saw.

The wall was full of mirrors, far more than had been there before. They were much smaller, however, which had me puzzled.

When I saw the figure inside the first glass, I nearly screamed.

My mother didn't have the same restraint. She gave a sharp howl before she collected herself. "Roman Picus?" she said, rushing up to the first glass.

Roman Picus, my old landlord from Wormwood, was indeed inside the glass. He was writhing and moaning, evidently in great pain. I had never been an admirer of Picus. He and I had been on opposite sides of every argument. But still, finding him here turned my stomach. In another mirror next to him was Cletus Loon. Like Roman, Cletus Loon and I had never seen eye to eye. But watching him now in evident agony, his eyes bulging out of his head with pain, our petty disagreements of the past wilted away. Next to him in another glass was Domitar, who oversaw my work at Stacks. He and I had reached common ground before I left Wormwood, and he had told me some important things that had aided me on my way across the Quag. Domitar was lying on his back with all his limbs clenched tight, as if he were on fire. Scream after scream escaped his mouth.

I gave a little cry when I saw who was inside the next glass. "Duf!"

It was Delph's father, Duf Delphia. His timbertoes, given to him to replace the legs he had lost in an accident, were gone, leaving him with his stumps. He was lying on his back, moaning.

I tapped the glass. "Duf? It's Vega. Delph is safe. I . . ."

Duf didn't make any sign that he could hear me.

Every inch of the walls was covered in mirrors. And behind each was someone who had lived in Wormwood. In fact, I saw every Wug I'd ever known who lived in Wormwood, except for Morrigone.

And John.

They all moaned and called out to make the pain stop.

But how could this be? These folks were dead and buried.

I looked at the floor, but there were no bottles collecting magical dust. That was because none of these people were magical. And again, they were dead. I doubted you could take magic from a dead person.

"Holy Steeples," said my mother, the horror of what she was seeing clear in her features.

"What is this, Vega?" said Archie, his features also screwed up in revulsion.

I shook my head. I felt sick to my stomach.

"They . . . they all lived in Wormwood. I know them all." I glanced at my mother. "*We* knew them all. But . . . but they're dead."

Archie said, "Well, part of them obviously isn't."

"Do you . . . do you think these are their souls perhaps?" said my mother in a hushed tone as she looked at Duf moaning in pain.

I shook my head. "I've seen souls. They don't look like this. And can souls even feel physical pain?"

"Can they be brought back, then?" asked Archie.

I shook my head. "Not if they're dead. There is nothing that can do that. Not even magic."

"And you're *sure* they were all killed?" said my mother.

Slapping my hand against the stone wall, I said angrily, "Thansius *told* me. He had to bury them all. He would never lie. And I don't believe the Maladons would have bewitched him to say that. What would be the point?"

"So why were, whatever they are, brought here, then?" asked Archie.

I had no answer to give him.

My mother finally drew her gaze away from Duf. "We can't leave them like this."

"No, we can't," I said.

I pointed my wand at Duf. "*Rejoinda*, Duf Delphia."

Duf remained firmly behind the glass.

I squared my shoulders and pointed my wand at one corner of the glass. *"Impacto."* The glass didn't even crack.

Of course it was not going to be easy.

I glanced at my mother. "Let's try it together."

We both fired off *Impacto* spells.

It had absolutely no effect. Duf continued to moan and writhe.

Bloody Hel, I thought.

"Let me add my wand," said Archie.

We fired off a trio of spells.

It still didn't work.

I felt the link of Destin under my shoulders.

I drew my fist back and let fly at the glass, bringing to bear all the strength that Destin gave me.

As soon as my flesh touched the glass, I was blown backward and smashed into the opposite wall.

Bloody Hel twice, I thought.

We tried every spell we could think of, and nothing worked. Absolutely nothing. And our spells made noise. I feared that at any moment the room would be filled with Maladons pointing their wands. Even invisible, we could still be struck by their incantations and killed.

As a last resort, I pressed the Adder Stone against the glass and thought wonderful thoughts, praying that if I couldn't free them from the glass prison, I could at least lessen their pain.

However, the Stone was powerless as well.

We were all exhausted and sweaty from so much spell work. I felt like I had fought a dozen battles. "Damn it!" I screamed, and then froze and listened closely while my mother and Archie glanced anxiously around.

When I heard nothing, I tried to pull a glass off the wall. It would not budge.

I stepped back, breathing hard and contemplating what to do.

I was still muddling over this when the door opened and three cloaked Maladons entered.

We immediately pointed our wands at them. I whispered, "Archie, left. Mum, right. I've got the bloke in the middle."

"*Impacto*," said Archie and my mother at the same moment I cast my spell at the middle Maladon and put his mind under my control.

As his mates slumped to the floor, my Maladon looked stupidly at the wall.

Archie paled a bit when I told the Maladon to let his hood down.

"Blimey," he said. "Do they all look like that?"

"Underneath, yes. That's a *real* Maladon, Archie."

I looked at my mother. She had obviously seen Maladons in death during the course of their battles with them. Still, I could see the revulsion on her features.

And they *were* revolting. It was like their bodies had been turned inside out and the foulness inside was now visible to all.

I said, "Okay, Maladon, explain the people in the glass. What are you doing to them? Why are they here?"

The bloke mumbled, "Bad 'un, they are. Punished."

"But they're already dead," I said heatedly. "Isn't that enough for you lot?!"

He shook his head, a demented grin spreading over his features. "We're always learning, ain't we?"

This response made me stiffen, and then I felt deeply intrigued. "How so?" I asked.

"How we survive. We always look for weaknesses. Then we take advantage." He pointed to the glass.

I looked at the suffering behind there.

"What have you learned from them?"

"Things," he said.

"What things? Tell me," I ordered.

"They ain't magical, for starters."

"That, I know. What else?"

He was about to say something when he clutched his chest and fell forward. I knelt down and checked him. His eyes were wide open and unseeing.

I looked up at my mother and Archie in shock. "He's dead."

"But how? You did nothing to him," said my mother.

I rose. It was true. I had done nothing to him.

I heard the footsteps.

I looked at the Wugs behind the glass. I had to free their spirits. But to do that, I needed to stay alive.

My heart was breaking, and tears welled up in my eyes as I drew near to Duf's glass. "I will be back, Duf, I promise."

"Vega, hurry," implored Archie.

I broke off gazing at Duf. "Come on!" I said decisively to my team.

We rushed from the room. As soon as we turned one corner, we saw a group of Maladons coming toward us. They couldn't see us, but they were spread out, filling the hall from wall to wall.

Well, two could play that game.

I lifted into the air, pulling Archie and my mother after me. We passed over the Maladons and continued on our way.

"Vega, what's going on?" hissed Archie.

"They know someone is here," I replied. "They must have placed some sort of curse on that Maladon back there. If he tried to divulge anything of importance, he would die. And he did."

We turned another corner and there they were.

A garm on one side and a jabbit on the other. And two huge Maladons leading them on chains. The beasts were sniffing the air heavily.

"*Odorous obstructo*," I said quietly, aiming my wand at their snouts.

This froze their scent capability, and we floated over them with no problem. We landed on the other side and rushed down the hall. We heard more footsteps coming, and I used my wand to look through the nearest door. What I saw inside made me gasp.

"This way," I said, pulling them into the room.

I shut the door behind us and stared at the objects I'd seen with my spell.

"Blimey," said Archie.

Blimey indeed, I thought. It was a pinstripe suit, white shirt and bowler hat hanging on hooks on the wall. Who did they belong to?

I drew closer and studied the hat and the clothes. They looked familiar.

I used my wand to flip over the hat so I could see the inside lining.

I gasped again.

Written out in silver handwriting along the inner rim's band was a name.

Mr. Endemen.

I whirled around, half expecting to see the man coming at me. But there was no one there. I placed the hat back on the hook with a flick of my wand.

I looked around. This surely couldn't be where Endemen lived. It was small, cramped and musty. More a closet than a room.

I had a sudden inspiration.

Using my modified wand wire, I contacted Victus.

When he answered, I said, "Victus, what has happened to Mr. Endemen?"

His answer nearly made me collapse to the floor.

"He has been imprisoned."

"What? Why?"

"I told you, Vega, that Necro was upset with him. Well, that upset has turned to anger and the anger has now led Necro to strip Mr. Endemen of his powers and his freedom."

"Where is he?"

"In the same tower I spoke to you about before."

The tower where my grandfather had been imprisoned.

"Thanks, Victus. Um, do they know we're here?"

"They know someone who should not be here is, Vega. Please take care."

I led Archie and my mother from the room and down another corridor. Burned into my memory was the way to the tower where I had nearly been crushed to death.

We made our way swiftly toward it. Along the way I wondered what sort of guards would be stationed outside the tower room. If they were already looking for us, they would be on high alert. And if we fought our way into the tower room, we might never get out.

But when we arrived I saw no guards.

This made me extra wary.

I took out my wand and cast the spell to see inside the tower room.

I had to shake my head at what I was seeing, my wand twitching in my hand.

Endemen *was* in there. He was stripped down to his underwear.

And he was bound by thick black chains that were attached to the floor. .

I approached the door and used my wand to open it. I was surprised that it yielded so willingly, which put me even more on my guard.

My mother whispered in my ear, "We need to take care, Vega. Something is not right."

I nodded, and we slowly entered the room, our wands in defensive positions, our gazes revolving around the space.

Endemen had not looked up at the door opening. He was simply staring at the floor. He was in his disguised state, not his original Maladon form.

In a few words, I explained to Archie and my mother who and what Endemen was. Though we were invisible, Endemen turned his head toward us when I spoke.

I gasped again, because his face was blank. I had identified him as Endemen by his hair and the line of his jaw and the rest of his profile.

But his face, the slash of his mouth, his dangerous eyes, were no more. He was like all the other slaves I had encountered, faceless, their magic taken from them. I wondered if they had encased Endemen behind glass and collected his powers in one of those awful bottles.

I kept my wand pointed directly at him, because face or not, he could be deadly, as I well knew.

Yet there was something so pitiable about him that I could no longer stand it. The last person I wanted to feel sorry for was this bloke.

I readied my wand and said, *"Origante."*

It was as though a lightning spear had entered my wand and the bolt of energy had hit me directly in the chest.

Endemen had not turned into a grotesque creature, as was the case with the other Maladons.

I nearly dropped my wand.

Jason, Necro's son and Uma's love, stared back at me.

No Way Out

"V EGA. VEGA!"

I came around and stared stupidly at Archie.

"What?"

"Does it feel funny in here to you?"

I looked back at Endemen. Or Jason. At first, I thought it must be some sort of trick. There was no way the gentle, handsome Jason could be the wicked, grotesque killer that I knew Endemen to be.

Yet as I looked into that face, I saw something strangely real. Pain.

True pain. The kind of desperate, hollow void that forms an abyss that you think you can never claw your way out of. I know. I've been in one myself.

"Vega!" said Archie more urgently.

I refocused on him, pushing the tortured features of Jason from my mind.

"What?"

My mother answered, "Vega, the air. It's getting hard to breathe."

I drew in a breath, gasped and instantly knew she was right. *Necro.*

I looked frantically around. There were no longer any windows in the tower room. We heard footsteps coming up the stairs.

This had been a trap. Or else we had triggered some warning spell that the Maladons had cast around the room.

Thinking quickly, I spun my ring around, rendering us visible once more.

I ran over to Jason and looked down at him.

"Why . . . why are you here?" he gasped.

"You're supposed to be dead. Uma saw you dead. Then she killed herself."

Jason groaned, and if it was possible, his pain deepened.

"Uma killed herself?"

"Yes, didn't you know?"

Jason shook his head, the agony of my revelation clear on his features.

"What happened to you?" I asked. "How did you come to be here?"

Jason shook his head as tears rolled down his face.

Archie edged up to me. He gasped, "Uh, Vega, it's really getting bloody hard to breathe in here. And the sounds are getting closer."

I ignored him as my mother peered over my other shoulder.

"Your father turned you into Mr. Endemen, didn't he, Jason?" I said.

He slowly nodded.

"Why?"

"To make war. And then to silence me. He took . . . he took my mind."

I thought back to the town of True and the room under the train station where the Maladons led groups of people to have their minds stolen.

My mother said, "Have you seen my son? Is John Jane here?" she added in an urgent whisper.

Jason only shook his head. "I . . . I don't know."

"Please, you must think." My mother put a hand out to grip his shoulder, perhaps shake him into remembering.

But I grabbed her arm and held her back.

My mother shot me an angry look.

I met that look with one of my own.

"I'm the leader here, Mum, not you."

"We're here to find John," she said forcefully.

"And we will find him. But we need to do it in the right way. And we need information."

I looked back at Jason and said, "But didn't you serve Necro faithfully? As Endemen, you and I have fought on many occasions. Why are you chained?"

"I . . . Uma."

"What about her?"

"Um, Vega, they're right outside the door," Archie warned.

I was totally focused on Jason.

"What about Uma?"

"She . . . she . . ."

"I have seen her," I said, hoping to prompt him.

He stared up at me, his eyes full of hope one moment and hurt the next.

"You have seen Uma?"

"Her spirit. She calls it regret. She loved you more than anything. With you gone she had nothing to live for."

"Can you tell her . . . can you tell her that I loved her just as much as she loved me? Perhaps more."

"I will, if we get out of here alive."

"Then I will do all in my power to ensure that you will be able to do so," he said, his voice for an instant growing firm and strong.

The door flew open.

I whirled around to see Necro standing there.

178

Our gazes locked, since I was not invisible.

I saw triumph on his features. But not necessarily immediate recognition. But then again, the last time I had seen him had been eight hundred or so years ago.

He slipped off his hood. "You must be Vega," he said. "I have heard much about you from various sources." He looked at me more closely. "And I believe that we might have met at some point."

Words coming out of that terrible visage were nearly unbearable.

"Where is my son?!" screamed my mother.

Necro's gaze pivoted to her. "Madame, you have the advantage of me. I would be delighted to reunite you with your son. Tell me who he is. I might have him under glass in the castle."

"Like your son?" I said.

Necro glanced at his son, and froze.

He bared his teeth like a dog about to attack.

I whipped my ring around, and we disappeared from view. But it was a small space and Necro knew we were here.

He raised his wand, and the air around us began to grow even heavier. I felt my lungs heave. Next to me, Archie and my mother gasped.

I lifted off the ground and took aim at Necro.

Then he simply vanished. Behind him were a dozen Maladons, all Bowler Hats. They streamed into the room, took aim and started firing spells all around.

Archie and my mother screamed as I dove, ducked, flipped, turned and hurtled us around the room, trying to avoid their curses.

The problem was the air was growing so heavy that I was having a difficult time staying up.

179

I looked at Archie.

"Vega, what can we do?" he gasped.

"Take out as many of the Maladons as you can. Fire left, Mum. Archie, you go right."

They nodded, pointed their wands and began firing away. I knew that each spell cast would reveal our position, but we kept moving. And if we didn't fight back we would be slaughtered regardless.

I added my wand to the fight and Maladon after Maladon fell, their wands rolling away across the floor.

But more crowded in to take their place.

We kept firing and taking fire. I cast a shield spell, but it only partially held against all the incoming curses.

"I can . . . barely breathe, Vega," Archie gasped.

I too was starting to flutter in and out of consciousness. For some reason, this did not appear to be affecting the Maladons.

And that was the moment he returned.

Necro stood in the doorway. He looked around at all his fallen followers and showed no concern at all for them. Indeed, a smile played over his lips. He raised his wand slowly into the air.

This would be it, I supposed. We were like birds trapped in a cage. Helplessly flying with no way out.

I didn't know what spell he would use, but I imagined it would finish us off.

I had escaped such a situation before, using my Elemental as a spear to blast my way through the high dome of the castle.

Now I tried to line up my wand to take aim at him. To finish *him* off before he did the same to us.

But I had made a critical error: I was about out of air. And I could no longer see or think clearly, and my wand wobbled in my hand.

"V-Vega," mumbled Archie, his eyes closing as he grew limp against the magical tether keeping him both invisible and in the air.

I refocused on Necro with my wand.

Come on, Vega, you can do it. Finish the bloke. Rigamorte *and it's over. Do it.*

Necro said, "Vega, your spirit is admirable. Come and join me in my crusade to bring us to our true destiny."

I couldn't believe it. This murderous fiend wanted me to join him!

I answered his call with a blast from my wand, which he easily blocked.

Rigamorte, *he can't block that. Do it.*

But the death spell required a concentration that I could simply not give at the moment. I was barely conscious. There was not enough wind left in my lungs for another breath.

Next to me, Archie slumped unconscious. His deadweight sagged against the tethers, stretching them to their limits. On the other side, my mother was still casting spells, but I could see that she was about to faint.

They pulled me down like lead, even as I felt my eyes fluttering and my chest struggling to rise once more.

"A pity, Vega. You would have been useful."

I looked down to see Necro aiming his wand toward us. He apparently could sense exactly where we were even though he couldn't see us.

"No!"

I saw a blur of movement to my left.

It was Jason. Despite his chains, he had managed to reach one of the wands dropped by a Maladon. He pointed it at his father.

There were bursts of light from his wand and that of Necro, who was momentarily distracted from killing us.

I took this opportunity to marshal my focus and transformed the Elemental into a lance. We hurtled upward, bursting through the ceiling of the tower room and out into the fresh air.

I didn't waste a moment. I reduced the Elemental back to a wand, tapped my leg and uttered the incantation with one image firmly in my mind.

The next thing, we were standing on the steps of Empyrean.

"Bloody Hel," exclaimed Archie.

"Yes, bloody Hel," gasped my mother.

I twisted the ring around, we became visible once more and we stumbled inside, collapsing onto the floor. None of us moved for a few long moments.

Pillsbury rushed into the room, gasped and hurried over to me.

"Mistress Vega, are you all right?"

I sat up and nodded. "Just a bit out of wind, Pillsbury. I'll be fine." I slowly rose and gave a hand to my mother, helping her up, while Pillsbury did the same for Archie.

Archie looked at me in a sort of awe.

"I don't know how you got us out of that place," he said. "But I'm very glad you did."

My mother put a hand on my shoulder. When I turned to look at her, there were tears clustered in her eyes.

"I know, Mum. I'm sorry we didn't find John."

"It's not that, Vega. You . . . you were wonderful back there."

I felt myself actually blush. "Th-thanks."

"I didn't know what it would feel like, having my little girl lead us," she admitted.

"I can understand that. I certainly was no warrior or sorceress back in Wormwood."

"Perhaps not outwardly, but clearly you had what it takes inside of you, Vega."

I didn't know what to say to this, and apparently my mother didn't want to add anything to it. She merely hugged me.

Archie appeared over her shoulder. "Well, if you don't mind, I think I'm going to go have a lie-down. This almost dying stuff has me knackered."

He staggered off.

My mum said, "I need to go check on your father."

She hurried off, leaving me alone with Pillsbury.

"Are you quite sure you're all right, Mistress Vega?"

"I'm a lot better than I would have been a few minutes ago, Pillsbury."

He seemed to grasp my meaning. "Did you . . . did you escape him again?"

"I did. But it was very close."

I thanked Pillsbury for his concern and then hurried off. There was someone I desperately needed to talk to. And I didn't want to waste a moment before doing so.

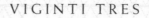

Twining

U MA?"
　　I looked around the chamber where I could usually find her. She didn't appear.

"Uma. I have news. Of Jason."

The next moment, there she was. Shimmering, nearly transparent. Nearly gone, actually.

"Jason?" she said breathlessly. "News?"

I nodded and leaned back against the wall, more for support than anything else. I was still feeling pretty wobbly actually.

"What I'm about to tell you will not be easy to hear, but it's the truth. I swear it."

She hovered there frozen in front of me.

"Please tell me, Vega," she said.

And I did. With some trepidation, because I knew it would come as a great shock, as it had to me. When I got to the part revealing Endemen to be her supposedly dead fiancé, Uma visibly shuddered. Then she broke down in sobs for such a long time, I finally said urgently, "Uma, Jason asked me to tell you something."

As I had hoped, this made her stop crying. She looked up at me, her chin trembling, and her face as flushed as a spirit could manage, I suppose.

"What?"

"He told me to tell you that he loved you just as much as you loved him, perhaps more." I paused as she took this in. "And I would not be here right now if he had not attacked his father. By doing so, he allowed us to escape."

Uma sank down to the floor, perhaps with the weight of all that I had revealed.

I sat next to her.

"I don't understand any of this, Vega," she sobbed. "He was dead. Jason was dead. I saw his body."

"I know. It seems inexplicable. But I think we can work it out." I paused, marshaling my thoughts. "Necro wanted to start a war between our kind and the Maladons. Pillsbury told me that he believed Necro came here to talk with Gunther Adronis under the pretense of preventing the war. But he ended up murdering Gunther instead. Now, that would normally have started a war on its own, but I think Necro was cleverer than that. How to blunt the outcry against him about one murder? Commit another one that seems to be directed at his own family."

"So he pretended to have Jason killed and blamed the death on us?" said Uma.

"Yes. How he did so I don't know, but with his magic it wouldn't have been too difficult to substitute another body for Jason's and make it look like him."

"But you say that he turned Jason evil and made him serve his father?"

"Jason was a good man, Uma. I've heard the stories that his father was worried that Jason would take over and commit to a peace. That was something Necro could never tolerate. But I also don't think he could let Jason's treachery — which is how he would see it — go unpunished. He took Jason's mind from him, made him wicked and then made him serve in doing

185

evil." I paused and drew a breath. "And when I saw you both in town the day I traveled into the past, Necro seemed very eager for the marriage to happen. I wondered about that. But clearly it was all an act, perhaps to avoid suspicion. He never intended to allow the two of you to marry. He instead made certain that your love would be subverted to his own purposes."

"But you said Jason told you he loved me? So has his sanity returned?"

"Apparently so. Somehow he finally defeated whatever his father had done to him."

"But how? After all this time? Necro is so very powerful."

"It must have been very recent. It wasn't all that long ago that Endemen and I were fighting to the death."

"So how, then?"

"Uma, I just don't have a good answer for that. What's important is that he *did* manage to throw off Necro's yoke."

"What happened to him, after you escaped the castle? Is he alive?"

"I don't know, but I have a way to find out. And as soon as I know, you will too, okay?"

"Thank you, Vega."

I left her there and rushed back up to the main floor. I found Delph and Petra and quickly told them what had happened.

Delph was absolutely stunned when I got to the part about the Wugs behind the glass.

"My . . . my dad was there?"

I nodded.

"Are they . . . are they alive somehow?" he said hesitantly. "But . . . but how could they be? You saw their graves."

I knew my features reflected the pain, no, the agony he was feeling. My eyes filling with tears, I said, "I don't know, Delph. I don't know what has happened to them. But I told him that we would be back to . . . to rescue all the Wugs, in whatever . . . form they happen to be."

He stood there breathing hard, his hands curled into fists. I thought he might start punching the wall. He cried out, "They've suffered enough. The bloody Maladons have already killed them. Why can't they let them rest in peace now? The bloody bastards."

"We *will* do something, Delph. I promise you. I tried everything I could think of to free them while I was there, but we will find a way to help them."

Petra shuddered. "How could Endemen, or Jason, suddenly become himself again? We've both faced Endemen. He was a demon, as evil as I've ever seen. But you described the man far differently."

"He was no longer Endemen," I replied simply. "He was back to being Jason."

"And you don't think it was some trick?" asked Petra.

"Hardly. Jason saved our lives. I doubt that Endemen would have done that."

"No, he wouldn't have," agreed Petra.

"What made him change back into Jason?" asked Delph.

"I don't know. That's the same thing I told Uma. But I'm telling you that the person I saw was Jason, not Endemen. Somehow, he threw off whatever his father had done to him."

"Do you think he's still alive?" said Delph.

I shook my head. "In a duel with Necro, I doubt Jason would win. He wasn't even using his own wand. I've bested Endemen in a duel before. And I don't think I'm at Necro's level."

"I'd wager on you, Vega Jane, just like I did in the Duelum."

I smiled at his comment.

"But what did you learn that can help us?" interjected Petra, looking quite serious.

My smile vanished. She had a point. I had gone at great risk to the castle, nearly losing my life and my mother's and Archie's in the process. But what *had* I gained? Was it worth it?

"I'm not sure. Victus did tell me that there was a lot of activity at the castle, as though something important was underway."

"What could it be?" asked Delph.

"I'll ask Victus to try and find out." Something else occurred to me. "If Jason was able to break free from his father's control, that shows that Necro isn't invincible."

Petra said, "That's true. But it doesn't mean we can defeat him."

"And it doesn't mean we can't," I retorted.

"Why would they have brought the souls or spirits of all the Wugmorts and put them behind the glass?" said Delph slowly.

"I — I don't know, Delph. And Victus said he hadn't seen anyone resembling John, so he may not be at the castle at all."

"Then we need to look other places."

"I'm going to send search parties out looking for him right now."

And I left it at that.

Or so I thought.

As I walked off, I turned back to see Delph and Petra in deep conversation. And something told me it wasn't about what we had just discussed. When Petra looked like she had been slapped at something Delph said, I hurried on, because something told me this was not going to end well.

However, I heard running footsteps behind me as I was racing up the stairs.

Of course it was Petra. She stopped running and faced me.

"How did you know?" she said fiercely.

I turned to her. "Know what?"

"That I suffered so much in the Quag? That's what you said to Astrea at the dinner."

My face screwed up in confusion, I said, "You told me yourself. And I found you in there. You were hardly in the best of circumstances."

Her eyes flashed at me. "According to you?"

"What is your problem?" I shot back.

"You're lying to me."

"I am not lying to you."

"Delph just told me!" she screamed.

My spirits sank. *Holy Steeples, Delph, can you keep nothing in confidence?*

"Delph told you what?" I said miserably, though I well knew the answer.

"About your going back in time. About your seeing . . . me. And the others, and what they called me. And yet here you stand lying to me."

I felt my face redden. "Look, Petra —"

She suddenly shoved me so hard, I nearly toppled over the banister.

I caught myself and jerked forward.

"Petra, stop!"

She shoved me again. My back hit the banister, and I felt pain shoot up my body.

I pushed her away and she stood there, fists clenched, chest heaving, but at least she was no longer attacking me.

"Look," I said calmly. "I'm on your side. I saw what they did to you. It was wrong. I felt so sorry for you, Petra."

As soon as the words left my mouth, I knew they were a mistake.

The look on her face became as murderous as Necro's!

Her fist lashed out, catching me in the belly and doubling me over.

Then she punched me full in the face.

"You feel sorry for me? To Hel with you. To Hel with you, Vega. I don't need your sympathy. You're pathetic."

I slowly straightened and looked at her with the blood pouring down my face from my bloody nose. She was staring madly at me, angrier than I had ever seen her.

But then, so was I.

Before I could catch myself, I grabbed her by the throat, and with the strength that Destin gave me, I lifted her right off the floor. She kicked and punched at me, but I held on. She grabbed my hair. And still I did not break my grip.

I felt something pulling at me, grabbing, punching.

Someone screaming my name.

"Vega Jane!"

The next moment I felt a terrible pain in my head and a spurt of blood shot out from my forehead.

I felt myself growing weak and then faint.

"You're killing her!" someone shouted.

Battling the pain in my head, I looked first at Delph, who was next to me, and then at Petra, who was hanging limp in the air.

I instantly let go, and she fell to the floor.

Delph knelt beside her.

"She's not breathing," he cried out.

My mind seemed to return, and I grabbed the Adder Stone from my pocket and waved it over her.

Please, Petra, don't be dead. Don't be dead. Please.

With a gush of air, she sat straight up, almost hitting me in the head with hers.

As she sat there regaining her breath, Delph whirled on me. "What was that about?"

"Why the bloody Hel did you tell her what I saw?" I shouted at him.

He blinked. "What?"

"*That's* what this is about," I snapped. "You told her what I had seen. And she went nutters and attacked me."

Delph looked over at Petra, who was holding her throat and shooting daggers at me.

"Pet, I wouldn't have told you if I'd known this would happen."

"What did you think I would do?" she gurgled, still holding her throat.

"But Vega didn't know she was going to see you in the past."

"And I certainly didn't do anything to you," I said.

Petra jumped up and raced off before I could answer. Just like she had when those awful folks had called her names.

"I'm sorry, Vega Jane," said Delph. "I didn't mean for that to happen."

I let out a long breath. "It's not your fault." I looked around at the empty hall. "I'm just glad no one else saw this. I could hardly expect them to follow me into battle if they saw me trying to kill Petra." I looked down at my hands, which were still shaking.

"I've never lost my temper like that before, Delph. I can't believe that I almost . . . almost killed her." I looked up at him, tears now mixing with the blood. "I mean, I love Petra. I would do anything for her. I . . . I did the Oath of Oblivion with her."

I touched my forehead, where the blood had come from. Under my fingers, it almost felt like a wound was closing up. If

I had killed Petra, I think I would have died, because I would have violated the Oath.

"I need to go after her," I said.

"You think you should let her calm down first?" said Delph anxiously.

"No, because we might all be dead from old age before that happens. So I think I need to deal with this right now."

A minute later, I knocked on Petra's door. I could hear her inside, but she didn't reply to my knocks.

Finally, I used my wand to open the door.

She jumped up from the bed and glared at me while I closed the door behind me.

"Get out."

"No, we're going to talk this out."

"I have nothing to say to you."

"Why are you embarrassed?"

"Embarrassed? I'm not embarrassed."

"Who's lying now?" I said calmly.

This retort made her stiffen.

"Delph was right. I had no idea I would see you in the past."

"Yet you told him about it and not me! Not me!"

Now I flinched. "You're right. I should have told you. I was wrong not to."

"You're just saying that."

Now I really wasn't even listening to her. I looked down at my shaky hands. Petra seemed to notice this too. I looked up at her. "I can't believe I did that. I was so angry. But that was no excuse. You're . . . you're my friend."

My earnest words seemed to take the wind out of her sails.

"We seem to bring out the anger in each other," she said.

"That we do," I agreed, staring at her.

"Perhaps we both have a bit of Maladon blood in us."

She sat down on the bed and looked at me.

"I'm sorry I hurt you," she said.

I waved the Adder Stone over my face, and felt the pain vanish and my injuries heal.

"I can't lose you, Petra. I worry about that all the time. And to think that it was me who almost did you in." A tear slid down my face.

Tears slid down her face too.

And then we met in the middle of the room and hugged.

She was definitely the sister I'd never had.

I MET UP with Archie later, and his eyes still carried the horror of what we had seen at the castle.

"I told Mum a bit of it," he said. "The part about Jason being Endemen stunned her. She said it was quite a bit of dark sorcery there."

"But Jason broke free from it."

"Yeah, he did. And Mum actually wanted to talk to you about that if you can spare a moment."

"I was going to see her now. I've been to see my father, and he's much worse. Whatever plan she has to cure him needs to happen soon."

"Right, follow me."

We made our way to Astrea's room, where I once more found her surrounded by piles of books and reams of parchment. She looked up from the pages of one tome when we entered and waved us over.

"Archie told me about what you saw and did." She leaned back in her chair. "Archie also told me that Necro came into the room, but then left so that his minions could take you on. He only came back in when the tide turned against his men."

I hadn't focused on this before, but I nodded. "That's exactly right. Is it important?"

"It very well could be," she said earnestly.

"How so?" I asked curiously.

"I have the benefit of having known Necro intimately. I also fought against him centuries ago. I well know that he was at the forefront of his followers. You could say many bad things about him, but one could never call him a coward. Yet he left you, his ultimate nemesis, to others. I wonder why."

"Why do you think?"

"That's the key. I must *think* on it, Vega."

I plunged into why I had come to see her. "Astrea, every Wug from Wormwood is imprisoned behind glass, the same glass where they take out the magic from our kind. But these Wugs aren't magical and they're also already dead, so it just must be their spirits imprisoned in there. How can I free them?"

Her look was despondent. "Freeing them from such a prison is difficult, Vega, though not impossible."

"Have you done such?" I blurted out.

"Are you asking me if I have rescued our kind from these glass prisons that take their magic? No. I wasn't aware that Maladons even did that. They certainly didn't do it during our time, at least that I know of. But I have freed our kind from other kinds of prisons the Maladons devised."

"How did you do it?"

"An eye for an eye, Vega."

"Meaning what?"

"To free a prisoner, you replace him or her with another prisoner. That is the only way to do it."

"Then you imprisoned another to save someone?"

"Yes."

"Who did you imprison?"

194

She looked embarrassed. "I only did it twice. And I used two of our kind who were very nearly dead from battle. Oh, I asked them if I could, and they readily assented."

"So you left them to be tortured forever?"

"Hardly that, Vega. As soon as the prisoners were freed, I destroyed the prison."

"I tried to free the spirits of the Wugs. I tried to break into the glass. But I could not."

"Clearly not. If it's like the other Maladon prisons I've seen, it can only be done one way."

"How?"

"There is a seam that opens as the prisoners are being exchanged. You must strike with an *Impacto* spell right before that seam closes. That is a Maladon prison's only weak spot. That is actually what I meant when I said I destroyed the prison."

"A seam. Like the one around the dome to the Quag?"

She stared sadly at me. "Nearly identical, in fact. The Quag's only imperfection."

"And the spell to exchange the prisoners?"

She took out her wand and used it to make three slashes in the air. *"Periculo nomadus."*

She set her wand down. "But freeing spirits? I do not know how it can be done, for you cannot exchange a spirit for flesh and blood. At least I have never done so."

My spirits plummeted.

She glanced at her book and started. "Oh, but where is my head? I think I might have something to help your father."

I drew closer and looked down at her work. "What?" I said eagerly. "Because time grows short."

"There is an ancient concept called *twining.*"

I looked puzzled, because I was. "Twining? What does that mean?"

In response, she held up a piece of parchment on which were drawn a series of symbols.

"What happened to your father was very rare, an anomaly of staggering proportion. In order to reverse the effects of such an odd occurrence, we must fight fire with fire, as it were."

"You mean an anti-incantation of similar rarity."

"Precisely, Vega, you've hit the nail directly with the mallet. And that is where the field of twining comes into play. Look at this."

She laid the parchment down and pointed to the various symbols.

"Now, the sphere here represents the totality of a particular subject, all factors and their variations and derivations. Of course here we would put in what happened to your father. Then the effects of two precise spells inter*twining* before impacting him. Now we apply the theory of twining to that."

"But how do we do that?"

She took out her wand and pointed to another sphere she had drawn on the parchment. It had all sorts of odd and indecipherable symbols around it.

"This is the twining sphere. What it takes into account is all the factors of the intertwining of the two spells and their variations, and applies it in coming up with an anti-incantation that precisely mirrors the problem."

"You mean like a formula of some sort?"

"Like the Elixir of Life. It is an exact way to reach a precise goal. Now, I do have to tell you that with something like this, there is no such thing as complete precision. Even the sphere cannot anticipate every single outcome. Therein lies the danger associated with doing this. But it is the best plan I can come up with, having looked at every other I could think of."

I looked over the drawing and nodded. "You have done

well, Astrea. I could never have come up with such a plan. Will it be ready soon?"

"Within the week. Once the calculations are fully complete and a spell is decided upon."

"So, you'll do the anti-incantation," I said, expecting her to simply confirm my statement.

"No" was her surprising reply.

"Who, then?" I exclaimed, giving her a sharp glance.

"It will have to be done by your mother."

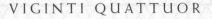

An Answer from Beyond

I HAD JUST ABOUT fallen asleep when I suddenly sat bolt upright, causing poor Harry Two, who was at the foot of the bed, to utter a low growl.

The reason for my sudden movement floated directly above me.

Uma, her eyes full of tears, was staring down at me.

"Uma, what is it?" I said a bit groggily.

"Now I know why Jason's spirit never came to me. Because he wasn't dead."

I sat up, and she floated down to sit beside me on the bed.

Harry Two returned to his sleep. I, on the other hand, was wide-awake.

"I guess that's right, Uma," I said, tugging hair out of my eyes.

"I should very much like to see Jason," she said, glancing sideways at me.

This request made my eyes widen.

"Uma, he's in Maladon Castle. At least he was the last time I saw him. I barely got out of there alive. And I've no idea what happened to him. But I told you that I might have a way of finding out. I just haven't been able to do it yet."

I felt guilty about this, because I had done nothing at all. Her next words drove this thought from my mind.

"I'm not asking you to go, Vega. I would never intentionally put you in danger."

"What, then?" I asked, confused.

"I can go alone."

"You?"

"They can't harm a spirit."

I thought back to my fellow Wugs behind the glass.

"I wouldn't be too sure about that. And if they did catch you and torture you, they could make you tell them things about us, about Empyrean."

She sat back, looking so forlorn that my heart went out to her. But my concerns about her going there were very real. And there was something else.

"Uma, there is no guarantee that Jason is still alive. He was battling his father when I last saw him. He might . . ."

"I know that, Vega. I know," she added quietly. "But when you love someone as I have —"

She gave a little sob and then vanished.

I sat back against my headboard and pondered all that she had said, particularly the last bit.

When you love someone as I have.

I rolled over and tried to go back to sleep, but it simply wouldn't come.

My thoughts turned to someone who I had loved as much as I had anyone.

My brother, John.

I had sent team after team to search for him. He wasn't in True or Greater True. There had been no sign of him in any of the surrounding villages.

So where could he be? There was nowhere else.

Once more this night, I sat bolt upright.

199

Vega, you git.

Of course there was somewhere else.

I leapt up, hastily dressed and ran out the door.

There was the bloody *Quag.*

I roused both Petra and Delph from their slumbers. Neither was happy about being awoken so abruptly, but when I told them what I had in mind, they forgot their lost sleep and seemed primed for an adventure.

We left Empyrean, and magically tethered together and rendered invisible, we lifted into the air.

The darkness was complete, the air still, the sky empty of clouds.

As we flew along, I said, "I can't believe I didn't think of it before."

"But the Quag," said Delph. "Why would he still be in there?"

"He didn't have the luxury of mentoring from Astrea for one reason," I replied. "She told us all about the circles and the dangers. John didn't have that. For all I know, he's still wandering around in there."

"If he left on the night the Maladons came to destroy Wormwood, that means it was long after we had gotten through the Quag," pointed out Delph in a worried tone.

"I know very well the dangers that lie in here," I said. "But I also know that once we got through the Quag, much of its magical force was expended."

Petra said, "But the beasts remain. It's not like the jabbits, garms, wendigos and lycans just up and died."

Delph said, "And, Vega Jane, the place is huge. Where will we start looking?"

"At the beginning, Delph."

"Wait a mo', do you mean . . . ?"

"Yes, I do."

And in keeping with my words, I pointed us toward the ground.

We landed a minute later and looked around into the darkness.

"What's here?" asked Petra.

"This is the spot where Delph and I really entered the Quag, after flying down a cliff with a herd of garms and freks after us."

Delph nodded and looked around. "Right, Vega Jane. This is where it all started. Feels like hundreds of years ago. But it looks the same. Doubt the Maladons bothered much with this." He looked up the cliff. "They just wanted to destroy Wormwood," he added darkly.

"Okay, but what's here that's so important?" asked Petra.

"The Kingdom of bloody Cataphile," answered Delph.

"Cata-whatsis?" said Petra.

"Bones," I said. "The Kingdom of Bones. The creatures who live here are called ekos. They have grass growing off them."

"That's weird," said Petra.

"It's how they evolved, for protection from other creatures, and it also allowed them to more efficiently hunt. They are a very nice group of beings," I added.

Delph said, "And there are creatures down here called gnomes. They got knives for hands. And grubbs, which can eat through rock."

"Blimey," said Petra. "And I thought where I lived in the Quag was strange."

"Like Vega said, they're nice. Even the grubbs. I actually felt sorry for them."

I was only half listening to this, since I knew it all anyway. "It was around here, Delph," I said, using my wand to illuminate the dark. The way into the ekos's home was in the ground. We had literally fallen into a trap, ending up down below ensnared in thick ropes.

Delph joined me and glanced at the long grass here.

"This looks familiar," he said. "Maybe a bit farther to the left."

"Let's take a shortcut," I said, pointing my wand at the ground.

"*Crystilado magnifica.*"

And there it was, maybe ten feet from us. The open hole and the wooden machinery, metal pulleys and rope netting that had rendered us captives.

"Looks all rotted," said Delph as we hurried to this spot.

I flicked my wand, and the ground cover was removed. We stared down at the revealed abyss.

"Steps over here," noted Petra, peering through the gloom.

We took them down, our wands lighting the way, while Delph hefted his short-handled ax, his weapon of choice lately.

"Luc?" I called out. He had been the leader of the ekos, and had been instrumental in our escaping.

"Cere!" cried out Delph. She was Luc's daughter. Delph had saved her son, Kori, from certain death when he had been attacked by some freks.

There was no answer from the darkness.

"Who are they?" asked Petra.

"Ekos," I said. "Luc was the leader, although a git named Thorne came here with his mortas and proclaimed himself king."

"He was from Wormwood," added Delph.

"Why would he leave Wormwood? For the same reasons you did?"

I shook my head. "He murdered his wife, who was Morrigone's mother. He fled into the Quag. Then he built all

202

sorts of weapons using slave labor here, with the plan of attacking Wormwood and becoming its ruler."

"Truly a git," said Petra. "Was he still in charge when you left here?"

Delph smiled. "He was actually running for his life from the ekos after we got in the way of his plan to attack Wormwood."

"Let's explore a bit farther," I said.

We crept down the stairs and reached the bottom. I could hear nothing. I well knew what a labyrinth of tunnels and rooms lay down here. But I was also aware that the ekos community was a large one with many sets of feet running hither and thither. And yet, there did not seem to be any life left here.

"You don't think the Maladons came here, do you?" Delph whispered into my ear.

"I don't know, Delph. I really don't."

I couldn't really get into the head of such a murderous race as the Maladons.

With my lit wand, I led us down a passage that I knew led to Thorne's bedchamber. As we walked along, the memories of my harrowing escape from that place came rushing back to me.

It was also here where I had learned of the power of invisibility my ring held.

We reached the end of the corridor and there was Thorne's thick wooden door. It had been knocked off its hinges when Delph had thrown the Elemental against it. It had not been rehung. It was lying on the floor. That told me a lot, principally that Thorne had not regained his kingdom.

We cautiously approached and looked inside.

"There's no one in there," I said, shining the light from my wand around the small space. "And the place is full of dust and cobwebs. No one has been in there for quite some time."

My skin started to tingle. I had a sense of dread creeping upon me for some reason. I mean, it was gloomy and dark and unsettling down here, but that wasn't it. I just didn't know what we might find around the next corner. After seeing the remains of Wormwood, I never wanted to see another sight like that for the rest of my life.

We retraced our steps and then I led us down another corridor where I knew Thorne's arsenal of guns and ammunition was kept. The glow from my wand soon revealed that this room was empty as well, with nary a gun in sight.

But there was something else stacked high.

Bones.

We just stood there staring.

The thing is, the bones still had clothes on. And they were small in stature.

"They're . . . they're . . ." mumbled Delph.

"They're ekos," I finished for him.

I don't know how I found the strength, but I stepped forward into that awful place and drew close to the piles.

It was with a heavy heart that I saw clothing that I recognized. Indeed, I would have known who I was looking at anyway because the skeleton was larger than the others, though not nearly so large as a normal person.

The bones were Luc's. The head ekos who had risked his life so that Delph, Harry Two and I could go free. And next to Luc's skeleton I also recognized the clothes and the bit of hair left behind.

It was Cere, Luc's daughter, and mother to little Kori, who Delph had saved from the herd of murderous freks.

Delph came to stand next to me and surveyed the piles of death, even as the tears started streaming down both our faces. Petra too joined us. And though she had not known these fine

204

creatures, she could see how we were affected, and tears slipped from her eyes as well.

"Bloody Hel," I said. I lowered my lit wand, unable to bear the sight any longer.

"Do you think Thorne did this?" asked Delph.

He had no doubt seen what I had as well. There was no skeleton that would equate to the size of Thorne, who was a full-grown male Wug.

"I don't see how, Delph."

"Then it was the Maladons," said Petra simply. "They did it. The murderous, evil monsters."

I had rarely heard her so angry, but then I recalled it was in the Quag that she had lost her family, in fact her entire village.

I held up my wand again and looked over the piles of bones for anything that might carry the clothing of my brother, but saw none. I didn't think John had died here. He may never have made it this far. For all I knew, a beast had gotten him before he even had made it to the cliff that led down here.

"We can learn no more here," I said, wiping my face dry. "We need to head on."

"To where?" asked Delph.

"Astrea's cottage."

THOUGH THE DAWN was now breaking, we nearly didn't find it, because there was no longer a dome of emerald green over the structure.

Delph spotted it as we made our third pass over the area where I knew the cottage had to be. We all three landed near the front porch and looked at the now-dilapidated building.

"Blimey," said Delph.

"Remember," I said, "Astrea and Archie have been gone from here a long time."

We passed through the front door and looked around. Memories came swirling back to me from our time here.

We, unfortunately, found no sign that John had ever been there. We went back outside, where it was now fully light. As we were preparing to leave, we heard a voice. A very weak voice.

"Hello, dearie, dearie."

I whirled around to see where the voice was coming from.

"There!" cried out Delph.

We rushed over to a large tree located near where the emerald dome had once been. Lying on top of one of the massive branches was Seamus the hob. When we had last been visited by him, he was dressed in black trousers, a white shirt, a vest laced with golden threads and a well-brushed top hat.

Now his clothes were rags, his face puffy and his limbs a tangled mass.

"Seamus!" I called out. I turned the ring around, and we all became visible. "What . . . what happened to you?"

He said weakly, "The . . . the Maladons, Vega."

I raised my wand and pointed it at him. A few moments later he was being gently lowered to the ground. We gathered around him. It broke my heart to see how battered and in pain he was.

"What did they do to you?"

"They killed most of my kind. I . . . I was lucky. I escaped and hid in the Quag. But then the pain became too much. I came back here, hoping to have Mistress Astrea help me, but she was gone. I've been getting better, but a few days ago I was attacked by a garm and didn't have the strength to fully fight it off. I came here and climbed this tree to be safe."

"But how did you know it was us?" I asked him. "We were invisible."

In answer, he tapped his nose. "Your scent, Vega. Having smelled it once, I will never forget it."

He coughed and turned pale and seemed to stop breathing.

I dug in my cloak pocket and pulled out the Adder Stone. I waved it over Seamus and thought the best thoughts I could.

His eyes opened, his bruised face returned to normal and his limbs straightened out some, but not quite all the way. Still, he seemed to be breathing normally at least and his features were no longer screwed up in pain. He sat up and rubbed at his healed face.

"Thank you, Vega," he said with tears in his eyes.

"Astrea and Archie left the Quag. They've joined up with us outside the Quag," I said. "We're fighting the Maladons."

He shivered at the mention of the name. "I'd rather face a million jabbits than one of them blokes."

"Seamus, we're looking for my brother. Have you any idea where he might be?" I described John to him.

Seamus sat on a rock and considered this.

"I have not seen your brother, Vega," said Seamus. "But others might have."

"The hyperbores," exclaimed Petra. "Whenever I had a problem, I would go to them. What they can't figure out can't be figured out."

The hyperbores were large feathery winged creatures who could talk and were quite wise and kind. Maybe wiser and more kind than my lot!

"Well, let's hope the Maladons didn't get to them too," I said.

Seamus stood on unsteady legs. "Thank you for all you've done, Vega. I wish you luck against the Maladons."

I looked at him, dumbstruck. "Seamus, I'm not leaving you here to fend for yourself. You're coming with us. To Empyrean. You'll be safe there and well fed."

His eyes once more bubbled with tears. "Bless you, Vega. Bless you all."

I tethered him to us so he would be invisible as well. There could be Maladons lurking about.

I didn't bother to fly to the hyperbores. I had flown over the Quag because I wanted to see elements of it. But now I could sense we were running out of time. Whatever the Maladons were planning, I could not discount that it would be soon coming to fruition. And that its effects could be devastating.

"Pass-pusay," I said clearly, as I tapped my leg with my wand.

The next instant, we were at the hyperbores' encampment in the trees.

And the instant after that, we heard the screams.

Beyond Words

MY WAND AND Petra's were out in a flash as we gazed around, ready for a fight. Though how anyone could see us, as we were invisible, was beyond me.

"Over there," hissed Petra.

I looked to where she was pointing with her wand.

A half dozen bowler-hatted Maladons had encircled two hyperbores. I recognized one; it was Ishmael, a hyperbore who had taken us to see Micha, the leader of the tribe.

The hyperbores were trying to use their enormously strong wings to attack the Maladons, who were smirking and laughing as they pointed their wands for the kill. I saw two hyperbores lying on the ground, probably already dead.

I looked at Petra and she glanced at me. A simple thought was communicated.

Attack.

Spells blasted from our wands.

Two Maladons were lifted off their feet, flung a hundred feet through the air and smashed into trees, where they fell down, crumpled and quite dead.

The remaining Maladons spun around, looking frantically to see where our attack came from.

Petra and I fired off again, and two more Maladons were blasted into the ether.

I raised my hand to Petra, signaling that I wanted to try something. She instantly lowered her wand as I took aim, and with one flick of my wand I delivered a death spell to one of the Maladons. He fell to the dirt.

With another flick I sent out a lasso, which spun around the remaining Maladon's wand, and I pulled it neatly out of his grasp. I smashed it with an *Impacto* incantation.

And then I turned the ring around, revealing us to all.

I wasted not a moment but strode toward the surviving Maladon, my wand pointed at his heart. If the accursed creature had one, that is.

They were all Bowler Hats. I had seen him before, with Endemen, or Jason, I knew now.

He apparently recognized me too, because he started to shake with fear.

"On your knees, Maladon. Now."

He immediately fell to the dirt.

I looked over at Ishmael and the other hyperbore.

"It's been a long time, Ishmael."

He lowered his wings and nodded solemnly. "Vega Jane from before."

"Yes. Long before. I've changed a bit," I added.

He eyed my tall, strong physique and my wand and nodded once more.

"Which I am personally glad to see; otherwise, I would be no more."

I looked at the dead hyperbores and then stared directly at the Maladon.

"Your name?" I barked.

"Dragoon."

"You killed these hyperbores? Why?"

"We were ordered to do so."

210

"By whom?"

He put his hands together in a pleading manner. "You know by whom," he sobbed.

"Why? What does Necro care about hyperbores? They bother no one."

"It is his way," said Dragoon. "If it cannot be controlled, it must be killed."

And I actually believed him.

"And where is Endemen?"

On this he would say nothing, which I had expected.

With a flick of my wand and the proper incantation, it was quite different.

Dragoon, his eyes wobbly in their sockets and his manner unnaturally stiff, said, "Endemen is at the castle."

"He's alive, then?"

"Yes. Barely."

"His real name is Jason. He's Necro's son. Did you know that?"

Dragoon shook his head.

"Is my brother, John, at the castle?"

Part of me wanted the answer to be no. Perhaps all of me did.

Stunningly, Dragoon granted this wish.

"No."

"But there is something going on at the castle," I said. "What is it?"

The Maladon instantly clutched his chest and sank to the ground, dead.

"What happened to him?" said Delph as we looked down at the fallen Maladon.

"Necro has cursed his own men. If they try to tell us something about what is going on, they die."

"Bloody Hel," exclaimed Delph.

Petra said, "At least there are six fewer Maladons alive, and six Bowler Hats at that."

I nodded and then looked at Ishmael. "What has happened here? Do your kind still live here?"

Ishmael shook his head. "No. We came back here for some things we had left behind. That was when we were attacked."

"So you moved?"

"We had to. The Maladons attacked us when they came through the Quag. They killed many of us, as they did many others who call this place home."

"Micha?" I said. "He's still alive, though, right?"

Sadly, Ishmael shook his head. "Our great leader fought to the end, and he killed many Maladons, but unfortunately Micha died in battle."

"I'm so sorry, Ishmael. Micha was so good."

The large hyperbore nodded. "Indeed, he was. As were Solomon and Ibrahim, who lie dead over there. We must give them a proper burial."

"We can do that," I said.

Petra added, "It would be our honor."

Petra and I used our wands to dig twin graves and we gently placed the dead hyperbores' remains in them and then covered them with the dirt.

Ishamel said a few words over them and then the two hyperbores broke into a lovely song of love, warmth and friendship.

I looked over at Petra and Delph and saw their heads bowed and tears sliding down their cheeks. It was the same with me.

When the ceremony was over, Ishmael said, "The ones of us who survived fled. We have been in hiding ever since. As time has gone by, we have ventured out bit by bit." He motioned to the hyperbore standing next to him. "Dimitri and I came here to get some supplies that were left behind and to see if the Maladons had abandoned this place. At first, it looked safe, and then we were surrounded. We would have all assuredly perished if you had not shown up, Vega."

"To where did you flee?"

"I will show you." He added a surprising postscript. "And it was not only hyperbores who sought refuge there."

WE FOLLOWED ALONG as Ishmael and Dimitri soared through the clear skies.

"Where do you think we're going?" asked Petra.

"Well, we're heading back toward the First Circle," said Delph, who had always been stellar with sense of direction. "In fact, there's the maze down there, Vega Jane."

I looked down. The First Circle maze was a death trap. Enormous walls of impenetrable material rose to the sky. The maze zigged and zagged in unfathomable and always-changing ways. And one of the most sickening elements to it was that part of the walls was made of bones. Bones of the dead who were trapped in there, never to see freedom again. This is where Delph, Harry Two and I had nearly died. And Delph still carried a burned arm courtesy of a foul wendigo that had sought our destruction. It was an evil, vile creation, and it also made me repulsed to think that it was our kind that had brought it to life. In order to protect a few, they had built a trap that had ended up killing far more creatures, and most if not all of them innocent.

I saw Ishmael up ahead give a most searching look in all directions. Then he and Dimitri suddenly went into a dive.

I followed, with the others tethered to me.

We were heading right for the maze. In fact, I thought we were going to crash directly into the ground, but just before that happened, a hole opened up, and we followed Ishmael and Dimitri into the space revealed.

We landed next to the hyperbores.

They had led us into a vast cavern that seemed as big as the maze above it. It must have been more than two hundred feet underground.

As I looked around, I saw lights popping up from out of the darkness all around. They slowly started to make their way toward us.

Suddenly, there was a happy squeal and we heard someone running.

Out of the darkness appeared an ekos with a light in hand. He ran up to Delph and hugged him.

Delph looked down at the ekos, who looked vaguely familiar to me. He was so small he could only reach Delph's knees with his hug.

"It's me, Delph, Kori."

This was little Kori, Cere's son and Luc's grandson? He had grown some, and his features looked haggard.

"Kori?" said Delph, bending down and hugging him back.

I touched Kori on the shoulder. "We went to your land. We . . . we saw what happened."

Kori's large eyes teared up. "Luc and my mother and the others fought with all their might. But the Maladons were too strong."

"What happened to Thorne?" I asked.

"We imprisoned him. He went mad and died. It was probably fortunate for him that he did. Had he lived when the Maladons came, they would have done far worse." Kori looked

214

behind him. "But as you can see, the Maladons did not kill all of us."

As I looked around at the other approaching lights, I could see other ekos emerging, then hyperbores, then, astonishingly enough, a few folks who looked like me.

Petra gasped. "Chauncey?"

I gaped at the tall young man who approached carrying a lantern. He was dressed in tattered trousers, a filthy white shirt that did little to hide his muscular physique and long, dark hair that touched his wide shoulders.

"Pet?" he said, nearing her.

"Chaunce, I . . . I thought you were . . ."

"Thought the same about you, Pet."

Both of their eyes filled with tears, and they embraced for quite a long time while I stood by silently, feeling my own eyes grow watery.

"And Lack?"

She took his hand, her eyes filling with fresh tears, and shook her head.

"He's dead, Chaunce. I . . ."

I stepped in here.

"Hi, I'm Vega. My friend Delph and I found Petra and Lackland wandering the Quag. We teamed up and fought our way across it and then escaped. Right before we were free of the Quag, Lackland, who was a warrior of the very first order, sacrificed his life so that Petra and I could live. He was very brave and a real hero."

Chauncey took a step back as he processed all that I had told him. He ran a hand through his hair and touched his chest and then his lips, raising his hand upward.

"Rest in peace, Lack."

"Were you good friends?" I asked.

He looked at me. "He was my brother."

Now I took a step back. "Your brother?" I shot a glance at Petra, who nodded.

"Lackland and Chauncey Cyphers." She smiled tenderly. "The troublemakers, they used to call them. But whenever we needed to fight, they were right at the front."

Chauncey nodded. "Lack never backed down from a fight and that's the truth."

"And neither did you, Chaunce," said Petra, squeezing his arm.

I counted about twenty ekos, a similar number of powerfully built hyperbores, several blokes who looked like Chauncey but weren't with him and that Petra didn't know. There were also a couple of women, and Seamus called out to a half dozen Hobs who had appeared, dressed similar to him, and who held small balls of blue light in their hands, just as Seamus had when I first met him years ago.

Seamus exclaimed, "Fellows, I believed you all to have perished!"

The hob closest to Seamus, who looked older and grayer, nodded solemnly. "Many was the time we too thought we were done for, Seamus."

And then from the darkness appeared creatures, both large and small. Some I recognized, some I didn't. My eyes filled when I saw the birdlike creatures of light, called cucos. They swirled around, illuminating the darkness and lifting my spirits.

I heard the clatter of hooves. A few moments later, there it was.

A big, beautiful unicorn with a mane of gold and a horn of silver. As I looked closer at the glorious beast, I saw that it was the very same unicorn I had helped after it was injured. It had relinquished its horn to me, which I later used to save Lackland's life after he was bitten by a jabbit. I was glad to see the unicorn had grown another horn to replace the one it had given me.

The beast came up and nuzzled my arm with its snout. I gently patted its neck. I surveyed all these people and creatures and then looked at Ishmael.

"How did all of you come to be here?" I asked. "What is this place?"

"Did I not tell you, Vega?" said Ishmael. "We were led here."

"Led here? By whom?"

I heard the footsteps approaching, slow and measured.

When he appeared from the darkness, I felt my senses nearly leave me. As it was, Delph had to grab me by the arm or else I would have tumbled down.

"By me, Vega," said my brother, John.

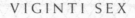

Grounds for Resistance

H E HAD GROWN tall and lean; his hair was long and dark, his eyes pinpoints of intensity.

My brother, John, came to stand before me. Now I had to look up to him for he was at least three inches taller than me.

I could not take my eyes off him, but in my peripheral vision I did note that all the others took a respectful step back from him and slightly bowed their heads.

"John, is it . . . is it really you?"

"Of course it is, Vega," he said firmly.

His tone seemed to jolt me out of my light-headedness.

I now appraised him with a more judicial eye.

Please don't let my worst fears be realized.

He wore a long cloak, and as my gaze traveled down his right arm, I saw what I thought I would see.

A slender, whiplike wand was held in his hand.

I stared back up at him and held out my arms, the tears rising to my eyes, a knot in both my belly and my throat.

"I never thought I'd see you again," I said.

I stepped forward and hugged him.

He did not hug me back.

When I stepped back awkwardly, he said, "It's good to see you too. I thought you were lost in the Quag."

"Morrigone's spirit told me that you had left Wormwood before the Maladons came. Or at least she thought you had."

"They've destroyed Wormwood," he said sharply. "All are dead."

"I know. I've been back there."

Delph put out his hand and said, " 'Tis good to see you again, John. You've certainly grown."

John looked at the hand but did not shake it.

"If I had not grown, I would be dead, Delph. But it is good to see you too."

Delph let his hand drop and stared uncomfortably at the ground.

"This is our friend Petra."

John glanced at her, seeming to evaluate Petra in barely a second. He looked over at Chauncey. "One of your mates, then, Chauncey?"

"Yes, Master John," said Chauncey quickly. "And a right good one."

Master John? I thought.

"How did you come to be here, *John?*" I asked. "And how did you manage to bring everyone here?"

"It is a long and complicated story, Vega," said John. "But to parse it to a relatively few words, I left Wormwood shortly before the Maladons came. It was pure luck that I was not there for the attack. I managed to make my way down the cliff to the valley below."

"How?" I exclaimed.

In answer, he lifted his wand to the ceiling and gave it a flick, and his feet left the ground and he floated into the air.

I gaped up at him.

"How did you learn to do that? And where did you get your wand?"

He floated back down to the ground.

"Incantations are born of necessity." He lifted his wand. "This came from our grandfather."

I looked at him, stunned. "Virgil left you a wand?"

"In a book he gave me when I was a child. It was hidden in the spine. The book was meant for me to read when I was older. I think he realized I would read all my books until they fell apart. And when it did, there was the wand."

"Why did you never tell me?" I said.

"I found it after you left Wormwood," he replied. He looked at my wand. "Did Grandfather leave you that?"

I felt my face burn a bit. Virgil had left me a ring but not a wand.

"No, I got mine another way. From an ancestor of ours." I paused. "When did you first learn you were magical?"

"When I lived with Morrigone."

"Did she tell you that you were?"

"Not in so many words. But it readily became apparent I could do extraordinary things. And when I found my wand, I could do *more* extraordinary things."

There was something off about his tone, but I had to admit, I was so happy to see my brother that I could not dwell on any misgivings right then.

"I have been looking for you for a long time, John."

"You left me in Wormwood."

I could not believe he was throwing that in my face.

"I wanted to take you."

"I didn't know that."

"The night I came to visit you. Your birthday. My birthday. I asked you to come and live with me."

"But you didn't tell me that you were leaving Wormwood."

"Would that have made a difference?"

"Perhaps, Vega, perhaps."

"Only I couldn't tell you, because I was afraid you would tell Morrigone. She tried to stop me as it was."

"So you didn't trust me, then?"

"You had changed, John. Morrigone had changed you."

"Morrigone allowed me to be as I was meant to be."

"No, she made you cruel and unforgiving."

As soon as I saw his face flush, I wished I hadn't said that. I thought I even saw his wand flick threateningly.

"John, you know what you were and you know what you became. Can you honestly claim you didn't change?"

He cast his gaze downward. When he looked up, his expression was calmer, more reasonable.

"I cannot say that your words are untrue, Vega."

Well, I thought that was something at least.

"I wanted very much to take you with us," I said. "I have missed you every day."

He nodded and said, "What have you been doing since you left Wormwood?"

"I have been trying to survive. And now I'm leading the fight against the Maladons."

"I know little of them."

"You know what they did to Wormwood." I pointed to the others. "And you know what they did to their families and their homes. So, really the only things you need to know are that the Maladons are incredibly evil and powerful and that they kill all who oppose them."

"Then perhaps we should not oppose them."

It was as though he had punched me in the face.

"You cannot mean that, John. They killed Virgil. And they nearly killed our father."

Now John looked like I had punched him in the face. He

221

took a step back, and something flashed in his features that reminded me of the little boy shuffling along beside me as I walked with him hand in hand through Wormwood.

"Virgil, dead? And our parents?"

"Dad is grievously injured. He is but a shell of his former self."

"But still alive?"

"Yes. And we are working on a counterspell to bring him back."

"And Mother?"

"She's fine."

"Can you take me to them?"

I looked around. "I think I need to take all of you."

"How is that possible?" John asked.

"There is only one way," I replied.

A Stranger in Our Midst

I USED A VARIATION of the same series of spells that I had employed to provide wands to all the formerly enslaved in Greater True and then transport them to Empyrean. I sent a wand wire ahead so that the others would be expecting us.

As I began to incant, I saw John looking at me curiously. When I reached the peak power of the spell, a huge dome of blue light descended upon all those who had fled there. I connected this dome to my golden tether, which I had reattached to Delph, Petra and Seamus. Finally, I uttered, *"Pass-pusay,"* and tapped my wand against my leg.

The next moment we were all standing in the front lawn of Empyrean.

"Quickly now," I said. "Inside."

The door opened and everyone, people and creatures and those, like the hobs, that were in between, were herded inside.

Inside, Pillsbury and some of the others were there to greet us.

I hurriedly explained what had taken place.

But what I really wanted to do was obvious.

"Come with me, John."

I told Delph to take over down here. "You can find rooms for the people inside, and the creatures, the unicorn and cucos and the like can be given free rein outside."

After that, I literally pulled John up the staircase.

"Where are we going?" he said, resisting a bit.

"You'll see," I replied.

I threw open the door to the room and pulled John in behind me.

Our mother looked up from the book she was reading, while our father lay swaddled on the bed.

The book fell from her hands as she stood, rushed across the room and embraced her only son.

"John, John," she said, weeping.

I stepped aside and took it all in.

John patted her on the back, and I could see his eyes grow watery and his features soften. With this sight, my spirits once more took a little leap.

She stepped back to look at him.

"My, you've grown so tall. Just like your father."

John looked over at the bed, and his features turned to dismay.

"That . . . that is Father?"

She nodded, the happiness at seeing her son after such a long time receded.

"Vega told me he has been injured but that a cure is being worked upon."

"That is so, John. And we all pray that it will work."

John looked at me. "Who is performing this? You?"

I shook my head. "Astrea Prine. The former Keeper of the Quag. Astrea is a very powerful sorceress. She is concocting the incantation, but she says that Mum has to actually perform it."

"This Astrea Prine did not stop the Maladons from destroying the Quag and Wormwood," John pointed out.

I could not argue with that, and I didn't. "She is still the best chance we have to bring Dad back."

John drew close to the bed and looked down. "What happened to him, precisely?"

"A confluence of two spells that struck each other before impacting him. That was why the result was so unforeseen."

To my surprise John nodded. "I have read of this."

"You have? Where?"

"In books provided to me by Morrigone."

"Her spirit is here, as I told you. She will be happy to see you, I expect."

John showed absolutely no interest.

"I would like to meet with this Astrea Prine."

"If you wish," I said. "We can go there now."

"I *do* wish it, Vega," he said, his gaze lifting to mine.

"You have not even told me how you found him, Vega," said our mother.

I explained in a very few words. "We were lucky," I said. "He more found me than I found him."

"But you kept your promise. You brought him back to us."

All this time John was staring down at our father, with more curiosity than pity or concern.

"Let us go see Astrea Prine," said John.

"Follow me," I said. My high hopes for who my brother would actually turn out to be started to fade once more. But I told myself I would not give up on him. Hel, I had just found him!

I led him down the hallway to Astrea's room and knocked on the door.

"Enter," came the imperious voice.

Astrea had set up an enormous table in the center of her room. On this table were stacks of books and parchment, ink sticks and various instruments of great delicacy. I also glimpsed the pewter cups that comprised her Seer-See.

When Astrea looked up and saw John, her jaw dropped. She left her desk and approached us.

"John Jane, then."

It wasn't a question.

"You know me?" he said.

"I know *of* you, yes."

"How?" I asked her. "Through Morrigone?"

"Not exclusively, no."

I quickly glanced at the cups. "You were watching him through the Seer-See."

She continued looking at John, her gaze seemingly taking in all facets of him.

"A Seer-See? What is that?" asked John, looking annoyed.

"A magical means to see faraway places. With it, I saw you in Wormwood. I watched you escape Wormwood. I saw you levitate down the cliff. And I observed you venture fully into the Quag."

"What else did you see?" asked John, in a tone that made me sharply glance at him.

Astrea came over to him and looked up at my tall brother.

"It is no sin to practice one's sorcery skills." She paused. "It is also no sin *not* to know certain parameters as a young sorcerer."

"Certain parameters?" I asked.

Astrea kept her gaze on my brother. "Most of us have gone through similar 'learning' experiences."

"What are you talking about?" I demanded.

Now Astrea looked at me. "Your brother was stretching his magical muscle, as it were."

"In the Quag, you mean?"

"Not just in the Quag," said Astrea.

I looked at John. "What is she talking about?"

John would not answer me.

Astrea said, "There was a reason why John left Wormwood."

"John, I thought you left Wormwood to discover what was outside it. And to find me and our parents."

"It's difficult to explain," said John, not meeting my eye.

I looked to Astrea for an "explanation."

Astrea said, "Let me just say that John exerted control over certain creatures that did not want his intervention, with the result that they did things that otherwise they never would have done."

"And what were these creatures?" I asked.

"I will not say, Vega," she replied firmly. "For it will do no good. To you, John or anyone else. I think John has learned his lesson — have you not, John?"

"I have," he said, though I did not note much sincerity in his voice.

"So there, now, Vega," said Astrea, looking as though the matter was settled. I could not believe she was giving in that easily. She had to see that John was just appeasing her.

She continued. "Now, you are undoubtedly here to talk about my researches into your father's condition and hopefully a cure."

"We are," said John before I could answer her.

"Well, I am happy to say that I have made progress. In fact, I believe that by tomorrow, we will be ready to give it a try."

"Tomorrow?" I said, astonished.

"I am fine-tuning a few things. But, yes, tomorrow seems right to me."

I looked at my brother. "Now, John, let's get something to eat. You look rather thin. And we can *talk* some more."

He didn't seem remotely pleased by this prospect.

But I didn't care.

After all, I *was* his big sister. And that status gave me certain inalienable rights with regard to my little brother!

VIGINTI OCTO

The Unmark

JOHN DIPPED HIS spoon into the bowl and scooped out some of the soup. We were sitting in the small dining room off the kitchen. It was just the two of us.

I had been serious about how lean he was. My brother obviously had not been eating well since leaving Wormwood.

Perhaps sensing this, Mrs. Jolly brought him some more bread and a rasher of bacon. I thanked her, and after she departed, I settled my gaze upon John as I sipped my tea.

"You rounded up that lot in the Quag and led them to a safe place under the maze in the First Circle?"

John swallowed his spoonful of soup and took a drink of the steaming tea before answering.

"As I said," he replied soberly.

"You also said that you were their leader. Where were you going to lead them?"

He shrugged. "I hadn't thought about it, really."

"And I really don't believe your answer."

He gave me a sharp glance but said nothing.

"So why don't you tell me the truth?"

"What business is it of yours?"

"You used to tell me everything."

"We're not children anymore, Vega. We haven't seen each other in years. We're no longer close."

"We *were* close. Which means we can be again."

He shook his head. "I've been on my own for a while now. I keep my own counsel."

"You *kept* your own counsel. Now we're in this together."

He shook his head again. "I don't know if I can be that way, with *anyone*."

"You can try, John. I need you to really try."

"Why? I don't understand the urgency."

I leaned in closer to him and started speaking quietly but firmly. I needed my words to sink deeply into that very large brain of his. "Because you need to understand quite clearly that we're in the fight of our lives. And the odds are not with us. We're heavily outnumbered by the Maladons. That's why we've stopped engaging them for now. We're running out of people to fight them."

"And you believe that we need to keep fighting them?"

"Unless you want to die, or be enslaved by them for the rest of your life."

John put down his spoon and wiped his mouth with his hand.

My heart fluttered when I saw the back of his hand.

There was no mark of the three hooks there.

He caught me staring and said, "What is it?"

"Nothing, John," I managed to croak out. "So, are you with me in fighting the Maladons?"

"Well, since I don't want to die or be enslaved, I guess that I am."

This was hardly an overwhelming endorsement, but I let it pass because a million horrible thoughts were flashing through my mind about his hand.

"What was Astrea talking about when she said you were stretching your magical abilities beyond certain parameters?"

"I don't know. You'll have to ask her."

I sat back. "When you were in charge of building the Wall in Wormwood, you pushed the Wugs hard. Duf Delphia lost his legs because of you, and other Wugs died."

"Why do you bring that up?" he said, scowling.

"Because you were 'pushing parameters' then, just not magically. So did you use your magic to do something similar? Push folks and creatures beyond what they wanted to do?"

"We are magical, Vega. That gives us certain rights."

"No, that gives us immense *responsibilities*, like never using our power to hurt innocent people or creatures. And that includes making them do your bidding."

"We can agree to disagree on such matters."

"No, John, we really can't. You have to choose. Do you want to be like our kind?" I glanced at his unmarked hand. "Or do you want to be like the Maladons? Because that is exactly what they do to all others." I stood. "Let me know when you've made your decision."

I left John and returned to my room. I sat on my bed stroking Harry Two's fur to calm myself. My brother did not have the mark. What exactly did that mean?

That he was a Maladon? Was that why he was so . . . unfeeling?

I blinked. But that could hardly be the case. He could *see* Empyrean. No Maladon could do that.

Yet why was there no mark on his hand?

I looked down at Harry Two and decided to try something.

I went to the door and called to him, he obediently followed me out.

I found John in the library, where he was staring up in wonder at all the books. This made me think back to our time in Morrigone's home, where John had been equally enthralled by all her tomes.

And this memory made me feel a little guilty about what I was about to do.

"Harry Two," I said. "It's John. Go and see him."

John turned at the sound of my words.

"Your canine," he said. "I remember him."

"My *dog*," I replied. "That's what they call them here."

I watched Harry Two closely, as he cautiously approached John. His nostrils were moving as rapidly as a pair of bellows in use. He seemed to be sucking in all of John's scent.

John said, "Hello, Harry Two. Do you remember me?"

And then my dog did something he had never done before. He sat on his rump and started to whine.

I looked up at John as he watched Harry Two.

"What's wrong with him?" he asked. "Is he sick?"

"I don't know. He's never done that before. Harry Two, are you okay?"

He looked up at me with a most pitiful expression.

It was also one I had never seen before on my dog's face, and it concerned me greatly, particularly in the context of my brother.

Harry Two was confused!

I said good-bye to my brother and took Harry Two back to my room. I sat with him on my bed and looked deeply into those beautiful mismatched eyes.

"Harry Two, with all of the wonderful things that you can do, I so dearly wish you could talk."

I sighed and sat back, more crushed than I had been a few minutes ago.

A knock came on my door. It was Delph.

Before he could say anything, I pulled him into the room

and told him everything that Astrea had said, and John had said, and also how Harry Two had reacted to John. And then I finished by saying that John didn't have the mark on his hand.

Delph surprised me by saying, "I already saw that, Vega Jane."

"Why didn't you say anything, then?"

"I didn't know what to say," he replied.

He might as well have added, *After all, he is your brother.*

I sat on my bed and glanced at Harry Two.

"And Harry Two was really confused about John," I said. "He was never that way before. Not even with Petra. What does it all mean, Delph?"

"It means that you just found your brother, after looking for him for a long time, Vega. And you have your mum and your dad back too. It's a lot to take in. You just have to give yourself a chance to, well, breathe."

As though putting action to his words, I involuntarily drew in a long breath and then let it go. I immediately relaxed, and my thoughts cleared a bit.

"Right," I said firmly. "Okay. Astrea is going to try and restore my father tomorrow."

"You said it could be dangerous."

"Well, apparently it is, according to her."

"How was your mum with John?"

"Thrilled to see him. Perhaps —" I stopped and shook my head.

"What?"

"Never mind."

"Maybe more thrilled than she was to see you?" Delph said.

I turned to look at him. I had forgotten how astute Delph was. How he often saw things that others didn't and then got right to the heart of the matter.

"Yes," I admitted.

"But see, your mum knows how strong you were, Vega Jane. How you always stood up for yourself. How you always protected your brother. She remembered him as he was. Small, weak and needing a guiding hand. Of course she would be more worried about him."

"I suppose you're right."

"And you're worried about him too," said Delph.

"Yes. No mark. Mysterious things he's done in the past. This is my brother, Delph. And I feel like I no longer know him."

"Well, you've been separated a long time. You'll just have to get to know him again."

"And what if I don't like what I find?"

"Then you'll have to deal with it. But don't prejudge him, Vega Jane. Give him a chance. John is complicated, that's easy enough to see. It will take some time."

After Delph left, I went to the window and looked out on the rear grounds.

I spotted John as he walked into my line of sight.

I continued to watch as Miranda Weeks walked up to him and started chatting. She was a bit younger than John, but confident and an excellent sorceress who fought bravely and well.

I saw John smile at something she said, and he used his wand to cast a spell. A fluffy white rabbit appeared on the ground and started to do tricks for them.

Miranda clapped her hands together and danced around with the rabbit while John watched.

The rabbit eventually faded away and Miranda and John walked off, chatting.

I turned away from the window, shaking my head.

My brother was indeed "complicated."

That evening I confronted him after dinner.

"It seems that Miranda Weeks and you get on."

"What do you mean?" he said defensively.

"Just that I saw you earlier in the garden. You were making her laugh with some magic you did."

"She's nice," replied my brother, not meeting my eye. "She is very young."

"She's not that much younger than you. But she is old beyond her years. And tough beyond them as well. She has turned into a formidable, battle-tested sorceress. Has she spoken to you of this?"

"A bit, yes."

"Her mother was murdered by the Maladons."

He shot me a look. "Really? How?"

I explained the Maladons' hideous process to take one's magic.

"It can go awry, and the person can die," I added.

He looked shaken by this. "They can take your magic? I did not know that was possible."

"Apparently, anything is possible. At least with those blokes. Delph found a book here that has the necessary incantations. Bloody awful stuff."

I watched my brother closely for his reaction to this.

Then my gaze dipped to his hand, where there should be a mark on him, but wasn't.

"Delph found a book?" he said.

I frowned. This was not the reaction I wanted.

"Yes. But you agree that it is bloody awful, don't you? You see, that's what the Maladons are, John, bloody awful."

He looked at me strangely but said nothing in return.

"Good night, Vega."

He turned and walked off, leaving me feeling worse than I had been, which was truly saying something.

Wand into the Water

I WOKE THE NEXT morning feeling as though I had not slept at all. Time was slipping away from us. And though I had successfully made a trip to Maladon Castle and learned some new information, and I had found my brother and more allies in the fight against the Maladons, I had made no real progress in winning the war with the foul creatures.

I dressed and went downstairs.

"It is time, Vega."

I turned to see Astrea standing at the top of the stairs.

"It is time to try and cure your father."

I raced back up.

A few minutes later, I felt my stomach knot and my throat grow dry as I watched her.

Astrea was preparing to cure my father.

Or else, she would kill him.

I was in my parents' room. Also there were my mother, John, Delph and Archie. Though I had a suspicion that right outside the door were many more people waiting to see if the morning's work was a success or a disaster.

Astrea had placed a large metal tub in the middle of the floor. In that tub now swirled waters of brilliant colors. They were moving all on their own, as no one was stirring them.

My father lay swaddled in a blanket on the bed. My

mother took turns staring at her husband, then at Astrea and finally at the tub, before starting all over again.

Her expression ran the spectrum from hope to abject terror.

I suppose my features bore the same looks.

Astrea looked up from a book she was consulting. "Nearly ready," she said in a casual tone.

I didn't see how she could be quite so cavalier about it all, but then again, it wasn't *her* father at risk.

"What are you going to do with the tub of water?" I asked as Delph peered into its depths.

"Why, *obviously* place your father in it."

"Of course," I said, thinking that it was not bleeding obvious at all.

"And then what?" I asked.

"Hmmm," she said. Not at me, but at the page she was reading.

My level of confidence in what she would be attempting dropped precipitously.

"Astrea, if you're not ready yet, there's no need to hurry into this," I said, glancing at my mother, who nodded in agreement at my statement.

She looked up from the page. "Vega, we are quickly running out of time. Look at your father."

I rushed over to the bed and looked down at him.

He was still small, and pale and disfigured.

But there was something changed about him.

He was barely breathing.

And his paleness was taking on another hue.

Blue.

"He's dying?"

"He's been dying ever since the twined curse struck him," she answered matter-of-factly.

"You . . . you didn't make that clear," I said, my voice cracking embarrassingly.

"I thought I did, but if not, it is quite apparent on its face, isn't it?"

I could only agree with her assessment. As I looked up into my mother's eyes, I expected to see terror. Instead, I saw calm and, perhaps, resignation.

I had forgotten that my mother had been dealing with this eventuality far longer than I had.

She said, "We can only pray to holy Steeples, Vega. It's all we can do."

She gripped my hand and that of my brother's as Astrea closed her book and came toward us. "All right, Helen, it is ready. Take your wand."

I said, "But why does she have to do it? Why can't you, or me?"

"Because your mother was with your father when it happened. She cast a shield spell that partially deflected the other two spells. Thus, part of her spell also resides in your father. We need her, using her wand, to precipitate the cure. That is simply how it has to be."

Well, that made sense, I thought. "You never really explained that," I said.

"Would the reason have mattered?" Astrea replied.

I started to say something before I realized that she was basically correct.

She nodded at Archie. "Prepare him, Archie dear."

We watched as Archie picked my father up from the bed and slipped off the blanket around him.

I had to look away from my father's naked, shriveled body.

Archie carried him over to the tub of water and held my father over it.

Astrea stepped forward.

"We can begin." She nodded at Archie. I suppose she had previously explained to Archie what to do, because Archie lowered my father into the tub.

My mother, John and I all took a step forward so that we could peer into the waters.

My father's head was visible above the level of the water. He appeared to be shivering, his small arms wrapped around his torso.

"He won't drown, will he?" I asked.

Astrea shook her head. "*That* is not the risky part," she said ominously.

She stepped forward and pointed her wand not at the water but at my mother.

"Helen, point your wand at your husband."

My mother lifted her wand, though her hand shook a bit as she pointed it.

"Calm yourself, Helen. All will be well."

"But I don't know the incantation," said my mother, her eyes suddenly wild with fear.

"Have no doubt, you will know it presently. Just let your nerves calm and your mind open."

My mother drew a long breath, let it go and focused on her wand and the water.

Astrea kept her wand pointed at my mother, and I could see her lips move, but no words or sounds came out.

Then I turned to my mother because she had started to speak.

Her eyes were closed, her face was tilted to the ceiling and she was incanting, but using words I had never heard before.

The water started to bubble and swirl faster and faster.

I gasped as my poor father was quickly sucked under the surface.

"No!" I cried out.

"Do not interfere," said Archie, grabbing my arm. "My mother knows what she's doing."

I shot a glance at Astrea, who was still moving her lips.

I looked back at my mother. Her face was still pointed at the ceiling. Her wand was now making long sweeping movements.

I looked down at the tub of water. It was turning black.

I glanced at John.

He simply looked curious, as though it wasn't our father in there fighting for his life.

I shook this off and turned back to look at the water, which was now green.

I glanced at Astrea. She was staring at the water and . . . frowning.

I did not take this as a good sign.

"What is it?" I hissed. "Is it not working?"

"I'm . . . I'm not sure. He should have reappeared by now."

This was enough for me. "Dad!" I cried out. I pulled my wand and said, "*Rejoinda*, Hector Jane."

My father shot out of the water, gasping for air, and flew into my arms. He had not changed one iota. No, I was wrong about that. He looked smaller and weaker. And his skin now looked burned.

I hurriedly carried him to the bed, dried him off and covered him with a blanket. I turned to Astrea, anger and mortification clear on my features.

My mother had opened her eyes and was staring down at her wand as though she had never seen it before. "Did . . . did it work?"

240

"No, it bloody well didn't," I said. I whirled on Astrea. "That . . . that was your solution!"

"I told you quite clearly, Vega, that there was no guarantee of recovery. Your father has been struck by a very complicated curse. There is no known antidote or reverse curse. I did the best that I could. I truly did. I am a very powerful sorceress. However, now I believe that magical power alone will not be enough to reverse his condition." She looked over at my father. "The good news is that he is alive. The failed procedure could have easily killed him." She glanced at me. "Your quick action saved your father's life, Vega. It truly did."

The anger seeped out of me with her sincere words. I nodded curtly and looked away.

"Now what?" said John matter-of-factly. "Will he die?"

I shot John a glance. Again, his face was like a mask. Not a trace of emotion on it. I could not understand. I truly could not. This was his father.

"We will find another way to cure him."

This came from my mother.

I looked at her as she stood there staring down at her husband. She reached out and touched my father's head. "We will find a way."

And at the precise moment, I believed that she was right.

I glanced at Astrea. "I thank you for trying to cure my father. I know you did your best and we appreciate your efforts." I looked at Archie. "And you too, Archie."

He nodded and thanked me with a smile.

"I have work to do," I said, and hurriedly left the room.

Delph rushed after me.

Outside the door, my suspicions were confirmed. A group of people, including Petra and Chauncey Cyphers, was waiting just outside.

My features answered Petra's question.

"But he's still alive?" she said quickly.

"Yes, but we don't have much time."

"Does Astrea have another plan?" she asked.

Delph said, "Not that she said. But we have to find some way to cure him."

"We will," I said far more confidently than I felt.

I hurried down the hall and went into my bedroom. I closed the door and paced my room, as Harry Two watched from the bed.

Astrea's words kept coming back to me:

I believe that magical power alone will not be enough to reverse his condition.

But if magic couldn't do it, what could? What other power did any of us possess to bring my father back to normal? And if we didn't have such a power, who or what did?

I had a sudden inspiration. It was one I had whenever I was confronted with a puzzle that I could not work out.

I raced to the drawer of my wardrobe and pulled out the single page of parchment.

"Silenus, can we speak?"

Silenus's aged features instantly appeared on the old paper. "Yes, Vega?"

"I have a problem that I need to solve, and I could use some advice."

The features perked up. "Present the facts to me, then."

I told him about my father's condition, how it had happened and Astrea's efforts to rectify it without success.

"She said that maybe magical power alone would not be enough to heal him," I added. "But if magic can't do it, what can?"

He didn't answer right away, and his silence eventually grew so long that I wasn't sure he was going to answer at all.

242

I had come to the point where I was thinking of sticking Silenus back in the drawer, when he stirred, cleared his throat and said, "Magic is not the be-all and end-all, you know. There are other things in existence that are more powerful than all the magic in the world combined."

Well, that was news to me!

"What are you talking about? What is more powerful than magic?"

"There are beings who were born with powers unimaginable to even the ablest and most skilled practitioner of magic."

"What beings?"

"They are called *celestial* beings, Vega. Gods, if you will. They are supreme spirits who need not rely on magic to accomplish what they want. Their power was created the instant they came into existence, because they were the offspring of similar celestial beings. Their power is in their every molecule. And they require no wands or incantations to do what they do."

And with that he added, "I hope that answers your question adequately."

The next moment Silenus disappeared from the parchment.

I looked dully at the paper.

"Well, that was no bloody help at all," I said to the blank page.

And then I nearly choked on my words.

Silenus had said gods were far more powerful than mere magical folks.

I actually knew that, because Astrea had already told me about the gods.

Well, if gods were more powerful, that meant that *goddesses* were too.

I ran out of the room.

Empchon

I RUSHED DOWN TO the lowest point in Empyrean, opened the door and slipped inside the dark space. I had been here so many times that it was no longer intimidating.

"Alice? Alice, I need to talk to you."

A moment later, Alice Adronis appeared before me.

"Yes?" she said curtly.

"Alice, did you know Elythia, Necro's wife?"

She stiffened at my query. "Why do you want to know?"

"Because Astrea told me that Elythia was actually not only a sorceress of exceptional power and skill, but also a *goddess.*"

Alice's gaze pointed to the cold floor of the chamber we were in. That struck me as odd, since she normally looked me directly in the eye, to such an extent that I often felt intimidated.

I said, "Astrea told me when Elythia found out how evil Necro was, and what he had done to her only son, that she cursed the Maladons so that the women would never be able to bear children. Necro found out what she had done and, in retaliation, killed all the Maladon women. I wondered why I had never seen any, either at the castle, or out with the other Maladons. And that would explain their absence."

Alice finally lifted her gaze to mine.

"I knew Elythia."

"Did you believe that she was a goddess too?"

Alice didn't answer right away.

"Elythia was . . . unique. She . . . she had powers that seemed beyond belief."

"You saw this?"

"Only accidentally. Elythia never drew attention to herself. Indeed, she never performed any magic that I ever saw."

"You said something about an *accident*?"

"It was a lovely day. Not a cloud in the sky. I was taking a walk along a path that took me close to Necro's estate. And that's when I saw something I never thought I would."

"What was that?"

"I heard a noise and ventured through the woods where they opened up into a small glen on the perimeter of Necro's land. I hid behind a tree when I saw two figures approaching."

"Who were they?"

"Necro and his wife, Elythia. They were arguing about something. I couldn't really tell what they were arguing about but with their raised voices, I did hear the names Jason and Uma."

"What happened?"

"The argument reached a crescendo, and Necro turned and abruptly walked off. Elythia stood there staring after him for a few long moments. I could tell from her heaving chest that she was still quite upset. She raised her fists to the sky, and I saw a pulse of black light erupt from each of them and shoot into the air." She paused and closed her eyes. "I remember this so clearly, Vega. Within a second the black light exploded and the blue sky was gone. An enormous storm covered the entire sky, lightning and thunder, torrential rain and winds that nearly blew me off my feet. It was the strongest storm I had ever witnessed. And through it all, Elythia stood there in that little glen and not a bit of the storm reached her, no rain, no wind, nothing. She lowered her hands, and just like that, the sky was blue, the sun was out and warming and there was not a trace of wind or rain. As I continued to watch, she walked off back toward her home." She paused. "It was as though she was releasing her anger to the heavens."

I had listened to all this breathlessly. When Alice was done with her story, I said, "So, she is a goddess, then? Because there is no incantation that I know of that could control the very heavens."

"If that defines a goddess, then Elythia was a goddess."

"Where did she come from?"

"No one knew. She simply appeared one day in our midst."

"And she chose Necro as her husband?" I said skeptically.

"He was different back then. He changed. Or else he hid his true nature very well."

"And she vanished, after Jason died?"

"Yes."

"Do you have any idea where she might have gone? I mean, could she be dead?"

"I do not think that beings such as Elythia can die, Vega. But why do you want to know where she is?"

"Because Astrea, powerful as she is, cannot cure my father. She said that a greater power was needed. Elythia is the only one I know of who possesses power such as that. If she can't help my father, I don't know who can. And I'm running out of time. My father will soon die if something isn't done."

"I see."

"And if she is so powerful, and she detests Necro so much, then she could simply use her great powers to destroy him and the other Maladons. Then the war would be over."

Surprisingly, Alice did not seem excited by my revelation.

"Don't you think?" I prodded.

"I think you need to find out for yourself."

I was frustrated by that response, but in my excitement, I just wanted to push forward. "So, you have no inkling where she might have gone? Where she might be now?"

"No, Vega, I don't. Soon after she disappeared, we were at war with the Maladons. Any thought I had of Elythia vanished as clearly as she did."

I stood there immensely frustrated. I could have the solution for not only my father's cure but the war against the Maladons right in my hands. I just needed to find Elythia. I was sure I could convince her to help us.

I finally turned to go as Alice remained silent.

"There is something," she said.

"What?!" I exclaimed, a flicker of hope coming back to me as I turned to face her.

To my surprise, she held up her wand hand. There I could see that she was missing a finger.

She touched the empty spot with one of her other fingers.

"You told me you know the story of my wand?"

"Yes," I said. "Your father would not grant you a wand. So you went in search of the tallest peak and the tallest tree on that peak. You climbed to the top of that tree and held up your hand in the middle of a raging storm. You pledged that if a wand was granted to you, you would always use it in the defense of good and against evil." I glanced at her hand. "And your wish was granted. Your finger was gone, and in its place was this." I held up the Elemental.

"That is all true."

"Why was your finger required in exchange for the Elemental?"

"Sacrifice, Vega," she replied. "I was given something incredibly valuable. Such things do not come for free. Without sacrifice. Part of my body was my sacrifice. It was my price to be paid."

"But how does that help me with Elythia?"

"I did not select that peak and that tree by chance, Vega."

"What do you mean?"

"That location was known as the most magical place of all in my time. It was well known that there was a power there that could be found nowhere else."

"But again, what does that have to do with Elythia?"

"That place was Elythia's favorite. It is said that she gave birth to Jason there. When one was looking for Elythia for some reason and could not find her elsewhere, she was always to be found in the small cottage next to the tree where my finger was sacrificed."

"A small cottage? Can you tell me how to get there?"

"Shortly after Elythia disappeared, so too did that peak and everything on it, including the cottage."

"Wait a minute," I said, mightily confused. "An entire mountain just vanished? Was it destroyed?"

"No, it just no longer was there."

"Do you think Elythia had something to do with its disappearance?"

"I am quite certain that she did."

"But if it's gone, how can I search for it?"

Alice's reply was only one word long, but it was enough to set me in the right direction.

"Empchon."

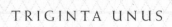

Elythia

I THOUGHT I MIGHT see you again, Vega."

I looked over at Eon with his hooded cloak, staff and light.

"Why?"

"Simply that I did not believe your work here was complete yet."

I didn't ask any more questions, because I knew that Eon would probably be equally cryptic. And, as a matter of fact, he was right. My work was incomplete.

As before, I elected to go into the past and I soon found myself walking through the gates and into the mist. I didn't know what would happen for sure, but I hoped that this journey would not entail multiple trips to different points in time. I was desperate to find Elythia, because I knew my father was dying. And Elythia was also the key to winning the war against the Maladons.

And yet my wish was not to be granted.

The mists cleared and my heart sank, even as the breath left my lungs.

She lay dead, on a slab of stone with a collection of white lilies and green laurels around her neck.

It was Uma. She was dressed in a pale cream burial robe. Only two people were with her.

Her mother and her father. Bastion and Victoria Cadmus.

They were kneeling next to the body of their dead daughter. Victoria was sobbing, while her husband stared off, the anger on his face terrible to behold.

Bastion was tall and strongly built, with a short black beard and a pair of flashing green eyes. I had first seen his countenance in a portrait at Empyrean. I had been told that Bastion was the greatest warrior our side had, even more powerful than Alice Adronis. But he had been betrayed by the woman kneeling next to him, his wife, Victoria. While under the *Subservio* spell, she had delivered her husband to the Maladons. He had died fighting and took a dozen Maladons with him before succumbing to his wounds. Victoria, once out from under the spell, and like her daughter, had killed herself in her despair.

The bereaved pair were grieving their daughter, not knowing that they too were both doomed.

My heart went out to them, yet I didn't know why I was here. What did this have to do with Elythia?

At the instant I thought that, the mists appeared once more, and I was at another place when they cleared.

It was similar to the one I had just left. With one stark difference.

There was but *one* grieving parent.

Jason was also lying on a slab dressed in his burial clothes. Next to him and sitting in a chair was someone I could only believe was the elusive Elythia.

She was tall and regal, and there was an aura about her that I had never seen with anyone else, not even Alice. It was as though she did not belong to our world.

And she was not sobbing like Uma's mother. Nor did she look in any way overcome with grief. She stared stonily at the body of her son. But in her eyes, which were like starbursts of blue, I saw something that was powerful, unassailable.

And terrible.

As I was watching, she stood, a figure of barely contained power the likes of which I had never before witnessed. Her hands were fists, her spine straight and her features granite.

I imagined that this was probably the moment she was going to curse all Maladon women into a barren state. And that would seal their fates at the hands of Necro.

I wondered if Elythia was even bothered by this. Or had thought through the consequences of what she was about to do. The effects it would have over other, innocent people.

But then again, I could often say the same about myself, I thought sheepishly.

With one last glance at the dead body of her son, Elythia turned and left.

The mists gathered around me once more.

When they cleared, I saw a mountain.

I looked around, trying to gauge where I was. But it was difficult to do so.

I walked toward the mountain until I thought of a better idea. I spread my arms and took to the air, the silent links of Destin moving slightly underneath my skin.

I alighted on top of the highest peak on the mountain and looked around.

And there it was: the tallest, straightest tree I had ever seen. This must be where Alice had come to receive her wand, the sacrifice of her finger the price that was demanded in exchange.

My heart fluttered when I saw next to the tree a simple cottage with two windows, a curved wooden door and a thatched roof. My senses tingled when I noticed smoke rising from the stone chimney.

I walked toward it on unsteady feet. I had to admit I was feeling a bit light-headed.

My gaze once more went to the tree, and I marveled at how Alice had managed to climb to its very top in the middle of a terrible storm and have the courage to lift her hand to the sky, willing to sacrifice anything — she didn't know it would only be a finger — in order to seize the life she demanded for herself. A life that her terrible father refused to give his only daughter, a person who would become her kind's greatest hero, besting all her male counterparts.

Men could be so stupid, I thought.

I reached the cottage's door and knocked. There was no answer. I put my ear to the wood but heard nothing from inside.

I steeled myself, put my hand on the doorknob and turned it. The door opened wide.

Necro sat in a chair by the blazing fire. His dead face and black eyes were staring right at me.

My wand came up, pointing at his heart, that is if he had one.

On my lips was the killing incantation.

"*Rigamo* —"

The air started hardening around me and I could not finish the curse. Just as it had when Necro was nearby. This really had been a trap.

And then, before my very eyes, Necro disappeared and another figure took his place.

Elythia quietly rose from her chair and looked me over.

She wore robes of pale blue. Her hair and features looked the same as when I'd seen her sitting with her dead son. I wasn't sure how we could be in the past because the image I had just seen of Necro was the one he now possessed.

But then I remembered that Elythia was a goddess. I supposed that time meant nothing to her kind and that she probably didn't age at all. Having eternal life seemed fitting for an all-powerful being.

"I apologize for what I just did," she said; her voice was low but it brought a pleasant ringing into my ears. "I had to make sure you were not one of them. A Maladon would never attack his leader."

I found my voice and said as firmly as I could, "I am not a Maladon. My name is Vega Jane."

She appraised me again. "Jane? You are descended from Alice and Gunther?"

"I am."

She nodded. "I see the resemblance."

"And you are Elythia." It was not a question.

She sat back down, steepled her hands and stared at me.

"You have come to see me. Why?"

"I have need of your help."

"Go on."

"My father, Hector Jane, is very ill. He was struck by a commingled spell. He lies at death's door. We have tried everything to cure him, but we have failed. I have come to you as my last resort."

"And who told you of me?"

"Two people did. Astrea Prine and Alice."

Elythia nodded. "And are they well?"

"Astrea is. Alice died in battle long ago."

She nodded again, seemingly unsurprised by this news. I had the feeling that she simply wanted to know if I knew the things she already did.

"Do you know *what* I am, Vega?"

I thought best how to answer this. "I know two things about you."

This was the first time that she seemed uncertain. And also the first time that she had to pay real attention to me.

"And what are they?" she asked.

"You are a goddess."

"What else?"

"You are a mother who believes she has lost her son."

She rose from her chair and looked across the planks at me.

"Believes she has lost her son?"

I had come up with my strategy for dealing with Elythia before going on this journey. I had to play it exactly right to get all that I wanted: my father cured and the Maladons vanquished.

"Your son lives."

"Jason lives?"

I cocked my head. Though she might be a goddess, she wasn't exceptional at hiding her true knowledge.

"You knew that, didn't you?"

"Of course I did not."

I have read the features of many people who were lying to me.

And I was convinced that Elythia just had.

In her anxiety, Elythia had floated up into the air until her head was near the ceiling.

But I looked up at her not in defiance and certainly not in sympathy, because I instinctively understood that such an emotion would not be welcome by such a person. I simply looked at her with resolution, with the certainty that I spoke the truth.

She slowly floated back down to the floor but did not take up her seat. She stood across from me with an aura of pure power.

Then this too passed, and she looked at me with a calmer eye.

"You are perceptive beyond your years."

"I've had to be. To survive."

She nodded and in that simple gesture much was communicated between us. Perhaps everything.

"You wish me to heal your father?"

"Yes."

"And that is all?"

I could tell that she knew this was not all.

"I want you to destroy the Maladons."

"Necro as well, then?"

"Yes. I don't have to tell you why. You know why they must be vanquished."

"I can help your father. I cannot destroy the Maladons."

"But you can, if you want to. You're a goddess. Your power is infinite."

"The thing is, Vega, you are wrong. I am *not* a goddess."

My mouth collapsed open, all my calm assurance and momentum in this confrontation gone. "But you said you were a goddess."

"No, *you* said I was."

"But you didn't deny it."

"It is not my task to deny or confirm what I am. But I repeat, I am not a goddess."

"Then what are you?"

"My mother was a goddess; my father was not. He was just like any other man."

Now something started to make sense. "Your mother, a goddess, fell in love with a man who was not a god?"

"That is correct. Such happens in life, Vega. Nothing is guaranteed, even for gods."

"And did you fall in love with Necro?"

"I thought that it was love. At least it was, on my part."

"How came you to be with our lot at all?"

"Isn't it obvious?"

I gaped as what she was implying struck me. "You were . . . shunned by the other gods because you had fallen in love with someone who wasn't a god?"

"Yes."

"Then Jason is at least part god."

"Blood runs in funny ways. He never exhibited any celestial tendencies." She paused and said in a measured tone, "And I do not necessarily consider that a bad thing."

"Why?"

"Gods cannot love, Vega. At least not like you can. Not even my own mother, who fell in love with my father, who was not a god. There was always an aloofness. The knowledge that a barrier would always separate their two hearts, no matter how much they may have desired otherwise."

"But you're not a goddess, at least not a full one," I pointed out. "So that rule doesn't apply to you. And you loved Jason. There was no barrier between the two of you."

"For me, love was mightier than any power."

I seemed to sense her now looking into the past, at a slab with a body on it.

"How did you know that I knew the truth about my son's fate?"

"You didn't cry at the sight of his body," I said simply. "You knew it wasn't him."

256

She nodded.

"Which makes me wonder why you can't destroy the Maladons. Even if you're not a full goddess, you are far more powerful than they are. Even than Necro."

She looked away from me. "I cannot answer that, Vega."

"You can't possibly love Necro. Not after all that he's done. He's enslaved Jason. He has him as a prisoner right now at Maladon Castle."

I thought this would cause her to fly into a rage, with the result that she would soar off and kill the bloody fiend. But she didn't.

"I'm sorry, Vega. I cannot."

I shook my head, my disappointment on this matter complete. "What about my father?"

"Reach into your right pocket, Vega."

I did so and pulled out a small bottle with clear liquid inside.

"Wash your father with this, and all will be well."

I held her gaze. "Thank you."

"I wish you luck in your battle with the Maladons."

"He killed all the women," I said quietly. "Because women struck barren were useless to him. Or so he believed."

I knew I didn't have to say *Struck barren by you.*

"This too I know," she replied.

And then the mists gathered around me.

And she was gone.

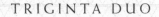

The End of the Day

B ACK AT EMPYREAN, I held the bottle over my father as my mother stood poised with a cloth.

I had told the others of my encounter with Elythia and her refusal to slay Necro. They were as disappointed and incredulous as I was, but there was also nothing we could do about it. We couldn't force a goddess, or near goddess, to do anything. But I would never understand her decision.

Love had nothing to do with it. Only selfishness, at least in my mind.

Behind us stood Astrea, Delph, Archie and my brother.

I let the liquid from the bottle drip onto my father's head. My mother used the cloth to wash him all over with it.

When the bottle's contents were exhausted, my mother and I stepped back and waited. At first nothing happened, and my disappointment and anxiety spiked. Had my trip to find Elythia been for naught?

Then my father started to squirm and his body began to gyrate violently. My mother reached out to him, but I grabbed her arm and held her back.

"Let it work," I said to her. "Trust Elythia."

Right before our eyes, the bottle's contents did indeed start to work. My father's tiny body started to stretch out, his skin lost its burned color, dark hair regrew on his head, his eyes started to flutter open.

When his body stopped vibrating, my father lay fully formed on the bed as my mother rushed to cover his nakedness.

She helped him to slowly sit up, tears sliding down her cheeks. It was the same for me. And I glanced around to see if John was experiencing something similar.

To my chagrin, he merely looked interested in what had transpired.

Astrea reached out and clenched my shoulder. "You have done well, Vega. You have brought back a miracle."

Delph added, " 'Tis a miracle. 'Tis."

Archie chimed in, "You did it, Vega. You did it."

I sat down next to my father and took his hand. He was still groggy and spent, and I could only imagine what he had gone through. He was terribly thin and weak, but we could sort that out soon enough with Mrs. Jolly's cooking and with tender care from the rest of us.

"Dad? It's me, Vega."

My father's gaze met mine. It had been so many years since my father had been able to truly look at me.

He gently touched my cheek, rubbed my skin, the familiar lopsided smile appearing at his mouth.

"Vega," he said in a weak voice. "My child. At last."

I put my arms around him and held him tight, even as my mother did the same from the other side. We three sat there holding on to one another, crying and shaking.

When I finally looked up, John had left the room.

And my sheer happiness turned into a troubled despair.

What the Hel was wrong with my brother?

But my melancholy didn't last long. My father was back. Hector Jane was back! And now my entire family was here with me. And we would fight together. And we would win together. And we would emerge from the war unscathed.

And I held that absolutely naïve thought for at least a good ten minutes.

MY FATHER WAS weak for the next few days, and he took his meals in his room with my mother. I visited him every day, spending hours talking with him, catching up on many things that had occurred in the years we had been apart.

My mother doted on him, but she was chagrined that John did not come by very often. I found myself defending my brother from time to time with her, but inwardly I was distraught that he was not more emotionally connected to his family.

And the absence of a mark on his hand was also weighing on my mind.

By contrast, the marks on my parents' hands were as robust as the one on mine.

I am sure that John had discerned that all the magical beings at Empyrean bore this mark. But then again, I remembered Petra did not have such a mark. That thought heartened me, because Petra was clearly not a Maladon.

I was sitting in front of the fire in the library after dinner one night when Astrea came in and took the seat across from me.

I had led a patrol of four to Greater True that day and returned with not much of value. But it had been good to have gone, because I had been feeling useless after my trip to see Elythia.

As it turned out, that was what Astrea wanted to talk to me about it and she didn't waste time coming around to the subject. She asked me quite pointedly about my time travel resulting in my meeting with Elythia. Astrea clearly wanted every detail.

After I described my multiple encounters in the past, she was quick to make queries.

"How did she look?" she asked.

"I really have nothing to compare it to, other than when I saw her in the past with Jason's body."

"She was not sad?"

"I think she was more angry than sad. And determined."

"And you say you told her that all the Maladon women had been struck barren? And that they had been killed as a result?"

"Yes. And she was aware of that, at least that's what she said. And she also knew that Jason was not dead. Whether she knew about him being imprisoned by Necro before I told her about it, I don't know."

"And still she will not move against him?" said Astrea, shaking her head in disbelief.

"Apparently not," I said.

"She was with him when it was clear that he was evil personified. Why did she stay?"

"Because of her son?"

As the flames flickered in front of us, she pointed a finger at me. "I think that exactly, Vega. Because of Jason. She would not leave him to Necro."

"And she may not have had a choice. She told me she was shunned by her kind because her father wasn't a god. But, Astrea, she could have taken Jason with her, started a new life."

"That's true. She could, for example, have even taken him to her cottage and lived there. But she didn't."

I sat back, puzzled. "That doesn't make sense."

"No, you're wrong. It makes sense . . . to Elythia."

She rose and walked to the door. She turned back and said, "It was quite brilliant what you did, Vega. Your father would not be with us if you hadn't thought of it."

Before I could respond, she had left.

I got up and sat in front of the fire. I had suddenly felt a chill racing through my bones, and the warmth of the flames was welcome. But I could sense that it wasn't merely a matter of cold permeating me. It was the thought of what was coming.

Would any of us survive? Had I collected my entire family here, only to see them perish at the hands of the Maladons?

The door to the library opened once more, and Delph looked in on me.

I started to get up, but he motioned for me to stay where I was.

He joined me on the floor.

"Saw Astrea outside," he began. "Did you two speak?"

I nodded and quickly filled him in on what had happened.

"That *is* a puzzler about Elythia," he said.

I told him of my concern about bringing my family here to die.

"Nobody can tell what's coming in the future."

"Jasper Jane saw me in the future," I blurted out.

"What?"

"He went into the future once and saw me. He told Alice. I think that's why Alice gave me the Elemental on that battle-field, Delph."

"Maybe Jasper saw you lead us to victory, Vega Jane."

"Or maybe he saw me perish, Delph."

Delph visibly shuddered at this remark. "Why won't he tell you?"

"Because if he did, he told me the results would be disastrous. For *me*."

Delph nodded and fell silent.

I put a hand on Delph's large shoulder. "The odds are against us, Delph."

Surprisingly, he gave me a silly grin.

"What?" I said.

"Vega Jane, when *haven't* the odds been against us?"

I had to smile. I mean I really smiled. And then I laughed. Like I hadn't in, I don't know, forever.

And then his silly grin inspired something inside of me and I leaned across and kissed him. Like I never had before.

He kissed me back. Like *he* never had before.

And we sat there in front of the fire, holding each other for the longest time.

I had never felt such warmth.

And it had absolutely nothing to do with the flames.

A Singular Request

I WAS ASLEEP WHEN I heard it.

I sat up. Harry Two was at the foot of my bed but he hadn't stirred, which was strange, since he usually sensed things before I did.

"Vega?"

It was Uma. She was hovering above me. As I watched, she slowly floated down to sit next to me on my bed.

"Uma, are you okay?"

"I was wondering if you had word of Jason?"

I felt something jerk in my stomach.

Jason. I had promised Uma that I would do whatever I could to find out about Jason being in Maladon Castle.

I had done nothing

"I'm . . . I'm sorry, Uma. What with my parents and my brother and all."

The lameness of this excuse was palpable. I felt it in every quarter of my being. And she made me feel it.

Her tone was sharper than it had ever been before. "You were the one to tell me that he was alive. That he loved me. You said you would find out more. I am running out of time, Vega."

This last was an odd comment for someone who was already dead. Yet I still felt guilty for having failed in my promise.

As my eyes adjusted to the darkness, I was startled by her appearance. Uma was barely visible now. It was as though she were vanishing bit by bit as we sat there.

"I'm really sorry, Uma."

"Better that you had never told me he was alive," she added in a hurt tone.

"Uma, you spoke before about visiting the castle on your own. I hope you didn't try. It could be very dangerous, even for someone . . . in your condition."

"I was persuaded by your words not to try," she said. "But since you've done nothing, curse me for not attempting it."

"Uma, I will try, but I do have other things that I'm trying to do. Like win a war with the Maladons."

"Bloody Hel, Vega, don't you see?"

"See what?"

"He's been with Necro all this time, doing his bidding. He knows everything that goes on there. Don't you think Jason would be a very valuable tool in helping to defeat his father?"

As she said this, her image actually seemed to burn a bit brighter.

And then she was gone.

I tried to go back to sleep, but it was impossible.

Uma was right of course; I had just been too stupid to see it.

I glanced out my window. It was still dark, but the dawn was coming. I decided to dress and go downstairs. I left Harry Two still sleeping on my bed.

I made my way into the entrance hall, where I was immediately confronted by Pillsbury.

"Yes, Mistress Vega. Do you require anything?"

"What, oh, no, Pillsbury. I'm fine. I just couldn't sleep anymore and decided to start my day."

"Ah, like sister, like brother, eh?"

"What?"

"Your brother is also up. He went outside not ten minutes ago after having some breakfast by the fire in the kitchen. Fascinating lad he is."

"He went outside?"

"Yes."

"Is he often up this early?"

"Almost always."

"What does he do outside?"

"I'm sure I don't know," said Pillsbury. "I, well, I don't watch him. He's your brother. If he requires anything, he lets me know."

"Right, thanks, Pillsbury."

"Do you wish to eat, Mistress Vega?"

"No, not quite yet. I think . . . I think I'll go for a walk and get some fresh air."

"Very good."

He clicked his heels and was gone.

I quickly headed outside.

The air was crisp and a bit cool, and I was glad of my cloak. I could glimpse a seam of the coming dawn against the blackened horizon.

I heard noises and thought it must be John. Then I heard two voices, and one of them was female.

I hurried forward and then ducked behind some bushes when I saw them.

It was Petra.

And Chauncey Cyphers, Lackland's brother.

They were snogging!

My heart leapt.

Not wanting to interrupt them, and a bit taken aback by the energetic scene I was witnessing, I hurried on in search of John.

I found him in the far back corner of the estate.

He was also not alone.

Miranda Weeks sat beside him once again.

They were talking, and I heard Miranda laugh at something my brother said.

I felt a bit guilty spying on them, but for some reason it seemed prudent.

John took out his wand and pointed it at a bush.

It suddenly lit up and snow began to fall down on it.

Miranda was delighted and clapped her hands.

Then John showed her how to perform the incantation, and a few moments later, I was watching bush after bush go through the same transformation as Miranda quickly got the hang of the spell.

This seemed to please my brother, and I could see him grinning and calling out encouragement to Miranda.

A few minutes later, Miranda took her leave and I quickly stepped farther behind my tree before she passed by.

I was about to call out to my brother, when something he did made me maintain my hiding place.

He had taken his wand, pointed it at the sky and made a whipping motion.

Suddenly, the sky was filled with fire. As I watched, both fascinated and appalled, the fire took shape.

My fascination ended, and horror took over completely.

It was the shape of an enormous jabbit.

What in the Hel?

I stepped out and said, "John!"

He whipped around, saw me and immediately dipped his wand. The jabbit vanished.

I walked forward, my gaze never leaving his face.

"What were you doing?" I asked.

"Nothing. Just . . . nothing."

My brother had lied to me before, so this was nothing new. But it still hurt me very much.

"Do you like jabbits?" I said, pointing to the now-clear sky.

"What? No, of course not."

"That's good to know. We will most assuredly have to fight some one day. Have you ever fought a jabbit?"

He looked at me goggle-eyed. "No. Have you?"

"Numerous times," I said. "I've certainly killed quite a few. And you saw me dispatch one at the Duelum in Wormwood," I reminded him. "Don't you recall that? It very nearly killed me and a great many other Wugs."

His gaze pointed to the ground. "I . . . do remember that, Vega. It was quite terrifying."

"Well, they're terrifyingly odious creatures. So, if I were you, I wouldn't go around incanting their image into the sky, all right?"

It wasn't quite an order, but close enough.

"All right, Vega."

"Have you seen Morrigone's spirit since you've been here?"

"No, I have not."

"I thought for sure that she would come and visit you, considering how close you two were back in Wormwood."

I did not mention that Morrigone had told me that John had left her home prior to leaving Wormwood.

"I don't know why she hasn't sought me out. Is it, um, *unusual* speaking with someone not living?"

"Not really," I replied. "One quickly gets used to it. Sometimes, it's more enjoyable and informative than talking with the living."

I continued to look at him, wondering what I was going to do with my brother. A brother I was having a hard time allowing myself to trust. And if I couldn't get over that hurdle, then what was the point of having brought him here?

"Have you fought anything with your wand, John?"

He looked first at his wand, and then directed his gaze at me.

"Yes."

"Have you killed with it?"

"N-no."

"You *do* know the death incantation, though?"

He nodded. "I read about it in a book."

"The difference between reading about it in a book and performing it against another is the difference between living . . . and dying."

He looked taken aback by my sharp words, but that was my intention.

I made up my mind right then and there.

"You and I are going on a trip together."

"Where, Vega?"

"To Maladon Castle."

If he wanted to be a Maladon, I was going to bloody well show him what they were like.

"Wh-what? Wh-when?" he stammered.

"Now."

John's Incantation

WE FLEW ALONG under the cover of my invisibility ring.

I could have used the *Pass-pusay* incantation and immediately delivered us to the outskirts of Maladon Castle, but the fact was, I wanted to spend some time alone with John.

"What will we do at Maladon Castle?" asked my brother.

"There is a man, Jason, the arch-henchman of Necro. We are going to rescue him."

"Why?"

"He can be of help to us. And, well, it's complicated, but I've found out he's not really who I thought he was."

"This could be very dangerous," said John.

"Every time we go against the Maladons it's dangerous."

He glanced at my hand.

"Why do you wear that glove, Vega?"

I had been wondering when he would ask me that.

"It's to cover a mark. The mark of the three hooks. Nearly all magical people who are not Maladons have that mark on them when they enter this world. It was the Maladons' doing. It is their way of tracking us. I wear the glove, which blocks the signal it would send to the Maladons. I have fashioned similar gloves for all the others."

My brother then did what I knew he would do. He looked down at his hands and saw there were no marks upon them.

He caught me staring at him, but quickly looked away.

And in that look, I saw the remnants of my little brother with feet far too big for his small frame. He had been unsure of himself, afraid of his own shadow. My heart went out to him, just like it used to on a daily basis when we had been children. I could not help myself, despite my suspicions.

But we were no longer children.

"I see" was all he said, his voice small and hesitant.

For the life of me I couldn't come up with anything to say in response.

As we flew along, him tethered to my golden lasso, I glanced over and studied my brother.

"You will be ready to fight them, won't you, John? If it comes to it?"

In answer, he held up his wand. "I will be ready, Vega."

"Just so you know, they have jabbits and garms in the castle. They're on leashes. The Maladons can control them."

"Interesting," said my brother. "But hardly surprising."

"What do you mean?"

"These are evil creatures, and the Maladons are an evil lot."

"I guess that makes sense," I said, staring at him warily.

"And what if this Jason is dead? What then?"

"Then we gather as much information as we can before we leave the castle. Every little bit helps."

He nodded, though I didn't detect in him much enthusiasm for my plan.

"You remember I told you about Miranda Weeks's mother dying?"

"They took her magic and things went wrong."

"Well, they also did that to our grandfather. And then Necro killed him."

Tears suddenly welled up in his eyes. "He killed Virgil?"

Now, that was the reaction I was looking for, at last.

"Yes."

I saw his fingers tighten around his wand.

"Do you think we will see Necro at the castle?" he asked.

"It's possible."

"I hope that we do," he said.

I looked away, my spirits considerably lifted.

WE LANDED WITHIN a hundred yards of the castle, and I took quite some time looking around. The place was dark, but that was not unusual. The gate was down, which was problematic. And there were no signs of activity or Maladons coming and going.

"How do we get in?" John asked.

Good question, I thought.

We took to the air once more, circling around to the back of the castle.

I knew that the dome of the castle could open, because I'd seen it happen once before.

I closed my eyes and sent a wand wire to Victus.

Victus, it's Vega. I need to get into the castle. I'm around the back. Can you help me?

Some minutes passed as I waited nervously for him to answer.

As time went by, my dread deepened. Had Victus been discovered as a spy? Had they killed him?

And then in my head came his reply.

There is a door. You will see it open presently. You must be swift.

I instantly flew John and me closer to the castle. We landed and waited.

Another minute went by and then I saw it.

A small door that I hadn't even noticed before opened at the rear of the castle.

I saw Victus emerge. He was carrying a bundle of something. He passed through the door, leaving it open.

Not wasting a moment, John and I shot through the opening.

A few moments later, Victus returned without the bundle. He shut and locked the door behind him.

We were in a low stone corridor off which a series of doors opened.

In a low voice I said, "Victus, thank you."

He said nothing but slowly nodded.

"Do you have any idea where Jason, I mean Endemen, is? The last I saw of him he was in the tower room."

Victus gave a searching look up and down the corridor. Though he had no eyes, I knew that he could still see. In fact, he saw more than most here, I wagered.

"He is in the Room of Removal."

"The Room of Removal?" I said, puzzled, but for only a moment.

I gasped. "Do you mean they're taking his magic?"

That was where my fellow Wugs were imprisoned. I would have another chance to free them.

Victus nodded and then said, "Whatever you mean to do here, Vega, you must do it quickly."

I knew better than to ask needless questions.

I said, "Thank you," and then hurried off with John right behind me.

"Where are we going?" he whispered as we darted left down a corridor.

"To find Jason."

I led us quickly to the hall that I knew the room to be in.

We were just about to reach the door when I grabbed John and pulled him close to the wall.

"Wh—" he began, but he didn't have time to finish.

The garm turned the corner and came down the hall. And it was not on a tether, and it was not being accompanied by a Maladon.

I could feel my brother breathing quickly behind me.

I put my hand over his and squeezed, to reassure him.

The garm grew closer to us. I could see its shiny blood on its chest, a characteristic that made the garm perpetually angry; it never stopped shedding its own blood.

And then the garm stopped. It sucked in its huge nostrils.

It was smelling us, I thought.

I held my wand at the ready. If the thing struck, I would conjure a shield to protect us. But I hoped that it wouldn't because that might give us away.

"It's okay, Vega," whispered my brother.

I turned to him in surprise.

"What?" I hissed.

"It won't harm us."

I started to respond, when a noise made me turn my attention to the garm again.

The garm had gone back the way it had come.

After it had left our sight, I glanced at my brother.

"How did you know it wouldn't attack?" I said.

"I'm not sure. It was just something I sensed."

"Have you sensed these things before?"

He nodded.

"Just with garms?"

He shook his head. "With garms, freks and . . . jabbits."

"Are you telling me that you could . . . what, read their thoughts?"

"I guess. Is that not normal?"

I didn't tell him that it was as about as un-normal as it was possible to be. Except perhaps for a Maladon.

I focused my wand on the door and cast my incantation.

Inside the room were two Maladons in long cloaks. On the walls were the hideous mirrors. I had to look away as I saw my fellow Wugmorts writhing in pain behind the glass.

Now the dilemma was, how did we get in without the blokes noticing?

Then I saw a gap under the door. I knelt down, pointed my wand through the gap and said, *"Paralycto."*

I cast the spell to see through the door. Both Maladons stood frozen.

I opened the door, and John and I went inside.

I passed by the paralyzed Maladons and surveyed the room.

John did likewise.

"Vega!" he exclaimed.

I turned to see where he was looking.

"I know, John."

It was the Wugs from Wormwood. They were still in the mirrors. They were still writhing in pain.

"Can't we do something to help them?" said John. The look on his face was one of stark horror.

"I've tried. They're all dead. I saw their graves back in Wormwood." I pointed my wand at the mirrors. "I don't know what exactly they are."

"Didn't you tell me that Thansius was alive when you went back to Wormwood?"

"Yes, they had him digging the graves of all the others. He died in my arms. I buried him myself."

John slowly nodded but continued to look at the Wugs in the mirror. "And yet there is Thanisus over there." He pointed to one of the mirrors.

"I know. It's inexplicable, John."

I moved around the room, keeping a watchful eye for the glass holding Jason.

"Morrigone's not here," he said.

"I know."

"Why not?"

"She was killed by the Maladons," I said.

"But, according to you, so were all of them. Why is her spirit at Empyrean and not here with the other Wugs?"

I pivoted on my heels, taking in all the Wugs behind the glass.

John glanced at me and said, "I don't believe these are spirits, Vega. I believe these are Wugs!"

My mind whirling, I said, "So . . . so they just dug those graves and put nothing in them. To . . . to fool us. But, as I said, Thansius was alive when I got there. *I* buried him."

"Dopplegang, or something like it," said John.

I knew of dopplegangs too. They could match their looks to anything.

"So, the Wug I buried was not Thansius."

"I don't think so." He pointed at the glass. "I think *that* is Thansius."

I thought quickly. "That makes sense actually. Wormwood was the one place the Maladons had been searching for for over eight hundred years. Merely killing Wugs probably wasn't enough for them." I looked at the glass. "But this was."

John said, "Can this be all of those who lived in Wormwood?"

He quickly counted the number of glasses. "One hundred exactly," he said. "Surely there were more Wugs before."

"I'm sure there were," I said. "But we have been gone from there for years now. We don't know what may have happened. The beasts from the Quag perhaps?" I glanced up and down the walls. "But regardless of their number, we need to free them. We *have* to free them."

John had passed down to the farthest end of the chamber. "Vega!"

I rushed to where he was standing.

Jason was lying unconscious in the glass. Underneath was the foul bottle collecting his magic. It looked to be very nearly full, with only a few grains now falling into it.

"So how do we free him? How do we free any of them?"

I gripped my wand, thinking back to what Astrea had told me.

Next, I sent a wand wire to Victus.

"How many Maladons are in the castle presently?"

The answer came back a few moments later.

"One hundred and forty-three."

I smiled grimly and looked at my brother. "This will be the biggest blow to the Maladons yet. Astrea told me how to free those behind the glass. I thought I would have to find Maladon spirits, but this is far better."

I told him the incantation and wand movements necessary.

"You will take that half of the room. Be quick with your wand, for we will have mere moments." I stared hard at him. "Are you ready?"

He took a long breath and stood up to his full height. In my eyes, he had just transformed from a little boy shuffling down the street to a man.

"Ready, Vega."

I opened the door to the room, and then we made three slashes in the air and cried out, *"Periculo nomadus."*

277

We ducked down as Maladons from all over the castle flew through the open doorway, their bodies catapulting into the glass, at the exact same time the Wugs and Jason were ejected. Right before the seams closed up, we cried out, *"Impacto."*

The spells shot out of our wands and, collectively, hit all 101 glasses. There was a shattering sound and smoke everywhere. Screams rang around the room.

When the air cleared, every single mirror had shattered and what remained was a blackened ruin.

But I wasn't really focused on that. There were a hundred Wugs slowly rising from the floor. Faces I hadn't seen in a very long time flooded my field of vision.

Thansius recovered before the others and stumbled over to me.

"Vega," he said, falling into my arms.

I hugged the mightiest Wug of all as tightly as I could.

Roman Picus, Cletus Loon and Domitar joined us at that moment. They all hugged me. And even though Loon and Picus had been enemies of mine back in Wormwood, we were apparently best mates now!

But we had no time for a lengthy reunion. There were still dozens of Maladons left in the castle and they would no doubt be converging on this room very soon.

And then I saw him. Duf Delphia was lying on the stone, for he had no timbertoes on which to stand. I rushed over to him, knelt down, and hugged him.

"Vega, is that really you?!"

" 'Tis, Duf."

I waved my wand over him and wooden timbertoes were neatly attached to what remained of his legs. I helped him to stand.

He gripped my arm. "Delph, is . . . is he alive?"

"Alive and well. And you will see him soon. I swear it."

The knowledge that my fellow Wugs were alive and not dead in their graves was intoxicating. I don't think I had been this deliriously happy in a long time. Even John, I could see, was delighted in greeting them.

I then hurried over to Jason, who lay still on the stone floor. And I knew why.

I grabbed up the bottle containing Jason's magic and tipped it over his body.

Just like they had with my grandfather, the grains of magic were instantly absorbed through Jason's skin.

I watched anxiously to see whether he would come around or not.

And then I heard what I had expected to hear. Footsteps running down the stone halls. The Maladons were coming. And perhaps Necro too.

Jason's eyes fluttered open, and he looked around before his gaze came to fix on us.

"I know you," he said, indicating me with his hand.

"I know you do. I'm Vega."

I pulled him to his feet. "We must hurry, the Maladons are coming."

I looked around at the others. "And now we have to get out of here."

The Maladons were almost upon us.

The magical tethers came out and attached themselves to each Wug and to Jason. I said to everyone, "I'm taking you to a place of safety."

"Wormwood?" said Roman Picus.

"No, my home."

"But Wormwood *is* your home," said Picus.

"Not anymore," I replied.

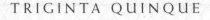

Reunited, Twice

AS WE ALL landed on the front steps of Empyrean, it suddenly occurred to me the enormity of what was about to happen.

Uma and Jason were about to be together again for the first time in hundreds of years. And on top of that, Uma was dead.

And Delph was going to be reunited with his father.

We went inside. I had a supportive arm around Jason because he was still very weak.

John followed us in. Along with all the others. I had sent a wand wire ahead to my mother, telling her that we would be bringing many people with us.

As soon as we stepped foot inside, Pillsbury came hurtling into the hall, his metal arms raised in an aggressive posture.

"Pillsbury, it's me."

But he wasn't looking at me. He was looking directly at Jason.

"Maladon. He's a bloody Maladon!"

You idiot, Vega, I thought. This hadn't even occurred to me.

Alerted by Pillsbury's shout, everyone came rushing into the front hall.

An array of wands was pointed at Jason.

All the Wugs jumped back, probably believing I had led them into a trap of gigantic proportion.

I put myself between them and the others.

"No," I shouted. "He's a friend. He saved my life. This . . . this is Jason — Pillsbury, don't you recognize him?"

Pillsbury dropped his hand and stiffened, well, as much as someone who was metal could "stiffen" even more. He took a step forward and peered more closely.

"J-Jason," he stammered.

Jason looked up at Pillsbury.

"Pillsbury? Is that you? Under all that armor?"

Mrs. Jolly toddled into the room and shrieked, "Jason?!"

"That's Mrs. Jolly," I said to Jason. "The household staff was enchanted during the war."

Jason slowly nodded. "I see."

But then his gaze fixed on something and he went rigid.

I saw where he was looking.

Uma had just floated into the room.

The look on her face was like nothing I had beheld before. It was a mixture of so many emotions that it was impossible to say which was dominant.

Uma drew close to us, and I watched as the tears started to stream down Jason's cheeks. He let go of my arm and reached out to her. I knew it would pass right through hers.

And then I was astonished when it didn't.

Their hands gripped each other's.

"But that's impossible," I said under my breath.

"No, it's not."

I looked around to where Astrea was standing.

"What?" I said. "But Uma is dead. That's just her spirit."

"That is what love can do, Vega. It can conquer all sorts of barriers, physical and otherwise."

"But . . . but she can't come back to life, can she?"

"Sadly, no. But they can hold hands. For now."

That last bit sounded ominous, but I said nothing in reply.

I could not even imagine what was going through their minds right now.

"Why don't you two go off somewhere private," I said. "I know you have a lot to talk about."

They slowly went off together, a man who was over eight hundred years old but still looked young, and his love, who was dead. I had to shake my head at the complete uniqueness of their situation. I had no idea what they would talk about, or ultimately what would happen to them.

And then Delph rushed into the room, with Petra close behind.

"Son!"

Delph stopped dead and turned to his right, where all the Wugs were crowded against the wall.

Duf slowly came forward on his timbertoes.

"D-Dad?"

I ran over and grabbed his arm. "Delph, they weren't dead. None of them. We . . . we rescued them from Maladon Castle."

I don't know if Delph even heard me. He stumbled forward, and he and his father met in the middle of the Great Hall, collapsing into each other's arms.

Petra hurried over to me.

"Vega, what happened?"

I quickly explained what we had done.

She put a hand on my shoulder. "Brilliant stuff, Vega. Absolutely brilliant."

My spirits soared because praise from Petra was never frequent and rarely effusive.

We had dinner in the dining room that night. John and I sat with our mother and father, who was looking much healthier than he had before.

We all ate heartily, and I sensed that the mood at Empyrean was far brighter. It might have simply been that we had successfully brought my father back. Or that John and I had made a brilliant raid on the Maladons and snatched from them an immensely valuable prisoner in Jason. *And* rescued all my fellow Wugs from their torture.

My parents, Delph, John and I spent time going around to all the Wugs, shaking hands and exchanging hugs, swapping stories and just catching up after all this time.

Domitar couldn't stop shaking my hand. "I always expected great things from you, Vega."

I wasn't sure he was telling the truth, but I took his comment at face value.

Dis Fidus, who had also worked at Stacks, sat down next to me after many of the others had gone off to their beds. It was an amazing aspect of Empyrean that no matter how many people I delivered to it, the place seemed to swell and add new rooms as needed.

Dis Fidus stared up at me with his ancient, wrinkled face. He had long been the oldest Wug in Wormwood and a kind and gentle soul.

"What happened to the other Wugs?" I asked. "There were assuredly more than this when I left?"

"The beasts from the Quag became much more aggressive, Vega. They came into the village with far more frequency. And many Wugs were killed."

"The Wall didn't prevent them?"

"The Wall turned out to be a pipe dream. It was never finished, for one. And then it quickly fell into disrepair. Guards placed on the towers were attacked by the beasts so regularly that no one wanted the job. Then Morrigone became more and more withdrawn, until she was rarely seen."

"And Thansius?"

"He did what he could, but the problems we faced were beyond any single Wug. The soil turned bad and crops failed. The water turned brackish. Stacks stopped employing Wugs. Domitar and I lost our jobs. Council grew increasingly erratic. Wugs were demanding things that no one could give. Some Wugs, including Jurik Krone and those like-minded, ventured into the Quag with their mortas and were never seen again." He sighed heavily. "It has been a trying time indeed."

I patted his hand. "But now you're here. And safe."

"I see your brother is now with you," said Dis Fidus slowly.

"Yes, we found each other."

Dis Fidus nodded but said nothing.

"Was John a help to all of you? I expected to hear that he was running Council." I said this last part in jest. Well, maybe not so much.

Dis Fidus did not answer right away. "I'm too old to beat around the hedges," he said. "So I'll come right to it. Your brother is magical no doubt, just as you are. Just as your whole family is. I have known that, Vega, since you were in pigtails and half as tall as you are now."

"All right," I said a bit apprehensively.

"The fact of the matter is, I often wondered on which side your brother would eventually fall."

"What do you mean?"

He looked at me. "Why do I think you know the answer to that query?"

"Are you saying my brother did bad things?"

"I'm saying your brother used his powers to hurt other Wugs. I'm saying he used his powers to make other Wugs do his bidding."

"Who did he do these things to?" I demanded.

"That is of no importance. But I will tell you that two of them were never right in the head after. They wandered off into the Quag and the beasts got them."

This shook me to my core, but I refocused. "He . . . had no one to guide him in the use of his powers. I . . . I thought Morrigone would do that."

"Morrigone! She was but a faded image of herself. She couldn't help herself, much less teach your brother."

I thought back to Astrea's cottage, when we had seen Morrigone looking a shell of herself.

"What happened to her?" I asked.

"All I can tell you is that the longer she was around your brother, the worse she became."

"Dis Fidus, what are you saying?" I snapped.

He looked at me, undeterred by the ferocity of my words. "I think my words are clear enough. I thank you with all my heart for rescuing us, Vega. But that does not change what I saw your brother do in Wormwood. Nothing can. Now, if you'll excuse me, I am very tired."

He rose and left me.

I could only stare helplessly after him.

After the meal, I was heading back to my room when they approached.

It was Jason and Uma. They were holding hands and looking immensely happy. My heart soared for them. It really did. It was a nice feeling to have and it helped me forget, or at least not focus on my brother for a bit.

I mean, there should be some unconditional love in this bloody world.

Uma said, "Vega, can we speak with you? In private?"

I led them into my bedroom and closed the door. Harry Two was on my bed asleep.

I turned to Uma and Jason and said, "You both look very happy."

Uma gazed adoringly at Jason. "I never thought this would happen. We don't know how to thank you, Vega."

I smiled. "I'm just glad it turned out as it did. But if Astrea hadn't told me the incantation to use, I couldn't have freed Jason or the others." I turned to him and said, "Why did your father imprison you and then seek to take your magic?"

"It was because of Uma."

"How could that be?"

"I saw her, in a vision."

I looked at him as though he were batty.

"You saw Uma, in a vision? Where? Surely not here?"

"I was in my chambers in the castle. I was about to go to sleep when I looked up and there she was, floating at the top of the ceiling. She beckoned to me, called out my name. My thoughts instantly cleared. I was no longer this awful Endemen. I was myself."

I turned to Uma. "So you went to the castle even when I told you not to?"

She shook her head. "No, Vega, I did not."

Puzzled, I turned back to Jason. "What happened then?"

"I called out to her, told her I loved her. The next moment, Uma vanished. A minute later my father walked in. He said, 'So you love Uma once more, Jason?'"

"Do you mean he was watching you?"

"No, he was the one who *conjured* the image of a fake Uma. To test me. And, in his eyes, I failed that test."

"You're sure it was he who had done it?"

"He told me himself. He was very proud of his deception," he added bitterly.

"That's when he locked you up?"

Jason nodded. "After you came to the tower room and I fought Necro to help you escape, he had me placed in the mirror. I was almost finished, I could feel that. And then you came along to save me."

He put a hand on my shoulder and directed those beautiful eyes of his to mine. "I owe you my life, Vega. I owe you everything. And I'm sorry for having fought you for so long as Mr. Endemen."

"You couldn't help it, Jason. Like you said, you weren't in your right mind. Now, what can you tell me about Necro's plans? I know something significant is in the making."

"That's true, but I don't know what it is."

"He must know that there are more Maladons than there are of us."

"Yes, but he also knows it's not a simple matter of numbers. He will not underestimate you, Vega. And you must not him. He is incredibly resourceful. He sits on his terrible throne and thinks deeply of things."

"I have no intention of underestimating him." I looked between him and Uma. "What are your plans?"

Jason shot Uma a glance, and she nodded.

Jason said, "I have been kept alive solely by magic."

"The Elixir of Life?" I said.

"Well, at least my father's version of it. Now that I have broken with him, the end cannot be far off. And I could be with Uma."

"I understand."

"No, I don't think that you do, Vega."

I stared at him.

He gripped Uma's hand. "We have discussed this. I am going to fight with you against my father."

"I am thrilled," I said. "We can always use another wand, particularly from so powerful a sorcerer. But are you sure that's what you want?" I looked between them.

Uma answered for them. "We are very sure, Vega."

I nodded. "Then I thank you with all my heart. But now I believe that there is one thing you need to do."

He looked at me curiously. "What is that?"

"I'd rather show you, Jason. If you will trust me."

"I do trust you."

I held out my hand to him.

WE PASSED THROUGH the gates and immediately entered the mists of time.

"Where are we, Vega," Jason said as he followed me over uneven ground.

"Normally, I could tell you that we were back in time. But that's not the case now. Nor are we in the future. Those are the usual choices when you pass through Eon's gates. But where we're going now is a third option I didn't realize existed: the present." I added, "A very special present."

Jason looked bewildered, but simply nodded.

"Take my hand," I said.

He did so, and we lifted off from the ground. With the power that the chain of Destin gave me, we sailed higher and higher until we alighted on the same tall mountain, next to the singularly tall tree where Alice Adronis had received her wand.

And next to the tree was the small cottage that I had already visited. I thought now that it was a humble place for even a *near* goddess to reside. But perhaps it was fitting, for a near goddess in eternal bereavement. What would a grand home mean to such a being?

We approached, and I knocked on the door. It opened of its own accord, and I was prepared to see the image of Necro, as last time. I was about to warn Jason of this, but there was no need.

The false Necro was not there.

But she was. She wore the same pale blue gown as before. She was seated in the same plain chair.

Elythia saw me first, and I saw her mouth curl in displeasure. She no doubt thought I was back requesting additional help that she would refuse.

But then she saw who was with me.

I saw the curl of displeasure give way to an expression of sheer astonishment.

She slowly rose, her features trembling, her limbs quivering.

"Jason?"

He was as astonished as his mother.

He stumbled forward. They met in the middle of the small room.

Their embrace was spontaneous. I saw Elythia's fingers curl into her son's back.

And when I looked at her face over Jason's shoulder, I saw what I expected to see.

Even with an almost goddess.

Tears. Tears of a mother finally reunited with a son she thought gone from her forever.

I went outside to give them some sense of privacy.

A great deal of time passed.

"Vega?"

At the sound of my name, I snapped my head around to see them both standing in the doorway of the cottage looking at me, their hands clasped together.

Elythia said, "Jason has explained all. You have given me back my son."

"I was glad to be able to do it."

Jason smiled at me and said, "I have told my mother of my plans with Uma. After I help you defeat Necro."

She looked at me. "Jason also told me that it was your idea that he come here."

"I thought it was the right thing to do," I said. "You're his mother. You deserved that. It allowed you to . . ."

"To cry?" she finished for me, wiping at her eyes. "People do not expect beings like me to have emotions. I am not a pure goddess, so what is inside of me, in essential elements, is what is inside all of you."

"But now it is your time to be with your son," I said. "And I'll wait here. For as long as you need."

Much time went by, but it didn't matter, I knew, because when we returned to Empyrean, only seconds would have passed. That was just how things worked beyond the gates.

When Jason finally came out of the cottage, his mother was with him. She kissed him on the forehead and then took my hand in hers and led us away from Jason.

There was such warmth, such ethereal power, in her grip, that it took my breath away.

We stopped near the edge of some trees, and she turned to face me.

"I will never forget this act of kindness, Vega. Never."

I wanted to ask her to use her powers to vanquish the Maladons. She could do it, easily, I believed. I looked at her, and she looked at me. And then she glanced toward her son with an expression that made me curious.

"I know what you wish to ask, Vega. And I am sorry that I cannot fulfill that request. Not even now, after you have freed my son." She pulled something from her robe. It was a small package. "But take this and do with it what you need to do."

I was so angry and bitter that I accepted the package without opening it.

As we flew away, Jason and I looked back once at Elythia. She stood there, on the tallest mountain I had ever seen, her gaze directly on us. She raised her hand in silent good-bye.

And then she was gone.

As we passed back through the gates, I looked at Jason.

"I'm sorry you didn't have more time with her."

"It was time enough, to say what needed to be said" was his reply.

We flew on back to Empyrean.

Even without Elythia's assistance, I felt a sense of hope that I had not experienced in a long time.

Unfortunately for all of us, it would not last.

A Memory from Metal

WHEN WE GOT back to Empyrean, I explained to Astrea what Jason wanted to do. She provided him with some of her Elixir of Life.

"I'm glad that you want to fight, Jason," said Astrea. "We will need as many wands as we can get to have a chance."

"Speaking of," I said as I handed Jason a new wand.

As he gripped it, he said, "From where did this come?"

"It was in a package that your mother gave me before we left her."

I could see Jason's focus intensify. "Then I will not let her down."

I turned to Astrea. "And I have some good news for you. Necro has a hundred fewer fighters."

I explained to her how I had accomplished this.

I had only rarely shocked Astrea Prine. This was one of those times.

"A hundred Maladons!" she exclaimed. "Not even Alice ever managed to topple a hundred Maladons in one fell swoop."

"Well, if she'd had the chance I did, she probably would have toppled at least two hundred of the foul creatures. I plan to tell the others. I hope it will lift their spirits."

"It has surely lifted mine, Vega."

DINNER THAT NIGHT was a raucous affair.

The Wugs were amazed at the opulence of Empyrean, and my fellow magicals were gracious and friendly hosts.

As my eyes strayed over so many familiar faces from my past, I somehow felt heartened. When I told the others of the one hundred vanquished Maladons, a cheer ran around the cavernous room. Mrs. Jolly and her team had a right time of it delivering the food, but they made an excellent effort, and the meal was enjoyed by all.

The only ones absent were Jason and Uma. Uma didn't eat of course, and Jason had had his meal delivered to his room, where, no doubt, he was with Uma.

I caught Thansius in deep conversation with my parents. When they caught me watching, they quickly changed expressions and smiled before returning to whatever it was they were discussing.

I frowned, for I thought their clandestine behavior was certainly strange under the circumstances.

After dinner that night, my mother approached and asked to talk in private. She led my father and me to the library and shut the door. With a flick of my wand I created flames in the fireplace, for dear old Empyrean could be nastily drafty.

We sat in chairs around the fire while I looked expectantly at my mother.

"What do you plan to do with all the Wugs?" she asked.

"I have given that some thought. They need to be taken to a place of safety. I was actually thinking of Jasper Jane's castle in the Quag. And then —"

I stopped speaking because my parents were shaking their heads.

"What?" I said. "And what were you talking to Thansius about at dinner? You were all acting very odd."

As if on cue, the door opened and there was Thansius. And behind him . . . was the spirit of Morrigone. This was the first time she had ventured to the main level, at least that I knew of.

I said, "Thansius, Morrigone? What are you doing here?"

"They came at our invitation," said my mother, though I could tell by the way she avoided looking at Morrigone that she was not pleased with her presence. And I was not surprised by this. After all, Morrigone had cursed her and my father.

"Your invitation?" I said. "Can someone please tell me what's going on?"

"Vega believes that the Wugs will be safer away from the war with the Maladons," said my father.

Thansius shook his broad head. I then noticed there was an immaculate silver sword hanging from a leather belt around his waist. I believed I recognized it from a collection of weapons hanging on a wall of Empyrean.

"We will not leave the field of battle," said Thansius. "We will stay here and fight."

I rose from my seat. "But the Maladons are sorcerers, Thansius."

"It matters not to me what they are. So long as they can be killed, I will be happy to accommodate them."

"You saw what they did to Wormwood. What they did to all of you."

"They caught us completely by surprise. This time they won't."

"It would be a slaughter," I said. "I can't allow you to make that sort of sacrifice."

"You saved us, Vega," he persisted. "And I hope you did not save us to watch us flee the battle that you will have to fight, because that is not in my nature."

"I didn't save you only to see you die unnecessarily at the hands of the Maladons."

"It would not be unnecessary."

This came from Morrigone. We all turned our attention to her wispy form.

"I was the only Wug the Maladons killed," she said. "I thought us all dead, but now I know that the Maladons took the other Wugs to torture them for eternity. Why did they do this?"

When she didn't respond to her own query, I said, "Well, why do you think?"

"Because they have nothing but contempt for those not magical like themselves. I've been told of what they have done to such people in the towns and countryside. It is wicked."

"But that doesn't mean Wugs have to fight them."

"We are not merely Wugs," said Thansius. "We are not magical, it is true. Just like those of which Morrigone just spoke." He drew himself up to his full and considerable height. "They destroyed our homes. They blackened our village. They tortured us beyond all reckoning. And I, for one, want to show them that though we may not have wands and incantations at our disposal" — he drew the sword and held it up in one massive hand — "that does not mean we cannot fight. I once led you, Vega. Now I ask you to lead me and the other Wugs to victory against the Maladons."

I sat back down, both humbled and stunned by his words.

"I will be honored to lead you and my fellow Wugs, Thansius," I said. "I truly would."

"Now," said my mother, "there is one other way we can augment our forces."

"How?" I asked warily. I felt like there was this grand conspiracy operating here that I was both irritated and intrigued by.

"While we were out there," she said, with a wave of her hand toward the window, "we met certain people."

"Who?" I asked.

"Villagers. There was one young man named Russell Everett."

I sat up straighter. "Russell! I met him before. The woman he was going to marry, Daphne, was killed."

I didn't mention that she had been killed by Endemen, meaning Jason.

"Russell told me about you. What you had done, warning him and the other villagers about the Maladons. He said he told you that they would be ready to fight with you against the Maladons."

"He *did* tell me that. I just don't know what they can do to help."

"You might want to talk to him about that, Vega."

"Where is he?"

"I can take you to him."

I thought about this but decided not to commit to a decision just yet. My problem was I didn't want to waste time and resources on something that would not end up helping our cause. I wanted to save the villagers. I wanted to save everyone from the Maladons. But my small army and I had to survive in order to do that. And though I had told Thansius I was honored to lead him and the Wugs into battle, I thought they would be more a burden than a help. I didn't want to commit to adding still other nonmagicals to the equation. I needed wands, not bloody pitchforks!

"I will let you have my answer soon," I said, and left them there to find my brother.

He was up in Jasper Jane's old laboratory going through our ancestor's old books.

He glanced over at me when I walked in.

"What are you doing?" I asked.

"Reading" was his simple reply.

"Yes, I quite get that. I mean, what are you reading?"

He held up the book.

"A History of All?" I read off.

"It talks about our kind and the Maladons," said John. "It delves into our differences, how we came to be like we are. I mean, it seems that we all started out quite the same, but then something happened."

"Right. The Maladons became evil and we didn't."

"I'm not sure it's quite that simple, Vega."

I took a seat next to him. "Then why don't you explain it to me."

"Did you know that before Necro came along, there weren't really two divided groups? I mean, they weren't even known as the Maladons. That was Necro's name for his following."

"I know. It means 'terrible death.' As if any death could be good."

"But if things were okay until Necro came along, and this book points out that Necro himself was relatively normal until he was grown, then something must have happened to change all that."

"Okay, let's say that I accept your argument. What do you think changed?"

"Power."

"What?"

"Power changes people, Vega. Necro was married to Elythia, a supremely powerful goddess. Much more than simply a sorceress."

"Well, she's not a full goddess," I corrected him. "But she's still incredibly powerful."

"How do you know this?"

"She told me herself."

"What else did she tell you?"

"That her mother was a goddess, but her father wasn't. Because of that, they were shunned. That was why she came to live with our kind. She met Necro and married him. It was really the same thing her mother did actually. Marrying someone who was not a god."

"Do you know what became of Elythia's mother's husband?"

"No. I don't."

"As a goddess, whatever mystic powers and auras and blood that runs through her veins is incompatible with what runs through ours."

"So, are you saying that simply being around Elythia made Necro evil? I've been around Elythia and I felt no evil compulsion."

"But you didn't fall in love with her, Vega. Necro did. Or else he fell in love with the idea that by marrying Elythia, he would himself become a god. At least that's what this book suggests."

"This is simply extraordinary, John. Do you mean to tell me that all of that is contained in that book? If so, why hasn't anyone told me about it? Astrea? Or Alice or someone like that?"

"Well, maybe because the book was only written about ten years ago. It says so on the first page."

"Ten years! But Empyrean has been abandoned for over eight hundred years. Who could have written the book only ten years ago?"

"There is no mention of the author's name in the book. But it is handwritten."

"But again, that's impossible, because there was no one here to write it ten years ago."

"That is not true, Mistress Vega. *I* was here. And I wrote that book."

I turned to stare at the figure that had appeared in the doorway.

It was Pillsbury.

The Ledger Falls

Y OU WROTE THAT book, Pillsbury!" I exclaimed.

My metal butler came into the room, his visored face staring at the floor planks.

"Yes, Mistress Vega. I did."

"But how? Why?"

"I had much time on my hands, as you know. With little enough to do. After the last of your kind left us enchanted, years and then centuries went by. And it occurred to me that perhaps no one would be coming back for us. Thus, about a dozen years ago, I took it upon myself to sit down and try to make sense out of what had happened."

"But, Pillsbury, what would you use as a basis for writing this book? A history of our kind."

"You forget that I worked at Empyrean for many years. I saw and attended everyone who came through those front doors. I saw them all, including Necro and many Maladons. I saw them in good times and bad. I overheard things. I observed things that many did not. And I have thought about all those things in the intervening years, putting them in context and sorting through them and putting them in their proper place in the grand scheme of things. Then I decided to chronicle those recollections, observations and conclusions." He pointed to the book. "And so, I wrote that."

"But why didn't you tell me?"

Pillsbury shook his visor. "I don't know, Mistress Vega. The conclusions in that book are my opinions only. I have no idea if they are correct or not."

John stirred and said, "They are very well thought out. If they aren't true, then the actual truth must be equally complicated."

John handed me the book. "You might want to read this," he said.

I took the book and idly thumbed through the pages before looking up at Pillsbury.

"Do you really believe what you wrote in here?" I asked.

"I do, Mistress Vega. For what that's worth."

"Well, to me, that's worth a lot."

TWO DAYS PASSED and the only thing I really did was read Pillsbury's book. There was much revealed in it. But though some of it struck me as unlikely, I had to admit that most of what I read seemed more than plausible. In fact, I thought it must be exactly what had happened.

Necro was a man ready to pivot to the evil side. When he married a being with far greater power than he possessed, this predilection to the dark side was immeasurably strengthened. It was shortly thereafter that Necro took his irreversible path to his evil ways. The Maladons were born, and the lives of our kind were inextricably caught up in this madman's thirst for absolute power and domination.

And all perhaps because of Necro wedding a near goddess.

I could only shake my head. I guess it was a good thing he hadn't wed a full-blooded goddess. Perhaps he would have been even more evil, I supposed, though that was hard to imagine.

301

I placed no blame on this with Elythia. It was Necro's weaknesses and desire for power over others that had made him become what he had. Elythia had simply fallen in love. It was Necro who had perverted that love into something hideous.

I went to the lowest depths of the castle to speak with Alice.

I found Alice in her typical state of scowling unrest.

I held up the book. "Any chance you read this over the last few years?"

She shook her head. "What is it?"

"Maybe an explanation for how Necro and the Maladons came to be."

"I don't understand."

I gave her a brief overview of what was in the book.

"And it was really written by Pillsbury?" she asked.

"Well, he was able to observe a lot and he certainly has had the time to think about it."

"I never thought Pillsbury focused on such things."

"I think he was trying to work out what had happened. I mean, he and the others were left alone for so long. They had to do something with their time."

Alice looked chastened by my observations. "I must admit, Vega, that I have never given much thought to those left behind at Empyrean. After I fell in battle and came back here, I have never once interacted with Pillsbury or the others."

"Well, like you said, you had died in battle. I'm sure you had a lot going on as well."

She shook her head. "There should never be enough 'going on' that we forget about the needs of others. That, essentially, is the essence of goodness."

"I think you're right about that."

"I knew Elythia, and liked her," said Alice surprisingly. "I often wondered why she ever came to be with a man like Necro."

"I think it was the worst of all possible outcomes," I said.

"What do you mean?"

"Elythia is tremendously powerful. Unfortunately, in Necro, she found someone uniquely suited to co-opting that power and using it for his own benefit. It's almost as if Elythia's nearly unlimited supply of power fueled Necro's already-innate desire to dominate and pushed it to incredibly high levels, far higher than they would have been had he not met Elythia."

"No one should be blamed for simply wanting the love and respect of another, Vega."

"I do not blame Elythia," I said. "I only look to Necro for that." But I suspected Alice was reliving the moment when her father had refused her a wand and with it his love *and* his respect.

I left her there and ascended to the main floor of Empyrean. I mulled over how Pillsbury's writings could possibly aid us in our fight with the Maladons. I wasn't sure it could, but I was at a point where I would seek out every advantage.

As I passed John's room, I heard raised voices and stuck my head in to see what was going on.

John was sitting in a chair and hovering in front of him was . . . Morrigone.

They appeared to be arguing.

"What is going on?" I asked, coming fully into the room.

They both looked at me. Morrigone seemed upset, John confused.

I walked over to them. "Why are you arguing?"

Morrigone said, "We're not arguing. We're having a *discussion*."

"Well, it's quite a *loud* discussion."

I looked at my brother. "John?"

"We were . . . we were talking about my last night in Wormwood."

"What about it?"

Morrigone said, "This is really between John and me, Vega."

I did not like her tone and decided to let her know it.

"John is my brother. Anything having to do with him also has to do with me."

Morrigone glared at me, but John said, "I was discussing with Morrigone her decision to let me go right before the Maladons showed up."

"I didn't *let* you go, John," admonished Morrigone. "You were no longer living with me at the time."

"But you tried to stop me," I said. "Before helping me to escape."

"And I explained my motivations to you," snapped Morrigone.

"And you also said that you didn't know my brother's fate. You said you didn't know for certain if he had left Wormwood."

"Because I *didn't* know."

"So why the loud discussion, then? Just about John leaving Wormwood? Why does it matter now?"

I looked at my brother, who was now studying his hands.

He said, "I was telling Morrigone that I wish I had been there to help fight them. To protect my fellow Wugs."

I was confused. "But why would that prompt an argument?"

I put my hand on top of his, and when I looked down, I gasped.

"John, your hand."

He looked down, and when he glanced up, the expression on his face was wonderful to behold. It was like my little brother was impishly beaming up at me as I walked him to the Learning.

The mark of the three hooks was as bold and legible on his hand as it was on mine.

Morrigone drifted over to see.

When I looked up at her, I could see a tear trickle down her cheek.

"John has made his decision." She looked up at me. "*That* was the reason for our loud discussion. I wanted him to know quite clearly the repercussions of that decision, particularly if it came out on the wrong side."

John said, "I have always known who I am. But I guess that I know better now." He paused and composed himself. "I think, in the end, it was seeing my fellow Wugs behind the glass. The pain they were in, how truly evil the Maladons were. I confess that I am curious about such things."

"As was your ancestor Jasper Jane," I pointed out.

John looked down at his wand. "And I have used my wand at times to explore those curiosities. I have done things that I'm now ashamed of. But . . . but I can never be like them. I . . . I truly don't want to harm others. It makes my heart hurt."

I hugged my brother. "Thank you, John. Because we need you. *I* need your help to win the war."

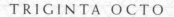

The Other Armies

L ET'S GO, DELPH."
I stared up at him after he opened his bedroom door.
"Go where?"

"True. And then Maladon Castle."

Harry Two followed along behind. I wanted him to come too.

It would be like old times, I thought. Me, Delph and Harry Two.

"Why go to True?" asked Delph.

"The Maladons are planning something. The bloke at Saint Necro's is a Maladon. I want to question him."

"But if you do, he'll just keel over. Like you said, Necro has cursed them."

"We have to try, Delph. We need information. And I don't think I'll find it at the castle. It will be too heavily fortified now after what we did there."

We stepped out of the front door of Empyrean. I magically tethered us together, after placing Harry Two in his harness. I incanted the *Pass-pusay* spell with my destination firmly in mind.

Seconds later, we were on the pavement in True.

We had been here so many times that we could easily find our way around. I released Harry Two from his harness and we set off. While it was dark, it wasn't terribly late, so there were some people on the streets.

We knew that the train carrying folks from the surrounding countryside would not be coming in until later, so we made our way to the church.

We found the little room where the loathsome Maladon's office was. There was a light on under the door.

I slipped out my wand and said the necessary incantation, and the door opened.

We took a step inside.

And froze.

The Maladon was indeed there.

And he was quite dead.

He was toppled forward at his desk. White spittle was around his mouth. And his neck had literally been slit from ear to ear. The blood had pooled on the desktop.

"Holy Steeples," exclaimed Delph.

I circled around to the other side of the dead Maladon and examined him more closely.

"He's gone back to his horrible self," I said, noting the vulture-like elongated features. "Maybe they all do when they die."

"But who killed him, Vega Jane?"

"Well, it wasn't by magic." I pointed to the jagged cut along his neck. "That was a knife, not a wand."

Delph nodded in agreement. "Didn't think it was possible."

"Delph, you've killed Maladons in battle before. With your hands and your ax."

"Right, Vega Jane. But not every nonmagical bloke is me."

"True enough," I said with a grin. Delph was enormously strong and a quite skilled fighter. "But somebody accomplished it."

"Like to thank the bloke who done it," noted Delph.

"But, Delph, the blood is hardly dried. This happened quite recently. Otherwise, someone would have found him by now."

"True enough."

Harry Two was scratching at the desk.

"What is it?" I asked my dog.

Harry Two jumped up, placed his two front paws on the desk and knocked a piece of paper to the floor.

I hurriedly picked it up and looked at it.

Now I knew who had done this.

I held out the paper to Delph.

He read, "This is for Daphne."

I said, "Russell did this. He must have found out this bloke was a Maladon. And he came here and killed him in revenge for them killing Daphne."

"And he might still be in True," pointed out Delph.

This put a whole new spin on things. Russell had promised that he and his fellow villagers would come to our aid in our war with the Maladons. I had never thought it a viable possibility, foremost because I didn't know what a nonmagical could do to someone with a wand. Well, now I knew. But I didn't want Necro to know what had happened, or else he might send his Maladons out to massacre every nonmagical in the countryside.

I tethered the dead Maladon to me and told Delph I would be back momentarily.

I said my incantation, and I was transported immediately to a dark wood outside of True. I buried the Maladon there and returned to stand next to Delph.

"Good thinking, Vega Jane," said Delph, after I told him what I'd done.

"Now we need to see if we can find Russell."

We left the church and began to walk down the streets of True, looking in all directions for anyone who resembled

Russell. It was difficult because most people were bundled up and, in appearance, Russell would look like many other men in True, at least from a distance.

We had covered about six streets when I put a restraining arm on Delph's shoulder.

"There."

He looked where I was pointing.

A man was walking along briskly. He was looking furtively in all directions to see if anyone was paying him mind.

I pointed my wand at him and said, *"Crystilado magnifica."*

His image swelled huge in front of us.

It was Russell. He had aged badly since I had last seen him. But I could understand that. He was fighting his own war, as was I. I also saw a knife partially hidden in his hand.

"Come on," I whispered to Delph and Harry Two.

We hurried across the street and soon caught up with Russell.

I waited until he turned the corner and entered a deserted avenue.

"Russell?" I hissed.

He jumped nearly three feet in the air, whirled around and brandished his bloody knife.

"Who's there? Show yourself, damn you."

I twisted my ring around and the three of us instantly appeared in front of him.

"Vega!" he exclaimed in relief.

"I have excellent hearing, Russell, so please keep your voice low."

I threw out a tether that attached to his arm. I turned my ring back around, and all of us vanished inside its embrace.

"Bloody Hel," said Russell. "What are you doing here?"

309

"Well, I didn't come looking for you, but I'm glad to have found you."

"What *did* you come looking for?"

"Maladons. And I found one back at the church." I glanced down at his knife. "As did you. You finished him off, didn't you?"

He slowly nodded. "Snuck up on the git and sent him on his way."

"How did you even know he was a Maladon?" Delph asked.

"I've been busy since last we met. I've put together a group of folks who lost people the way I lost Daphne. We've fanned out across the countryside, come to the other villages, towns and places like True. We observe everything and report back. We've built up a lot of information. One of my blokes saw the git from the church turn into his real self. What the Maladons really look like."

"How did you know about that?"

"Like I said, we listen. We watch. When you do that, good things happen."

"Look, Russell, are you and your lot still ready to fight with us?"

"I told you I would, and I stand by what I said. I have to admit, we've lost quite a few in the fight. But when we die, we take some of them bloody fiends with us."

"Where are your forces located?"

"I can take you there."

"Please do," I said.

We flew for well over an hour until we reached a place that was both isolated and covered with difficult mountainous terrain.

I followed Russell's direction and alighted in a valley.

310

"Let me call out," said Russell. "I have sentries posted."

He cupped his hands to his mouth and made an odd sound. A few seconds later a similar sound reached our ears.

"We'll need to show ourselves," said Russell.

I turned my ring around, and we all became visible. We followed Russell, who was striding quickly into a glen of trees.

As soon as we entered the canopies, we were surrounded by men holding bows and arrows and spears, while some hefted axes. They all looked strong, battle-hardened and resolute.

Russell said, "It's me. They're friends. Keep to your posts."

We walked single file through the dense trees until we emerged into a clearing that was as long and broad as the pitch back in Wormwood.

Here we could see an encampment, with tents, pots cooking over open fires, people talking in small groups and children huddled together and looking anxious.

Everyone seemed on edge, and all eyes turned to us as we entered the clearing.

All the adults grabbed weapons, but when they saw Russell, their tension disappeared.

Russell motioned for all to gather around.

"Vega is the leader of the magical opposition against the Maladons. She saved my life and the lives of my village. We can trust her. I told her long ago that I would fight alongside her if she ever asked. Well, she has come here to ask. And I put that question to all of you. Will you fight with me and Vega?"

No one said anything, but slowly, one by one, the men raised their weapons. I saw, to my great delight, that many of the women did the same thing.

Russell turned to me. "There's your answer."

I nodded and said to the crowd, "Thank you. Together, I know that we can be victorious." I said in a lower voice to Russell, "I'll be back soon to go over specifics."

He nodded. "Until then."

I tethered Delph and Harry Two to me and lifted my dog into his harness, and we set off.

As we flew along, I glanced at Delph, who was staring at me.

"What?"

"Just thinking."

"About what?"

"Seeing me dad."

I grinned. "I know, Delph, that was wonderful."

"Have you to thank for it. Have you to thank for just about everything."

"There's plenty of credit to go around."

His next words stunned me.

"If I don't make it through, Vega Jane, can you, will you, take care of my dad?"

I very nearly tumbled out of the sky at his words. As it was, I felt a chill run through my entire body.

"Delph, you're going to make it through."

He shook his head. "You don't know that. Nobody does."

"You're right. So, if I don't make it through, can you help take care of my family?"

He reached out his hand and touched my shoulder. "Would be my honor. But you're going to make it, Vega Jane."

"But you just said —"

He touched his chest. "I feel it here. You're going to make it, and that's as it should be."

We flew along in silence. Many thoughts were rushing through my head.

Chief among them was trying to come to terms with a life that did not include Delph.

THE NEXT TWO weeks were filled with preparations for the showdown to come. I had sent teams out to spy on the Maladons and to visit True and Greater True. They all came back with the same conclusion.

Something was going to happen. And it was going to happen soon.

I had told my parents of my finding the dead Maladon in True and the role Russell had played in it.

"They are standing by to help us," I said. "I thought that would please you since it was your idea."

"It does please us, Vega, but it does not guarantee victory," said my mother.

"Only *we* can do that," I said.

Delph was putting the Wugs through their paces. They had wanted to fight and so they needed training up. Thansius was still a formidable warrior, but many of the others left a lot to be desired. I remembered training with Delph for the Duelum. I had made progress under his tutelage, but I wasn't sure about this lot.

Roman Picus was okay as a brawler, but the soft Domitar and the ancient Dis Fidus were hopeless. As were many of the others. Most of the women were not adept at the brutality of physical combat. However, there were several who showed quite a penchant for getting in their licks in clever ways.

Still, watching them falling down, crashing into one another and sometimes simply weeping did not leave me too confident. And I wasn't talking just about the women. Yet Delph was patient and dutifully kept at it. However, he would throw me glances that showed me he was worried too.

Astrea joined us one day and watched along with me.

"It's not a pretty sight," she said.

"No, it's not. But they want to fight. I just don't want them to be needlessly slaughtered. Russell's people *have* been fighting. I've seen them. They're hardened and capable. But this lot?"

"Let me work on it, Vega," Astrea said.

I glanced at her. "Work on it how?"

"Just leave it to me," she said mysteriously, and then walked off.

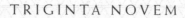

The Worst of Times

ANOTHER WEEK PASSED. Whatever Astrea was going to do with the Wugs was not readily apparent to me. Delph continued to train them diligently, and to my great surprise, I saw marked improvement in many of them.

Cletus Loon saw me watching and came over.

Out of long habit, I expected to hear insults sprout from his mouth. But they didn't.

"I just wanted to thank you, Vega, for all you've done for us. Getting us out of them glasses. And putting us up here. Never ate so good, well, since Ma died."

I had loathed Loon's father, but I had admired his mother. She had always been quite kind to me.

"What happened to your parents?" I asked.

"Garm got Dad one night. Mum got the sick, and then she died too."

"What did you do then? Where did you live?"

"Thansius got Ezekiel to take me in. I helped out with taking care of Steeples and all. It weren't so very bad. Lots of folks died since you left, Vega. Beast, the sick. Crops weren't coming in. Not enough food and such. No work to do."

"I heard some tried their luck in the Quag."

He nodded. "And were never seen again."

A question suddenly struck me, and I couldn't believe I hadn't asked it before. Perhaps I didn't want to know the answer.

"What happened when the Maladons came?"

Loon paled. "The sky turned real dark. Thought a storm was coming. But then the sky was filled with these . . . flying blokes. They landed and came at us. Most of the Wugs gathered in the square. We were ready to fight 'em. Some were calling 'em Outliers, you know like we were warned about by Morrigone."

I well remembered this lie. "Go on."

"They had wands like you got. Next thing I knew, I was behind glass."

"I know it was painful."

"Hurt even worse than when you hit me in the Duelum."

He grinned. I didn't smile back. He was an ally of mine now, but we would never be friends.

"We need to beat them, Loon," I said. "So, get back there and keep working."

In another part of the castle, Jason was honing his dueling skills with Petra while Uma watched.

Endemen had been a superb fighter and, of course, so was Jason. I smiled as I watched him easily block Petra's spell attempts. His would be a very welcome wand in the fight.

As I was leaving I thought I saw Alice watching from a far corner of the room. However, when I drew closer, there was no one there. I might have imagined it.

Perhaps.

That night after dinner, Delph, Harry Two and I visited True. I wanted to see if another Maladon had replaced the one Russell had killed. If so, I would try and get some more information from him. I wasn't particularly optimistic about it, since it seemed that Necro had hexed all his men to instantly die rather than reveal vital information about his plans.

However, the church of Saint Necro was empty. So, we next traveled to meet with Russell at his hiding place.

Around a small campfire, we sat and discussed tactics and strategies.

"The Maladons still outnumber us," I said. "If we are to beat them, we need to inflict maximum damage on them with limited losses on our side."

"How do we do that?" Russell wanted to know.

"We attack in small, concentrated forces that strike and then retreat while another force takes up the fight against another part of Necro's army. Divide and conquer."

"Blimey," said Delph. "Where did you learn that, Vega Jane?"

"How do you know I didn't just come up with it on my own?" I shot back.

Delph looked embarrassed and said, "Vega Jane, I didn't mean that. I —"

I smiled and cut him off. "I read it in a book on battle tactics I found at Empyrean."

I felt my smile widen. My spirits hadn't been this high in a while.

We landed back at Empyrean a bit later.

And that's when my life changed forever.

THE DOOR TO Empyrean was knocked clean off its hinges.

Inside, all we could hear was screaming and the sounds of spells smashing into things, and people.

The whole house was ablaze, as smoke poured from multiple points.

I stood there frozen, but only for an instant.

Then I released Harry Two from his harness, but not his tether. We all three raced through the opening. My wand was drawn and ready. Delph hefted his ax. Harry Two's fangs were bared, and his hackles had shot straight to the sky.

The Great Hall was absolute pandemonium.

Three Maladons lay dead by the stairs.

With a sickening feeling in my belly, I saw that next to them were the bodies of Anna Dibble and Clive Pippen.

A spell shot past my ear and I wheeled around and blasted a Maladon off the second-story balcony.

"Delph," I screamed. "To your right."

He let his ax fly and I watched it cleave a Maladon nearly in two.

Harry Two raced forward, leapt and grabbed a Maladon by the throat, ripping it out and leaving the stricken Maladon to topple over dead, with the blood running down the front of his cloak as my dog went in search of more prey.

Something flew past me, and I turned to see Dimitri, the hyperbore, seize a Maladon in his arms and lift him straight up in the air. He pinned the Maladon's wand hand to his side and watched with grim satisfaction as Dimitri's powerful arms broke his quarry's neck neatly in two. He let the Maladon fall, where he crashed to the floor on top of two of his brethren.

A bolt of light hit Dimitri directly in the chest.

He banked to the left and fell straight down to the floor.

His wings lifted once, feebly, and then he lay still, in death.

I killed the Maladon who had shot Dimitri out of the sky, even as a body rolled past me.

"Archie!"

"No!" screamed out a voice.

I looked at the top landing to see Astrea standing there. I had never seen her more stunned in her life.

"No, Archie! You cannot die. Not now."

She held her wand aloft and then gave a long sweeping motion across the entire lower floor.

I felt the floor beneath me heave up, as though it was no longer attached to the ground.

Everyone in the room was thrown off their feet.

A quartet of Maladons who had been trying to charge up the stairs at Astrea but were now trying to hold on to the stair rails for dear life were blasted to nothing by a huge bolt of light from her wand.

But the Maladons were still coming at us in waves.

Delph had retrieved his ax and, still invisible, was striking out at the enemy, culling several from the ranks.

The little cucos were swirling like bothersome gnats around the Maladons. They would shake their wings, and this made the light coming from them so blinding that I saw many Maladons cover their eyes. This allowed our lot to blast them away.

I raced across and knelt down next to Archie. He was breathing, though in pain.

I turned my ring around so that I became visible. "Astrea," I cried out. "He's alive."

She swept down to us, examined Archie and then, with a compacted sweep of her wand, she lifted Archie from the floor and I saw him soar away into another room to safety.

Then I lost track of Astrea because charging across the room were Seamus and his group of hobs. They were flinging their blue balls of flame at the Maladons, whose cloaks caught on fire. In mere seconds they were engulfed in flames, screaming and ripping at their burning flesh.

On the other side of the room Chauncey Cyphers was fighting valiantly with his sword as he dueled with a Maladon who only had one arm remaining.

Chauncey gave a gasp as a blast of fire struck him from behind.

I whipped around to see the garm bolt through the open doorway.

Chauncey, fully on fire, screamed, dropped his sword and raced madly around the room, as I aimed at the garm and took its life with my cast spell.

The next instant, Petra appeared on my right. She raised her wand and a cannon shot of water poured from it, dousing Chauncey. He collapsed to the floor, and she raced to his side, kneeling next to him as the battle continued on all fronts.

I watched Petra until she looked up and I saw the tears leach down her cheeks.

Chauncey was obviously gone.

Then, with a shriek, Petra leapt into the air and started firing spells at a brigade of Maladons who had just entered from another room.

Raining spell after spell, she caused them to disperse. But they found cover, turned and returned the salvos of spell.

But I had already cast my shield incantation, and a host of curses fell harmlessly off its toughened hide.

The look on Petra's face told me that she knew exactly what was happening.

I saw her glance around and then she mouthed, *Thank you*.

The unicorn charged into the room and caught one Maladon on its horn. The beautiful creature lifted its head, and the impaled Maladon flew across the room and crashed into the wall. He fell to the floor quite dead.

"John!" I exclaimed.

My brother was battling a large Maladon at the back of the hall.

I raced forward, but I needn't have bothered.

My mother appeared directly in front of her son and calmly and efficiently dispatched the Maladon to the hereafter.

Then I saw my father battling two Maladons, but deftly holding his own.

The next moment I was knocked off my feet by the front facade of Empyrean tumbling down around me as a huge gash was opened up in the stone.

I looked over my shoulder at the figure striding into the crumbled space.

It was Necro.

Something landed to the right of me.

It was Astrea.

She took a few steps forward and stared across the width of the floor as Necro drew to a halt.

The wands were pointed at each other.

Necro lowered his hood so that his terrible countenance was fully visible.

He looked around at the destroyed hall.

"Empyrean, at last. But, you must admit, Astrea, it has seen better days."

Astrea said, "I should have killed you during the first war."

"You never could, Astrea. And you well know it."

"My son lies badly injured," she said.

"Your son should have been dead long ago, as should you. I am here now to take care of that."

At the same instant, their wands slashed and the duel began.

But it was not the only fight going on, because a surge of Maladons had followed Necro through the opening. He must have brought every bloody one of them with him.

I leapt into the air and shot spell after spell upon them.

I saw the remains of my army charge forward and engage the Maladons on the floor. But they were quickly overmatched, and they started falling at a rapid number.

And then I looked over at Astrea, who was holding her own with Necro, matching him spell for spell. But Necro looked unworried by this, and I wondered why.

My panic increased as more of my lot fell. I was killing Maladons left and right, but there were just too bloody many of them.

Then double doors leading from the dining room burst open and in they charged. Thansius was leading the pack, in full armor with his mighty sword raised over his head. When I saw what was behind him I almost fainted.

It was all the Wugs, but they were . . . enchanted. Loon was a marble bull. Domitar was in a suit of armor like Pillsbury. Other Wugs were tall, reedy pieces of wood and all were wielding deadly-looking weapons.

Now I knew what Astrea had done to them.

A hundred strong, they smashed into the wall of Maladons and their sheer force of momentum drove the Maladons backward.

After flinging multiple spells that cut down a trio of Maladons, I turned to look at Astrea right as she seemed to have seized an advantage.

Necro had fallen back and stumbled over some of the wreckage he had caused by blasting the front of Empyrean apart.

Then, just as she was about to press this advantage, from out of nowhere, an enormous jabbit exploded through a wall and struck her in the back with its fangs.

Astrea looked stunned and stumbled backward as the serpent reared to strike again.

"Rigamorte," I cried out.

The spell hit the foul beast dead center of its chest. It froze for an instant, wobbled and fell to the floor with a great crash.

Astrea had fallen to her knees, and before I could make another move, Necro stepped forward and with a slash of his wand — he beheaded her.

Everyone in the place, Maladons and my lot alike, froze at this.

I was so stunned that I could barely think.

"Father."

Necro turned as Jason, who had just dispatched four Maladons, calmly walked up to him, his wand at the ready.

Necro snarled, "You dare to call me by that name? You are no son of mine."

"I quite agree. I take after my mother, don't you think?"

Necro glanced at his son's wand. "Do you really think you can beat me?"

"Let's find out, shall we?"

The next instant, Necro sent a spell that knocked Jason off his feet.

"No!" screamed a voice.

I turned to see Uma zooming forward, right at Necro. "You will not hurt him again!" she shouted.

Distracted by this, Necro took his eye off Jason, who sent a curse whirling at his father.

It struck Necro in the leg, and he dropped to his knees.

"Kill them!" roared Necro.

And the battle around us was engaged once more.

Necro pointed his wand at his leg, and the wound there vanished. He rose and aimed his wand at Jason, who still lay stunned on the floor.

"Say your last," snarled Necro.

"Go to Hel!" replied Jason.

The spell Necro was about to deliver I was sure was the killing one.

I flew up into the air and landed between Jason and Necro.

"To kill him, you must kill me first."

Necro appraised me coolly.

"I thought you must be around somewhere," he said, his voice low and mocking.

I raised my wand. He looked amused.

"You are beaten, but apparently are unaware of it. Look around, Vega — you are beaten, your army in tatters." He indicated Astrea's headless torso. "And you have lost the most powerful sorceress you had."

"You are mistaken on that point," I said.

His smile deepened. "How so?"

The fury inside me was so fierce that I never even heard the spell leave my lips.

My only regret was that I didn't use the right one.

That I didn't kill him.

My spell hit him so hard that Necro was lifted off his feet, flew twenty feet into the air and slammed against the one remaining section of the front wall.

To his credit he was back on his feet in an instant, but the look on his face was no longer amused.

"*I* am the most powerful sorceress we have," I said.

And then, it happened.

Pillsbury came charging into the hall, wielding a broadax. He ran straight toward Necro, screaming, "You will not befoul the House of Jane, you scoundrel!"

Unfortunately, he stumbled over a pile of debris and went flying.

And slammed right into me, as I was about to deliver the killing curse to Necro.

I was sent sideways, tumbling heels over ass. When I stopped and sat up, Necro had a dead aim on me. "No!" a voice cried out.

Light shot from Necro's wand directly at me.

The body flew across in front of me at the same instant.

The light hit the person right in the chest.

There was a gasp, a slight bulge of the eyes and then the body came to rest, never to rise on its own again.

I touched my chest, where I had felt a jab of pain so searing I thought that Necro's spell had hit me after all.

I slowly rose and looked down at the crumpled heap.

She had given her life for mine.

Petra was dead.

I looked up in time to see Necro lift his wand, and the air all around us started to harden. There was no escaping this, not unless I acted now.

The spell came to me instantly. It was the same one I had used to carry all the Wugs from Maladon Castle to here. The golden tethers shot out and connected with all those of my lot who remained living.

And we were gone from Empyrean.

Leaving the Maladons in victory.

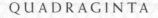

The Tolling Bell

I SAT ON MY haunches with the remains of my defeated army scattered around me. The trees were dense, which muffled somewhat their cries of pain and suffering.

And loss.

And it was staggering. Beyond belief, really. I had checked on all the survivors after we had escaped from Empyrean. It was only then that I truly understood how many were gone.

Seamus had survived, but had lost four of his band of hobs.

Little Kori and five other ekos had perished.

Ishmael was alive but injured. He and two other hyperbores were all that remained of his race.

Petra.

Astrea.

And a dozen more magicals, including Amicus Arnold, Clive Pippen and Tobias Holmes.

Cletus Loon, Domitar and Roman Picus were dead, though the still-enchanted Thansius and ancient Dis Fidus had survived. But of the hundred Wugs I had saved from the glass, a full forty were no longer with us.

This included . . . Duf Delphia.

Tears welled up in my eyes.

And I had suffered an even more devastating loss.

My father had died in a duel with two Maladons. After he had fought so hard to survive the commingled curse. After all the efforts to restore him. He was dead.

I didn't know until my mother had told me once we got to safety.

I had sat with her and my brother for a long time, holding one another.

John had cried freely. My mother was consoling him, which I think allowed her to escape her personal grief for a bit as she tended to her son.

I did not have the luxury of grieving for my father. I had to make the rounds of the survivors, lift spirits where I could, and console those who had lost others.

Delph was nursing multiple wounds and tearing up over his father.

Harry Two had lost his other ear and had deep gashes burned into his body.

The beautiful unicorn was battered and bloody, licking its wounds while lying on the ground.

I used the Adder Stone to do what I could to relieve the suffering. What that didn't cure, I tried to help with my wand. But many of the wounds were so cursed that my magic had little effect.

Archie had survived, though he was badly injured. I had been surprised that my magical tether had delivered him here with me, though it had faithfully executed my command that all of my lot living were to be rescued from Empyrean.

I knelt next to him for the longest time using the Stone and my wand to relieve his pain. He was ghastly white and shivered from head to toe.

"My mother?" he had asked me. "How is she?"

He obviously had been unconscious and not seen what had happened.

I took his hand. "Archie, she fought valiantly. She really did. She would have defeated Necro but for a bloody jabbit."

"My . . . mother is dead?"

I slowly nodded. Archie started to quietly sob. I had Dedo Datt, who had wounds across his face and neck, stay with him as I ventured on to see the other wounded.

Afterward, I looked around and counted all who were left with me. Our numbers were devastated. And some, like Archie, might never be fit to fight again.

In my head, I counted the Maladons killed. I shook my head. Their advantage over us had only grown.

And then it became apparent that none of the household staff had come with us. I had been so stupid, commanding only the living to come with me, not the enchanted. But then, the Wugs had all made it, at least those who were alive.

Of course, I thought. Astrea had just recently enchanted them. Pillsbury, Mrs. Jolly and the rest, though enchanted, had apparently outlived their "natural lives."

My mother came over to me. Her face was bruised and she was walking with a limp.

She said anxiously, "How are you, Vega?"

I shook my head. "I can barely understand what just happened. How did the Maladons break into Empyrean?"

"All I can tell you is that there was this enormous sound, like a powerful storm was coming. I was sitting on a bench in the rear grounds. I looked to the sky, but there was no storm. And despite the sound of the wind, there was just a gentle breeze. And then as I continued to watch, there was a huge gash across the sky, like someone had cursed it."

"Holy Steeples," I exclaimed.

328

She nodded. "And out of that gash they came hurtling down. Maladons everywhere. I ran inside and raised the alarm. By then they had burst into Empyrean and the battle had begun."

She put a hand to her face. "I saw Petra fall."

I nodded, tears gathering in my eyes. "She saved my life. She gave her life for mine."

"Friends do that for each other, Vega. As I would give my life for yours. Gladly."

I gripped her hand. "I can't believe Dad is gone."

"He fought hard. So hard. But he died a warrior. He would have wanted nothing less."

As she left me. I thought back to Petra. Those open eyes. And then I touched my chest. Because as soon as that curse struck her, I actually thought it had hit me, because my chest had felt very funny. Like something had died inside it.

I saw John sitting against a tree. His face was battered and one limb hung listlessly next to his side. Miranda Weeks leaned next to him. She only had a single arm left, but she resolutely clutched her wand in the one hand she had remaining.

I stood and looked down at my arms. They were gashed and bloodied. My face was cut and burned. Every muscle in my body ached wearily. I felt a century old.

And I had been one of the lucky ones.

Delph came over to me and put an arm around my shoulder, a simple move that drove pain to his features because of his injuries.

"I'm sorry, Vega Jane, about your dad. So sorry."

"We both lost our fathers this night," I said. "I still can't believe it."

"They went down fighting." Delph rubbed a tear from his eye.

"I know, Delph. I know."

"And we got to keep fighting."

I looked up at him with incredulity.

"With what, Delph? Look around. We really have nothing left to fight with."

"We can't give up now, Vega Jane. We can't."

"Why not?"

"Because then all of them, my dad, your dad, they would have died for . . . for nothing."

Tears seeped from his eyes as he said this.

And I felt them fall from mine.

He took me in his arms and held me.

I clutched at him.

I was holding on. To something. Anything.

But really, I had nothing left.

It was all gone.

THOUGH NONE OF us really wanted to sleep, we all did, falling into an exhausted slumber. Midway through the night, I awoke and relieved Sybill Hornbill, who was on watch. We said nothing to each other. A simple nod and then she left to lie under the trees and sleep.

As I sat there, my gaze swiveled in all directions because I knew another attack would finish us. And I would put nothing past the Maladons.

In the dark before the dawn came, I noticed something.

A gleam of light started to materialize about a foot away from me. I hurriedly stood and aimed my wand directly at it, wondering if I should strike before it fully formed.

I'm glad I didn't.

Uma appeared in front of me.

Jason rushed up. He had apparently seen her as well.

Jason was battered and bloodied, but the curse from his father had fortunately not killed him.

"Uma, what are you doing here?" he said.

She looked at him sadly. "I came to tell you something, both of you."

I said, "About the Maladons?"

She nodded. "I know the reason that Empyrean fell."

"What was it?" I exclaimed.

She pointed her finger at Jason, who took a step back.

I was so stunned my brain stopped working for a few seconds. I felt myself lift my wand and point it at Jason's heart.

"No!" shouted Uma. "He didn't know."

I kept my wand on Jason, my reason returning, and along with it came anger.

"Then explain," I said icily.

To his credit, Jason looked just as stunned as I did.

Uma said, "I overheard Necro." She glanced at Jason. "My love, he placed a curse within your body. Then he allowed you to be rescued from Maladon Castle. He knew they would take you to Empyrean."

"I still don't understand," I said.

"Nor I," said Jason.

"When Vega carried you past the enchantments protecting the house and grounds, you were accepted because you were no longer a Maladon. In that way, Necro used your breaking from him as a strength for him. You could fool the enchantments, only on his behalf. And the curse within you destroyed the enchantments from the inside out. It revealed Empyrean to your father. And it allowed him to breach the protections."

I nodded dumbly at this. An enemy from within had given us away. And I had fallen right into Necro's trap. I had been so stupid. Now of course it made sense. It had been too easy rescuing Jason. Far too easy.

I groaned and slumped down.

"Please, Vega, do not blame yourself," said Jason, obviously distraught.

"There is no one else to blame," I said. "Except me."

They looked around at the others with us, all battered and injured.

"I'm so sorry," said Jason as tears fell from his eyes. "My accursed father. I've ruined everything."

"It's not your fault," I said, staring off before I could bring myself to look at Uma. "I thank you for telling us." I paused. "What is happening at Empyrean now?"

Uma said nothing, but she looked extremely nervous.

"I really need to know. Do not spare my feelings, Uma."

"They've enslaved Pillsbury and the others," said Uma. "And . . . and they've desecrated Gunther's remains."

"Gunther's remains! Have you seen Alice since it happened?"

"No," said Uma.

"Please keep us informed, Uma."

She and Jason embraced before she vanished.

Jason turned to me. "Vega, I . . ."

"Jason, it was not your fault. You fought valiantly. You took on your father. I could ask nothing more from you. Now go get some rest."

After he left, I pulled out the pewter cup that constituted part of Astrea's Seer-See. I had performed the "*Rejoinda*, Seer-See," before escaping from Empyrean.

I placed the cup on the ground and used it to spy on Empyrean.

332

Outside the building, I could see the swirl of rainbow colors comprising the protective enchantments. The Seer-See must show all such magic. The Maladons must have placed the enchantments back over Empyrean after they had vanquished us.

Inside, the place was now filled with Maladons. I saw in the dining hall that they were having a victory feast and poor Pillsbury, now battered and blackened, was forced to serve them as they threw objects at him and called him vicious names.

Mrs. Jolly came out with the food cart and was subjected to this same harassment.

I could see that the portraits of our kind on the walls had been slashed and burned or else had foul names painted across them. My beautiful Empyrean was no more.

And, in a scene that actually made me retch, I saw that they had piled all the bodies of the dead in the Great Hall, and set them . . . afire. Some of them actually danced around the flames, hooting and calling out horrid names.

However, Necro was not there and I wondered why.

I manipulated the Seer-See until I finally found him.

What that creature was doing was more diabolical than even I could give him credit for.

He was in Jasper's laboratory. Astrea's headless body was behind a glass.

There was an enormous bottle under the glass collecting Astrea's magical dust.

As I watched, the bottle filled. Necro waved his wand over it and the dust swirled out and . . . was absorbed into his body.

He had just taken Astrea's considerable magic for his own.

I had no idea such a vile thing was possible.

Necro had been a force to be reckoned with before this.

Now, now he would be truly invincible.

I watched as he smiled, pointed his wand at the wall and gave it a tiny wave.

I could see that he had conjured a shield enchantment in front of the wall.

Next, he pointed his wand at the shield and flicked it.

The blast of power that came out of the wand was so strong that the shield enchantment was instantly punctured and the massive stone wall was obliterated. I mean there was nothing left.

I dispensed with the Seer-See and resumed my watch.

It seemed likely to me that the Maladons, after celebrating their victory, would commence their hunt for us. They would know how few there were left of us, and that we were injured and hardly prepared to fight. They would think they could finish us off easily.

And they might not be wrong about that.

"Vega?"

I turned to see my brother standing there.

"Yes, John?"

"We have to continue the fight."

"I know that."

"We have to avenge Dad."

"We have to avenge many."

I told him what the Maladons were doing right now. When I got to the part about their burning the bodies, my brother turned to the side and vomited.

He wiped off his mouth and straightened.

"Do you think they'll be coming after us?"

"I think it quite likely, yes."

"We need to have a plan."

"Yes."

"Do you have one?"

"I'm trying to come up with one, John! Do you realize what just happened at Empyrean? Do you understand how many people we lost? Including our father?"

"I understand all of that, Vega. And I think we need to find the villagers you met. Russell? Delph told me. They can help us fight."

"I was thinking about that. But they're not magical. They can fight and I know they can kill Maladons, but I'm not sure that it will be enough now. Not with our depleted numbers. To fight would be sending them to their deaths."

John squatted down next to me and clasped his hands, his head bowed as though in deep thought.

"Better to die than be ruled by the Maladons."

I mulled over his words. "I guess I should give Russell and the others the choice. But there's something else," I added. I told him about Necro taking Astrea's power for his own. "Now he will be even more formidable. I'm not sure that he can be stopped at this point."

"He *can* be stopped, Vega."

"How?" I demanded.

"*You* will stop him."

"How can you be so sure of that?"

"Because it's the only reason you're here. It's the only reason you've survived everything that's been set against you. It was why you lived tonight when so many others died."

"No one can know the future," I said.

"One person can."

I looked more closely at John until the truth hit me.

"You were in Jasper's laboratory. You were reading through his books. What did you find?"

"I found that he went into the future. I found that he knows your fate. But he can't tell you, because that would mean awful consequences for you."

"And how can you be sure that in the future I'm the winner and not Necro?"

"Because I've never known you to be beaten. Ever. Every time you were knocked down, you got back up. Every single time when it would have been easier to stay down, you stood again. And you won. You fought Necro today. You knocked him into the air and slammed him against a wall, Vega. *You* did that. You stunned him. He knows how powerful you are. That was why he sought out Astrea's magic." He paused and then simply said it. "He fears you."

He rose, his gaze downcast, but for some reason I could feel the burn of its intensity.

"That's what I think anyway," he said.

And he turned and walked off.

I watched him go for a long while, until I could see him no more.

Then I huddled in my cloak, for it was chilly here, and thought about all that he had said.

It was true that I had survived much. That I had always gotten up after being knocked down. That I had come up with some way to emerge victorious when all looked dark against me.

And still, the future was guaranteed to no one. I could come all this way and still lose. I knew that.

But my brother's belief in me, well, it bolstered me. It made me feel that what he was saying at least could be possible.

Maybe, at this darkest point in my life, that was enough.

All I could do was try.

As One

B LIMEY," SAID RUSSELL.

Blimey indeed. I had flown to Russell's hiding place to meet with him. I had just told him of the Maladon attack against our stronghold.

"What will you do now?" he asked.

"Regroup. Join our remaining forces with yours, if you're still willing. We're not as strong as we used to be, Russell. The result might be a slaughter. I just want you to know that. And if you decide not to help, I completely understand."

"Are you nutters? Didn't we already pledge our allegiance to you, Vega? Do you really think we'd go back on our word simply because you lost a battle? Hel, you need us now more than ever, I reckon."

"Thank you, Russell. And you're right, we do."

"What do you need right now?"

"Give me five of your best fighters," I said.

"What are you going to do?"

"I'm going to take the fight to the Maladons."

"How?"

"Leave it to me."

I had a plan, just not one I wanted to divulge.

He said, "When do you want them? And by the way, that number will include me."

"Tomorrow night."

"Do you need shelter, food?"

"That would be good, yes."

"Then bring your army here."

I thought to myself that when he saw my ragtag band, he might use a different word than *army*.

I returned to the others and told them of the plan to unite with Russell's group.

I gathered all the survivors, tethered them and did the requisite incantation.

Seconds later, our feet, and in Harry Two's case, paws, hit the dirt smack in the middle of Russell's encampment. They were expecting us, as a crowd had gathered around with Russell at the head.

I will never forget the kindness showed to us that night. They could see that we were battered and bloodied, tired and hungry.

The outpouring of food and water and blankets and tents to sleep in was instant and overwhelming. In some cases it was simply a helping hand, a kind word of sympathy or encouragement.

One lad who couldn't have been much older than John came over to me. He was dressed in rags and already bore the wounds of battle.

He said eagerly, "You're Vega. I heard you speak last time you were here."

"What's your name?"

"Donovan. Donovan McDougal."

"Well, I appreciate you fighting with us, Donovan."

"Appreciate? Blimey, Vega, 'tis an honor. If I survive this, I'll be telling me kids, 'Oi, your father, he fought with Vega bloody Jane.'"

I kept smiling at this comment long after he left.

Before I really knew it, my lot was fully integrated with Russell's people. They were chatting away as though they had known one another their whole lives.

I watched as my mother sat in front of a small campfire warming her hands and sipping from a tin cup she had been given. She had spent most of her time nursing the wounded, and I was glad to see her take a moment for herself.

I looked around at the primitive camp. It was certainly not the grandeur of our existence at Empyrean, but I was even more moved by the beauty of acceptance.

John and Miranda were under a tree having a conversation with some of the younger members of Russell's band.

Delph was sharpening his ax with a tool given to him by a bloke who was nearly as large as he was.

Harry Two lapped water from a bowl while two other dogs sat peacefully watching him.

I took Russell by the arm and led him over to a private spot to discuss matters.

"Okay, have you got your five yet?"

He nodded. "All good fighters. I spoke to them after you left. They're ready to be led by you, Vega. As am I."

"I'm not sure you coming is a good idea, Russell. If something happens to both of us, we'll have no one to lead the survivors."

Surprisingly, he smiled. "Well, Vega, I reckon if we fall, there are others here who can take up the mantle. I'm not saying you're not special, a lot more than me actually. But leaders aren't so much born as made, I believe. They rise to the occasion. Daphne was like that. She had her opinions. And she stood up for others. But she wasn't the only one in the world. And neither are you or me."

His statement struck me on a number of levels. I

involuntarily glanced over at Delph and John, and then my mother and Thansius.

Russell was right. In their own way, they could all lead, given the chance. They did rise to the occasion, doing what needed doing.

You git, Vega, I thought to myself. A bit of humility never hurt, did it? And on the other side of the ledger, a bloke like Necro no doubt believed that he was the only possible one to lead his lot. He would never believe that he had an equal. Maybe I had fallen a little too much into that trap.

I shook my head clear. "You're right, Russell."

"So you said tomorrow night, then?"

"Yes."

"Right you are. Well, you and your lot should get some sleep. Will any of them be coming with us?"

"Yes, they will," I replied.

I bade Russell good-bye and took up a place with my mother.

She handed me a cup of hot tea, and I drank it gratefully.

"Empyrean?" said my mother. "Will we attempt to take it back?"

I shook my head. "I have seen what they are doing there. It is too well protected now. There is another, better target."

"What?"

"Maladon Castle," I replied.

My mother said, "Do you think that wise, Vega? What will we have to gain by attacking there?"

"I think several important things," I answered.

"Such as?"

"Do you trust me?" I said suddenly.

"What?"

"Do you trust me?"

340

I didn't expect a quick answer and I didn't get one.

"Mum, I know that when we last parted, I was still a little girl who needed her nose wiped and her hand held."

She smiled. "You haven't needed your nose wiped or your hand held since you were two, Vega."

"I can do this. I *have* been doing this."

My mother looked at me wistfully, running a hand through my hair. "I think all parents believe their children will always need them, even when they're all grown. We just want to feel like we're still a part of your lives. That we're still necessary."

I took her hand. "You will always be a part of my life. And I actually need you now more than ever."

"Then Maladon Castle it is," said my mother. "When do we leave?"

"Mum, you're not coming."

"What do you mean? You can't go there alone."

"I'm not. I'm taking Delph, Harry Two, Miranda and John. And five of Russell's blokes."

"Your brother?" said my mother anxiously.

"John can fight. He's not a little boy anymore either."

"And if you are successful?"

"Then we will undertake the next step."

"Which is?" she asked breathlessly.

"We take back our home. And we destroy the Maladons, once and for all."

I SLEPT FITFULLY that night, lying under the stars, my body pressed into the dirt.

By the time the dawn broke, I was already up and taking a short walk through the dense trees. I needed to be alone right now as I contemplated what lay ahead.

I took several deep breaths and drew in the scents of the flowers arrayed all around. The path I was following was well worn and meandering.

I had just followed it to veer around a large poplar tree when I stopped dead.

Shimmering right in front of me . . . was Alice Adronis.

"Alice?" I said.

She nodded curtly and strode forward.

I could never see Alice without glancing at least once at her awful mortal wound.

"I'm so sorry about Empyrean," I said.

She cut me off with a dismissive thrust of her hand.

"It is not your fault. Uma has explained matters to me. Necro's plot was quite brilliant, I will give him that."

"Insanely brilliant," I added, for I had long since concluded that the man did indeed have to be insane to do all that he did.

"I have seen what they have done there. And I was told of . . . of Gunther's remains."

This was the first time I had ever seen Alice look the way that she now did, as though she were about to cry. But she composed herself and said, "Fortunately, my dear husband knows nothing of it. They desecrated his mortal remains. They did nothing to harm the spirit and legacy he left behind."

"Alice, why didn't Gunther come back as you have, in spirit form to Empyrean?"

"I died in battle. Gunther was murdered by Necro."

"I know that, but what does that matter?"

"By murdering Gunther, Necro was able to keep his spirit from his rightful home. He wanders elsewhere, but always looking for his home. Always looking . . . for me. All this time."

This saddened me almost more than I could bear.

"So Uma and Morrigone?"

"Uma was not murdered. She is free to go where she pleases. But she chooses Empyrean because her father, Bastion, was killed by the Maladons, and thus cannot return to his home. Morrigone can never go back to her home in Wormwood."

"What about our side?"

"Our side does not slit the throats of unsuspecting people," snapped Alice. "We fight honorably. And we die honorably. When you murder, you are a coward, but the victim of a murder will never be free until . . ."

"Until what?" I said.

"Until his murderer is, in turn, killed."

"So if Necro dies?"

"I will be reunited with Gunther. And Uma with her father."

"Then I will do my best to see you reunited with him."

She gave a curt nod.

I said, "I also saw what he did to Astrea. He took her powers."

Alice did not seem all that upset about this startling development. In fact, I could have sworn that a tiny smile had escaped her lips. But it was gone so quickly that I convinced myself that I had imagined it.

"Tell me your plans, Vega."

"To destroy Maladon Castle, absolutely and completely."

I was prepared for her to argue with me, to voice her opinion that another tactic would be superior to mine. To my astonishment, she nodded.

"Good, Vega, I quite agree."

"You do?"

"Of course I do. Do you know how you will accomplish that objective?"

"I have a pretty good idea, yes."

She scrutinized me for several long and uncomfortable moments. Why was it that Alice always put me on guard, as though I had to continually prove myself in her eyes?

Do you really have to ask that question, Vega?

"I believe it would need to be somewhat better than 'pretty good.'"

The next instant, she vanished.

I sighed. Leave it to Alice to make me feel like a git.

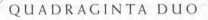

A Face Returned

WE LANDED SOFTLY and looked around.

There were ten of us, all tethered together.

We were invisible. I hoped we'd stay that way.

Delph was right at my shoulder, as always.

I unharnessed Harry Two and set him down.

Russell was at my other shoulder. He gazed carefully over the castle.

"So this is it, eh?"

I nodded.

"Where they took Daphne and killed her?" he said grimly.

"Yes."

"How do we get in?" asked one of Russell's men.

I took out the Elemental and sent a wand wire to Victus.

A few minutes passed before I received an answer in my thoughts.

"This way," I said.

I led them to the rear of the castle.

Victus was there holding the same door open. We hurried inside, and he closed the door after us.

I whispered, "Thanks, Victus. Can you tell us how many Maladons are here?"

"Fewer than a dozen. Most left two days before, for some reason. Including Necro."

I well knew where they had gone.

"Can I assist you in any way, Vega?" he asked.

"No, Victus, you've done more than enough for me. But you must do one thing for yourself."

"What is that?"

"You must come with us when we leave here."

Though he had no face really, I could still sense the shock in him.

"Go with you?"

"Yes, Victus. Because once we leave here, there will be no castle left."

To his credit, Victus asked for no explanation. He simply nodded and said, "I shall be ready, then."

As we moved down the hall, Russell said, "He was an accommodating bloke. But where was his face?"

"Long story," I replied.

"Where are we headed?" asked Delph.

I hadn't really filled the others in on my plan. There were several reasons for this, including the fact that I was still finalizing it in my head. I did have a purpose. I did have a goal. But so much of what I had accomplished while being here had been done on the fly, reacting to what I was confronted with. I guess I had accepted that as a normal state of affairs.

"You'll see," I said. "It's just up ahead."

We reached the door, and I looked through it using the *Crystilado magnifica* incantation.

There was no one in there.

I used my wand to unlock the door, and we went inside.

This was the room where magic was taken. The shattered mirrors stared back at us.

With waves of my wand I restored twelve of them.

That finished, I lifted my wand and looked at John. "Are you ready?"

He nodded and lifted his wand too.

I *had* prepared John for what we had to do, and terrible though it was, he did not shy away from it.

We said the spell at the same time and cast our wands in a wide arc with the tips touching at the end of the sweep. Then we whipped them across the fronts of the restored mirrors.

Soaring into them were the dozen Maladons left in the castle.

I went over to the shelf, and with John's and Delph's aid, I gathered a dozen bottles and we set one down under each glass. As soon as they touched the stone floor, the men in the glass started to scream in agony.

And grain by grain, their magical lives started to drain down into those glass jars.

I knew they were suffering. And I also knew they had done the same thing to my lot. And had loved every minute of it.

I did not love this. I did not wish to see anyone in such agony.

But my heart had been set in stone a long time ago. Only time would tell whether I'd get it back to normal or not. And I also knew that their suffering would not last long, for we still had work to do.

"Let's go," I said to the others.

I summoned Victus and inquired if there were any others of his kind in the castle.

"Only I," he replied. "Even the terrible beasts are no longer here."

I pulled out my wand. *"Rejoinda*, necessary bottle."

A glass bottle appeared in my hand, an especially large bottle.

On the side the tag read, *Geoffrey Tremaine.*

I took off the top and cast my spell, and the dust inside returned to its rightful owner.

Victus turned stiff as a tree, but only for a moment as his pores absorbed what had always belonged to him before the Maladons stole it away.

I watched as Victus's face returned to normal.

He was quite handsome.

And he was also crying.

"Welcome back, Geoffrey Tremaine," I said.

He hugged me, sobbing into my shoulder quietly for a few moments before righting himself.

"Thank you, Vega. Thank you. However can I repay you?"

"I will need you to fight with me, that's how. Against your former masters."

He looked uncertain. "I don't know how to fight, Vega."

I had expected this too.

In answer to that I had something else to give him, besides his freedom.

And a face.

The first time it had been an incredibly difficult spell to cast. But all the hard work on that one had been done. And the presence of a certain wand was still potent in the magical ether.

"Hold out your hand, Geoffrey."

He did as I asked.

I incanted what needed to be said.

A wand of gold appeared out of the air and sailed into his hand.

"Your wand, Geoffrey, courtesy of Bastion Cadmus. And with the size of your bottle, I think you will be one powerful sorcerer indeed."

He looked down at the thin reed of gold.

When he looked back up, Geoffrey was a changed man. Gone were the tears, and along with them, the uncertainty.

"I will fight with you, Vega. It will be my honor."

I HAD RUSSELL and his men go room by room and find all the wood they could. With Delph's help, they stacked it in the throne room. Using my wand, I levitated Necro's hideous throne onto the top of this pyre.

"Stand back," I cautioned.

John and I raised our wands and pointed them at the stack.

"*Ignito*," we said together.

Flames shot from our wands and the stack instantly caught fire. Higher and higher the flames rose until they reached Necro's wretched chair. When it burst into flames, I smiled, for the first time in a long time.

"Outside," I said.

We left the way we had come.

I raised my wand again, along with John.

We said together, "*Vernetigen*."

The ground shook as our twin spells slammed into the wall of the castle.

The stone vibrated violently. And then it fell in upon itself.

John let his wand drop at this point.

But not me.

I kept my wand pointed directly at the collapsing mass as the ground underneath it opened up. I knew that if Necro were still here with his army of Maladons, that what we were doing would have been far harder, perhaps impossible. But Necro had made a tactical mistake leaving such a small force to guard his castle. And now I was taking full advantage of that mistake, knowing there was no more magic left in the accursed place to stop me.

My focus was complete. I would only relinquish my aim and my magical prowess when every bit of Maladon Castle was no more.

With a long clattering sound, the last vestiges of the castle disappeared into the dirt. I used my wand to fill the hole with dirt, as over a coffin.

They had taken my home. Now I had taken theirs.

That was my rough form of justice.

I lowered my wand and looked at the others.

"This is the first step of the last," I said quietly. "None or all of us may survive what is coming. But what I will tell you is that no one will fight harder than I to make sure that what we did here today will be like child's play compared to what the Maladons have coming for them."

Delph raised his ax; the magicals, their wands; and Russell and his men, their fists. Sometimes it was as simple as that.

Then I soared into the air, carrying all of them with me.

We had been ten to start. Now we stood at eleven.

Including my friend Geoffrey, a slave no more.

In small victories lie the deeds of lasting good.

What Archie Wanted

I STOOD UNDER A tree, watching the seam of dawn appear.

"Vega Jane?"

I looked up as Delph came toward me. Most of the others were asleep. They had cheered when we told them what we had done to Maladon Castle. But now they were resting. They would need their strength. We did not have the option of waiting too long to finish this. Time was not on our side. Already, the Maladons had sent out teams to track and kill us. Garms and freks and jabbits had pounded through the forests in pursuit of us. It was only by skill and some luck that we had managed to escape.

"Yes, Delph?"

He had a weird expression on his face. And his hands were behind his back.

I rose. "Are you okay?"

"I'm fine. I just wanted to tell you something."

"What?"

"Happy birthlight."

This simple phrase nearly knocked me off my feet.

I was eighteen this day.

With everything going on, I had completely forgotten.

Delph pulled his hands from behind his back. In them was a bunch of fresh flowers.

"I wish I had been able to get you a proper gift, Vega Jane, but this was all there was."

I took the flowers from him, sniffed them, and a wide smile broke across my features.

"They're beautiful, Delph. Thank you so much."

I hugged him.

And then the hug quickly turned to a snog that lasted far longer than probably either of us initially intended.

When we drew apart, I said, "That was an even nicer present than the flowers."

He looked down solemnly at me.

"What is it, Delph?"

"The last is approaching," he said. "Not all will survive."

"We've talked about this before."

"Yes, we have, but now we need to do something about it."

"I'm coming up with a plan to —"

But he placed a hand on my mouth to shush me.

"This isn't about fighting the Maladons. This is about us."

"I'm not quite following, Delph." And in truth, I was bewildered by his words.

"I didn't quite tell you the truth just now."

"What?"

"I do have something else for you."

He drew something from his pocket and held it up in front of me.

It was a ring with a bit of stone atop it.

"This belonged to me mum. Dad gave it to me after you rescued him from the castle."

"But why?"

"Because he knew I would have need of it one day." He paused and looked deeply into my eyes. "And this is the day."

Delph got down on one knee.

And I lost all the breath in my lungs.

"Vega, will you do me the honor of becoming my wife?"

I could barely see him as the tears slipped from my eyes. I tottered on my feet as though I'd absorbed a dozen *Impacto* spells.

My entire life seemed to flash past in my mind. Delph and me as young friends. Then older. We had been through so much together. Now we were battered and hardened by a war neither of us had wanted. I couldn't think of anyone I would rather spend my life with.

So . . .

"Y-yes, Delph."

He slipped the ring on my finger. I liked it far better than my ring of invisibility.

He rose.

And then we fell into each other's arm. A kiss was shared and our hearts truly became as one.

"I love you, Vega."

Just Vega now, I thought. Delph had only ever called me Vega *Jane.*

"I love you, Daniel Delphia."

I TOLD MY mother first, showing off my ring and telling her exactly everything that had passed between me and Delph.

She was overjoyed for me, and we hugged and laughed and cried together.

And I could not stop looking at my new ring, which had become a permanent part of me the instant Delph placed it upon my finger.

"And on your birthlight too, Vega, how wonderful. I was coming to wish you a happy one when you arrived here with such truly beautiful news."

I pushed the tears from my eyes and then it struck me.

"Holy Steeples, it's John's birthlight too."

"Yes, it is, I've already seen him. He will be glad of your news."

I FOUND JOHN perched on a tree limb reading a book, using his wand tip to write notes in the margins. This did not surprise me. John was happiest when he was reading.

I called up to him, "John, can you come down?"

He glanced down at me and then slowly made his way to the ground.

"What is it, Vega?"

"I wanted to wish you a happy birthlight."

He smiled. "Mum has already been by. And that means I will wish you the same, Vega."

"Thank you."

He glanced at my hand. "Is that a new ring?" he asked.

I was positively beaming. "I have news, John. Oh, do I have news."

After I told him, my brother said he was very happy for me and that he looked forward to Delph officially joining the Jane family. There was a bit of a sad undertone in his words, however, and I well knew why.

We might not live to be married.

I SPENT THE rest of the day planning out my assault on Empyrean.

As my lot had, I had to assume that the Maladons would have encased Empyrean in protective spells.

I could have used Astrea's advice on this, along with other items. She had used such a shield to protect her cottage in the Quag. She might know ways to defeat such spells.

I had a sudden thought and unrolled the old parchment.

I had taken it with me on the mission we had gone on before Empyrean was attacked later that night.

"Silenus? I have a query."

His aged face appeared on the paper.

"Yes, Vega?"

"There have been some developments since we last talked."

"Such as?"

I briefly filled him in on the Maladon attack, our loss of Empyrean and how few people we had left. I also told him about our destruction of Maladon Castle.

I watched as his bushy eyebrows rose with each of my revelations.

"Indeed, Vega?" he said. "I marvel at your calling all of this mere 'developments.'"

"Well, 'catastrophes' might be a better term, but I'm trying to stay positive."

"And your query?"

"Though Astrea has been killed and her magic transferred to Necro, is there a way for me to communicate with her? Though she died in battle, her spirit has not come to see me. I thought that she might."

I could see Silenus mulling this over.

"The answer would be an easy one and a positive one for you, Vega, but for one factor."

"Which is?" I asked.

"Necro claiming Astrea's magic for his own. You see, it is the magical core that allows you to converse with those technically dead."

"And without that magical core, all is lost?" I said, feeling more depressed than I thought possible.

Surprisingly, Silenus shook his head. "There might be one way."

"What?" I said eagerly.

"Astrea is dead, you say. What about her son, Archie?"

"He lives, though he is badly injured."

"But his magical core remains intact?"

"As far as I know. Why?"

"It is a delicate business, Vega, very delicate."

"What is?" I exclaimed.

"You can use the son's magical core to communicate with the mother. That is clear."

"That's great," I said.

But the ominous look on his face told me that I was missing something.

"What?" I said aggressively.

"This comes with a price. A heavy one."

"What?" I said far more quietly.

"What I propose is not a natural magical event, Vega. You are relying upon a conduit to make the connection. It requires an enormous amount of power and sacrifice. It will, in fact, extinguish the conduit's magical core."

I said slowly, "Meaning that Archie will no longer be magical?"

"Not just that. I seriously doubt that his life can be maintained."

This stunned me. "But I have seen the Maladons take the magical dust from others. And I have returned it to them."

"This is different, Vega. Necro took Astrea's magical core as his own. Were she not already dead when he did so, that act would have made Astrea perish in and of itself. That is irreversible. Using Archie as the conduit means that you will be transferring his magical core to the remaining ether of his mother. It can only be done among the closest of family. That connection can remain alive even after death. But that is also irreversible. It cannot restore life to her; nothing can. But it will allow you to communicate with Astrea." He lifted one finger. "For a single time only. Then the core will be extinguished."

I slowly shook my head. "I can't ask that of Archie. I can't ask him to give up his life so that I can ask his mother for help."

"One can always ask, Vega. It is his answer to give."

"But —"

"Just in case you require it, here is the incantation."

The words appeared on the parchment in spidery handwriting just below his image. I committed the spell to memory and then put the parchment in my pocket. I looked around, because it felt like someone was watching me, but there was no one there.

I sat for a long time contemplating all of this. Then I made up my mind and went and found Archie. He was lying under a tree where one of Russell's blokes was tending to him.

I took over for the man, and when he was gone, I turned to Archie.

"I'm so sorry, Archie."

"I should have died a long time ago."

"Don't say that."

"I know why you're here."

"What?"

"Your brother came by. He saw you talking to that piece of parchment."

I was jolted by this. *So someone* had *been watching me? And listening to what Silenus had said.*

"He told me everything."

I looked down at his poor, wretched body, and I just couldn't ask it of him.

"It doesn't matter, Archie. You just rest now."

"D-doesn't matter?! It matters more'n anything at the moment."

"What do you mean?"

"I'm dying."

"No, Archie, you'll be fine. You just need —"

He cut me off once more. "I'm dying and you bloody well know it. You needn't lie to me. I don't deserve that."

I remained mute because he was right. He *didn't* deserve that.

He swallowed with difficulty. "I spent centuries in that cottage in the Quag, when I should have been out here fighting against the Maladons." A tiny smile crept over his lips and he looked directly at me. "Fighting next to you, Vega. This has been the best time of my whole life."

I felt tears creep to my eyes in the face of his heartfelt confession. "You fought well, Archie. I was proud to have you with me."

He drew a replenishing breath, and then his tone became more workmanlike, as though he knew he had a limited amount of time to accomplish what he wanted to.

"The point is, there's still more to do. Only I won't be around to help." He started to cough violently and abruptly sat up. I knelt next to him and waved the Adder Stone over him, wishing the best thoughts I could. His breathing eased a bit, but he was clearly in a great deal of pain. Pain that I could do nothing about.

He drew another shuddering breath and said, "You need to talk to my mother. If she can help you get into Empyrean, then you need to try."

"But you know what will happen if I use you as the conduit."

He smiled bitterly, his eyes seeming to glass over as I stared into them.

"That I'll die?" He laughed until he coughed.

After he recovered, he said, "Let me put what life I have left to good use. To help you. To help our lot. I'd much prefer that to lying under a tree until I breathe my last. What bloody good is that?"

I could see the logic in all that he said. Still, I sat there for several long moments as I mulled this over. Finally, I reached my conclusion.

"When do you want to do it?" I asked.

He touched his chest. "I think we best do it now, Vega. My time is dwindling. I feel it in every bit of me."

I helped him to his feet and led him into the trees until we found a small clearing where we could be alone. He lay on the ground and looked up at me.

"Thank you, Vega. Thank you for letting me do this."

Tears were spilling down my cheeks now, as what was about to happen fully set upon me.

"Thank you, Archie, for being so good, and brave."

He closed his eyes and I raised my wand.

A Talk with a Fawn

I HAD NEVER EXPERIENCED anything quite like this. I had been in mists before that held surprises. In the Quag, I had ventured under a river into the lair of Orco and his wall of the dead. I had seen horrors that would drive most people starkly insane and yet never lost my nerve.

But this was somehow different.

The mists were there, and I beheld no terrors sprouting from them. But an undeniable dread rose up in every pore of me as I walked along.

"Astrea? Are you there? It's Vega. I need to talk to you."

There was no answer and my spirits plummeted. Had I just sacrificed Archie for no reason a'tall?

Just as I was thinking of turning back, I sensed movement to the left of me. I turned in that direction and strode through the mists with purpose. Surprisingly, my footfalls made no noise. When I looked down, there was nothing there. No dirt, no floor. Just my feet lost in mist.

I seemed to walk for hours, but it couldn't have been that long. Finally, the mists parted, and I glimpsed a small pond set in the middle of what looked to be a broad meadow, though nary a single flower grew there that I could see.

"Astrea?" I called out again.

"Yes, Vega?"

The voice was unrecognizable to me, and I had no idea from where it was coming.

"Astrea? Where are you?"

"I am here, Vega."

I looked in every direction until my gaze fell upon something in the distance coming toward me.

I ran in that direction, my legs and heart pumping furiously. As I neared it, I slowed and then stopped.

It wasn't Astrea. At least as I knew her.

It was a fawn.

The creature drew close to me and then stopped.

"Astrea?" I said, bewildered.

The fawn nodded its head.

"But you're a —"

"A living thing that I admired greatly when I too was alive. An innocent creature with not a shred of hatred in its heart. It simply wants to run into the sunshine and live at peace with all other things. How glorious for me."

I could not see the fawn speaking these words. They were just echoing all around me. But the creature was undoubtedly the source.

"So you chose this . . . form?"

The fawn nodded. "I did indeed. For all of eternity."

"Astrea, I'm sorry that you're dead."

"I should have been dead long ago, Vega. My only regret is that I did not dispatch Necro while I had the chance."

"I killed the jabbit that bit you."

"As I knew you would."

I could see the fawn looking me over. My battered body seemed to give it pause.

"I see that things have not gone well for you."

I took a minute to tell her what had happened.

The fawn nodded but then gazed at me sharply. "Who has sacrificed in order for you to be here?"

I knew that so accomplished a sorceress as Astrea Prine was bound to ask this question.

I swallowed the lump in my throat and said, "Archie. He was badly injured. He was dying. And he insisted. I didn't want to do it, but . . . but he wanted his death to have a purpose. A purpose that would help our kind."

I thought I could see a cluster of tears in the fawn's eyes.

"My son did the right thing. A brave and honorable man. As you know, much of his life was spent doing things with which he did not agree. At least at the end he was able to do as he wished."

"I agree."

"What did you want to talk to me about?"

"The Maladons have taken over Empyrean, as I said. They have made it their new home."

"But surely their castle . . ."

I had forgotten to tell her that part.

"We destroyed their castle. It is no more."

"I applaud you, Vega. I truly do."

"But now we need to attack the Maladons and take back what is rightfully ours. I know that in the Quag you had the green dome, which kept your cottage safe."

"Yes."

"Empyrean had such protections, but they were broken."

"Tell me how it was done."

I told her what Uma had said.

She said, "It is an old ruse. Hiding your enemies inside an innocuous object that is then used to breach the desired target."

"Well, it worked. But Empyrean has been covered once more with such protections, so I can't see how we can successfully attack now. Our numbers are few, so the element of surprise is critical if we are to be victorious. We can use my invisibility shield to our advantage. But we need to get in first."

"I see your dilemma. But there is a way, Vega, there is indeed."

"What is it?" I asked eagerly.

"Look to the sky."

I did so. It was a breathtakingly beautiful blue with nary a puff of anything to mar it.

I looked back at the fawn, well, at Astrea.

"What am I looking for?"

"What did you see when you went to Maladon Castle?"

"I saw the castle," I replied, puzzled at the inquiry.

"And that was all?"

"Yes."

"No, it wasn't. You saw the sky over the castle."

"Well, of course. But so what?"

"And nothing else?"

"Look," I said, growing irritated. But then it struck me. I had seen nothing else. Only the castle and the sky.

"Why didn't the Maladons use a protective spell around their castle?" I asked.

"The answer to that is the Maladons are arrogant beyond belief. And they felt no need for protections like that. They have ruled this world for so long and no one has ever challenged them. They have grown complacent and lazy in their superiority."

"I guess that's true enough, though even without the protections the castle was well guarded. I could never enter without my invisibility ring. And they had garms and jabbits as well. They didn't need bloody enchantments."

"Correct."

Then I thought about it some more. "But that can't be right," I said. "I used your Seer-See. I saw the protections around Empyrean. They're there."

"I'm sure that you did."

"So *they* must have put them there."

"Why? When they thought you were defeated?"

I was immensely frustrated because it appeared we were talking in circles. "But there are protections there. I just told you that."

"I know. I was the one who put them there initially."

My head was growing wonky. "Astrea, can you please just explain this to me?"

The fawn drew closer to me.

"I drew up those protections to hold against anything, Vega. But, in the rare chance that they were broken, for any reason, I did something else."

"What?"

"I conjured the protections so that, if ever defeated, they would grow *back*. The spells you are seeing around Empyrean through the Seer-See are mine, not the Maladons'."

I looked down at the fawn, stunned.

"You're . . . you're sure about this?"

"Absolutely. But you can test it for yourself with a simple spell once you return."

She told me the spell. "If the light around Empyrean turns green, the protections are mine."

"Green, like the dome around your cottage?"

"Yes. And if the protections are mine . . ."

"Then they form no barrier for us," I finished for her.

The fawn nodded and then drew closer still.

"Vega, I'm sorry that I fell in battle. I would have much preferred to be with you fighting."

"I know."

"And since this will likely be the last time we will ever meet, I need to say this."

I stood there rigidly, since I had no idea what she was about to say.

"It was an honor to first be your teacher in sorcery, Vega. And it was an even higher honor later to be your follower. I can't think of anyone better suited to lead our kind than you."

Before I could say anything back, she said, "Now go on and finish off the bloody Maladons once and for all."

My thoughts swirled, my head spun and my eyes closed.

When they opened, I was lying on the ground looking up at the sky.

No mist. No fawn. No Astrea.

I wondered for a moment if I had dreamed it all.

But then I sat up and looked to my right.

And went rigid.

There was Archie.

Dead.

His glassy eyes were staring, lifeless, up at the darkness as well.

I used my hand to close them. I stood, lifted my wand, used it to dig a grave and placed Archie's body in it and then covered it over.

I found a chunk of wood and set it in the dirt at the head of the grave.

Using my wand, I burned an inscription into the wood.

Here lies Archie Prine. Who at the end of his life lived as he wanted. Your bravery will never be forgotten.

I looked down at the mound of freshly dug dirt.

I had buried others before.

Many.

Too damn many.

Yet Archie's death was different somehow. He had sacrificed himself so I could talk to his dead mother, and give us a fighting chance against the Maladons. For a man who had spent hundreds of years in complete drudgery, I wondered if the short time he had existed on the outside of that stillborn life had made up for all those centuries.

Somehow, I thought they had.

I turned away from the grave.

I had thought Empyrean impenetrable to us because of those enchantments. We would not have the element of surprise. But if Astrea was right and those were *her* protections?

I prayed to holy Steeples that she was not mistaken.

Because I had business to finish.

I had the Maladons to finish.

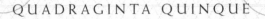

Return to Empyrean

INVISIBLE, I HOVERED over Empyrean in the dead of night.

I was here for one reason, and one reason only.

I raised my wand and pointed it at the dome of protection and uttered the spell that Astrea had told me.

Tears of joy appeared in my eyes when the color green emerged over the dome for the briefest of moments before vanishing.

I had my answer. Now it was time to act on it.

I returned to our camp and gathered my army together, including our newest member, Geoffrey Tremaine. I had fifteen magicals, including me and Jason. I had Delph, an assortment of creatures like hobs and ekos and the unicorn, and sixty Wugs led by Thansius.

Russell's contingent was a hundred strong, but none of them could perform sorcery.

I calculated the Maladon army at over two hundred, all sorcerers.

Still, I actually considered this as fair a fight as we were ever likely to manage.

I faced my troops and told them about what I had learned.

"We will take them by surprise, but it won't be easy, and it won't be without loss. This is our last chance to defeat the Maladons, and we have to take it. They have the fewest number of sorcerers they have had yet. And with Russell's group and my fellow Wugs, we have nearly an equal number of warriors as they."

I looked around at my lot, wounded, battered, still reeling from the loss of comrades and friends. And all I saw in their countenances was a steely resolve that caused the hairs on my neck to rise and my cheeks to flush, and my own spine, always abnormally stiff, to harden even more.

"Are you ready?" I asked.

They held up wands and weapons and fists.

Silently.

To me they represented something far stronger than shouts. They heralded a group of people who would never submit to defeat, who would fight on so long as one of them still stood.

"Let's finish this," I said.

IT WAS THE darkest part of the night. It was so black, in fact, that sky and ground seemed to have melded into one.

Indeed, the stars above seemed to have moved to below.

To cluster with us.

Having drifted right through the protective incantations, we landed softly on the front grounds of Empyrean. The front of the house had been repaired, and the door was solid and presumably locked.

All magically tethered together, and hence invisible, we made our way to the back.

As we stared at the rear of Empyrean, Delph took my hand and leaned in.

"Whatever happens this night, Vega. If one of us doesn't make it —"

"Delph, we'll be fine."

"Vega, if one of us doesn't make it, I want you to know that I love you with all my heart. I have always loved you."

I felt my heart thudding inside me. And tears rushed to my eyes.

Just leave it to Delph to make me all wonky right before I was to go to war!

"I love you too, Delph. With all that I have."

We exchanged a kiss and then focused on the task at hand.

We searched around for sentries and finally happened upon two Maladons sleepily at their posts. Necro must have truly believed we were not strong enough to attack. He was probably focused on seeking us out and finishing us off, never truly contemplating that we were going to do the same to him.

We pointed our wands at the Maladons, and said the words.

The two sentries lost their lives never knowing who had taken them.

Two down, about two hundred to go.

Next, I said softly, "Pillsbury?"

The armored man appeared next to me a moment later.

"Mistress Vega," he said softly, gazing around for me.

"We're over here, Pillsbury," I said very quietly.

I cast a tether over him and Pillsbury instantly became invisible too.

"Mistress Vega, thank all that is good in the world that you are safe."

"We're here to attack the Maladons," I said.

He looked around at the others. "How may I assist?" he asked gamely.

"We need to get in the house without anyone knowing," I said.

He nodded. "There is the rear door by the conservatory. There is no one there. They are most derelict when it comes to security."

"Where is Necro?"

"I am not sure, Mistress Vega. I have the pleasure to say that I have not seen that awful creature for some time."

That information worried me, but there was nothing to do but continue on.

Pillsbury got us into the house through the conservatory door.

We moved silently into the Great Hall from there.

"Where are the Maladons?" I asked.

"Some are sleeping in their rooms upstairs. Others are in the lower level. About a dozen are eating in the dining hall."

"Eating, at this hour?" I said.

"They do not adhere to any normalcy of schedule, the louts. I mean, can you imagine the indigestion? I hope they choke on it."

Delph said, "Well, they're not bloody *normal*, are they?"

I looked at my troops. I had already conceived a plan pairing off magicals and nonmagicals in clusters of attack groups. And had gone over the tactics and techniques that I wanted them to employ. There was great risk with this, and many things could go wrong. I knew that better than anyone. But the greatest risk of all would be to do nothing. Then the Maladons would simply hunt us down and kill us at their leisure.

We divided up into three forces to take on the lower level, the dining hall and the upstairs.

I was in the group going to the lower level. Pillsbury had also told us that was where the greatest concentration of Maladons were. With me were Miranda, John, Geoffrey and my mother. Also a third of Russell's men and the Wugs.

In the brief time I'd spent training Geoffrey in the art of battle, he had proved to be an apt student. Though I would only truly know when the battle began.

We headed to the lower level as quietly as possible. I felt the chain links of Destin silently moving under my skin. I would need every bit of power I had to survive this night.

We reached the lower level, and I immediately felt a presence.

Alice Adronis appeared in front of me.

"Follow me, Vega," she said quietly. "I will lead you to them."

I nodded. In her features, I could see the pain and I knew its source.

Alice was unable to fight these monsters herself. I could sense that she wanted Maladon blood on her hands tonight.

We moved quickly down the hall, Alice right next to me.

She whispered something in my ear. I nodded at this and then quietly passed this information down the line of my fighters.

We reached a door behind which I knew there was a large room.

Alice turned to me and said, "What they're doing in here will sicken you if you allow it. But do not turn away. Do what you came here to do. If only I could wield a wand with you."

The look on her face was so fierce that I thought it was very good indeed that I wasn't about to do battle against *her.*

I drew a quick breath before looking at the others. I could see they had the same tense expressions on their faces as I did.

"Are you ready?" said Alice.

I inclined my head.

"Give me five moments," she said.

I nodded again and sent a wand wire to the other two groups, telling them that the time of attack drew near. It had to be precisely coordinated or else we would be lost.

Alice passed through the door.

I counted off the moments in my head.

Five . . . four . . . three . . . two . . . one.

I opened the door, and we all surged inside.

There were approximately fifty Maladons there.

And I was glad of Alice's warning, but still I was so revolted by their actions that I nearly screamed out in fury.

Gunther Adronis's body had been pinned against the wall, and the Maladons were using the corpse for target practice, hurling spell after spell against it.

Russell's men, led by a large man who simply went by Cull, split off to the side, raised their axes and swords and awaited my command.

The Wugs, still enchanted by Astrea's spell, and the creatures, including Seamus and the unicorn, had hung back on my orders as the rearguard. The room could not contain all of us. But they had orders to take up the fight if it looked like things had turned against us.

I, along with the other magicals, raised our wands.

I sent a wand wire to the other two groups.

Now.

We opened fire with our wands.

The Maladons turned and stared around at where the attacks were coming from, though they could see nothing until the lights from our wands passed our protective invisibility shield.

Our first volleys took out ten of them.

Cull and his men rushed forward and their axes and swords slammed into unprepared flesh.

A score more Maladons went down under this onslaught.

And then, as I knew it would, the return spells started blasting across the room.

Invisible or not, we could still be hit. And killed.

We conjured protective shields, but the Maladons had done the same.

Cull's men were repelled.

Cull was slammed into a wall and his magical tether was broken.

He died when a black light nearly split his broad chest in two.

Geoffrey charged forward, shooting spells at every Maladon within reach.

My mother dropped two Maladons with a nifty reverse curse that hit one and ricocheted off the other.

"Triangle!" I shouted.

I shot into the air and fired spells down, drawing the Maladons' attention. All their wands pointed upward and they commenced hurling spells as I dodged out of the way.

My lot had formed a three-sided attack formation and fired spells into the mass of Maladons at a frenetic pace.

The Maladon dead were so many now that bodies lay on top of corpses.

A spell whizzed by my face and I heard someone cry out below.

Miranda Weeks had been backed into a corner by a group of Maladons who had concentrated fire on the site of the lights emanating from her wand.

I could see the desperation on Miranda's features even as she fought bravely.

I soared down and ripped apart this Maladon blockade, not with my wand, but the strength that Destin gave me.

"No!" I screamed.

The light had shot right under my arm. I saw Miranda's face tighten as the spell hit, and then it relaxed. She gazed at me for a second. Her mouth moved, but I could hear nothing.

"Miranda!" I yelled.

Miranda's wand dropped from her hand as her knees struck the stone.

I caught her before she hit the floor.

"Miranda!" I fought the tears before just letting them flow.

I took the Adder Stone from my pocket and waved it over her, thinking the absolute best thoughts I could.

"You cannot save her, Vega," said the voice. "She is gone. And you have others to save. Quickly."

I looked up to see Alice hovering over me.

Tears were blinding me, but as I focused on her and then on what was going on around us, I knew that she was right.

I laid Miranda down, closed her eyes with my hand, gripped my wand and returned to the fight.

Despite our advantage of being invisible, the Maladons' superior numbers and the close quarters of the place had turned the battle against us.

There were only a dozen of Russell's men left alive.

My mother, John, Geoffrey and I were still in the fight, but there were fifteen Maladons still firing spells at us.

But I had something in reserve.

"Now!" I shouted.

The Wugs and creatures surged forward from the rear-guard positions and smashed into the Maladons. Seamus hurled blue fire at two of the Maladons. Their shrieks of pain rang through the room. The unicorn galloped into three other Maladons, impaling each on its magical horn.

An inspired and metallic Domitar plunged his sword into the belly of another Maladon and drove the blade in to the hilt.

I gathered my mother and John with me. My brother had not yet seen that Miranda lay dead. And I didn't want him to.

"Fire and move instantly," I said. "Mum to the left; John, you go to the right. Geoffrey, in the center. The very instant," I added forcefully.

They nodded, knelt down and aimed their wands.

I soared upward and hovered over all as the Maladons looked around warily for the next sign of light heading their way.

I could see only one way out of this.

I readied my wand and said the incantation. Since it came from above, the Maladons did not see it immediately.

Yet as soon as they did, they fired.

And every single one of their spells rebounded upon them, because I had cast a shield incantation around *them*.

Maladons fell left and right, done in by their own spells.

However, my shield spell had broken and the remaining Maladons would not be fooled twice by the trick. And they still outnumbered us. I was racking my brain for an answer when someone cried out below.

Mum had been thrown back against a wall and slowly slid down it to lie unconscious on the floor.

A moment later a battered Geoffrey joined her on the floor.

The shriek that followed this drew all of my attention away.

I hovered there mesmerized as a figure soared across the room.

It was Alice astride her steed, the same one I had seen her riding on the battlefield where she had died.

The Maladons could see her, of course, and fired up at her, not realizing that she was already dead.

I was about to fire spells at them, but they were so dispersed, I would give myself away. Then Alice called out to me.

"The Elemental, Vega. The Elemental. On the battlefield."

I instantly willed my wand to its full Elemental size, cranked my arm back and let fly.

Following my thoughts, the Elemental soared downward. It passed right through one Maladon, and then another and then another.

Until there were none left.

The last body toppled as I alighted on the floor, my hand instinctively rising up to catch the Elemental as it returned to me. It shrank back to a wand and I thrust it into my cloak.

I raced over to my mother and knelt down next to her. Her head was bleeding, but she was breathing. I took out the Adder Stone and waved it over her. The bleeding stopped, and her eyelids fluttered open.

She gripped my arm. "Vega, you're alive."

"Yes. I'm fine."

"And John?"

"He's fine too."

She tried to get up, but I held her down. "You're hurt, Mum. You need to stay right here. I'll be back for you shortly."

"No, I need to fight."

My mother had fought enough. I could not afford to lose her again. I just couldn't. I surreptitiously pointed my wand at her and said the spell.

Her eyelids shut once more, and she feel into a deep sleep.

I rose and checked on Geoffrey. He too was alive, but his fighting was over for now.

It was just me and John left.

Or was it?

"John, John, where are you?"

I looked frantically around the darkened room until I saw him.

376

He was huddled in a corner cradling Miranda's head in his lap.

I ran over to him.

"John, oh, John, I'm so sorry."

He looked up at me, tears streaming down his face.

"They killed her, Vega. She's dead."

I knelt next to him and put my arm around him, as I had so many times when he was a child.

"I know, John. I know they did. And now we have to finish this. For her. For everyone we've lost."

John's own internal struggle was vast, I knew. He and Miranda had grown quite close. But he finally set her down gently on the floor and stood.

He pointed his wand at her.

"What are you doing, John?"

Snow started to fall over her.

When I looked at him, he said, "She thought it was pretty."

I gripped his shoulder. "Are you ready?" I asked.

He nodded.

Alice appeared next to me.

"The fighting still rages above," she said. Then she looked over at the wall. "Could you return Gunther to his place of peace, please?"

I nodded and used my wand to lift his body from the wall and return it to his coffin.

"Thank you," said Alice. "Now go and fight. I will be there with you."

John and I led Russell's remaining men, the creatures and the surviving Wugs out of the room and we all dashed up the stairs.

It was time to triumph or die.

All In

W E REACHED THE main floor and looked frantically around.

Shouts and screams were coming from the dining room.

"Quickly," I said.

We raced down the hall and entered the dining room, where a terrible fight was taking place.

The air was filled with a blur of lights, screams and the sounds of falling bodies.

I was stunned to see that my invisibility tether had broken and that my side was having to fight against a block of Maladons that outnumbered them dramatically. I also saw that the group I had sent to the top floor of Empyrean were now in the dining room. Delph and Jason were two of them, thank the holy Steeples.

But they were losing badly, being driven into the far corner with no escape.

Before we could strike, there came a scream as Pillsbury, Mrs. Jolly and the entire household staff came charging into the room.

Two of the horse statuaries slammed into a group of Maladons, sending them sprawling.

Pillsbury used his sword to run another Maladon through, while Mrs. Jolly clubbed another with a metal ladle.

A contingent of Wugs, led by Thansius, took up the fight,

and the two forces collided in the middle of the room like two large boats crashing together.

Russell and his lot attacked from another flank.

Still, we were outnumbered when it came to wands.

"Now, John," I cried out.

Invisible, we charged forward, firing off spells at the mass of Maladons surrounding the others, while Domitar and his group hacked away at them. This was followed by Russell's regiment hurtling at them from another direction.

Spell after spell, ax and sword, fist and clubs thinned the Maladons, and finally, finally, the tide began to turn, and they started to fall back.

I watched proudly as Harry Two flew through the air and sank his fangs into a Maladon who was about to cast a spell at John's back.

"Bleeding awesome, Harry Two," I cried out.

Inspired by this, Delph used his ax to cleave a hole in the wall of Maladons in front of him.

"Come on!" he cried out, right before a spell hit and blew him across the room, where he slammed into a wall and fell senseless to the floor.

"Delph!"

I finished off the Maladon who had taken down Delph and raced over to him. He was wonky, but alive.

I held up my ring. "You had better not bloody die," I said. "Or I'm going to kill you."

" 'Tis okay, Vega Jane," he said. "Just give me a mo'."

I turned just in time to shoot a Maladon who was about to hurl a spell at us.

And minutes after that, the last Maladon fell when I hit him with a curse and Delph finished him off with his ax.

It was over.

"These blokes weren't that good," said a grinning Delph. "Right good thing they didn't have Endemen anymore."

His words shook me to my core.

Don't have Endemen anymore?

Where were the Bowler Hats? The most elite fighters the Maladons had? I had never seen them at Empyrean through the Seer-See.

To my horror, the front wall of Empyrean crumbled and through it zoomed twenty flying Bowler Hats. They started to blast everything in sight with skill, speed and a murderous efficiency.

Three of my magicals fell almost immediately, as did ten of Russell's men.

It soon became apparent that this had all been planned. They had allowed us to attack them but kept the Bowler Hats in reserve. And now they were intent on slaughtering us.

I saw Jason backed into a corner with Delph, both fighting desperately.

My brother was aiming his wand at the Bowlers, but they were zooming around so fast that he could not bring any of them down.

Russell's men had fallen back, and the Wugs had been completely driven out of the room by the Bowlers.

Things looked hopeless. I couldn't think. I couldn't act. The only thing in my mind was that I had led my people to their deaths, through my own stupidity.

Alice appeared next to me.

"Vega, you must fight."

"It's hopeless, Alice. We've lost."

"We haven't lost."

"But they tricked us. They kept a secret weapon, the Bowler Hats."

"We also have a secret weapon."

"We do? What?"

"You, Vega! This is your time. This is what you've been waiting your whole life for. Now go and finish them."

She vanished.

I looked down at my wand. And then I looked up to see Harry Two growling and backing up as two Bowler Hats descended on him. They were laughing, leisurely taking aim at my dog. They were jabbering about who would kill him first.

I felt my nerves calm, my heart slow, my thoughts clear.

When I looked back down at my wand, it wasn't merely something I was holding in my hand.

It was totally and completely a part of me.

I flexed my shoulders and felt the links of Destin ripple across my broad back.

I was Vega Jane. And my moment had finally come.

I turned my ring around, showing myself to the Maladons.

As soon as the Bowlers turned to me, I lifted off the floor at an explosive speed I had never felt before, and I went on the attack.

I was not going to allow anyone else I cared for, anyone I loved, to fall to these miserable, evil bastards.

The Maladons who were threatening Harry Two never knew what had killed them. And as soon as they fell, I forgot about them.

I was a machine now. I was a *killing* machine.

I willed the Elemental to full size and crushed another group of Bowlers with it as I thundered in between them.

I accelerated and charged right toward the next cluster. They saw me coming, but it did them no good.

My mind was the clearest it had ever been. The confidence in my skills, my magic, had achieved a level I never thought I could.

I roared right at them, deflecting their multiple spells with ease. Three I killed with my wand, rapid-fire death spells emanating not from my mouth but from my mind. That was the level I was at now. The other three I hit so hard with my left fist that I smashed their skulls with the force. They toppled from the air and landed in crumpled heaps like dead birds.

I kept racing around the room, somehow conscious of the fact that all eyes down below were upon me.

But my focus never strayed from my prey.

Maladons. Bowler Hats.

I had a dozen left. And every move that I would take to kill them was already firmly in my mind.

I went into a steep dive as they shot spell after spell at me.

But right before I hit the floor, I shot upward, into their midst.

My wand was moving so fast, it was a blur. Every time light shot from it, a Maladon died.

I twisted and turned and ducked and pivoted and bounced off walls, to avoid all that they were throwing at me. Spells passed right by my ear, my arm, my leg, my heart.

I was never afraid. I was never indecisive.

I knew . . . I mean, I knew that I was going to vanquish them. In my mind I saw the last of them fall.

Now I simply had to do it for real.

I tossed the Elemental into the sky and then sped to the other end of the room.

The Elemental passed completely through three Maladons, dropping them as though they had been tied together. I caught the Elemental at the other end of the room, shrunk it and blew up another Maladon who had dared to race toward me screaming, his wand raised to do me in. When my killing spell hit him dead center, he stopped in midair, looked at the hole in his chest and then plummeted.

I lowered myself to the floor and stared up at the three Maladons left alive.

"*Rejoinda*, Maladons."

They were jerked out of the air and pulled to the floor, where they slowly stood to face me.

I held my wand up.

They did likewise.

But I could see it in their faces.

There was no confidence there, only fear. Only the understanding that I was about to kill them.

There was no fear in my face, for there was none in my head or my heart.

Their shaky hands held up their equally shaky wands.

I could have spared them, I supposed.

I could have had mercy, I supposed.

But I didn't. Right then, I did not care about mercy.

My wand flashed with a speed that no eye could follow. I did not kill them separately. I killed all three with one spell, for it was so overwhelmingly powerful, it passed through the first and then the second and then the last.

They fell to the floor, their wands falling from their dead hands.

I lowered the Elemental.

"NO!" someone screamed.

I turned to see the spell heading right for me.

But before it struck, someone cast a shield spell that blocked it. The light ricocheted off and blasted a hole in the wall.

I looked behind me to see a Bowler Hat that I had apparently missed standing there, his wand raised.

But who had saved me?

As I looked to my right, I gasped. I don't think I have ever been that stunned in my life.

"Petra?"

The Ultimatum

IT WAS INDEED Petra.

Together we turned our wands on the remaining Maladon. Our combined spells struck him so hard that he simply evaporated.

I turned to Petra, who was standing there beside me.

I gripped her arm, if only to make sure she was flesh and bone.

"You're . . . you're alive, but how?"

She smiled and shook her head. "I don't know how. One minute I thought I was dead. The next minute I was up and fleeing from Empyrean."

"Where have you been all this time?"

"Searching for you. I finally gave it up as a bad job and came back here and waited. I didn't see you come."

"I was using the invisibility ring."

"Of course. I finally left to get some sleep, but then I heard all the fighting and came running back. I got here just in time, I guess."

"You did. Or else I wouldn't be alive."

I hugged her. A moment later we were being crushed in another embrace.

We both looked up to see Delph.

"Pet, thought you were a goner."

"Me too, Delph. Me too."

I looked over and my smile widened.

A bloody and battered Geoffrey staggered up the stairs carrying Mum in his arms.

I hurried over and reversed the spell I had placed over her.

She opened her eyes.

She put a hand on his cheek and returned the smile as John came over to hold her other hand.

"We survived," she said.

Then all grew quiet.

I saw Geoffrey stiffen. He was looking over my shoulder, so I slowly turned and looked there too.

Necro was standing in the ruins of where the front door to Empyrean used to be.

His hood was down and his vulture-like features were clear to all.

He surveyed the damage, the fallen, the devastation that accompanied every battlefield.

I held up my wand as my lot gathered behind me, their wands and weapons raised as well.

It was us against Necro, and I liked my odds just fine.

Until thirty creatures suddenly appeared behind him: jabbits, garms, freks, giant amarocs, and the dreaded lycans, whose bite would turn someone mad.

"My new army, Vega," said Necro. He looked at the carnage. "Conveniently so, since you appear to have dispatched my other one. But then your numbers have been culled dramatically." He looked us over. "Not that many wands. And of course you have many who have no wands. Which stands for nothing."

One of Russell's men stepped forward and raised his ax. "Well, we'll see about that, won't we?"

"We will," said Necro. "You first of all."

He never even moved his wand. He never said a word, didn't move a muscle.

The man suddenly gurgled, blood poured out of his mouth and he fell forward, dead. His ax clanged against the stone floor.

"No," I cried out as I rushed toward him.

Necro's voice stopped me in my tracks.

"He is nothing. Do not waste your time with nothing, Vega. You have far more important issues to confront."

I looked across the width of the hall at him.

"No life is worth nothing," I said.

"Well, that is the difference between you and me."

"That is the only thing on which you and I will ever agree."

And without another word from Necro, all thirty beasts attacked.

I sprang into the air and willed my Elemental to full size.

I heaved it at the charging beasts. It smashed into the wall of flesh, bone and ferocity and took out ten of them with the blow.

My lot surged forward to take up the battle.

The Elemental flew back to my hand even as Necro entered the fight, and with sweeps of his wand he felled four of Russell's men and two of my sorcerers.

Harry Two had latched on to the throat of a frek and had knocked the beast over. I finished it off with a spell. The jabbits were heading toward Geoffrey and Petra, their foul, fanged heads hissing and jabbing at the pair.

I swooped in to help but then saw that John was in very real danger of being torn apart by a trio of lycans.

I was about to help them when I saw that my mother was very nearly being done in by a garm, her shield spell the only thing keeping the beast at bay.

And then there was Delph battling two giant amarocs and on the verge of losing the fight.

And there was Jason, who had recovered from his injuries and rejoined the fight, taking on a frek and a garm.

I couldn't be in all those different places at once. I would have to choose who to save.

My mother? My brother? Delph? Petra?

I hovered frozen in the air, my wand darting in all directions and accomplishing nothing.

And then it happened.

At first, I thought that Necro had used his air-hardening spell, the one that I found virtually unbeatable. But it wasn't that. It was something else altogether.

Something else even more powerful.

And everything in that room, people and beasts, grew still as corpses.

I looked up from my high perch at something even higher.

The orb of light had come in through a hole in the ceiling.

It descended downward until it alighted upon the floor right in the middle of the frozen battle.

When the shimmering dissipated, I could see what, or rather, *who* it was.

"Elythia!" I gasped.

She wore a hooded cloak of the palest blue. It was so pale in fact that it almost looked like a sheet of ice with light dancing through it.

I glanced over at Necro, who was staring at his former wife.

And for the first time ever, I saw something in his eyes that I never thought I would.

Fear.

"Elythia?" said Necro.

I looked around the room. My lot just stood there and stared at her.

Even the beasts were frozen in place, unable to look away from the pale blue cloak and the woman inside it.

Elythia stepped forward and surveyed the death all around her.

Then she turned to Necro and the look on her face made me weak at the knees. Never have I seen such fury, such poisonous venom, not even in a thousand jabbits.

"There stands *my* son, Necro." She pointed at Jason. "As he fights against your kind."

"He is misguided," snarled Necro, regaining a bit of his bravado.

"I had been told for eons that Jason was dead. That her lot" — she pointed to me — "had killed him."

"Elythia, you always knew the truth," began Necro.

"Silence!" she spat.

And Necro shut his cruel mouth.

I almost smiled at how weak he now looked.

Almost. Since I had no idea what Elythia planned to do. For all I knew, she would kill us all. And I knew there was absolutely nothing I could do to prevent that.

"My son was brought to me by Vega," she continued. "She wanted a mother to see her son. And for that I thank you," she said, glancing at me.

She turned to Necro and advanced upon him.

"I now know Jason had been enslaved by you. Turned into one of your followers, your hate-filled leeches that utter your name as though you were a god. Are you a god, Necro? Are you?"

He shook his head. "I am not a god," he said.

I found my voice because I was confused. "But, Elythia, you had to know the truth about Jason. You struck all the

Maladon women barren because of it. Because you knew he had taken your son."

She turned to me. "I always knew that Jason was alive and that Necro had wrongly blamed his death on your kind. That was why I did what I did. I did not want any more babies born to these fiends, who would raise them to be Maladons."

"Blimey," said Delph. "Why didn't you just kill the bloke? Him!" he added, pointing at Necro.

Elythia turned to Necro. "Shall I tell him, or will you finally tell the truth?"

"Curse you!" said Necro.

"Jason," she said. "Come to me."

Her son dutifully crossed the room and took the hand of his mother.

Elythia said, "What I'm about to tell you I have never told anyone, ever. Only I and Necro knew." She turned to Delph. "And it will explain why I did nothing to him."

She looked back at Jason. "Your father performed a spell on you when you were born, my beautiful son. It is a complex spell. It is a dark, hideous, evil spell. And of course, he knew how to do it because that is who he is." She paused. "Do you want to tell them what you had to sacrifice in order to accomplish this?"

Necro remained silent.

Elythia turned back to me. "He had to voluntarily relinquish his soul."

"Blimey," exclaimed Delph.

"It is a terrible thing. It's like cleaving yourself in half. He did it to protect himself against me, for not even my power is enough to overcome such a curse. But the price he paid means that when his physical body dies, he will live forever in a Hel of his making, never able to escape, never able to have even a moment's respite from the pain, the agony, the horror of having done something so foul."

I glanced at John, who was watching this all, mesmerized.

"But what did he do?" John asked. "What was the curse he made?"

Elythia turned to Jason. "My dear son, the curse irreversibly connected your soul, your life, your spirit, with that of your father's."

I gasped. "But that means —" I began.

Elythia nodded sadly. "That if I killed Necro, Jason would die."

"Bloody Hel," said Delph.

"I was powerless. Trapped. But not entirely. Not now. As you can see."

With a mere sweep of her hand, all the dangerous creatures aligned against us simply vanished.

Now it was Necro, all alone.

Jason came forward. "Mother, I am prepared to die. I have been alive far too long as it is. I want to join Uma in death. Kill him and I will die happily."

Tears started to slip down Elythia's cheeks. "I cannot kill you, Jason. I cannot. I could utter the words, but there would be no force behind it." She glared at Necro. "Which he very well knows."

Jason took her hand. "I understand."

"I looked for you, Jason. I went to Maladon Castle, the hideous place he built after he won his terrible war. I knew what Necro had become. But never did I think that he would have completely transformed you into another. Into someone of his own image." She once more glared at Necro. "He used my love for you against me."

I stepped forward. "But if someone else kills Necro?"

All eyes turned to me.

"Then only Necro dies," said Elythia.

"Then that is how it must be. I will duel Necro, alone."

Delph said, "No, you won't. We got a lot more blokes ready to fight this one. We'll all take him on."

"But, Delph —" I began.

"Vega, it's your bleedin' army. Lead us against him. We'll tear him apart."

I started to waver.

Necro said, "Yes, Vega, by all means. And then when I kill all of your friends, then and only then will I kill you. Because I want you to watch them die."

My wavering halted.

"No, Delph, I will fight him alone."

"But —"

"I will fight him alone," I said in such a ferocious tone that Delph instantly stepped back, his head bowed.

"Where do you wish to do this, Vega?" Elythia asked. "Here? In your ancestral home at Empyrean?"

I shook my head. "No. It must be done . . . in my real home."

Elythia nodded once more. She obviously knew exactly my meaning.

"Then so be it."

She turned to look at Necro.

"Should you prevail, I will not intervene."

At this, Necro's mouth curled into a smile. "Delightful, Elythia. And once I'm done with Vega, I will be free to rebuild my empire."

Elythia looked at him with a face of stone.

"Do not be too assured, Necro. I do not like your chances against Vega. Truly, I do not know."

She waved her hand in the air.

And Necro and I vanished in a cloud of smoke.

Back to the Beginning

I ROSE FROM THE cobbles of the High Street in Wormwood.
I watched as Necro did the same.

I looked down at myself because I felt different, a bit heavier.

And what I saw made me understand why.

I was wearing battle armor.

I stood tall and firm there on the cobbles, my hair hanging down around my shoulders.

We stared warily at each other.

"You remind me of someone," he said.

"Do I?" I shot back.

"I think you know who." He paused. "Alice."

I looked down at the armor and could understand his observation. This was identical to the armor that Alice was wearing on the battlefield when I'd first encountered her.

"I hope to wear it as bravely as she did, then."

He sneered, "Remember that she died on the battlefield."

"A lesson I have learned from."

"Why here?" Necro demanded, looking around.

"Like I said, it's my home. And because of you, it became my prison."

"Well, now it will become your grave."

But I was ready for him.

The spell shot out at me, but I was already gone.

I had taken to the air at the same time I'd turned my ring around.

I could see Necro looking everywhere for me.

"You can't run forever," he said.

I felt the air hardening around me.

But I was prepared for that too.

"*Pass-pusay.*"

I tapped my leg with my wand and vanished.

I reappeared at Stacks, next to my old workbench. My brass nameplate was still on it. The Maladons had defaced it, but I had burned their foulness off it.

I looked around the cavernous space. The Maladons had toppled the towers and smashed in the massive wooden gate, but I already knew that and didn't care. I had spent two years of my life laboring here.

I now knew that Necro could command beasts. Perhaps this was due to his also being a fiendish creature without a heart. Really, in all essential respects, he was no different from a garm, frek or jabbit. He was simply even more deadly than they were.

I walked into Domitar's old office with its ink bottles, parchment and ink sticks. It was at Stacks that I had learned from Domitar and Dis Fidus some of the truth of this place. Which was one reason I had come here until I could finalize my plot against Necro.

I had no intention of simply dueling him until one of us fell dead.

I wanted him to understand exactly why I chose this place as the site of our final battle.

I ventured to the hole in the dirt where our pretty things were laid to rest. I placed an article from the hole into a small bag, tapped my leg once more and said, *"Pass-pusay."*

I landed in front of Morrigone's old home. The ornate gate was gone and the front door blasted away, thanks again to the Maladons. I walked into the home and went up the stairs to my brother's old room. The Maladons had left it untouched, perhaps hoping to enlist my brother as one of their own.

But I knew my brother better than anyone. And despite how he had changed while under Morrigone's tutelage, inside that chest was a heart that was bigger than mine even. He might have been tempted by the sorts of black magic they performed, but he could never be like them.

I found in John's room a journal that I had given him for his birthday right before I left Wormwood. My brother had always been such a voracious reader of books that I had told him he might want to write one of his own.

I opened the journal and started to read what he had written.

I did this with some trepidation because this had been the period of time when my brother had, I believed, been sorely tempted by the darker side of sorcery.

Despite that, what I found in his writings and drawings were not about such things, but about his thoughts on his family, his mother, his father and . . . me. He had drawn animals in the pages with surprising skill. He had discussed his thoughts of what Wormwood was and wasn't. Like I had, John had figured out that Wormwood and his life here were built on lies.

I got to the bottom of one page where John had written lines that struck me hard.

My sister is the only one I could ever really count on. For everything. To tell me the truth when I didn't want to hear it. But for her, I would have chosen a different path that I now, with her gone from my life, find dangerously tempting. Wherever you are, Vega, please know that though I may draw close to the line that separates us from them, I will never cross it. And that is due entirely to you.

I sat on the floor and read these lines three more times, my tears increasing with each pass. I finally rose, and tapped my leg with my wand.

I reappeared in my old home.

I found what I was looking for in the corner.

One of my dead father's old hats.

I tapped my leg with my wand, and I appeared outside of Delph's house.

I stared up at the front porch, where the objects that I had seen there before filled my line of sight.

Duf Delphia's wooden timbertoes. They had replaced the legs he had lost while working on the Wall around Wormwood. A wall that we had been told was to keep these creatures called the Outliers out. But it was really meant to keep us in.

Duf would need the wooden legs no longer, but I required them.

I raised my wand and said, *"Rejoinda,* timbertoes."

They flew to me. I reduced them in size and placed them in my bag.

My last stop was the Hallowed Ground, where Wugs buried their dead.

It was here that I thought I had buried Thansius.

I had conjured and then carved his headstone. I read off the words that I had written with my wand.

"Here lies Thansius, the best and mightiest Wug of all."

And perhaps the one with the biggest heart of all too, I thought.

I tapped my leg and appeared back in the High Street.

Under my armor was my cloak. And in my cloak pocket was the Seer-See.

I set it on the ground and manipulated the cup. As the flaming liquid seeped across the cobbles, he appeared in it.

Necro was roaming the village at the other end, near where the Council building used to be before the Maladons destroyed it. He was hunting me, but Necro had no idea I was doing the same to him.

I studied him closely, something I had never had the opportunity to do before, seeing as how I was normally running for my life from the git.

His terrible features seemed strangely enlarged and even more deadly white in the bright sunshine that hung over my little village.

There were several breaches in the wall. I don't know what had caused them, whether beast, sorcerer or some other evil.

I continued to watch Necro walk along, his wand always at the ready. In my mind's eye, I saw him take Astrea's magic for his own, which had rendered him infinitely more powerful.

Still, for a variety of reasons, I never doubted my ability to defeat him.

The blow that hit me the next second was so stunning that my ring spun around, cutting off my shield of invisibility.

Barely ten feet from me stood Necro.

But how was that possible? I looked down into the flaming liquid and there was Necro as well, still walking through the village.

Then it struck me.

He had conjured a doppelgang of his very own.

Another thought struck me as I stood on shaky legs.

He had absorbed Astrea's magic. Did that mean he knew all about what she could do? If so, he was well aware of the

Seer-See. Perhaps he had known all along that I used it to spy on his lot at Empyrean.

"I can see that the truth has occurred to you, Vega. Astrea was a brilliant sorceress with a far-reaching mind who could conjure things that even I could not. But for you, this is not a good thing."

He hurled another spell at me, a killing spell that I managed to dodge by flying into the air.

Necro leapt into the sky and met me a hundred feet off the ground.

"No doubt you thought it to your advantage to duel me in your old village," he said. "You know the 'lay of the ground' as it were. But so did Astrea, and thus so do I, seeing that she created it."

"You will never know this place as well as I do."

"You were not a match for me even before I took her powers, Vega. You are overconfident. You will find that was a fatal mistake because I have never truly unleashed my full powers on you. But take heart, I will not kill you immediately. I want you to suffer," he added, with a snarl. "Because you have taken much from me. And I want you to know that after I finish you off, I will return and kill every single member of your lot left alive."

The air started to seize up around me. And this time I could not escape its effects. I grabbed my throat because I could barely breathe. I became senseless. Right before my eyes closed, I could sense that I was falling . . . a very long way.

And then there was nothing.

Death Finally Comes

WHEN I OPENED my eyes, I was bound head and foot by golden lashes. I struggled against them with all my might. With the strength that Destin provided me, I could feel them give, but only a little. Then I fell limp, exhausted by the effort.

I looked around and saw that I was at Steeples. The last time I had been at our place of worship, the pretty glass had been melted and the building gutted by the Maladons.

I was up on a stone slab on the altar where Ezekiel, the Sermonizer, would preach to us, basically telling us that no matter what we did, we were doomed.

I could actually relate right now to the feeling of being doomed.

I sensed movement to my left and flinched when I saw it.

The jabbit was enormous. And it had wings, like the kind I had seen long ago on the battlefield where Alice had been killed.

The creature sat coiled up barely ten feet from me, but all of its hideous heads were staring right at me. Hundreds of forked tongues slithered out of the serpents' hundreds of heads and the fangs were revealed, pointy and full of venom so deadly that one drop could kill just about anything.

To my right, I also sensed movement.

This time it was Necro who was striding up the center aisle of Steeples directly toward me.

"Vega, I trust your rest has been pleasant?"

I just stared at him, the fury in me overtaking the fear.

"I'll take your lack of response as a no," he said.

He twirled his wand between his fingers.

"Now, let me see, I have taken some items from you and would like an explanation."

He flicked his wand and a series of objects appeared above of me.

They were the things I had collected around Wormwood. A brass candlestick, my father's hat and Duf's timbertoes. He also had taken out the Adder Stone. And my wand.

"Tell me what these mean to you," he said.

I looked away.

"Ah, some prompting, then."

He lowered his wand and pointed it at me. It was as though someone had set me afire. I had never felt such pain in my life.

I screamed and pulled against my bonds. Tears fell down my cheeks.

"Please, stop," I cried out.

The pain did indeed stop.

"Answer," he said.

"The candlestick represented things that I labored for years making for no reason at all, other than to occupy my time in useless endeavors. Because your lot made my lot hide."

"Dear me. But that's what those who lose wars do. They run and hide like the frightened little weaklings that they are. The hat?"

"My father's hat."

"Your *dead* father, let's not forget that little fact. I burned his body, along with all the others. And after I kill you, I will go back to Empyrean and slaughter your mother and brother too. I will tell them how you begged for your life. How you would have gladly sacrificed them to survive."

"You bastard!" I roared.

I screamed again as the fire returned. I had to cry out for him to stop for nearly a minute before he relinquished the spell.

"The other items?" he asked calmly. "You will tell me."

"Duf Delphia's timbertoes for the legs he lost."

He laughed. "You have so much to learn. But you never will. But I'll tell you who will learn at my knee. Your dear brother. I have high hopes for him, very high indeed, provided he swears his loyalty to me."

"He would rather die."

"Then I can surely accommodate him."

It suddenly struck me what this was all about.

"You want *him* to replace Jason, you vile monster!"

The next moment the fires returned to my insides, this time even hotter and deeper. It was as though I was being cooked from the inside.

When he let go of the spell, I managed to catch my breath. I told myself that the next time he did that, I would not cry out. I would not beg him to stop. I would just die. But what tore at me was the fact that I would be leaving the others to deal with Necro. In my mind's eye, I saw a fresh pile of bodies aflame. That was more painful than anything that Necro could do to me.

"And why would you want to collect these things?" he asked.

402

"Because I wanted to show them to you right before I killed you. I wanted you to see how much evil you had wrought. I wanted them to be the last things you ever saw."

"Hmm. Grandiose plans, Vega. Quite ridiculous, in fact. Now, your wand I know," added Necro, using his own wand to spin mine in a circle. "The Elemental. Alice's old wand. I hardly think you worthy of it, Vega. Hardly."

"It's my wand," I said between gritted teeth.

"Which only leaves us with this."

With his wand, he made the Adder Stone spin around like a top in the air. "What does this do?" he asked.

"I don't know."

"Come now, Vega, don't be stubborn. It could be useful to me as I rebuild my empire."

I thought quickly.

"I'll never tell you."

He pointed his wand and the fires returned.

I didn't scream. I didn't cry. I didn't beg for him to stop.

When I looked at him defiantly, he said, "Well, you're a bit tougher than I would have thought. We'll see how you withstand the jabbit."

He flicked his wand, and the creature unwound its coils, rose up fifty feet into the air and then descended over me, such that its hundreds of pairs of eyes and its lethal fangs were but an inch from me.

I watched as a drop of venom gathered on one of the fangs.

Necro said, "I will not let it be absorbed into you, Vega, not yet. But I can tell you that the pain it will cause will make my spell seem as nothing."

I didn't answer. I just stared up at all those eyes an inch from me.

I watched the drop of poison cling to that fang. It started to stretch as gravity pulled it downward, toward me. In another second it would break free and fall.

Wait, Vega, wait.

Right before the venom fell, I screamed out, "Don't, please."

"Tell me!" he barked.

"It's the torture stone! You wave it over the person and think bad thoughts. Whatever you think will happen."

Necro flicked his wand, and the jabbit drew away from me.

"Bad thoughts? I have a great many of them. What a useful object."

He plucked the Stone out of the air and held it over me.

"Shall we try it out, Vega?"

I braced myself.

He waved it over my body and no doubt thought the vilest thoughts he could.

There was an explosion of power that ripped me free from my bonds. I saw the jabbit hurled the length of Steeples, where it slammed into the wall with such force that it burst apart into a mountain of blood, venom and gore.

Necro screamed like I had never heard anyone scream before.

As I rose off the stone slab, I snatched the Elemental out of the air.

When I saw Necro, I had to gasp.

His hooded cloak was gone. His skin was gone. His eyes were gone. All that was left was bone. And in his skeletal hand was his wand.

He was still screaming, and pointing his wand around.

"Damn you, Vega. Curse you, Vega. I will destroy you. Where are you?! Where are you?!"

It was then I knew that without eyes, he could no longer see.

Now I had him.

Or at least I thought I did. My problem was, I kept underestimating him.

He waved his wand and a murderous swarm of creatures flew through the empty windows of Steeples.

I recognized them immediately.

A chontoo, an inficio, a manticore and a swarm of dreads.

"Kill her!" screamed Necro as he stumbled around.

I shot into the air and zipped out of Steeples with the creatures right on me. I tried to turn my ring to become invisible.

Only it wasn't there.

Necro must have taken it.

I looked back to see the beasts gaining on me.

I had faced all these vile beasts before. And I knew what they could do and couldn't do. They had all nearly killed me before. Now they had a second chance.

The manticore could read minds. This gave me an idea. I flicked my wand back over my shoulder at the chontoo, a creature that consisted only of a head. It hunted prey in hopes of gaining the necessary body parts to make it whole.

What I had just done was transfer a thought of mine to the chontoo.

The manticore turned on its neighbor. They spiraled out of the sky, battling each other.

Now I was faced with the dreads and the inficio. Again, I had an idea.

The inficio breathed out poison. The dreads would simply claw me to death if they could catch me.

I shot upward and then flipped over and headed right for them.

405

The inficio opened its mouth.

Come on, come on, do it.

Poisonous vapor poured out.

I immediately conjured a stiff wind that blew the gas right over the dreads.

They fell from the sky and thudded into the ground.

I shot downward, pointed my wand up at the belly of the inficio and muttered, *"Jagada."*

Slashes opened up in the gut of the foul flying beast. It turned over, banked to the side and plummeted downward.

I watched it until it struck the ground with an enormous crash.

Then I turned and headed back to Steeples.

And to Necro.

When I got there, I found the building demolished.

And rearing up from the back of it, I saw why.

It was the largest colossal I had ever seen. And I'd seen some gigantic ones indeed.

And in the grip of the brute's right hand was blind Necro, screaming in pain as the thing was crushing him to death.

I hurtled forward, my wand ready.

This was going to be a little tricky, but if anyone was going to end Necro's life, it was going to be me, not some git colossal.

I zoomed in low with the intent that I would fire upward into the creature's arm, severing it from the rest of it. While he was preoccupied with losing a limb, I would conjure a shield to soften the landing of the arm, freeing Necro.

And then kill the bloody bastard.

"Severus."

The forearm of the colossal came neatly away from its upper arm. Necro plunged to the ground. However, I conjured

406

the shield, and the severed limb landed gently on the dirt as the colossal danced away, raging in pain at what I had done.

I used my wand to free Necro, and then, as I zoomed toward him, I realized that this was the moment of truth. Soon, it would all be over.

And I was right about that.

For all the wrong reasons.

The light hit me straight in the chest.

I looked down and saw the mortal wound pierce my armored chest. It seemed identical to the one Alice had suffered.

And then, just like Alice Adronis, I died on a battlefield.

The Truth

IF THIS TRULY was dying, then it wasn't so terrible.

I could remember what had happened to me.

Necro had tricked me with the colossal.

And then he had killed me.

I would see Astrea and Archie. So many who had fallen fighting with me.

I would see my father.

But then I thought about those I would be leaving behind.

My mother and John, Delph, Petra, Harry Two and the others.

Necro had sworn to go back and kill them.

Could I warn them somehow?

But I was dead.

I could help no one.

The mists were thick here, but then they cleared and what I saw was clean and cheery. Not terrifying at all.

There was a quiet serenity here that I had never found in life.

I walked along, not hesitant or anxious at all.

I was bound to run into the other dead.

Still, Necro had beaten me. And something burned inside of me that I could not reconcile with the blissful atmosphere of where I was presently.

Or perhaps for all eternity.

That would make Astrea's and Archie's time at the emerald cottage in the Quag seem quite short by comparison.

I saw a bench up ahead that was set by a pond of still water.

I suddenly felt tired, so I sat down and looked around.

But my gaze returned to the mortal wound on my chest, where my armor had been punctured, and my flesh and heart along with it.

It didn't hurt. I was in no pain.

But I was still dead.

And there was a distinct sadness associated with that.

I had failed everyone. Necro had won.

I frowned as I stared at the still water.

"Vega?"

I looked around.

I saw no one, but the voice calling out to me was vaguely familiar.

"Vega Jane?"

I rose and looked in all directions.

A figure appeared from out of the mists and started walking toward me.

I flinched when I saw who it was.

"Jasper?"

Jasper Jane drew close. He looked as he had when I had seen him in the Quag.

"You told me you saw me in the future?"

He nodded solemnly.

"Now I know for certain. You saw me when I was dead, didn't you?"

"That is true."

"You said you couldn't tell me because something bad would happen to me." I added angrily, "But what's worse than being dead?"

"Many things," he replied matter-of-factly. "A great many things."

"That doesn't help me," I shot back.

"What I can tell you is restricted to one thing and only one thing."

"Which is?" I said suspiciously.

He pointed to the wound in my chest.

"Your mortal wound?"

"Undoubtedly."

"Do you feel dead?"

"No, but I am. I know I am."

"Yet you are in your original form?"

"What do you mean? Alice and Uma are in their original form."

"No, they are no longer flesh and blood. They are spirits. In Uma's case, she is regret. Yet you are flesh and bone. Don't you see?"

I slowly reached out a hand and touched my leg. I could feel it.

I glanced up at him. "How can that be? I was killed. Necro killed me."

"Petra too was killed. And yet she rose again, did she not?"

I stared at him. "That's because she only thought she was dead. She was stunned, that was all."

"No, she was dead. The spell that hit her was a killing spell."

I shook my head. This was nonsense. "That's impossible."

"When Petra died, did you feel anything?"

"No, I —" I paused, because I had felt *something*. "I . . . I felt something funny in my chest."

Jasper nodded. "That would make sense."

"Why?" I said quickly.

"Because it is a condition of the Oath of Oblivion that you both took. That you both made to each other."

I drew in a sharp breath. "The Oath of Oblivion?"

He pointed to my forehead. "There is a solemn vow, an exchange of blood, a pact that one will die for the other. And if not, if the pact is broken, then terrible consequences will follow. But on the other hand, good can come from it. Because it can offer extraordinary protections that can be found nowhere else in the magical world."

I tried to follow what he was saying, but it was difficult.

"Do you . . . do you mean what I think you mean?"

"A bit of you and a bit of Petra were exchanged when you made the promise to each other. That bit of you and that bit of Petra serve to protect you against the most dire of consequences."

"Death?" I said in a hollow tone.

He nodded. "Petra lived because the killing curse hit that bit of you, Vega. And that bit of you absorbed the full force of the spell. It killed that piece of you, but it allowed Petra to survive."

"So Necro's spell?"

"It killed that bit of Petra."

"Then why am I here? If I'm not really dead?"

"A part of you *is* dead, Vega. And death requires you to come here. But unlike virtually all others who arrive at this place, you will not be required to stay."

"But Petra didn't mention any of that happening to her."

"But you are not Petra. Her coming here would have garnered the barest of recollection. Perhaps she would not remember it all. But you, you are different."

"Why am I different?"

411

"You are Vega Jane, and with that comes complications. But chief among them? You have a choice to make."

"You mean I can leave and go back to the living?" I looked around. "Or stay here?"

"Yes. But should you die once more, it will be final."

I nodded, because that made perfect sense. "By taking that oath, we saved both of our lives?"

"Yes."

"I guess it was lucky that we did so."

"Oh, I think luck had little enough to do with it."

"Did you know I would triumph over Necro because you saw that in the future?"

"No, Vega, but having met you, I thought it a pretty good bet."

I smiled at his confidence in me.

I wish I could have known him when he was alive. I think he would have been quite wonderful to have been around.

"I've made my choice, and I have to get going, Jasper. But I would like to ask you one more question."

"Yes?" he said expectantly.

"How did you die?"

"What does it matter? Life and death are just states of mind, Vega. I will see you again at some point, but not for a long time, I suspect."

The mist swirled around me so fiercely that I had to blink to be able to see.

The next moment the image of Steeples appeared before me.

The colossal lay dead in the field next to the building.

And at the doorway to the building stood Necro.

He appeared to have healed himself, for he was nearly back to his original form.

He seemed to be searching for something. Perhaps he was wondering why, having vanquished me, he was not free to leave this place.

His voice boomed out. "I have won, Elythia. Fair and square. And now it is time for you to set me free to do as I wish. I demand that. Now."

"I don't think so," I cried out.

He turned slowly to face me. When he saw who it was, he grew still.

"This cannot be."

"It certainly can be," I said as I started walking toward him.

He shot a spell at me that I flicked away with my wand. He fired another and another. I deflected them with ease.

I had never felt stronger. It was as though all the power of the entire Jane family now rested within me. It was palpable.

"You are dead!" he screamed.

"No, I'm not. But you are."

I stopped when I was only five feet from him. We stared across the width of ground at each other.

"I killed you once. I can do so again," said Necro.

"You killed me by trick. That won't happen again."

He held up his wand. "You will never get through my defenses. I have the power of not just myself, but dear Astrea inside me."

"You took her power out of fear."

Necro curled his lip. "You are mad."

"Out of your fear of me."

He laughed shrilly.

"Because you were afraid your magical powers would not be equal to mine."

"You are deluded. There is no magical being more power-ful than I."

"But you made a mistake," I said, ignoring his self-aggrandizing comment.

"You talk in circles."

"Then let me make it clearer. You and Astrea are not compatible."

"What does that mean?" he sneered.

"It means that you took inside of you the magic of a mighty sorceress who hates you. Can you feel that, Necro? Can you understand your colossal blunder? You have killed yourself from within."

He started to laugh, but then stopped and looked down at his wand. His hand shook just a bit. His brow creased in worry. This garnered his full attention.

And that was all I needed.

I flexed my shoulders. And at the same time I willed something to happen that I never had before.

Destin, freed from my body, shot straight out at Necro. The chain wound around and around his wand. With a sweep of my hand, Destin propelled into the air, taking Necro's wand with it.

"No!" screamed Necro.

I willed the Elemental to full size. I took my time in so doing. And I had no need to even tell it what to do.

It already knew.

The Elemental hurtled directly at the now-defenseless Necro.

He didn't have time to scream again.

When it struck him, I have never seen a flash of light that bright. It was every color of the rainbow and then some.

Out of this burst of light wheeled the Elemental.

It flew straight and true right back to my waiting hand. To its rightful owner, where it once more became my wand.

When the lights fell away, Necro was no more.

I stared at the spot for a few moments, just to make sure.

Then, recalling Destin to me, I took Necro's wand, pointed the Elemental at it, and the thing simply vanished, never to be wielded again.

I lifted into the air and set my route directly back toward Empyrean.

I didn't use the *Pass-pusay* spell because I had something to do.

I reached the wall at the end of the Quag and breached the seam.

On the other side of the wall, I read the words I had burned there before.

THIS TIME WE WILL TRIUMPH

I used my wand to erase this and then used it to burn new words in their place.

PEACE HOPE FREEDOM

Then I rose into the air and headed home.

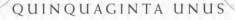

Another Beginning

M Y FEET STRUCK the dirt in front of Empyrean. I was feeling exhausted but thrilled.

Our enemy was gone.

I walked through the hole where the door had once been.

Inside the hall, a group of people was waiting.

Delph gave a cry of delight and rushed toward me.

He lifted me off the floor in a bear hug and spun me around.

"I knew it," he cried out. "Didn't I tell you?" he called out to the others. "Didn't I?"

"You did indeed," said my mother. She rushed over to give me a hug once Delph let me down.

"I'm so very glad to see you back, Vega," my mother said.

Petra joined us and took my hand.

"Are you okay?" she asked.

"I was about to ask you that," I said. "You look very pale."

She touched her chest. "I felt funny here," she said. "It was like something had . . ."

"Had died inside you?" I said.

She shot me a glance. "How did you know that?"

"It's a long story. But I will explain it to you later."

She touched my ring. "Delph told me the wonderful news. Congratulations, Vega."

"Thank you, Petra."

"So, what happened with Necro?" asked Delph.

I told them briefly about what had taken place between us back in Wormwood. I left out the part about dying. That one would take a bit of explanation, which I didn't care to get into right now.

"That is bloody amazing, Vega Jane," said Delph.

"I'm just glad to be back."

I looked around at the remains of Empyrean.

"We have a lot of work to do on this place. To get it back up to snuff."

My mother nodded. "But we will."

"There aren't many of us left," I pointed out.

"There will always be new ones to come along," said Delph.

I touched his arm and smiled. But he didn't smile back. In fact, he looked pale and sad.

"Delph, what is —"

But at that moment, I saw John come into the room, and I ran over to him. "John, where have you been?"

"Tending to some of the wounded. I quite think I'd like to be a Healer, Vega."

"That's wonderful, John. Our lot is certainly battered and bruised. Why, if —"

The rest of my words got caught in my throat as I saw Delph coming toward me.

He was carrying a limp body in his arms.

As he grew closer, my lips started to tremble and large tears gathered in my eyes.

Delph drew to a stop in front of me and then gently set the body down on the floor.

Now I knew why Delph had been pale and sad.

I dropped to my knees.

"Oh, Harry Two," I moaned. "Not Harry Two."

417

My beautiful dog was lying in front of me. His glorious mismatched eyes were open and glassy, his chest was not moving. Harry Two had never failed to rise from his wounds. Several times he had been so close to death, usually after saving my wretched life, but he had always managed to get to his feet and labor on.

Always.

Until now.

I put my hand on his head and ruffled his fur.

"Wh-what h-happened?"

"He was fine," Delph said. "He got hurt some in the fighting, but nothing bad."

Petra added, "But then a few minutes ago, he got really tense and his eyes focused like I had never seen before. And . . . and . . ." She looked miserably at Delph.

"And he just fell over, Vega. And died."

Petra said, "But there was something shimmering around him."

"Something shimmering. What are you talking —"

I stopped in midsentence.

I knelt down close to Harry Two and stared directly into his still blue eye.

And somewhere in those depths, I saw something, just a glimmer of something that I had seen once before there and that reminded me of someone I dearly loved. And dearly missed.

My grandfather Virgil.

I sat back and looked at my wand. I recalled the power that I had felt upon coming back from the dead. Right when I was to battle Necro for the last time. It was as though the entire Jane family was inside me. And maybe they had been.

I looked at Harry Two again. I had never known where my beautiful dog had come from. He had just appeared in my life one day when I was all alone and really, really needed someone.

And Harry Two and I had found each other.

And then I remembered that my first dog, Harry, had been killed by a garm, sacrificing his life for mine. And my grandfather had been with us then. He had held me that day while I sobbed into his strong shoulder at my unfathomable loss.

I buried my face in Harry Two's wonderfully soft fur and sobbed once more. I held on to him as tightly as I could. I didn't want to let him go. Death, after all, was only a state of mind.

I don't know how long I was there until Delph gently lifted me up into his arms.

At first, I fought him.

"No, I can't leave him. You don't understand. He needs me."

"What he needs, Vega Jane, is for you to let him move on to where he needs to be. Will you do that? Because he loved you so much. You need to do that for him. He deserves it. Let him be at peace."

I stopped fighting him. As he carried me up the stairs, I peered back down where the ball of fur lay on the floor with everyone gathered around it.

Finally, Geoffrey gently picked up Harry Two and took him away.

As I lay in bed that night, I stared up at the ceiling. I had finally stopped crying. I knew that some would think it silly that I was so heartbroken over a dog. But he and I had been through so much. He was often the only friend I had. And he had fought with me, helped me survive.

He was not simply a beast.

He was my friend. He was my family. And I would miss him till the day I died.

As it should be with those you love, beasts or people. It didn't matter. What mattered was what was in your heart.

And in theirs.

THREE YEARS LATER

DELPH AND I walked hand in hand through the gardens of Empyrean. The *fully restored* Empyrean.

After discussing it long and hard with them, we had restored the household staff to who they had once been. Then Pillsbury and Mrs. Jolly and the rest died peacefully and gratefully. I, for one, thought they had labored long enough.

We had traveled to True and Greater True, and though it had taken a long time, we had finally freed everyone's minds from the Maladons' vicious handiwork. Now folks still scrubbed floors and washed windows, but they did it with a free mind and an ambition to seek other jobs if they so desired. The elites of Greater True had been made to understand what had happened, and they opened their fine homes, which had been given to them by the Maladons, to their fellow citizens.

The guards, both adult and boys' divisions, had been disbanded.

The trains that ran from the countryside into the towns now did so merely to transport folks to and fro.

There were more magicals in the countryside and the towns, but they no longer sported the three-hooks brand, because when Necro had died, so had that curse.

Those magicals came to Empyrean to live and learn their craft, and to understand how to use their magic responsibly.

My brother became a Healer in record time and spent a great deal of his time treating folks in the towns and country-side. But when I saw him at Empyrean, where he had taken over Jasper Jane's old digs, his face was still always buried in a book.

Some things never changed. And bully for that.

My mother lived with us at Empyrean and really managed the place. She also helped Delph with the teaching of those who came to stay with us.

Jason stopped taking the Elixir of Life and soon joined Uma in death. I feel that now she has no more regrets. And neither does he.

Elythia visited once and thanked me again for all that I had done. She blessed me, which I guess coming from a near goddess is not such a bad thing.

Sadly, once Necro was gone and the threat of the Maladons was vanquished, all the spirits that walked the halls of Empyrean left, never to return.

I had sat with Alice the night before she would leave for good.

With Necro dead, Gunther had finally returned to her and his home. They had both come to thank me for this. But for a few moments it was just Alice and me.

"Why do you have to go?" I asked.

"It is time, Vega. I have been around far too long. The old must give way for the new. You will do so one day too."

"But I will miss you, terribly."

"No, you won't." She had stroked my hair. "You need only look in the mirror, Vega. And I believe you will think of me."

I have done as she asked, and she was right. Our resemblance is remarkable. But no one could ever truly be Alice Adronis. She was clearly one of a kind.

It took two years, but we magically worked our way through the Quag, ridding it of all the deadly creatures that my kind had conjured to protect us from the Maladons. And when that was done, we removed the dome over it so that anyone who desired could visit. It is actually quite beautiful now that one doesn't have to worry about being eaten by a beast!

The surviving Wugs had wanted to return to their home, so Wormwood has been fully restored and Thansius is once more its leader. But unlike in the past, when our real history had been withheld from us, the new Council building has a complete chronicle of everything that happened. For all those who come, it stands as a critical lesson that when a people grow complacent and less than vigilant, evil can quickly take root and come to dominate. I do not wish to learn that lesson a second time. And I never want to live through again what I already have.

Russell and his group now live in peace. Some in True and Greater True. Some in the country. Some in the Quag. And a few even moved to Wormwood.

And Petra and Geoffrey seem to be growing very close. Another marriage may be in the works.

"Are you happy, Vega?" Delph asked as he put his large arm around my shoulders while we walked.

Ever since he had asked me to marry him and I had accepted, he had stopped calling me Vega Jane.

And I have to say, it was about bloody time!

I looked up into his face, his features full of love and warmth.

"I don't think I've ever been happier, Delph."

He smiled and we continued our walk.

It took us to a small glen that held special significance for me.

There was a grave here that I visited every day.

I had placed a bench in front of it so that I could sit and talk to my friend.

I took my seat while Delph stood.

I looked at the headstone and the now sunken plot of dirt. "Hello, Harry Two."

The first year I had come to this spot I had cried. Often uncontrollably. Harry Two had not been my pet. He had been my friend, my equal in every way.

It was not his fault that people thought of him as merely a dog. He was far better than just about any person I'd ever met.

And it wasn't just Harry Two I was talking to and missing.

It was my grandfather, who, I now knew, had played a large role in Harry Two coming into my life. Virgil had once told me that he thought of me every day after he had left Wormwood, and me, behind. I had not truly believed him.

Until I had realized the truth behind Harry Two.

Delph put his hand on my shoulder as I started to tear up. I shook my head.

Vega, it's been years. You need to move on. And you can. Harry Two will always be part of your life. He may not be with you physically anymore. But he will always, always be here. As will Virgil.

I touched my chest. I touched my heart.

I will always love you, Virgil. I will always love you, Harry Two. And I will never forget either of you.

"What's that?" said Delph suddenly.

I looked toward the spot where the tall grass had started to quiver.

Though we had not been threatened by anything or anyone in a long time, I still instinctively pulled out my wand and pointed it in that direction.

"Show yourself," I said.

The grass parted and out it trotted.

My mouth fell open.

"Harry Two!" I exclaimed.

But then I looked at the grave and knew it couldn't be. Even magic could not do that. Nor should it.

This dog was the spitting image of Harry Two, except it had two intact ears.

It came toward me slowly, its mouth open, its long tongue hanging out. It seemed to be smiling at me.

It stopped at the bench and sat down next to me, exactly as Harry Two would have done.

I looked at its eyes. And they were mismatched! One blue, one green. Only it was the other way around from Harry Two.

I glanced up at Delph.

"What is this, Delph? Where did he come from?"

Delph smiled and said, "I expect he came from love, Vega. *Your* love."

I slowly reached down and stroked the dog's ear. It licked me in reply.

"I can't believe this," I said, the tears sliding down my cheeks. Tears of joy this time.

"What will you name him?" asked Delph.

My answer was immediate.

"Harry *Three*, of course," I said.

When I said the name, Harry Three perked up, turned and looked at me full in the face with those beautiful, those wonderful mismatched eyes.

Even though he couldn't speak, I could hear his response clearly in my head.

And a right wonderful name it is.

I knelt down next to Harry Three and hugged him,

breathing in his scent. And letting my face burrow into that soft fur.

When I looked back up at Delph, he was grinning broadly.

"Let me ask you again. Are you happy, Vega?"

I didn't have to answer.

I just had to smile.

A Wugmort's Guide to Wormwood and Beyond

adar \\'ad-ər\\
A beast of Wormwood often used as a messenger and trained to perform tasks by air. Although they appear clumsy on the ground, adars are creatures of grace and beauty in the sky, owing greatly to their magnificent height and wingspan. Most remarkably, adars can understand Wugmorts and can even be taught to speak.

Adder Stone \\'ædər-ston\\
A stone known to possess healing powers, capable of erasing all traces of a wound when held over the injury.

alecto \\ə-'lek-tō\\
A lethal creature in the Quag characterized by serpents for hair and blood-dripping eyes. The hypnotizing sway of the serpents atop the alecto's head can drive its prey to commit suicide.

amaroc \\'a-mə-räk\\
A fierce and terrifying beast of the Quag, known to possess the ability to kill in many ways. Amarocs have upper fangs as long as a Wug arm and are rumored to shoot poison from their eyes. When captured, their hides are used in the production of clothing and boots in Wormwood.

attercop \\'a-dər-käp\\
A type of venomous spider indigenous to the Quag.

Bimbleton Station \\'bim-bəl-tən ste-ʃən\\
A ramshackle station where people wait to take a train to what they think will be a better life.

Bowler Hats \\'bolər hæts\\
The most elite fighters the Maladons have. They wear three-piece pin-stripe suits and bowler hats, hence the name.

Breath of a Dominici \\'breTH əv ə dä-mən-'ē-chē\\
A long-stemmed flower with a fist-size bloodred bloom that gives off the odor of slep dung. The Breath of a Dominici grows only in viper nests.

Campions \\'campions\\
The insurrectionists focused on causing as much strife as possible for the Maladons.

Care, the \\'ker\\
A place where Wugs who are unwell and for whom the Mendens at hospital can do no more are sent to live.

celestials \\se-'les-tiəls\\
A godlike, ageless people born with innate supernatural ability. Celestials are the most powerful magical figures and do not tend to mix with other peoples, magical or nonmagical.

chontoo \\'chən-too\\
A flying beast in the Quag composed only of a head, the chontoo is said to wildly attack its prey in the hopes of using its body parts to replace the ones the chontoo does not have. Spawned over the centuries by the intermingling of different species, the chontoo is characterized by a foul face with demonic eyes and jagged fangs, and flames for hair. The chontoo is primarily found in the Mycanmoor.

colossal \kə-'lä-səl\
An ancient race of formidable warriors, of an origin largely unknown to the average Wugmort. The average colossal stands about sixty-five feet tall and weighs nearly seven thousand pounds.

Council \'kaun-səl\
The governing body of Wormwood. Council passes laws, regulations and edicts that all Wugmorts must obey.

creta \'krē-də\
An exceptionally large creature used in Wormwood to pull the plow of Tillers and transport sacks of flour at the Mill. The creta weighs well over one thousand pounds and is characterized by horns that cross over its face and hooves the size of plates.

cucos \'koo-kōs\
Small birdlike creatures that inhabit the Third Circle of the Quag. Brilliantly colored as if small bits of the rainbow are embedded in their feathers, the cucos are best known for glowing wings that can illuminate their surroundings.

Dactyl \'dak-til\
A Stacks worker whose job entails shaping metal with hammer and tongs.

Destin \'des-tin\
A magical chain that bestows any who touch it with increased strength and the ability to fly.

dopplegang \'dä-pəl-gaNG\
A dangerous creature in the Quag, marked by hideous rows of black-ened, sharp teeth, that morphs into whatever it sees. The power of the

dopplegang lies in its ability to trick its unsuspecting victim into injuring or even killing itself, since striking the beast in its altered form is tantamount to striking oneself.

dread \\dred\

A black flying creature in the Fifth Circle created by Jasper Jane. About the size of a canine, dreads are characterized by their screeching cries and clawed wings that they use to cut their prey to pieces.

Duelum \\dool-əm\

A twice-a-session competition occurring outside of Wormwood proper that pits strong males between the ages of fifteen and twenty-four in matches against one another. Viewed by many Wugs as a rite of passage, Duelums can often be brutal.

ekos \\ē-kōs\

A small creature in the Quag exceptional for the mats of grass that grow on its arms, neck and face, and sprout from its head. The ekos have small, wrinkled faces and bulging red eyes.

Empchon \\emp-chon\

Sometimes known as the Fates, Empchon is the force of connectivity that binds people and events to preordained paths.

Empyrean \\ɛmp-ir-e-ɛn\

The ancestral home of Vega Jane. Once the residence of Alice Adronis, it has remained safely under a spell that has rendered the grounds undetectable by Maladons over the years.

Elixir of Life \\ē-ˈliks-ər əf līf\

A potion made of dangerous substances, such as the venom of a jabbit, that can extend one's life span indefinitely.

Event \i-ʹvent\

A mysterious occurrence in Wormwood that has no witnesses. Wugmorts presumed to suffer from an Event disappear entirely, body and clothing, from the village.

Excalibur \ek-ʹskal-ə-bər\

A rare type of sorcerer born with extraordinary magical powers already intact and a profound knowledge of Wug history embedded in his or her mind. It may take years for an Excalibur to become aware of his or her innate abilities.

Finisher \ʹfi-nish-ər\

A worker tasked with "finishing" all objects created at Stacks. Finishers must show creative ability at Learning, as the requirements for the job range from painting to kiln firing items intended for the wealthiest Wugs of Wormwood.

Finn, the \ʹfin\

A magical element consisting of twine knotted in three places and looped around a tiny wooden peg. The untying of one knot brings a force of wind powerful enough to lift objects off the ground. Untying the second knot produces gale force winds, and undoing the third brings a wind of unimaginable strength with the ability to level everything in its path.

firebird \ʹfi-yuhr-burd\

A huge flying creature in the Quag known for its colorful plumage and sharp beak and claws. It's said that the firebird's feathers are so brilliant they can be used to provide light and warmth. A firebird can be a harbinger of tragedy.

frek \\'frek
A huge, fierce beast of the Quag characterized by an extensive snout and fangs inches longer than a Wug finger. The bite of a frek has been known to drive its victims mad.

Furina \\fuhr-'ē-nə
A Wug-like race indigenous to the Quag, made nearly extinct because of continuous attacks from beasts. The Furinas are descendants of a group of Wugs and Maladons who became trapped in the Quag while migrating from the great battlefields to the village of Wormwood.

garm \\'gärm
A large beast of the Quag, thirteen feet in length and nearly one thousand pounds in weight. The garm is a hideous creature, its chest permanently bloodied, its smell odious and its belly full of fire that can cremate its victim from several feet away. Wormwood lore maintains that the garm hunts the souls of the dead or guards the gates of Hel.

gnome \\'nōm
A creature of the Quag known for long, sharp claws that allow it to mine through hard rock. The gnomes are characterized by deathly pale and prunish faces and yellowish-black teeth.

Greater True \\'gretər tru
The land of the elites. Many of the people living here have slaves to serve them. The Maladons regularly patrol here as well.

grubb \\'grəb
A peaceful creature that lives primarily in tunnels beneath the Quag and can eat through rock faster than most any other species. Twice the size of a creta, the grubb is known for its strong, expandable hide; long slithery tongue; enormous jagged teeth; soft, slippery body; and eye color that differentiates males (blue) from females (yellow).

High Street, the \ˈhī ˈstrēt\
A cobblestone street in Wormwood proper lined with shops that sell things Wugmorts need, such as foodstuffs, clothing and healing herbs.

hob \ˈhäb\
A creature in the Quag about half the height of an average Wug, characterized by its thick frame, small but powerful jaw, stout nose, long peaked ears, spindly fingers and large hairy feet. Hobs are typically amicable creatures that speak Wugish and make themselves of assistance in exchange for small gifts.

hyperbore \ˈhī-pər-bȯr\
A blue-skinned flying beast indigenous to the Quag characterized by a lean, muscled torso and lightly feathered head. More closely related to Wugs than any other creature, the hyperbore may serve as an ally or enemy and responds favorably to respect and kindness. Hyperbores set on their prey quickly, beating them to death with their compact wings and ripping them apart with their claws. The hyperbores live in nests high in trees.

inficio \in-ˈfish-ē-ō\
A large fiendish beast indigenous to the Quag that can expel poisonous smoke potent enough to kill any creature that breathes it. The inficio has two massive legs with clawed feet; a long, scaly torso with powerful webbed wings; a serpentlike neck and a small head with venomous eyes and razor-sharp fangs.

jabbit \ˈja-bit\
A massive serpent with over 250 heads growing out of the full length of its body. Although jabbits rarely leave the Quag, little can halt their attack once they are on the blood scent. Jabbits can easily overtake Wugs and have fangs in each head full of enough poison to drop a creta.

Learning \ˈlər-ning\
The institution youngs attend until the age of twelve sessions. It is at Learning that youngs gain skills necessary for work in Wormwood.

light \ˈlīt\
The time of sunlight between one night and the next.

Loons, the \ˈloons\
A boardinghouse on the High Street.

lycan \ˈlī-kin\
A beast of the Quag covered in long, straight hair, whose bite turns its victims into its own kind. The tall, powerfully built lycan walks on two legs and wields its sharp fangs and claws to attack its prey.

Maladon \ˈmal-ə-dän\
From the Wugish word for "terrible death," an ancient race whose highest calling is to inflict terrible death on others. A sessions-long war between the Maladons and Wugmorts forced the Wugs to found the village of Wormwood, around which they conjured the Quag for protection.

Maladon Castle \ˈmal-ə-dän kæ-səl\
The headquarters of the Maladon race. It is here that Necro dwells, and also where the Maladons torture and enslave their enemies.

maniack \ˈmā-nē-ak\
An evil spirit that can attach to a body and mind, driving a Wug irreversibly mad with every fear he or she has ever had.

manticore \ˈman-tə-kȯr\
A swift, treacherous beast indigenous to the Quag with the head of a lion, the tail of a serpent and the body of a goat. Over twice the height

of an average Wug and three times the width, the manticore's most formidable features are its abilities to read minds and breathe fire.

Mill, the \mil\
A place of work in Wormwood where flour and other grains are refined.

morta \mȯr-tə\
A long- or short-barreled metal projectile weapon.

Noc \näk\
The large, round, milky-white object in the heavens that shines at night.

Ordinaries \ȯrdənɛriz\
Those who do not possess magical abilities.

Outlier \aut-lī-ər\
A threatening two-legged creature that lives in the Quag and can pass as a Wugmort. Outliers are believed to be able to control the minds of Wugs and make them do their bidding.

Quag, the \'kwäg\
A forest that encircles Wormwood and is home to all manner of fierce creatures and Outliers. It is widely believed among Wugmorts that nothing exists beyond the Quag.

remnant \rem-nənt\
A collection of memories from an assortment of Wugs; an embodied record of their remembrances.

Saint Necro's \sәint nɛ-kros\
The church in True where the people come to worship. It is named after Necro, the leader of the Maladons, who insists on being worshipped by all.

Seer-See \sē-ir 'sē\
A prophetical instrument used by sorcerers to view other places. The Seer-See consists of sand thrown into a pewter cup of flaming liquid, the contents of which are then poured onto a table to display a moving picture of a distant location.

session \se-shən\
A unit of time equal to three hundred and sixty-five lights.

slep \slep\
A magnificent Wormwood creature characterized by its noble head, long tail, six legs and beautiful coat. It is said that sleps were once able to fly, and that the slight indentations noticeable on their withers now mark the spot from which their wings grew.

sliver \sli-vər\
A small unit or brief period of time.

Stacks \staks\
A large brick building in Wormwood where items for trade and consumption are produced.

Steeples \stē-pəls\
A place the majority of Wugmorts go every seventh light to listen to a sermonizer.

True \tru\
The first town that Vega and her friends encounter. It is seemingly filled with happy people, but has sinister secrets.

unicorn \yoo-nə-kȯrn\
A noble and gentle beast characterized by a brilliantly white coat and mane of gold, with shiny black eyes and a regal horn the color of silver.

The soft horn of the unicorn is known to defeat all poisons, but can only be obtained by convincing the unicorn to surrender it freely or by killing the beast outright.

Valhall \val-hal\
The prison of Wormwood, set in public in the center of the village.

Victus \vɪk-tus\
The name given by the Maladons to those they enslave.

wendigo \wen-də-gō\
A malevolent spirit that can possess whatever it devours. This ghastly, quasi-transparent creature lives throughout the Quag but is predominant in the Mycanmoor. Signs that a wendigo is nearby are a vague feeling of terror and a sense that the facts stored in your head are being replaced by residual memories of the prey the wendigo has devoured.

whist \wist\
A large, domesticated hound of Wormwood known for its impressive speed.

Wugmort (*Wug* for short) \wəg-mort\ (\wəg\)
A citizen of Wormwood.

Acknowledgments

Writing the fourth and final installment of the Vega Jane saga was both euphoric and bittersweet for obvious reasons. I will miss Vega and her cohorts and the fantasy world they inhabit. But the good news is I still get to hang out with all the cool and supremely talented people listed below, who helped mightily in bringing Vega's world to all of you.

To Rachel Griffiths, you have been so wonderful and made the experience of publishing Vega as good as it could be. For that I thank you. And I look forward to many more sessions of Ritz-Bits!

To David Levithan, Julie Amitie, Charisse Meloto, Dick Robinson, Ellie Berger, Lori Benton, Maya Marlette, Dave Ascher, Elizabeth Parisi, Jackie Hornberger, Jessica White, Joy Simpkins, Kerianne Steinberg, Sarah Jospitre, Evangelos Vasilakis, Melissa Schirmer, Alan Smagler, Sue Flynn, Nikki Mutch and the whole sales team at Scholastic, for being truly a dream publisher. I hope we can do it again one day.

To Venetia Gosling, Alyx Price, Kat McKenna, Amber Ivatt, Sarah Clarke, Jade Tolley, Charlotte Williams, Rachel Vale, Tracey Ridgewell, Daniel Jenkins, Anthony Forbes Watson, Jeremy Trevathan, Trisha Jackson, Katie James, Alex Saunders, Sara Lloyd, Claire Evans, Sarah Arratoon, Stuart Dwyer, Jonathan Atkins, Anna Bond, Leanne Williams, Natalie McCourt, Stacey Hamilton, Sarah McLean, Charlotte Williams and Neil

Lang at Pan Macmillan, for bravely going where this author had never gone before.

To Steven Maat and the entire Bruna team, for bringing Vega to Holland.

To Aaron Priest, for always having my back.

To Arleen Priest, Mitch Hoffman, Lucy Childs, Lisa Erbach Vance, Frances Jalet-Miller, John Richmond and Juliana Nador, for being great advocates and, more importantly, dear friends.

To Sandy Violette and Caspian Dennis, for working seamlessly with the crazy Yanks!

To Kristen White and Michelle Butler, for doing what you do better than anyone else.

About the Author

David Baldacci is a global #1 bestselling author. His books are published in over forty-five languages and in more than eighty countries, with over 130 million worldwide sales. His works have been adapted for both feature film and television. He is also the cofounder, along with his wife, of the Wish You Well Foundation®, which supports literacy efforts across America. David and his family live in Virginia.